MR.
MURDER

A SALLY HARRINGTON NOVEL

MR.
MURDER

LAURA VAN WORMER

MIRA®

ISBN 0-7783-2177-0

MR. MURDER

www.MIRABooks.com

Printed in U.S.A.

First Printing: January 2006
10 9 8 7 6 5 4 3 2 1

For Chris, who makes it all work.

And wonderfully so.

PROLOGUE

"He's in," a giant of a man said. "Delafield's paying him six bucks an hour under the table as a handyman."

"Ripping people off right up to the last," the man muttered, rolling his leather chair back from his desk. "No great loss to mankind. What about the house?"

"Got it. Everything's set."

"And the cameras?"

"But if you're taking her—"

"Who said I was taking her?"

The giant looked confused. "So what are you going to do with her?"

"The question is," the man said, "what are you going to do with her after I'm through with her."

The giant seemed to falter somewhat. "You mean—you mean kill her?"

"Why the hell would I step in to save her life if I was going to kill her?" he half sneered. "Look, I want a couple of days with her and then I'm gone. But I'll want tapes." His eyes narrowed. "What? What is it now?"

"This is costing a fortune."

The man shrugged. "I can't take the American accounts anyway. Spend it all, I don't care, just get it done." The man smiled a little, looking down, examining the nails of his right hand, one after the other. "I just have this last piano recital with my kid I want to see tonight and then I'll be ready to go. Tomorrow."

"Tomorrow," the giant repeated, scratching behind his ear a minute. "I guess we can do it."

The man looked up. "See that you do."

"But what if she doesn't come?"

"Oh, she'll come," the man said with some certainty.

"But what if she doesn't?"

He waved his hand through the air. "So I'll do her another favor. What does it matter?" He frowned. "What the hell is the matter with you? This should be kid's play for you."

"I know, but—"

"I *pay* you a goddamn fortune," the man suddenly yelled, slamming his desk with his fists and jumping to his feet, "and I'm *giving* you a goddamn fortune, so what is your problem? Just do what I tell you!" He paused, breathing heavily. "Got it?"

The giant looked unsure, but said yes, he understood, and took the cue to leave the office, closing the door behind him.

The man walked briskly around his desk and crossed the office to lock the door. Then he went over to open the doors of an ornately carved mahogany wardrobe, revealing an entertainment center. He walked back around his desk to sit down and pulled open a drawer, removing a remote control, a box of tissues and a bottle of body oil. Slamming the drawer shut, he turned on the TV and DVD player.

"Good evening," the attractive young woman said on the screen, "and welcome to *DBS News Magazine.* I'm Sally Harrington, sitting in for a vacationing Alexandra Waring." As the woman continued to talk, the man undid his belt, unzipped his pants and adjusted the opening of his boxer shorts. Eyes glittering, attention focused on the screen, he pumped oil into his right hand, grabbed a wad of tissues with his left and sat back in his chair.

I

CHAPTER

1

"I hate to be the bearer of less than good news," my studio producer, Haydn Cooke, says, appearing in the doorway, "but I wondered if you had seen this."

I glance at our chief film editor, Clem, who sighs and drops his hands from the console to wait. This is our third interruption since we sat down, but this is what happens in television when you are a producer for DBS News in New York.

I look at the papers Haydn hands to me to read:

Harrington Hammered In Hometown

Since my name happens to be Sally Harrington, I read on:

Everybody with a television set has by now seen the great white hope for DBS News in the shapely form of the blue-eyed, almost-blond Sally Harrington. You know the one. The sensational witness from the Mafia Boss Murder Trial that audiences found so compelling the network decided to launch an early morning newscast to showcase her? Unfortunately for DBS, however, a bitter debate has broken out in Harrington's hometown of Castleford, Connecticut—a debate that has pitted residents who believe Ms. Harrington worthy of emulation against those residents who believe her worthy of deportation.

I read on to an editorial that has evidently run in the *Herald-American*:

The Castleford Women's Club recently awarded its highest honor to part-time resident and DBS News maven Sally Harrington "for her extraordinary professional achievements, outstanding contribution to the community and overall excellence as a role model." While the *Herald-American* (as her former employer) is also proud of Ms. Harrington's professional achievements, we must question the motive behind the organization's selection. Given the highly publicized trials and tribulations of Ms. Harrington's personal life, one can only shudder at what kind of role model the Women's Club would consider unsavory. Scribbling a big check to the club from a recently inflated bank account does not, in our opinion, constitute a good role model.

I am left almost breathless by the attack. My old boss, Al Royce, and I have always rubbed each other the wrong way, but I served him and the paper well. Certainly I have done nothing to warrant this kind of viciousness. At least I don't think so.

I lower the paper and cover my eyes with my left hand for a moment. *Given the highly publicized trials and tribulations of Ms. Harrington's personal life, one can only shudder at what kind of role model the Women's Club would consider unsavory.*

Well, let's see now, what could be considered unsavory about my personal life: I broke up with a Castleford favorite to take up with a slick New York insider; a tape of him and me having sex was distributed all over town; the defense attorney in The Mafia Boss Murder Trial set me up to come across as a nymphomaniac, making me an instant media sensation; and, finally, that slick New York insider was involved in a very messy and very public divorce trial into which my name was dragged.

"Sounds like sour grapes to me," Haydn says sympathetically. Of course Haydn's still pretty new and probably isn't yet familiar with my unsavory personal life.

I drop my hand. I have a feeling if Haydn's skin was not black, I might see that he is blushing on my behalf. He's a good guy. "When I graduated from high school," I explain, "the Women's Club gave me a renewable scholarship for four straight years. I couldn't have made college work without it."

"I'm with you," Haydn assures me. "Mine was from our Rotary Club."

"So then my mother tells me that after a hundred years the club can't meet in the cultural center anymore," I continue, "because the air-conditioning is shot and a lot of the older women can't breathe without it. So fixing the air-conditioning seemed like the least I could do."

I look down at the wire service release again—*one can only shudder at what kind of role model the Women's Club would consider unsavory.* I check my watch and look at Clem. "Can you give me five minutes?"

"Sure," he says, turning back to the console. "I've got the Puget Sound piece to finish, anyway."

I leave editing and walk down the short hallway into the central newsroom. "Sally—" an assistant begins.

"Give me five," I beg, swerving around him to head into what we call the Fishbowl, a conference room constructed of soundproof glass. I close the door, pick up the phone, punch in my office ID number and make a long-distance call. I look at my watch. It's 4:02 p.m., Friday. Mother stays late at school Tuesday through Thursday to supervise the English lab, but today she should have left right after the bell.

"Hello?" Mother answers with her usual warm grace, giving me, today, somewhat of a pang. How she ended up with a daughter with a temperament like mine is beyond everybody's understanding, although Mother maintains it is our differences that allow us to be so close. (I think our closeness is much more likely due to long-time combat fatigue, the kind remaining family members share in the trenches when the father dies young.)

"Hi, it's me."

Pause. "Oh, darling heart, I am *so* sorry. When I saw the paper at lunch—"

"At lunch?" I yell. "Are you telling me this editorial ran today and was submitted to the wire services yesterday?" *Son of a bitch, I'll kill him.*

"Sally, what do you mean?"

"I mean that sleazebag Royce submitted the editorial to the wire services before he even ran it because he knew he'd have to write a retraction. And you can bet your bottom dollar the retraction will never make its way to the wire services."

"Oh, no," Mother says quietly.

"Oh, yes." I drop heavily into a chair. "And it beats me what I've done to set him off."

"It isn't anything you did, Sally," Mother says. "It's what I did."

"Mother, it's okay, I'm a grown-up, I can handle this."

"No, really, darling."

"Alfred Royce adores you, he always has."

"Stop it, Sally, *please,*" she pleads. "You're breaking my heart."

I blink, taken aback.

"Al wrote it to hurt *me,* not you. Al is mad at *me.* Do you understand?"

"I don't understand at all," I tell her. The newsroom assistant is trying to get my attention by waving his arms at me through the glass. I make a swatting motion for him to go away.

"He's been harboring this—this *feeling* about me for years," Mother says. "It's ridiculous."

It's nothing new for a Castleford man of a certain age to have a thing for my mother, not even now that she is in her early sixties. Mother is one of those kind and gentle beauties men always wish they had married.

"Something happened, Mother, didn't it?"

Pause. "Yes." Silence.

"Are you going to tell me what?"

"Only if you promise not to do anything, Sally. And to let me handle it." She pauses for a moment, expecting a protest from me, and incorrectly assumes my silence means I agree. "He begged me not to marry Mack. He said he was in love with me and it was our last chance for happiness."

I think I'm going to scream. Alfred Royce III is one of the worst kinds of human being. He is one of those self-centered brats who inherited enough money and power to make everyone's life miserable.

"Does Al not remember, perhaps, that he already has a wife?" I ask. "A second wife, I might add? For whom he traded in the first?"

"Actually, he's been married three times," Mother says almost conversationally, "but the first was over so fast no one remembers it. She was some kind of lady of the evening and your father thought it was just hilarious, and of course his parents were beside themselves."

"Mother," I nearly shout. "Tell me what happened."

"I went to the club with the Levys Saturday night for dinner. They knew Mack was at a conference and they asked me if I'd like to join them." (I'm trying to be patient.) "Al was at the bar with the golf committee, and when our group was leaving he walked me out to the car." Faintly. "He had had a few and he made a pass at me and I told him to stop it, but then he grabbed my arms and said all these things about us having one last chance."

What makes it worse, in my mind, is that I have no doubt Al felt that he was *entitled* to Mother. That's the way he is.

"I had to slap him across the face. And then he stared at me, as if he couldn't believe it—"

I feel the stirring of rage.

"And then he stormed off." Her voice comes close to breaking and so does my heart. "He said some loathsome and wicked things and I'm not sure I will ever be able to forgive him, Sally."

The newsroom assistant is now moving along the glass wall to keep in my line of sight, making entreating motions. I turn my back on him. "Why didn't you tell me about this, Mother?"

"You were in the field, Sally," Mother says, upset. "I didn't want to upset you."

Suddenly the conference room door bursts open and I turn around to see the assistant. "I'm sorry," he says in an exaggerated whisper.

"Could you please hang on a second, Mother," I say, impatiently covering the mouthpiece. *"What?"*

"Somebody's been murdered," he says breathlessly, "and Will says it's got something to do with you."

I rush across the newsroom—from much practice neatly avoiding desks and computer stations—to reach our executive producer, Will Rafferty, who is standing with Haydn in front of the affiliate monitors we use to view any "film" (everything is digital these days) our affiliate newsrooms submit to use on *DBS News America Tonight with Alexandra Waring*. Will is talking into a headset while looking into monitor 4 at what appears to be the charred remains of a small house or cabin. Monitor 4 means the image has come from one of our affiliates in the Southern Atlantic region. I grab a headset and Will looks over at me gratefully while I plug it in. "Sally's here now, Kit."

He must be talking to Kit Whitehawk, a rookie reporter from our affiliate in Gainesville, Florida. He recently assisted me on a story I covered for *DBS News Magazine*.

"What am I looking at, Kit?"

"All that remains of Wilson Delafield."

I glance at Will and then focus back on the screen. The story I did for the magazine had been about Wilson Delafield, a jet-setting playboy and horse breeder who lived outside Gainesville. "You mean he's dead?"

"Someone locked him in his garden shed and torched it."

I flinch. "When was this?"

"About five before three."

Just over an hour ago.

In my story on Delafield I showed how he had been on the verge of bankruptcy when his highly prized stable of Thoroughbreds burned to the ground, killing all seven of the horses in it, and how he received a little over thirteen million dollars in insurance money. Delafield denied any connection between his pending financial ruin and the fire, maintaining, "The insurance payment is proof the entire tragic event was completely and thoroughly investigated to the satisfaction of all parties."

Well, er, no, that wasn't quite right. Wilson Delafield had been born Warren Drubber and, I discovered, was distantly related to the supervisor in charge of the insurance investigation. Not only did I learn that Delafield and the insurance investigator supervisor had met four years before at a wedding, but I even had pictures of them sitting together at the reception dinner. That meeting alone should have prompted the supervisor to abstain from working on the Delafield fire, but he hadn't. Instead he conducted the investigation himself with the assistance of a relatively new company trainee.

I had no hard evidence proving Delafield arranged for the fire. The evidence was circumstantial: Delafield's disastrous financial situation before the fire, the fact the supervising insurance investigator knew Delafield personally, and a long trail of brokenhearted wealthy women and furious former business partners who said Delafield was a liar, a cheat and a crook. Because the evidence was only circumstantial I was tempted to put the story on the shelf until something more concrete turned up, but then my boss, Alexandra Waring, who has always kept horses, explained to me exactly what those poor animals had to endure before they finally died in the fire. After that I was ready to go with what I had.

So under the guidance of the DBS lawyers, I stayed on the right side of slander while still getting the message across that something highly irregular had gone down and a group of trusting domestic animals had essentially been tortured to death. The story ignited an immediate criminal investigation into the possibility of insurance fraud and within forty-eight hours of the broadcast the authorities had frozen all of Delafield's assets.

And now, it seems, the eminently smooth-talking jet-setter had been trapped and slowly burned to death just as his horses had been.

Renegade animal activists, I bet.

Kit tells me how he heard the fire company call on his scanner while running an errand for the station owner (it is a very small station), recognized the address from when he assisted on my story and took off immediately, arriving at the horse farm just behind emergency rescue. The cedar roof and walls of the garden shed were already mostly gone and the firefighters were extinguishing what remained. The maid was running around, hysterical, screaming Delafield had been in there. She said he received a phone call and then the millionaire had gone to the shed to retrieve a log he kept there on the gardens. The next thing the maid knew the garden shed was a wall of fire and she could hear her employer screaming inside.

"How do you know he was locked in?" I ask Kit.

"A fireman said the door was padlocked from the outside."

I take in a slow breath and let it out just as slowly; Will flicks to a dramatic picture of responding fire trucks, police cars and ambulances, against a backdrop that can only be described as pastoral. "How many pictures do we have?"

"Just the two," Will says. "He took them with his cell phone."

"Nicely done, Kit," I say into my headset.

"I would have taken more," he says, his voice wavering slightly, "but as soon as the cops knew there was a body they kicked me off the property."

"Are they calling it a homicide?" Will asks.

"I think so. They think the fire was intentional, and if he was locked in...?"

Man, Kit sounds young. Well, he is. Like twenty-three.

"Where are you now?" I ask him.

"Front gate. With everyone else in the county." We can hear people in the background. "Are you guys still looking at the shed?"

Will flicks the remote to bring the shed back on the monitor. "Yes."

"You can see Delafield's arm. It's that long black piece resting on the inside of the door."

I lean closer to the monitor, grimacing as Will asks which side had the door been on.

"Far side," Kit answers. "You can see his elbow replacement. There's a shiny thing? In the black stuff?"

"Good God," I murmur.

"Talk about poetic justice," Alexandra Waring murmurs from behind me, blue-gray eyes riveted to the monitor. I bring her up to speed while handing over my headset and picking up the phone to call the Gainesville affiliate. "Kit, Alexandra here," she says into the mouthpiece. "How are you holding up?"

"We should do a newsbreak on the half hour," I tell Will while checking my watch, "which is in exactly seventeen minutes."

"Agreed. Haydn!" he yells.

"I'm right here," Haydn says from behind him.

"Greg," I say into the phone to Gainesville, "it's Sally Harrington. Where are you on the Delafield fire?" Will shoves his headset at me and takes off with Haydn to galvanize the studio. "Why not?" I say into the phone.

"Who else is there?" Alexandra is asking Kit.

I hold Will's headset against my left ear while continuing to listen to Gainesville in my right.

"Everybody," Kit tells Alexandra.

"And who else got to the fire?"

"I don't care if you have to *buy* a camera, get one out there!" I shout into the phone.

"I think I was the only one," Kit says. "And the only one who got pictures."

"He sent them over his cell phone," I whisper to Alexandra, "so they could have been intercepted."

My pager goes off. The on-duty crew is being summoned to studio A.

"What about helicopters?" she says in the headset. "Kit?"

There is a lot of noise on his end. "I'm here."

"Any helicopters yet?"

"One. I think it's ABC."

"Damn," Alexandra says.

"Call ABC in Gainesville," I yell to an assistant, "and find out if they have a helicopter at the Delafield fire. Make up something, just find out."

"Newsbreak at four-thirty!" Will calls across the newsroom.

I spot Clem across the newsroom and wave him over. "Lock in the pictures on monitor 4—there are two, one of the burned shed and one of the rescue scene. Call them two and three and feed them into control. We're going to use them in the news-break."

"Sure."

"Wait, Clem!" He wheels around. "Also call up the Delafield magazine story and pull a close-up of Delafield as a still and call it one. Then pull an aerial shot of the Delafield farm, call it four, and stream them into control, as well."

"Got it!"

"You've got to be kidding me!" I shout into the telephone. I turn to Alexandra. "Sports took all the Gainesville cameras to a NASCAR qualifier a hundred miles away."

The anchorwoman grimaces.

I hang up on Gainesville and yell at the news editor on desk duty to call Miami and see if their helicopter is available. I glance at Alexandra. "Maybe they can get us something in time for the newscast tonight."

"Kit," Alexandra says urgently, "do you see any stringers around with a camera?"

"It's a mob scene," he says helplessly.

"They'd be freelancers, Kit, by themselves, no logo," I say into the headset.

"I don't know!" he says, sounding rattled now.

"It's ABC's helicopter," the newsroom assistant confirms.

"Kit," I say, "take pictures of the scene, recharge your cell phone and we'll get back to you."

"But—" he starts to say.

I yank the headsets out of the monitor plugs. "We'll get him sorted in time for the newscast," I promise Alexandra.

"Miami's helicopter is covering a cruise-ship fire ten miles out," the news editor reports.

"CBS Radio just reported Delafield's death," someone calls out.

"Your black suit is back from the cleaners," I tell Alexandra.

"Cleo's waiting for you in Makeup," Haydn says, disappearing through the door to the studio.

"Go," I say, gently shoving Alexandra to get her moving. Then I swing down behind a computer terminal and start drafting copy. "Can somebody get Clem for me?"

"Everything's cued in Control," Clem confirms when he appears.

I scramble out of my chair to lead him over to monitor 4. "That's Delafield's arm," I tell him, pointing it out. "That's his elbow replacement. What do you think?"

"Gruesome," he says. "But we run it and just not point it out."

I hesitate. "No," I finally say, "crop it out. Double-check with Will, but I think we should leave that to the cable ghouls."

Clem dashes off and I return to drafting copy, watching with one eye the people rocketing around me.

This is the kind of situation when the business of news is, well, for the lack of a better phrase, sort of revolting. A human being has been cruelly murdered and we're on the adrenaline high that comes with a scoop. But this is what we are paid for. We are to choke down our personal feelings and reactions until the story has been safely delivered to the public. Only afterward are we allowed to fully absorb the news we have covered. At that point, sometimes days later, the adrenaline is long gone and only the sick feelings remain.

And people wonder why news people have a tendency to drink.

The editor on duty checks my copy, makes some minor changes and sends it into the system that will produce it on the prompters over the studio cameras. We also print out hard copies and I send a production assistant with one for Alexandra and hand-deliver the others myself.

"So we're definitely not talking to Kit during the newsbreak?" Will asks me in the control room.

"He's breaking down and he's alone, so no. But we'll pull him together by the newscast. And we should have a decent camera there by then."

He stares at me. "Where is our decent camera now?"

"Sports took every single camera to a NASCAR qualifier a hundred miles away."

Will swears.

"Let's just get this done," I suggest, handing him the copy.

"I want you on a plane to Gainesville as soon as the news-break is over," he says.

"Fine," I acknowledge, thinking of the suitcase I have stashed here at West End exactly for that purpose, to bolt into the field. Since I just got back this morning from our D.C. affiliate, most of the clothes in it are already dirty. And poor Scotty's been stuck in doggy day care here for two days already. Well, it can't be helped; I need to get down there.

I hurry into studio A, and even now, this pressed for time, I can't ignore the sensation I always feel. Entering studio A is like being launched into outer space, into an entity of deadened sight and sound, but a huge emptiness with an all-permeating vibration in it, not electric exactly, but something like it.

The sets for *DBS News America Tonight with Alexandra Waring* take up a quarter of the studio space. On the far side are the sets for the magazine show and special news programming. There are also three sets used by Sports, a group we haven't been overly fond of since they recently defected from our division, taking their revenues with them.

Hanging thirty feet over the studio is the maze of our mech-anized lighting grid. When the lights on the grid are shut off, you can see the two floors of inside offices looking down on us from sublevels 1 and 2 (the newsroom is on sub 3).

"Five minutes to air!" the floor manager calls.

"Sally?" Lighting calls, pointing hopefully toward the set. I hop up to sit in Alexandra's chair. A lot of anchors these days stand up while giving the news, supposedly to energize the newscast, but as our ratings will testify, the somewhat legendary eyes of our an-chorwoman evidently already accomplish this. Besides, when the anchor is seated it's easier for the rest of us to crawl around on the set when things go awry.

The three camera operators are in position. We have to use all three whether we need them or not. Union rules.

Lighting holds a meter in my face.

"Who was your field producer on Delafield?" Will's voice asks over the studio speaker system.

"Tell him it was Margo Shande," I say to the floor director, who has his studio headset on.

"There's a shadow on the right side of her nose," Camera Two tells Lighting.

"My right or her right?"

"Her right, your left."

"I'm pulling Margo from Houston and putting her on a plane to Gainesville," Will tells me over the studio speaker system.

"Four minutes to air!" the floor manager calls.

"Seventeen to the left!" Lighting yells to the lighting director, who is standing in the shadows, manning the computerized lighting board like the great and powerful Oz. Union rules say we have to use him, too, because of his union seniority and despite the occasional difficulties we have working with him.

Looking up at the lighting grid, Lighting swears, frustrated. "Nothing's happening on seventeen!"

I frown, shielding my eyes to look up into the lights. "What's the matter with the grid?"

"It's screwed up," comes the highly technical answer from the shadows.

Lighting and I exchange glances. "Maybe you should see if he needs some help," I say quietly.

"Get your ass over 'ere," the lighting director yells at Lighting, who hurries down off the set.

I ask the floor manager where the monitor is. I am told to hold my horses for two seconds. *One, two,* I count. Excellent, here is the monitor.

Lighting comes running back with a long pole. I frown. "Why do we have to move the light in the first place? I thought these were locked in place."

"They were," Lighting says, gritting his teeth as the pole slips and gives a nerve-racking whack to one of the barn doors on the light.

"Three minutes to air!" the stage manager calls.

"You're on a six-o'clock flight out of LaGuardia," Will announces, crossing the studio. "With any luck you and Margo will get there around the same time."

"Is this getting any better?" Lighting asks.

"A little," Camera Two reports.

Audio comes running into the studio and hustles onto the set with a metal suitcase. He quickly kneels to the floor and throws open the case.

"Nice of you to join us," Will tells him.

"Nice of you to care," Audio mumbles, pulling out a microphone pack.

"Lighting's good!" Camera Two announces.

"Finally," Lighting mutters, jumping off the set with a thump and running off with the pole.

"You'll need to personally hold Kit's hand to prep him for the newscast," I tell Will.

"No," Alexandra says, entering the studio, heels sounding dull over the floor. "*You* need to personally prep him, Sally." We all watch the anchorwoman cross the studio floor. She is in full makeup and is wearing the black suit, an off-white blouse, gold earrings and a strand of pearls. Hurrying behind her is our hair-and-makeup artist, Cleo, who contrasts with the boss nicely in her leopard-colored tights, multicolored hair and butterfly glasses. Tied around Cleo's waist is a gray apron carrying tools of her trade.

Audio taps my shoulder for me to vacate Alexandra's chair.

"But Sally will still be en route to Gainesville," Will tells Alexandra.

"Sally is staying put," Alexandra says, stepping onto the stage. She puts her copy down and slips off her blazer so Audio can fix a microphone pack on her skirt band. Cleo, in the meantime, stands with her hands outreached as if she is scared Alexandra's head might fall off. "The affiliate convention is too important."

"Two minutes!" the stage manager calls.

"We'll just have to go with Kit."

"Kit!" Will cries.

The cool look Alexandra offers him evidently gives Will pause for thought, for he shuts up.

"Margo can whip him into shape," she says, slipping her blazer back on and sitting down. Lighting sticks a meter in her face.

"But can she teach him how to be a reporter?" I say.

"I would hope you taught him something while he worked with you," she says to me.

"We need a sound check," the stage manager calls.

"Here I am, audio man," Alexandra says in a slightly deeper, richer voice, "yippee-yi-yo-yi-yea. Essess, essess, puh-puh p's and buh-buh b's and sh-sh-shushes."

Will tries one more time. "But it was Sally's story that probably got Delafield killed in the first place."

"Gee, thanks," I say, turning away from the set.

"One minute!" the stage manager calls. "One minute!"

"Sally," Alexandra says.

I turn back, watching as Cleo circles the anchor desk to stand in front of it and then lean over to move Alexandra's chin slightly to the left, to the right and then dab a little something on her cheekbones. Then she fusses with the neckline of Alexandra's blouse and fiddles with her pearls. Cleo makes a sound of approval and backs down off the set, stiletto heels clicking on the studio floor. She stoops over to slip them off.

"Thirty seconds!"

Alexandra is watching the studio monitor, waiting for the DBS News Special Bulletin logo to appear. "It is best you focus on the affiliates right now," she says, apparently to me.

"Fifteen seconds!"

Alexandra neatens her copy and looks straight ahead at camera two.

"Ten, nine, eight…"

I leave the studio before I kick something in frustration.

CHAPTER

3

It is now almost one o'clock on Saturday morning, and to say the events of the day have been tiring is putting it mildly. All I want to do is get my dog and go home to bed.

I can see through the glass door ahead of me that the West End park is deserted. The park is in the middle of the West End Broadcasting Center, which is the home of DBS Television as well as headquarters for the other Darenbrook Communications companies. Three three-story office buildings face out toward the Hudson River in a gigantic U; beneath the buildings are three subterranean floors containing offices, technology labs, engineering, the satellite rooms, production suites, dressing rooms, conferences rooms and storage areas. The boundaries of the park roughly outline studios A and B. While we share studio A with Sports, studio B is used by the entertainment division.

Darenbrook Communications is a family-owned-and-operated media empire comprised of newspapers, magazines, textbooks, electronic information systems, broadcasting and, of course, the Darenbrook satellite, which makes most of the aforementioned financially viable. The print companies are housed in the building to the south, Darenbrook II; Broadcasting is in the one to the north, Darenbrook III; and the executive offices and employee common areas (dining room, day care, health center) are in the center building of the U, Darenbrook I. I have a small office overlooking the park next to Alexandra's on the third floor of Darenbrook III.

As soon as I exit the doors of Darenbrook I into the park there are the telltale sounds of a ninety-pound dog jumping up on a chain-link fence (cha-*ching,* cha-*ching*). And in case I might somehow miss my Scotty boy—stretched to a full five foot eight against the dog run—he offers a single deep, barrel-chested bark to let me know he is there.

Scotty is a beautiful collie, German shepherd and retriever mix (with, the vet tells me, a good dose of wolf), which gives him exotic, black-lined, almond-shaped eyes, scary-looking fangs, but a disposition so sweet it makes you want to cry. He is a big love. His long hair is brown and tan and black, his legs are golden and his tail is splendidly feathered. Whenever a New Yorker asks me what he is I'm afraid I almost always say he is a New Zealand Highlander, to which people usually smile and nod, murmuring something like, "Oh, right."

There are, you see, all of these terribly chic purebred dogs running around in Manhattan, and Scotty's papers come from the Castleford Humane Society. ("Breed: Several.") Scotty and I have both found out that although good looks can help immeasurably in New York, no one ever seems very interested in anything unless it has an immediately recognized and impressive-sounding label attached to it. So saying, "Hello, I'm Sally Harrington of DBS News," for example, works a great deal better in terms of being well received than saying, "Hi, I'm Sally Harrington from Nowhere, Connecticut." Just as, "This is Scotty, a New Zealand Highlander," is much more effective than, "This is Scotty, a banged-up stray from the streets of Nowhere, Connecticut."

The poor guy is the only dog left out there. "Hello, handsome," I tell him, opening the door of the run. He jumps down from the fence and can barely contain himself—doing a frantic little dance to the left and to the right—while waiting for me to bend over and wrap my arms around his neck in a big hug. (Dog hair, at this time of night, is no longer an issue.) "I know, I know," I whisper, "it was one of those days for me, too." I pull back to look at him and scratch him behind the ears. "Yes, yes, I missed you, too," I say as he licks my face, "but no more—yuck, Scotty—stop."

"I wanted to thank you for everything you did today," Alexandra says.

My boss, you should understand, specializes in suddenly appearing over my shoulder at the oddest times. As my friend she is a little less sneaky. "You're welcome," I tell her without turning around.

"I thought it went off well."

The Delafield story grew with each newsbreak and we devoted a full ten minutes to it during the newscast at nine. I think it was with a mixture of pride and sullen fury that I helped twenty-three-year-old Kit make his national network debut. We got a camera there finally and he went on the air live during the newscast. Margo was in Gainesville by then and coached him well. He was scared to death and still seemed somewhat immobilized. And since I was the original reporter covering Delafield, that means I must now turn over all of my hard-won contacts to him. It also means that I have to cover the story from here and send him what to read on the air.

The story's a good one. We know it is definitely a case of murder and the leading suspect is a casual worker who disappeared. The list of who might want to see Delafield dead is rather long. We've got ex-wives, ex-girlfriends and ex-business partners. There is a drug cartel for whom he performed the occasional transaction when money was tight and in whose good graces he had not been in lately. There are several swindled investors who have been too embarrassed to publicly admit what happened to them, but who might well have been angry enough to have wished Delafield harm. And then, of course, there is the radical fringe of the animal rights movement.

"I wanted to explain why I'm making you stay," Alexandra says. I glance back at her to see she hasn't taken her studio makeup off yet.

Alexandra is forty now and looks absolutely great except for the deepening creases at her eyes, which no TV camera will ever learn to forgive. She is scheduled for a—*shhh*—minor eye lift next month, which will be her first physical concession to television. In this business (for news is a business) eye lifts and face-lifts are mandatory maintenance.

Even the guys have to do it. Later, but they have to do it, too.

Speaking of concessions to the business, the Suits (as corporate is called) have been hinting they may ask me to graduate my light brown hair to blond. Research shows blond morning hair might provide a better contrast to Alexandra's black hair at night. (Aha! The morning *yin* to Alexandra's nighttime *yang!*) Since I have blue eyes and fair skin I would look fine as a blonde, but I am annoyed that no one seems to think my co-anchor, Emmett Phelps, needs to change anything. He can just go on the air as his frumpy law-school professor self.

"Before you try to apologize," I say, standing to retrieve Scotty's leash from the board and snap it on his collar. (I can just hear the anchorwoman's mind now, *Who said I was apologizing?*) I turn around to look at her. "I have a confession to make."

One eyebrow goes up. "Which is?" She opens the cage door and holds it open for us.

I murmur thanks as we pass through the door. "I feel terrible about what happened to Delafield. And I know he's dead because of my story."

She looks at me a moment before turning to close the door and latch it. "He's dead because of the way he lived his life." She steps next to me, slinging an arm through mine in a rare gesture of comraderie and setting us walking. "Evil often begets evil," she says, "and you're not responsible because you warned society of the evil in the first place."

I sigh. "I know." We walk a few paces. "And although I was ticked off at first I couldn't go to Gainesville, I realize now that I'm sort of relieved." I look over at her. "I think I've lost my appetite for murder."

"I don't blame you," she says, stopping to face me. "And given the fact you are soon to be an early-morning news anchor, I think the cereal sponsors thank you for losing your appetite for murder stories."

I smile a little, petting Scotty behind the ears. "It's going to be an uphill climb at the affiliate convention, isn't it?"

"Yes."

A lot of our affiliate stations have balked at the idea of carrying *DBS News America This Morning with Sally Harrington and Emmett Phelps* because they already produce a news hour locally in that slot, six to seven. This allows them to keep the advertising dollars for themselves. On top of that, DBS has an unfolding disaster with *The Jessica Wright Show,* which follows our nightly news Monday through Friday and until now had been the network's ratings leader and biggest moneymaker.

Jessica Wright, the television sensation of the past ten years, is married to our Will Rafferty (the concept of spouses not working at the same company seems unknown to the Darenbrooks), and the couple had terrible trouble carrying a pregnancy to term. They finally succeeded with this last pregnancy, and Jessica took leave from the show to give birth to a healthy little girl. Jessica then told DBS she wasn't coming back anytime soon (and maybe never) and suggested they try me in her place. I turned the job down and the affiliate managers know this—and they also know the stand-up comedian DBS hired for a ton of money to host *The Jessica Wright Show* has been an unmitigated disaster. The long-time executive producer recently quit and the ratings now appear to be in a bit of a free fall, which is also starting to erode Alexandra's ratings.

Thus, in the minds of many of the affiliated station managers, DBS not only failed to prop up the network's single most successful show by drafting me as a replacement, but the network is now jamming me down their throats in an early-morning newscast they don't want.

Uphill climb at this affiliate convention, indeed.

There is more to *DBS News America This Morning* for the network than what immediately affects our American affiliates, though. The early-morning newscast is also a vehicle to recycle the best from *DBS News America Tonight* the night before for additional ad revenues. We are also producing a half-hour newscast later in the day that will be seen live in the United Kingdom through our overseas partner, INS, which will focus on news out of Wall Street, Washington and Hollywood. In return, INS, who already supplies us with the half hour of international news we run at eleven, will expand their newscast to a full hour.

Scotty, sensing this might take a while, lies down on the ground, sighing, and rests his chin on his paws.

"I try not to think about it," I admit, "but sometimes I wonder how this is ever going to work."

"It does sometimes feel like a dog chasing his own tail." She leans over slightly. "Begging your pardon, Scotty." At the sound of his name he raises his head, smiling. "We need big sponsors to recruit the affiliates," she continues, squatting to pet Scotty, "but we need signed affiliates to land the big-name sponsors. We have to convince the affiliates the newscast will work and eventually make them more money than they make now, and when we come back we've got to convince sponsors we have the reach and power to deliver." Scotty raises his paw to shake hands, which makes Alexandra smile—and accept his paw in a handshake. "We need to keep you fired up and at your best."

"When I was little and my father was teaching me how to play tennis…" I begin as she stands up. Scotty gets up as well and we resume walking. "He always told me to visualize myself as the winner of the match long before I started playing. I was to *assume* I would win, regardless of the skill of my opponent, and take it from there."

She glances over. "You were good, weren't you?"

I nod. "I try to do the same thing here. Assume I will win and take it from there."

"So you're not scared?"

"What, are you on drugs? Of course I'm scared. If it doesn't work I'll be stuck being your handmaiden for the rest of my life."

Alexandra throws her head back to laugh. It's good to see her do it. I've been a little worried about her lately. We're friends, we've come a long way, but recently she's seemed quiet. Unnaturally quiet.

"Nothing's wrong, is it?" I ask her then.

Her laughter disappears. "Why would you ask that?"

"Because you've seemed withdrawn."

"Withdrawn?" She frowns.

"How is Georgiana?" I ask her, alluding to her love life. It's a very long story, but Alexandra is sort of out with her actress friend, Georgiana Hamilton-Ayres, although no one, including themselves, say outright they are gay. If anything, it seems to have increased Alexandra's viewership with younger generations.

"She's in Bali."

"I know that, but how is she?" I ask, reaching ahead to open the gate.

"Working hard."

Do I dare ask her about their plans to have a baby? It's been a couple of months since Alexandra has said anything about it. I close the gate behind us. "What kind of movie is it?"

"She's playing the queen of Atlantis," she says with a laugh.

We aren't allowed to walk our dogs through the buildings so we have to walk all the way around Darenbrook I to the front entrance of the complex. After a while Alexandra says, "I saw the wire-service story about the *Herald-American*."

"You mean *given the highly publicized trials and tribulations of Ms. Harrington's personal life, one can only shudder at what kind of role model the Women's Club would consider unsavory?* As you can tell, I've scarcely thought about it."

"Why are they attacking you like that?"

"Not they, him. Al Royce," I tell her as we approach the driveway. "He declared his undying love to Mother, she slapped him and he goes after me to get to her."

"What is the matter with people?" she asks rhetorically. "Well, I'm sorry."

I shrug. "Thanks." After a moment, "So you know where I'll be all weekend." When she looks at me, I add, "Here. Pretending not to be covering the Delafield story."

She waves to her driver, who is standing, waiting, by the passenger side of her limousine. "If you need me, you can call my pager," she says as the driver opens the door for her.

I stop short. "Pager? What pager?"

"The option you have on my voice mail?" she says, climbing in.

This is bizarre. Not once in all the time I have worked for Alexandra have I ever been told to use her pager. I call her at the farm or call her at her apartment or if she's in transit, on her cell phone. Pager?

"Good evening," my driver says to me and Scotty.

"Hi," I say, walking over to the town car and handing him Scotty's leash. Then I walk back to the limo where Alexandra has lowered the window. "About this pager," I begin.

"Let it go, Sally," she says quietly, sounding tired.

"But where are you going to be that I can't call you?" I persist. I lean closer, resting my arms on her window. "It hasn't come back, has it?" I say quietly. I am referring to cancer. When she had it before she asked for my help to disappear for a few days.

"No!" she says, eyes widening.

"Don't look at me like that. How am I supposed to know? This is new for me, okay? You being unreachable."

"I will not be unreachable," she argues. "I just don't want to be disturbed. Page me and I'll call you right back."

I openly frown. "This is very suspicious."

"No it's not."

"Yes it is," I tell her. I straighten up. "Well, go on," I say, waving her away. "Go disappear mysteriously." I smile. "And please think of those of us who will be here slaving tragically away."

There is a flash of the famous Waring smile. "Page me if you need me," she says one more time.

I am still subletting a studio apartment on One Hundredth Street between Riverside Drive and West End Avenue. Since the guy I'm subletting from has just had his contract renewed on a soap opera taped in Burbank there's no rush for me to vacate and, frankly, I am content to spend thirteen hundred a month and use his stuff. There is a school of thought that believes I am throwing money away by renting, but any New Yorker will tell you that thirteen hundred for a furnished studio is more than a Dixie deal. And although my immediate fortunes have recently and vastly improved, I still need to budget my money carefully.

Three years ago our family home in Castleford was appraised at between $225,000 to $260,000. Interest rates have been so low and Fairfield County has been so invaded with new money that even Castleford, some ninety miles away from New York, is beginning to be considered a suburb! Our house, which I am to buy from my mother (she is getting remarried this summer), has just been reappraised for four hundred thousand. She is selling it to me for $350,000.

Now, when you understand how doubtful it is that I could even find a two-bedroom apartment in Manhattan for $350,000, you may understand my reluctance to consider buying a place where Scotty and I virtually just crash for the night. Certainly if it is a choice between owning the house my father designed and built—four bedrooms, two and a half baths, two fireplaces, five acres—and owning some hole in the wall with taxes and monthly maintenance charges, I'm choosing home. At least until that time when, which people say is coming, the real estate market tanks.

With my new DBS contract I will be paid $300,000 the first year. If you can believe it, this staggering amount of money is not considered to be a lot in my industry. If I anchored the local news in New York, for example at our New York affiliate, WST, I would probably make around a million. I know, I know, it seems all out of whack. I certainly am not complaining, although you might be interested in how I will spend that first $300,000.

First, I will pay roughly $80,000 in income taxes, which leaves $220,000. My agent takes fifteen percent of my gross income, $45,000, leaving me with $175,000. The network covers most of my union dues (while there isn't a union for producers, I belong to three unions—I appear on camera, I write copy and I edit film—and I also maintain a third-class engineer's license), which means my part of the fees run about $8,000. That leaves $167,000. Then $18,000 goes into retirement savings, which leaves $149,000. I'm putting $70,000 down on Mother's house ($40,000 has already been paid), which leaves $119,000. Property taxes will run me $6,000, which leaves $113,000. My fifteen-year five percent mortgage will be about $19,000 a year, home insurance $2,000, utilities in Connecticut $4,000, which leaves around $88,000. Overhead on my apartment in New York, including utilities and food for me and Scotty, runs about $20,000 year, the parking garage $4000, which leaves $64,000. Car insurance $1,500. Dental bills, vet bills and gym membership, around $3,000. We are now down to $59,500.

Now we get to the part where I have no job security after a year. If the newscast fails, I'm out, which in my mind means a necessity of savings to cover rock-bottom expenses for six months—which would be $25,000, leaving $34,500.

I have already pledged $5,000 to my church in Castleford, $15,000 to the United Way ($5,000 in New York, $10,000 in

Castleford), $2,500 to the Castleford Humane Society, $2,500 to ASPCA in New York and $5,000 to medical causes (cancer, leukemia, mental illness), which will leave me a grand total of $4,500 mad money (which I've already blown on Christmas and my intern Margarite).

DBS News gives me a clothing allowance—you know, *clothes befitting a successful anchorwoman*—and I travel so much for the network that the only vacation I want is to stay home!

So there you have it. While I will make $300,000 a year, cost-cutting measures and bargain hunting will benefit me just as much as they did when I made $35,000 and had college loans and car payments.

But wow, it is a whole different world. I earn, I live, I invest, I give, I will own.

The studio apartment is on the ground floor of a brownstone built in 1890 as a single family home. (The brownstone was most certainly from Castleford or very near to it; half of our brownstone mountains are missing because so much stone was excavated from them.) There's no doorman or anything; there are simply two sets of doors with an intercom system. DBS pays for me and Scotty to be taken back and forth to West End each day, which is a good thing since almost all cab drivers in New York are terrified of Scotty and refuse to pick us up. (Sometimes I am nervous about the cab drivers that *do* pick us up, because they peer at Scotty in the rearview mirror as if he could be something tasty.)

We are dropped in front of the brownstone and I wave at the security guard the block association employs at the end of the street near the fireman's monument. The driver waits until I have unlocked the front door of the building and the outer door is closed safely behind me before he takes off. I unlock my mailbox—very exciting, electric and telephone bills—and unlock the second door to get us into the foyer. We walk past the staircase to our door.

Sitting on the floor by the door is a vase of flowers wrapped in cellophane. A note from one of my upstairs neighbors is balanced on top, saying she signed for them Tuesday afternoon around four. Great, they've been sitting here without water for

three and a half days. I insert all the various keys required to open
the three locks on my steel door—a simple lock, a sliding bolt,
and an illegal police lock—drop Scotty's leash and pick the flowers up, pushing the door open with my hip.

The studio is spacious, with ten-foot ceilings and a large bay
window facing south. There are bars on the outside and no
drapes on the inside, but the jungle of plants left behind by my
actor-landlord effectively blocks the view from outside. Extending back from the big main room is a Pullman kitchen, which
gives way to a large bathroom, which in turn has a door leading
out to a tiny walled-in yard. Over the door to the yard is an air
conditioner that, in the summer, gives a whole new meaning to
the term cold shower.

Two other noticeable features of the apartment are a shallow
fireplace and a nine-foot round bed. Nothing in here, save the
food and the clothes and toiletries, belong to me, but the actor
has nice things: a glass table and four decent chairs, wooden
bookcases, a desk, lovely cotton sheets and towels. His glasses and
china are nice, too.

All in all we've been extremely comfortable here. (Scotty
thinks the bed is the biggest L.L. Bean dog bed in the whole universe.) The only drawback, in my book, is the lack of a dish-
washer.

I put the vase down on a counter in the kitchen, take Scotty's
leash and collar off (the jangling of his license and shot tags wake
me up) and throw him a couple of Milk-Bones. I cut the cellophane and wince; they had been beautiful white roses with deep
green leaves, but now are almost dry and wilting. I read the card:
"Looking forward to seeing you again." No signature. Great. Who
are they from? I fill the vase with cold water in (false) hope it
might revive the roses and take them out to place on the table.

I notice the blinking light on the combination phone and answering machine and hit the playback button while arranging
the half-dead flowers.

"Hi, Sally," my beau, Paul Fitzwilliam, says. "I just got back to
the station house and got your message. I can't believe they're
making you work this weekend when they already have you
working next weekend!" He makes a sound of frustration. "And

you don't even get to cover the Delafield story, which I hear is really something. Anyway, I'm going to be here until at least four doing paperwork, so if you want, call me when you get in." Pause. "I understand about this weekend. It just seems like lately we're jinxed—if it isn't you, it's me. Well, whatever, give me a call when you can, beautiful lady."

I pick up the phone and punch in the police precinct number, which by now I know by heart. Paul is working full-time as a cop in New Haven while going to law school. He's right, between the two of us we aren't seeing very much of each other.

I prop the wireless phone between my chin and shoulder and clear my ancient breakfast dishes from the table in front of the fireplace. "Paul Fitzwilliam, please." When Scotty walks over, ever hopeful for some sort of scrap, I say to him, "I can't believe the maid didn't clean up while we were gone, can you?" I am, of course, the maid in question. I walk back into the kitchen to put the dishes in the sink.

"Fitzwilliam," he says.

"Hi," I say softly, smiling a little.

"Hey," he says, tone immediately brightening. "How are you?"

"Still bummed I'm stuck here for the weekend."

Paul is seven years younger than I am. I met him when he was working as a police officer in West Hollywood, California. While I found him overwhelmingly attractive, I must confess it never entered my mind the relationship would ever or could ever lead anywhere. It certainly did not occur to me at the time that the twenty-six-year-old would take it into his head to move East.

Sometimes, when Paul agonizes over this first semester of his law studies—agonizing over whether he'll ever "get the hang of it"—I worry that his life would be very different had he not met me. At the very least he would still be a police officer, going to law school, but still frolicking in the sunshine with his surfing pals and endless girlfriends.

"As it turns out," he says, "I'm not sure how much I would have seen you this weekend even if you did come out. I was asked on a stakeout, and I was asked by the captain in a way that I really couldn't say no to. You know?"

"I know," I assure him, feeling a twinge when I realize he is not going to try to come into town to see me.

It's crossed my mind that by now there must be other women who have caught Paul's interest. Although he traveled a heavily populated trail of women to get to me, I'm confident he has not slept with anyone else since we met. Paul simply is not a liar and in this day and age—with all the disease and conditions running around—you must be sure of a person's character at least in this one regard.

I wonder how long it will be, though, until Paul moves on.

One Friday last month I was to meet him at The Anchor Bar in downtown New Haven. I arrived almost a half hour before I thought I would and through the window I saw this lovely young woman in thoughtful conversation with Paul—her face inches from his—and for half a second I thought about leaving. Then I thought about simply standing there watching them until—*if*—Paul ever took his eyes off her to notice me looking in through the front window. I told myself I was being stupid and went in. Paul introduced Vanessa to me, who, he explained, was working on her master's degree in history at Yale. He then introduced me to Vanessa as, "My friend Sally." Vanessa's eyes had widened a little when I came in and I know she recognized me from somewhere but she coolly dismissed the possibility of saying anything about it. At least to me.

I don't blame her. I was the competition, I understood that. Paul and I had a sexual commitment and that was it—either we were on or we were off, and for the moment we were a couple. No, I wasn't bothered by competing with a twenty-three-year-old; it was that for the first time I knew without a doubt how much better off Paul would be with someone like Vanessa. Someone young and fun, someone with a hell of a lot less miles on her, someone Paul could live with if he wanted. He had little to lose with a Vanessa and an awful lot to gain. A lot more control over the relationship, certainly.

"Things will be better when you're doing the news," he says, as if to remind himself why he is in this relationship. "You'll have regular hours and weekends off."

"Right," I say, wishing I could believe it, too, but as I warned him you just don't go into this line of work expecting a smoothly operating work schedule.

My eyes fall on the white roses. I could say, *someone sent me flowers this week* as a prompt, but if Paul didn't send them it will only bother him. I certainly hope he didn't send them because they must have cost a fortune.

White roses. Not necessarily romantic. Could be from any-one. My super maybe? (I got one of the guys from the studio to fix our building intercom system for free.)

"When exactly are you going to L.A. to meet with the affiliates?" he asks.

"Next Saturday."

"And your meetings are at the Manning Convention Resort?"

"That's what they tell me."

"Jack says they've got a great golf course there."

"How is Jack?" I walk through the kitchen to let Scotty out to do his last business for the day.

"Unemployed," he says, starting to laugh. Jack, Paul's former roommate, is always unemployed. He has a trust fund.

"So now that you're not out there," I say, "what does he do all day?"

"He's got two TVs in the living room now, both with a split screen, so he can watch four games at once."

"Maybe he needs another roommate, just to have someone to talk to."

"He's got two girlfriends—they come on alternate nights." He stops laughing and says something to someone on his end. "Sally?"

"I'm here."

He lowers his voice. "You have no idea how much I wish I were there, right this very minute."

He makes me smile and redden slightly as I feel an immediate response below. For whatever aspects of our relationship I fear are faltering, the sexual aspect is not the one. I know men—and women, too, I guess—are supposed to like sexual variation, but for months Paul and I have, without discussing it, gotten into a routine that gets us both, well, so aroused and ultimately so well satisfied I think we're scared to jinx it by talking about it. How

can I explain? That we can lie around, watching a movie, cud-
dled up together eating popcorn, and it won't enter our heads
to make love. But say we go into the kitchen to make popcorn
and somebody calls and says they're on their way over, and, well,
more likely than not we will soon be on the table.

I know. It's strange. The more wham-bam-thank-you-ma'am
the encounter, the more we both seem to get off on it.

On the rare occasion we can actually spend the night together
it feels more like a slumber party than one night in a love affair.
We have fun, but we almost never have sex. I mean, maybe if in
the morning I'm all showered and dressed and have to catch a
plane or something we might hastily succumb, but when we have
all the time in the world…nothing happens.

"But I gotta go," Paul finishes. "My partner doesn't know how
to spell *inebriated*." A laugh. "Seriously, we've got to roll. I'll call
you later because I might have some news."

"What news?"

"Not yet, not until I know for sure."

Scotty is scratching at the back door and I let him in, carefully locking the door behind him. "That's not fair, you can't
just—"

"Gotta go, babe—" And he is gone.

I hang up the phone and get ready for bed. My eyes keep going
back to those roses, trying to figure out who they're from. I make
a mental note to call the florist tomorrow and ask them about
the order, but when I go through the wrappings the flowers came
in I can't find anything with the florist's name on it. Strange. Very
strange.

I say my prayers and climb into bed. Scotty comes up on the
bed at my feet, circles around a few times to trample the imaginary grass, and lies down for the night.

There is an elegance to white roses and I can't help but think
of someone I don't allow myself to think about—David Waring,
Alexandra's older brother. He is definitely the kind of man to
whom stunning white roses would appeal; he would view sending them as a message he is thinking about me, but not in the
suggestive sense that red roses would.

No, they can't be from David, I decide. No married man sends white roses to a woman he asked to go away with him. And certainly not to the woman who not only turned him down, but sent him away. Permanently.

II

I think I've been on the phone about the Delafield murder for six straight days. It's all well and fine to give Kit, who's a cute kid, the career break of his life, but the result depends on how well an experienced crew can—or is willing to—cover for his lack of experience. Half the contacts I've given to the team in Gainesville call me to complain they only want to deal with me. Fine. Deal with me, then. So they do. I write it all down, hang up, call Kit, who then tells me to hold on while he gets Margo on the phone, too. "Kit, we don't have time. Just listen to me," I think I've said about thirty times.

When I succeed this Thursday afternoon in keeping him on the phone long enough to listen to what I have to say, I am so surprised I almost forget why I called. "Listen, Kit, Karen Mayer is willing to meet with you today—"

"But I've got to go on the air tonight."

"That's seven hours away. I want you to go over to her home now. She's there and expecting you. You need to watch her face very carefully when you ask her about—"

"But I have to rehearse," he says. "Alexandra wants me to change my delivery."

This is where I grit my teeth and ask him to have Margo call me. Three minutes later Margo is on the phone. "Did that guy from the Ponce de Leon reach you?" she asks me.

"What guy from the Ponce de Leon?"

"Everybody and his aunt at the Ponce de Leon keeps asking me if you're staying there under another name. There's some guy who keeps calling and showing up, looking for you."

"I have no idea what you're talking about."

"I don't think he's a contact." Pause. "While you were down here you didn't hook up with anybody, did you?"

"No," I tell her. "Now, about the kid, Kit—"

"He's overwhelmed. The story's fanning out in different directions and Alexandra's throwing stuff at him right and left."

"She's only telling him to do what I told him to do the day before," I say irritably, hurling an eraser across my office. I don't like working Monday, Tuesday, Wednesday, Thursday, Friday, Saturday, Sunday, Monday, Tuesday, Wednesday, Thursday…

"Sally." Margo pauses a moment. "He's what we have to work with."

This ticks me off even more, the implication that I am not making the situation better. Well, I am. And I'm not. *All right, Margo, I'll let it go.* "Caleb should be back from Tampa any minute, so send him with Kit to Karen Mayer's and *make sure* Kit goes through the questions properly. He's got to learn. Then have Caleb work on his report with him instead of you. He's scared to make a move without you, but Caleb's a great editor."

"Okay."

"Did you get the clothes wardrobe sent?"

"Yeah. He looks good."

"Tell him they're his to keep." I can't help but smile. It will be quite a windfall for the kid. Well, let's face it, the whole thing is a windfall for the kid, and as much as I might question Alexandra's decision to keep Kit on this story, it was his actions and no one else's that gave us the scoop on the murder in the first place.

"Do you suppose I'll ever be allowed a day off?" Margo asks.

"No," I tell her, "you have to work until you drop in your tracks. Death is the only way out." I check my field book. "How would Saturday suit you? You'll have to stay in reach in case something breaks—"

"Of course," she says eagerly.

"And you know we're all leaving for L.A. Saturday night."

"Yes."

"Then it is done," I tell her, "and I will tell Clem and Kit. You have Saturday off."

There is a cheer on the other end.

The Delafield story is a beaut. After six days the only suspect the authorities have is the missing casual laborer hired three days before the murder. As for the list of suspects who may have *arranged* for Delafield's murder, the list is rather lengthy: one ex-wife (from whom Delafield was somehow receiving alimony), two swindled former partners, a contractor Delafield owed four hundred fifty thousand dollars to (we are wondering if Delafield knew of this contractor's ties to a Miami crime family), a Saudi prince, an insane Dominican drug dealer and the husband of the woman Delafield had been sleeping with.

What gives the story its special sizzle, though, is how for years Delafield slid and sleazed his way around the rarefied "horsey set." ("I did think he was a rather ill-bred, smarmy sort of a person," one woman listed in the blue book said on camera, "but I didn't think he was a crook. He was rather good-looking, actually.")

So the Delafield story has everything—money, sex, drugs, murder, fashionable society—but she, the correspondent who started it all, is sitting here in New York working on these stupid presentations for the affiliates' convention. To be fair, though, the presentations are extremely important, particularly the five-minute video that introduces *DBS News America This Morning,* but I've reworked them so many times in an effort to get them right I'm starting to see them whenever I close my eyes.

For Alexandra's big presentation, covering the overall news division, we had to review the entire year for highlights to use in a montage of narrative, clips and sophisticated graphics that at this point seems more reminiscent of a major motion picture trailer than a TV newscast. But that is what it takes to keep the attention of the affiliate managers, particularly when the entertainment division will be there, too, bringing all of its Hollywood glitz with it. We've only just got the soundtrack fully sorted and now it should be a matter of tweaking it with Clem.

"Excuse me—Sally?"

I look up from my computer to see my intern, Margarite. Since there is currently a hiring freeze at DBS News, an unpaid intern is the closest thing to an assistant I can have. I just love this young woman. She's a senior at NYU and an absolute wonder. I know first-hand what it is like to juggle school, paying jobs and internships under the pressure of knowing that if your grade-point average slips, the entire endeavor can collapse with a rescinded scholarship.

Margarite graduates in May and formally signs on with DBS News as my full-time assistant on June 1. I can only hope she'll stay long enough with me to learn something before she is lured elsewhere. Margarite is not only acutely bright and capable, but has those stunning good looks of the new America—light brown complexion, large hazel eyes, dark brown hair and high cheekbones—that TV is scrambling to find and for which smaller markets will gladly skip the experience part of a résumé to acquire.

No, I think, looking at Margarite in the doorway, there's no way I will hang on to her for long. "What's up?"

"I thought you would like to see this," she says, walking over to my desk with a piece of paper. "It's another letter that ran in the *Herald-American*."

To the Editor:
I taught science at Castleford Junior High School for forty-two years and wish to say that Sally Harrington was a wonderful child and student and *Herald-American* publisher Alfred Royce III was not. After reading Alfred's editorial last week I gather absolutely nothing has changed.
Isabel Millar
Castleford

I burst out laughing. "You go, Miss Millar." I look up at Margarite. "You've made my day." This is the kind of thoughtfulness that makes me happy to slip Margarite a hundred and twenty-five bucks a week under the table to help keep body and soul together. The other interns always seem to be wealthy kids somehow related to the Darenbrooks, and when I was an intern I *swore* I would try to help students like me.

"Too bad I can't submit *this* to the wire services," I say.

"Sally," Margarite apologizes, "I'm sorry but I've got to go. I have that exam in an hour."

"Oh, right." I look at my watch; it is a little after three. "Go on, then, scoot. And thank you for all your help."

"I have a class at ten tomorrow," she says, backing out of my office, "and then I'll come straight here. Around noon."

"Excellent," I tell her. "Because tomorrow I want you to sit in on our run-through of the presentations. Ask us questions we can't answer, you know the drill. Be a mean station manager."

She smiles. "Great. Now, don't forget to call Mr. Peterson's office at three-thirty."

"I won't," I promise.

"Oh," she says, turning around again. "Human Resources wants to know if you'll run the blood drive again this year."

"Sure," I say, flipping my calendar open. "Tell them—" I stop myself. "Margarite, go! I'll call them myself. Just go! Don't be late."

After Margarite leaves I call over to Human Resources to set up a meeting for the blood drive and then, at three-thirty, call the office of Langley Peterson, the chief operating officer of Darenbrook Communications. "Ms. Harrington," Langley's ancient secretary, Adele, says in her ladies-should-always-wear-white-gloves-to-church kind of voice, "Mr. Peterson wishes, if you have time, that you would come to his office for a short meeting."

"Sure." Next to Jackson Darenbrook and the board of directors, Langley Peterson is as far up the corporate food chain as you can go. I'm going to say no? "Do you happen to know what it is in reference to, Adele?"

"He only asked that you come to his office as soon as possible."

★ ★ ★

The office of Langley W. Peterson is one of the two largest at West End. It is on the top floor of Darenbrook I and has a floor-to-ceiling view of the park and the Hudson River. His office favors dark furnishings—bookcases, conference table, leather chairs and couches—which give it a lawyerly feel.

Langley is a funny sort of a man. He is tall and slender, with dark hair heavily streaked with gray. He always dresses in a suit and tie and wears heavy, black-framed glasses that serve only to perpetuate the ongoing joke that he looks like Dennis the Menace's father. (It's been said that Langley has worn glasses like that for so long he's accidentally been on the cutting edge of fashion twice.)

He has his jacket off when I am shown in. He is sitting behind his massive mahogany desk, talking on the telephone. His pristine white shirtsleeves are fastened with gold cuff links. He gestures for me to have a seat in front of him, which I do.

We have a special connection, COO Langley Peterson and I, in that Scotty is the only resident in doggy day care who has successfully befriended the scruffy little black mutt Langley found a year ago in Central Park. (Langley named the dog Blackie, which gives you a pretty good idea of his creativity beyond things financial.)

"I see," he says into the telephone with some seriousness. "What else could we reasonably expect? They're not going to come up with a solution. If they did they'd be out of pocket for what it will cost to replace the entire system." He pauses, his lips pressing into a line, his eyes riveted to his desk. He shakes his head. "No. No way. Anybody but those guys—and tell them that I said so. Tell them I'm sick of their bullshit and if the problem isn't fixed in three days I'm bringing in someone else and will drag their sorry asses into court." He looks up suddenly, as if remembering I'm here. "Right. Let me know." He hangs up the telephone. "I'm sorry."

"It's fine," I tell him.

"It's a messed-up world out there," he says, clenching his fists. "How rational people can believe short-term thinking produces real solutions to anything is beyond me."

"They're looking for immediate results to make themselves look good *immediately*," I offer. "Why do long-term planning when they have no intention of sticking around to do any heavy lifting?"

He stares at me a moment. "Sometimes you surprise me, Sally."

I smile slightly.

"At heart you *are* a team player—Cassy's always said so," he says, starting to look through papers and folders on his desk. "It's often difficult to see while you're careening around from one crisis to the next."

I think this is a compliment, particularly the endorsement from our elegant network president, Cassy Cochran.

"I appreciate you've stayed away from the Delafield business," he says. "The morning sponsors hate that sort of thing, I'm told."

"So I understand."

"And I'm told you're still doing all the work on the story."

I shake my head. "It's the field producer, Margo Shande, you should thank. She's terrific."

He leans forward to pick up a pen.

"S-h-a-n-d-e," I spell for him. "But please don't promote her out of the field. She's the best we have. And Caleb Gorst is there now. He's a great writer and editor." I lean forward slightly as a hint. "G-o-r-s-t."

"Good, thank you." Then he puts his gold pen down, looks around his desk and suddenly snatches a piece of paper and pulls it in front of him. It is an oddly dramatic move for a man under such control. "Right," he says loudly, reading the paper to himself.

I wait.

Langley leaves the paper on the desk and sits back in his chair. He pushes his glasses higher on his nose, rests his elbows on the arms of the chair and knits his hands together, watching me. "Tell me your view on the current situation of *The Jessica Wright Show.*"

I blink. This comes out of nowhere. "Well," I begin, "the ratings are down, Denny's gone and the format changes and new producers are not helping—not the show or the host." I pause. "It's like watching people change seats on the *Titanic.*"

Behind his black glasses Langley's eyes widen slightly. He takes off his glasses to cover, and reaches into his back pocket for a white handkerchief to clean them.

So here we sit, Langley cleaning his glasses and me looking at a nice picture of his wife and twin children.

He puts his glasses back on. "I had yet to hear an opinion quite as brutal as that, Sally."

"The only way to save the show is to get Jessica back in the studio. *Not* me, Jessica Wright. She's only the one who can do it."

"She said she's not coming back."

"So everybody keeps saying." I lean forward, resting my arms on his desk.

"She's been asked, Sally," he says coldly, looking down at my arms.

"Sorry," I mumble, sitting back in my chair. I meet his eyes. "Jessica needs someone she loves and trusts above all others to talk the situation through with her."

"Who do you have in mind?"

"Will. For once maybe one of these inter-company marriages might work to our advatage." Whoops. Langley's married to the youngest Darenbrook sister. "I mean—Well, you know what I mean. If there's anyone who can influence her decision, it's Will. Because he wanted her to leave." I lean forward. "The thing is, Jessica Wright thrives on people, and on contact with people. Her work here was a source of great joy for her. I know she had trouble carrying a pregnancy and everything, but Alexandra says working had nothing to do with the miscarriages, that it was a genetic condition."

"She carried this child to term with four months of bed rest," Langley says.

"So they have a healthy little girl now," I say. "But what do you think the chances are that someone like Jessica is happy at home talking to the baby, the nanny and the maid?"

"I understand she's doing some fund-raising for charity."

This time I deliberately rest my arms on Langley's desk. "We're talking about Jessica Wright, a woman who considers twenty million people her intimate friends." I hit his desk once with my fist. "Somebody's *got* to talk to Will. Jessica, part-time, baby and nanny come to work with her three days a week."

There is a knock on the door and Adele tips her head in. "I am very sorry to interrupt, Mr. Peterson," she says, "but the police are here to see Ms. Harrington."

"We have a Detective Fitzwilliam out here to see you, Sally."

I suppress a smile as I respond to front-gate security. "Paul Fitz-william?"

"Yes, ma'am."

"Send him right through, please, thank you." I hang up Adele's phone and look up at her. I don't want Adele to think I'm bring-ing shame and disgrace to her beloved Darenbrook Communi-cations, but I don't think I should say my boyfriend is making an impromptu visit, either. "It's a police officer who has helped us in the past," I explain, speaking the truth. "If Langley should need me further, he can reach me in my office." Then I skedaddle.

Just as I come out of the complex into the driveway, I see Paul's old LeBaron convertible swing into view. I wave, smiling; he stops the car and jumps out, still dressed in his blue uniform (sans gun and hat). The security guard, alarmed at Paul's swift entrance and flash of uniform, comes tripping out of his hut.

"Police officer!" I call to security.

"Yeah, but from what country?" the guard says sarcastically.

"U. S. of *A.*," Paul says, giving me a kiss. Over Paul's shoulder I see the guard is mugging kisses at me. He is a dope. I turn my attention back to Paul.

When I first met Paul in Southern California during the trial for the murder of crime boss Nick Arlenetta, he was perpetually tanned, but since his move East he has turned the same pasty color as the rest of us after a long winter. He's added a line or two to his young face, most likely from patrolling one of the worst inner-city beats in Connecticut. His soft brown eyes look tired, but are filled with a degree of excitement I doubt is entirely due to seeing me.

"Sorry to crash in on you like this," he says, flashing his gorgeous teeth and reaching into his back pocket, "but I couldn't wait." He whips out a black leather wallet and flips it open for my inspection: it is the heavy silver shield of a detective in the New Haven Police Department.

"Security *said* Detective Fitzwilliam!" I cry, hugging him.

Oh, Paul! the security guard mimes behind him, clutching his hands under his chin like a swooning girl.

"Hey!" I shout. Paul turns around to see what I'm looking at. "You better not mess with Detective Fitzwilliam, because he'll bust your chops. Show him your badge, Paul."

"Sally," Paul growls, embarrassed.

"You made detective?" the guard says, coming over and looking at Paul with new appreciation. "Hey, that's great. But you're still wearing your old hardware."

"It just happened," Paul says.

"Congratulations," he says, giving Paul a hearty handshake. "What division?"

"Narcotics."

I turn to look at Paul. Even the security guy says, "Narco, whoa," and ducks his head a little, as if he might catch a bullet.

"It's where most of the action is," Paul explains, avoiding my eyes.

"I bet," the guard says.

"May I have a pass for him?" I say without enthusiasm.

He takes Paul's driver's license to scan through the machine, which then spits out a pass with Paul's picture on it. He affixes it to Paul's uniform pocket. As we enter the building, Paul puts his arm around me.

This is unusual for him, to display affection for me here. But is it affection, I wonder, or is it a new sense of possession? Interesting how people's behavior changes when they feel good about themselves.

"It's where the action is," I mutter as we cross the lobby. "You don't need any more action, it's hard enough to be doing all that you are."

"What could be better experience for a future prosecutor?" he asks, pulling his arm away to push the button for the elevator.

"A longer life," I suggest.

A few years ago I wrote a three-part feature for the *Herald-American* on the new gangs that had moved into central Connecticut to deal drugs. What most distinguishes these gangs from the ones of the past was that none of their members appear to have a conscience. They slaughter people they perceive as rivals and cut them up into pieces; they murder witnesses, including children; and they carefully train dealers to recognize the preteens and adults most likely to become addicted to their products in the shortest period of time. Their methods of operation are so debased even the major organized crime families are scared of them. They have no code of honor, not even among themselves.

"Come on, Sal," Paul says, "drugs are the single biggest cause of crime. Muggings, burglaries, murders—someone has to deal with it."

The elevator arrives and I don't say anything as we get in. As soon as the doors close Paul reaches for me, but I clear my throat and look up at the security camera.

"Forgot," he murmurs, backing away. Then he looks at me. "You should be happy for me, Sally. There's a nice raise that comes with this."

"I hope to God you didn't apply for Narcotics so you could make more money," I blurt out. "The idea is to stay alive until you finish law school." The elevator doors open and I walk out.

He doesn't follow, but stops just outside the elevator, silently demanding I stop and turn around to look at him. "Are you coming?"

"I don't complain about the stuff you have to do on your job," he says in a low voice, walking over. "I haven't complained about the stupid chances you take in the name of doing your job."

"You mean like having *your* ex-girlfriend run us down?"

"Risk is part of doing your job well," he says, ignoring my cheap shot. "It's the same with me. I'm better than most cops and better cops need to take greater risks in order to get the worst guys, okay? You do a good job and they throw money at you. We do a good job and maybe a few lives are saved down the road."

"Is that why you think I do what I do for a living? Just to make more money?"

"Don't give me grief on this, Sally," he warns. "It's what I want to do and it's what I'm going to do."

"Is that you, Paul?" a voice says. We turn around. While we have been arguing in the hallway Cassy Cochran has snuck up on us.

While it's normal to see a lot of good-looking people in television who never made it as on-air talent, it is very unusual for someone as beautiful as Cassy Cochran is to spend a thirty-year career avoiding the camera. During a writers' strike in the 1980s, legend has it a certain blue-eyed blonde news producer sat in for a striking anchor and by the end of the strike had actually *increased* WST's news ratings. That producer, Cassy Cochran, never appeared in that role on camera again, and it is only because I wrote an in-depth profile of her once for a magazine that I know the reason why.

Cassy had been one of those children blessed with great beauty and cursed by a horribly unhappy mother who wished to kill any semblance of vanity in her only child. Mrs. Littlefield had been a great beauty herself and had banked on that beauty to marry well. Her fairy-tale marriage to Prince Charming, however, ended up in alcoholic and financial disaster, and by the time Cassy's father died, Mrs. Littlefield had lost her beauty and easy ticket to another marriage. She thus became bound and determined to make her only child fear her beauty, and pounded it into Cassy that her brains counted for everything.

It also became plain to me when I interviewed Mrs. Littlefield that she had hammered her daughter's sense of self-esteem to pieces. And since Cassy's only ally growing up was her alcoholic father, it was no great psychological mystery that she came to marry an alcoholic herself.

It's amazing, isn't it? How people who appear to have every-thing often had so little to start with?

Cassy Cochran has been Mrs. Jackson Darenbrook for about eight years now, a period of her life synonymous with skyrock-eting professional success. And since prior to coming to DBS she had worked her way up from the news department at WST—our largest affiliate—to station manager, she had been no slouch to begin with.

She is now fifty-two, and while I know for a fact she is not the most uncomplicated person in the world, she is everything I hope I might one day become. I'd like to be happily married. I'd like to have children. I'd also like to continue a career that is meaningful to me, and to surround myself with people I admire and care for, as Cassy has done.

Kind is the first word that comes into my mind in relation to Cassy. She's wicked smart, but *kind* is the first word. *Strong* might come next. Then *wicked smart* and, finally, *elegantly beautiful*. She still has long straight blond hair—streaked with gray—that she always wears up on the back of her head.

Kind, strong, wicked bright and elegantly beautiful... Yes, that's what I'd like to be.

"We met at Sally's engagement party for her mother and Mack," Cassy reminds Paul, extending her hand.

Mother's fiancé, Mack Cleary, is a retired physicist who now teaches at Weslyan.

"Oh, I remember," he assures her, shaking her hand, "I just can't remember if I'm supposed to call you Cassy or Ms. Cochran or Mrs. Darenbrook or Ms. Darenbrook or—"

Cassy laughs.

I smile a little, proud of him. "Guess what?"

"Don't," he says under his breath, pointing a finger at me.

I wrest his arm down, holding it to my side. "Paul was just promoted to detective."

"Already?"

"I've been fortunate," Paul says, skipping the part about Nar-cotics.

"Law school, promoted to detective—" Cassy smiles, her eyes twinkling. "We always knew Sally had excellent taste."

"And so do you," he says smoothly, "since Sally tells me it was you who gave her her first big chance."

"Luck is for people who are ready," she says graciously. Changing gears, she turns to me. "I was wondering how the presentations are coming."

"Great," I say, meaning it. "I think you'll be pleased. We're just polishing them now. I can show you either one, or both, whenever you want."

"That's great." She turns to Paul. "It's nice to see you again, Paul. And congratulations again."

"Thanks. And it's good to see you again, too."

"*Cassy,*" she emphasizes, edging sideways down the hall. "You're not going to make me feel like a dinosaur, are you, Paul?"

"Never!" he declares, grinning. I forget how charming he can be.

"Sorry I put a damper on your news," I tell him on our way to Darenbrook III.

"Sorry I was a creep about the money thing," he says, briefly touching my hand. "I only care about it because I would like to know I can take care of you."

I blink a couple of times; this is out of left field. Has something progressed in our relationship that I missed? We reach the elevator banks of Darenbrook III and I push the button. "Can you stay over?"

"Sorry, no can do." He glances at his watch. "If you could offer me a cup of coffee, I'd be grateful. But then I have to take me and my new badge back to New Haven."

"You drove all this way, just to tell me?"

He nods. "Hell, it's three thousand miles to my parents' house. I wanted to show somebody!"

He is darling, I decide. He's not that traditional tall-and-handsome combination, but is simply attractive and appealing and strong, but with a warmth, too. And when he is wearing his uniform there is something irresistible about him, maybe because you know he's one of the good guys, or maybe because he looks like the kind of man you first thought, as a little girl, you wanted to marry when you grew up. You know, someone who liked to help people.

Our shoulders briefly touch as we walk down the hall to my office. When we turn into the area where Margarite usually sits, I find Alexander's assistant, Benjamin, standing there; evidently he has been waiting for me. "Benjamin," I tell him, "I'd like you to meet my friend Paul Fitzwilliam. Paul, this is Benjamin Kim, Alexandra's assistant."

"I believe we've met once before," Paul says, stepping forward to shake Benjamin's hand.

"Yes, I believe I have had the honor, Mr. Cutie-Wonderful," Benjamin tells him, making Paul laugh. Now I know they've met before; a lot of people can't tell when the Korean-American with a vague southern accent and advanced degrees in literature and a deadpan schtick is trying to be funny. "Here, this mess is for you," Benjamin says, shoving a sheaf of papers in my hands. "Big Kahuna Lady would like this translated into English before tonight's newscast so the Kidlet Whitehawk can read it. The new sales guy took her to see a sponsor." He turns to Paul. "We're all supposed to pretend the Delafield story isn't Sally's."

Paul just nods, but doesn't comment. I tell him to go ahead into my office and make himself comfortable. When he is out of earshot I turn to Benjamin. "We can disagree within the family," I quietly remind him, "but never ever in front of the neighbors."

"I think you need some kind of twelve-step program," Benjamin says, walking away.

In my office I find Paul looking at the photographs on the wall. "Who's this guy?" he asks.

I walk over. "You've met him. That's Jackson Darenbrook."

Paul frowns. "Why don't I remember him?"

"'Creepin' crickets, Sally ol' girl,'" I say, dropping my voice, "'what's with this rotgut vodka?'"

"Oh, right," Paul says, nodding.

"And these are the guys who own everything?" he asks, stepping back from a photograph of the whole Darenbrook clan. "Darenbrook Communications?"

"Yes, sir, that's our board of directors." I take a last look at the picture. "They've been very good to me."

"Then they are the most wonderful family in the world," he

says, taking my hands and turning me around. He looks down at my mouth, taking a breath and letting it out slowly. His eyes come up. "I've missed you."

"I've missed you, too," I say.

He glances behind me at the doorway and then pulls me close to kiss me. A few moments later I feel a hand sliding over a place that makes my spine stiffen.

It's like this with Paul sometimes, like the tumblers of a lock suddenly falling into place and it opening whether I want it to or not. One simple motion can make everything start sliding in the same direction. "Paul," I sigh, pulling his hand away.

"No one's here," he murmurs, grazing his lower body against me once, just to make sure I know what is on his mind.

"No, I can't," I say, swallowing, stepping back.

He smiles, slipping around me, making an exaggerated effort to silently close the door and—*click*—lock it. Then he leans back against it, waving me over.

I shake my head, feeling a little weak. "I can't."

He keeps waving me over, eyes half closing in an almost sleepy look I know so well. I look down at the floor, shaking my head no, but my face is burning because I know that I want to.

But not here! Maybe we could go down to a dressing room.

Now he has breezed past me to the window to close the vertical blinds, and then spins around with a mischievous smile.

I hesitate. He comes to get me and pulls me toward my desk, turning me against it. He holds my breasts in his hands and begins to move against me, and then backs off slightly to slide one hand up my skirt and into my panties. I haven't worn panty hose since Paul moved here; I wear thigh-highs. "You can't?" he whispers happily, kissing my ear.

His hands are all over me. Then he guides my hands down and I undo his belt, unhook his uniform trousers, pull down the zipper and bring his swollen state into the outside world. As I hold him, he looks at me and then closes his eyes, making a sound in the back of his throat. He roughly pulls up my skirt and yanks down my underwear. He presses me back against my desk and pulls my legs up around him. He mutters something I can't hear, shoves his pants down farther and directs himself, and then I feel him pushing in a little, making sure of the way.

Then he regrips me and pushes himself all the way in, making me crumble completely, feeling helplessly, divinely impaled. He pushes me down on the desk, lifting my knees a little higher, but then pulls me forward into his arms, creating an angle of greater friction, of greater contact, and almost immediately his thrust begins to falter. "Six times seventeen," he says, trying to hold back.

"Please," I gasp, and he holds me so tight I can scarcely breathe, but then he resumes thrusting and my desk starts making squeaking noises that almost make me laugh but that familiar ache is beginning to transform under him, pounded into something heavy, something heavy being torn loose and dragged to the surface.

I cry into his shoulder when the release happens so suddenly, and then clutch him as I spasm in waves around him and suddenly he freezes—and collapses on top of me.

"Oh, man," he sighs, holding me.

My face is buried in the side of his neck, wet.

Everything is wet. Warm and wet. And as Paul turns his head to kiss my cheek, I feel warmth seeping down between us.

My desk! I tense so abruptly Paul is startled upright, falling out of me. I lunge across the desk to grab the box of Kleenex. He starts to laugh and reaches to hold the box in place so I can pull the tissues out. "I still have my shoes on," I say under my breath, making us both start to laugh, our happy laugh, and then we pull our clothes together and sheepishly look at each other over all the incriminating Kleenex.

Someone tries my office door. We freeze. Whoever it is gives the doorknob a jiggle or two and goes away.

I open the blinds and the small window to let in some fresh air. I run my hands through my hair a little, trying to smooth it down, and walk over to do the same to Paul's. He hasn't stopped smiling. He slides his hands around my waist. "Was that the best or what?"

"I think I've got third-degree burns from your five o'clock shadow," I complain, touching a particularly raw area on the side of my face.

He kisses the end of my nose.

"You're going to get me into a lot of trouble some day," I whisper, kissing him back.

"If it's anything like this, I'm all for it," he tells me, taking me into his arms and kissing me one last time as if he means it.

I drop Paul off at the men's room and head into the ladies' room. When we emerge we both look presentable enough and smell only of soap. I walk him down to the driveway and wait for his car to be brought around, and then kiss his cheek goodbye. I watch him drive away and wave when I think he might be looking in the rearview mirror. He honks twice.

I've got to get a move on, I think, looking at my watch. But I have to admit I certainly feel better than I have for the past several days. I hurry back to my office in Darenbrook I to hunt for the copy Benjamin gave me to work on. I sail into my office and stop short when I find Alexandra sitting in a chair in front of my desk. She turns around, looking at me with an expression that can best be described as something between apprehensive and incredulous. There is a glint of something else in those eyes, too, as she says, "And was it good for you, too?"

My way of dealing with embarrassment is to pretty much not deal with it all, but simply work twice as hard until whatever prompted it has largely blown over. So I have doubled my efforts to make Kit Whitehawk look great tonight on the newscast. By the time we go on the air Kit's thoroughly rehearsed the copy I rewrote for him, he is sporting a sharp new haircut (sketched and faxed to Gainesville by Cleo) and he is wearing one of his four new out-fits (tailored suit, dress shirt, conservative tie, black oxford shoes).

"It's hard to believe he's the same guy," Clem remarks as we watch the newscast on a monitor in the newsroom. "He used to look like he was twelve."

"He still writes like he's twelve," the news editor on duty says.

"That's enough," I say sharply. "Kit scooped everyone on the Delafield murder and until one of you delivers like that I don't want to hear anything more about it."

The newscast goes smoothly and afterward, as she always does, Alexandra makes the rounds to thank everyone for their efforts. When she comes to me, that dreadful smirk is still playing at the corners of her mouth. "Kit looked and sounded great," she tells me. "Can we try to take a clip from his report tonight and work it into our presentation?"

What she means is, Sally, please reedit the presentation for the hundredth time and not complain about it.

"Sure," I tell her.

"He looked great!" Will declares, coming in from the control room. "Sally, do you think we can—"

"I've already asked her," Alexandra says.

"Excellent," he says, moving on.

As a rule the production crew breaks down quickly after the newscast and then the skeletal night shift slips in to take over. I amble over to Editing to see what I can do about adding Kit to the news division's presentation for the affiliate convention without hopelessly messing up the sound track. I've been sitting at the console for a while, trying to make things work, when I hear Alexandra clear her throat. I take one look at her expression and turn back to the console. "You're just going to torture me for the rest of my life about this, aren't you?" I say.

"To the contrary. I was thinking no wonder he's crazy about you."

I hazard another look at her.

She's leaning against the door frame, arms crossed over her chest. "Do you think you guys will get married?"

"Come again?" I say, flinching at my unfortunate choice of words. She comes into the editing bay and slides the glass door closed behind her. "I wondered how serious you are about Paul," she says, sitting in a chair and rolling it closer to the console to look at the screen. She leans closer to the screen. "That haircut really made all the difference, didn't it?"

"It helped a lot," I agree.

She reaches forward to advance the newscast.

"We won't get married," I say. "Paul will get sick of me never being around and will want someone who is really there for him." I look at her. "What about you and Georgiana?"

"Since we don't have sex in the office I don't think I have to answer that," she says without looking at me. "Somewhere around here Kit had his first confident smile."

"A little farther," I tell her. "There. Is that what you were thinking of?"

"That's it." She's right, Kit does look confident here. Trouble is it only lasts about two seconds. "Can you work this in?" she asks me.

"Sure." I mark the place.

She pushes herself up out of the chair. "I'm calling it a night," she says. "I've got a lot to do before we leave."

"Okay, see you tomorrow," I say, making a note on my pad.

"Even if we could get married, we won't," she says quietly, leaving.

"Wait, Alexandra!" I call, scrambling out of my chair and going out to the hall. She is waiting, but her expression is unreadable. I struggle for what to say. "I'm sorry" is what comes out.

She shrugs. "It's complicated."

She was going to have a child with Georgiana Hamilton-Ayres and now their relationship is simply "complicated"?

"I'm sorry," I say again.

She smiles a little sadly. "Thanks," she murmurs, turning to go.

It is almost one o'clock. I finished adding Kit to the DBS News presentation long ago and am now once again searching for a clip of me and Emmett from a particular half hour we did after the Mafia Boss Murder Trial. It was the half hour where I was supposed to interview organized crime figure Michael Arlenetta, the younger brother of the slain mob leader, but they arrested him outside the studio. As I scroll through the 492 hits on the video index that resulted from a "Harrington-Phelps Mafia Trial Arlenetta Police" search, I decide I am now so sick of these affiliate presentations I officially hate them.

I leave Editing to stretch my legs and see if anybody in the newsroom has cookies. "Some guy named Devon Clarke called," the news editor tells me. "He sounds drunk." I accept the slip of paper he offers. Devon is a photographer I used to work with at the *Herald-American* in Castleford. I glance up at the big newsroom clock. Something must be happening for him to call at this hour.

I pick up a phone and dial the number.

"Hello?" he shouts. There are voices and a great deal of noise in the background.

"Devon, its Sally."

"Oh, man, Sally, you're missing it!" he cries gleefully. "Hey, guys, it's Sally!"

"*Our* Sally?" a female voice asks.

"Hi, Sally!" a variety of voices call. They all sound drunk.

"So what's going on?" I ask, feeling tired suddenly and a little lonely.

"The *Herald*'s been evacuated!" Devon says. "Somebody called the police and said they were going to blow it up!"

Just about everybody in Castleford has at one time or another threatened to blow up the *Herald-American*, but no one has ever actually done it. I look at the clock again, thinking what an odd time it is for a bomb scare. They usually happen during the day so employees can take the rest of the day off.

"Tell her we figured it was her!" a guy laughs in the background.

She, I think

"Shut up," Devon says loyally. "I'm sure Sally has nothing to do with it. Although," he adds into the phone, "whoever it was specifically said they were blowing up Al's office."

"Where are you?" I ask.

"Across the street in the parking lot. The cops won't let us leave. But we have a bottle of tequila and the cops let Mary go to the Mobil station for potato chips and dip."

I smile, well able to imagine the scene. Anything is an excuse for a party with this crew and most any kind of food and booze will do.

"I'm telling ya, Sally—" Suddenly there is a lot of commotion on Devon's end and somebody screams. "Holy shit!" Devon says.

"What?" I say, bolting upright in my chair. "Devon, what is it?"

"There *was* a bomb," he says, sounding in awe. "The second-floor windows blew out. I gotta go—"

"Wait!" I cry, jumping up. "Devon!" The duty editor and night producer are looking at me, but Devon's hung up. "Damn it," I say, slamming the phone down and diving for the newsroom Rolodex. "Call Alexandra and tell her to get down here," I tell the editor. "A bomb went off in Castleford, Connecticut. Where's Eric?"

"He's working on the equipment inventory."

"Find him," I tell the producer, "and tell him we need a camera and mobile transmitter." I punch a number into the phone. "It's Sally Harrington from DBS. We need the helicopter to cover a bombing in Connecticut. Yeah-yeah-yeah, I have permission." *From myself,* I think, hanging up.

Thirty-eight minutes later our DBS van swings through the gates of the Hudson River helipad. The Darenbrook helicopter is just arriving from across the river and is descending. I've got our affiliate newsroom in Springfield, Massachusetts, on Eric's cell phone and Alexandra on mine, and I practically have to kneel on the floor of the van in order to be heard.

"We have to know first thing if it's a terrorist bombing," Alexandra is shouting.

It seems highly unlikely any terrorist would target my hometown as a means of rendering America helpless, but in this day and age who the hells knows? I promise to find that out while Springfield, in my other ear, is confirming they will dispatch a news crew immediately.

A few minutes later we take off, dizzily ascending and then sweeping across the northern end of Manhattan toward Connecticut. Devon doesn't answer my repeated calls to his cell phone.

When Castleford comes into view I direct the pilot to fly under the local NewsCenter 3 helicopter so Eric can get a clear shot of the scene. Downtown Castleford is a sea of flashing lights—police cars, fire engines, ambulances, the SWAT truck and a bomb-squad wagon are all in attendance. "Land there!" I shout to the pilot, pointing to the vast parking lot of Castleford's abandoned downtown shopping mall. "On the far side of the building!"

As soon as we touch the ground, Eric and I jump out and run across the parking lot in the direction of the newspaper. The *Herald-American* is housed in a renovated brick complex just two streets over, and as we circle a police blockade, I see the main entrance is mobbed with spectators. I also spot Al Royce standing near the front entrance with a state trooper. Since he's the last person who will help me get inside I neatly duck him.

"Sally!" A teenage boy appears at my side. I think it's young Sam Laurencelle, but he looks so much taller than the last time I saw him, at first I'm not absolutely sure. I love this kid, and his parents. (I should. They only saved me once from freezing to death.) "Devon's looking for you," Sam says. "The bomb set off the alarm at Dad's business so we came down and Dad was talking to him. They're around back. If I found you I was supposed to bring you. Come on," he urges, "follow me!"

We follow Sam, circling the newspaper complex and heading for the back perimeter of the campus. I spot Buddy D'Amico of Castleford PD, a friend since childhood, but there's no way he's going to help me get inside, either, so we duck him, too.

"I don't see your dad," I tell Sam, looking around.

"There's Devon," he says, pointing his arm in a flash.

I whip around and see Devon waving at me from behind a concrete retaining wall across the street. We jump over the parking lot guardrail and cross over, where Devon pulls us back into the shadows. "I found a guy who will get us in."

"Why haven't you gone in?" I whisper to Devon.

"Because the guy wouldn't take him unless he brought you," Sam pipes up.

"He said if I found you he'd take us in," Devon acknowledges.

"Whatever, who cares, let's go!" Eric urges.

I punch some numbers into my phone. "Will? We might be able to get inside with a camera. I'm handing the phone to Sam Laurencelle to tell you what he knows about the bombing." I thrust the phone at Sam. "Tell him everything you know and then try to answer his questions if you can. Do you think you can do that?"

"No problem," he says, taking my cell phone.

"And then find your dad and have him talk to Will," I add.

"Mom's around here, too, somewhere," he says, raising the phone to his ear. "Hello? This is Sam Laurencelle speaking."

"Let's go!" I whisper to Devon.

He takes us down an alley and we're doing yet another wide circle around the *Herald-American* campus, skirting around several boarded-up buildings. I glance behind me to make sure Eric's doing okay lugging his equipment. We seem to be leaving most of the noise behind us.

Devon hustles us across Zemke Street to the entrance of what in Castleford's industrial heyday had been a machinery-parts warehouse. Devon knocks sharply on the plywood nailed over the entrance. There is a thumping sound and then the whole boarded mass parts a crack. "I've got Sally Harrington," Devon whispers loudly.

The opening widens but I can't see anything in the dark.

"Sally Harrington?" a man's voice rasps.

"Yes," I confirm, stepping forward. "Devon said you could get us into the *Herald-American* building."

The door swings open entirely and I take the cue to stumble into the building. It smells damp and like—well, I guess like abandoned old industrial buildings do in the cold, a cross between a basement and your grandmother's well-oiled sewing machine. Devon, Eric and I gently collide with one another in the dark; the door slams and it sounds like a crossbar has been dropped across it. A flashlight comes on, blinding me. The guy is shining it right in my face.

"Please," I say, holding a hand up.

"Sally Harrington," he rasps again, swinging the flashlight away. He's under six feet tall, and while I can't really see him, I get the impression he might be homeless. "This way," he says gruffly, turning so suddenly I trip again.

"Watch out, there's a lot of junk lying around," Eric whispers. He offers to turn the camera floods on, but our guide shouts "No!"

"Give me your hand," the rasping man says to me.

"No, that's okay," I tell him.

"Give me your hand," he rasps again.

"Give him your damn hand, will you?" Devon says impatiently.

This is creepy. "All right." I hold out my left hand. He snatches it with surprising strength, a grip which is firm but does not quite hurt, and guides me to a set of stairs descending into a basement. With our eyes growing accustomed to the unsteady light, Devon and Eric keep close as we grope our way down the stairs.

Mr. Raspy pulls me off the last stair and I step into fetid water. When the gook floods my shoes I suppress an urge to gag. The walls are ancient brick with mortar oozing down the sides. There are spiderwebs so thick they cast shadows from the flashlight. Mr. Raspy keeps pulling me, his hand now getting sweaty. "I really can see now," I whisper to him. As a response he gives my arm a violent yank, and pulling me forward he catches me just before I go headlong into the gook.

"You okay, Sally?" Eric asks.

"Yep."

Mr. Raspy has now roughly linked his arm through mine and we slog along over squishy slippery stuff. He pushes open a big wooden door and pulls me into a round brick tunnel. The ground graduates uphill and mercifully we leave the squishing goo behind, although we all reek of it. The floor levels out for a while, and then suddenly the man stops and shines the flashlight on a set of six brownstone stairs. They lead up to a door, hung on iron fastenings, which is secured on this side with a crossbar. He pulls me up the stairs and finally lets go to take down the crossbar and jam a screwdriver into the iron keyhole. Something clicks, and with a shove from his shoulder the door opens.

Mr. Raspy shoves me through the door. "I need the flashlight," I tell him. He takes my hand, slaps the flashlight into it, grabs me by the shoulders and forces his mouth on mine. I don't know if the soreness is left over from Paul, but, whatever, it hurts. He pulls me closer and much to my shock and dismay, I feel his arousal. Abruptly he then releases me and jumps off the stairs. A moment later we hear him running through the tunnel in the darkness.

8

I wipe my mouth for about the tenth time with the back of my hand as I lead Devon and Eric through an area I never saw while I worked at the paper. It is a dry and musty storage area and has cardboard storage boxes piled five high in double rows. Labels read: Miscellaneous 1959, Correspondence 1959-60, Editorial Page 1959. Evidently these are records from the publisher's office, going back to even before the *Castleford Morning Herald* merged with its rival, the *Castleford American*. "I think we're under Circulation," Devon whispers.

I sweep the flashlight beam around and spot a set of concrete stairs on the far side. Quickly we climb these and find a fire door at the top. I turn off the flashlight and push it open. It is the circulation office. The emergency lighting over the doors is on and there are swirls of red lights coming in through the glass doors from the outside. I kneel and find that the carpet is soaked. The sprinkler system must have come on after the blast. I can only imagine how much damage that alone has done to the equipment in the building and fleetingly consider the possibility of Al engineering this for the insurance money.

"That's the staircase we want," Devon whispers in my ear, pointing across the room to the luminous Exit sign.

"Right," I acknowledge. "Do you need me to carry anything?" I whisper to Eric.

"I'm good."

I crawl along the floor, keeping out of the line of sight from the glass doors. I rise to my knees and open the door to the stairwell. We can see perfectly well on the stairs with the emergency lighting, but there is a horrible acrid smell of burning plastic that's making my eyes tear. We pause on the third-floor landing to get ourselves sorted.

While the guys ready their cameras, I touch the fire door. Cool. I put my ear up to it but can't hear anything. "Devon," I whisper, "we're on the northwest corner of the newsroom, right?"

"Yeah."

"Al's office is that way, right? Far side?"

"Right."

There are no windows in the newsroom proper, but Al's office is right off it and it was his windows that were blown out by the bomb. It must have been planted in or around his office at that end of the floor.

"We should have at least thirty seconds," I whisper. "As we go in, Eric, the site of the explosion is probably around two o'clock, far side. The partitions around the desks are only four feet high, so you should be able to get the shot. I want you to focus tight at two o'clock and then zoom out to take in the whole scene in context. Ready?"

"Got it," he assures me, mounting the camera on his shoulder and turning on the floodlights.

"Devon?" I whisper, shielding my eyes against the glare.

"Ready."

"Okay, here we go," I say, quickly opening the door and holding it open for Eric. The powerful beam of light from the camera cuts a swath through the lingering smoke and debris of what used to be the newsroom. The cubicle walls are blasted, computer screens smashed, papers are all over the place, and there is that horrible acrid smoke that makes Eric start coughing. We've caught the authorities by surprise; they are standing near what used to be Al Royce's office and are wearing gas masks and haven't quite yet distinguished our TV camera light from emergency lighting carried by rescue workers.

As soon as Devon's camera starts flashing, though—he's shooting a series, sweeping the room in an arc, flash-flash-flash-flash-flash—a firefighter, I think, raises the alarm and people start picking their way through the wreckage toward us. Devon hightails it back out the door and I have to keep yanking Eric's shirttail to get him to back out. We dash down the two flights of stairs to the classifieds office. As we cut across Circulation a searchlight blazes through the glass doors; Devon flings open the door to the basement and we stumble over each down the stairs—I whack my knee but good—but I get the flashlight on and limp my way back to the big wooden door. The guys are right behind me, handling their equipment well and knocking over only a couple of boxes.

We hear the thundering boots of rescue workers overhead in Circulation. I open the door for the men and see flashlights shining down the stairs. I pile in behind the guys and pull the massive door shut behind me. "The bar," I say, but Devon's way ahead of me, shoving his camera into the crook of my arm—making the flashlight swing crazily—and picking up the crossbar to drop it in the steel braces.

Devon takes his camera back and I lead them down the stairs into the tunnel. Our pursuers have reached the big door and are pounding on it. We run into the slimy stuff again and slosh through the basement and take the stairs up to ground level, where this time Eric slips and falls on one knee. We hesitate at the front door of the building while Devon opens it a crack to look outside. Then he pushes it open and slips outside, Eric following. I snap off the flashlight and suddenly feel myself being lifted in the air by two sets of hands. There is one really big shadow and someone else. I jam my heel on somebody's instep and he swears, and I yell for Eric.

"Get her other arm," a man says.

Standing in the doorway, Eric turns the camera lights on, blinding me and whoever it is that is holding on to me. Devon pushes past Eric and butts the guy holding me and he falls back, letting go. Devon grabs my arm and pulls me out the door after

Eric. "This way!" he says, yanking me around the corner as Eric switches off the camera lights.

We hurry down an alley and then Devon takes us around the back of another boarded-up building.

"Who the hell was that?" I ask Devon.

"The guy who took us in and a cop, I think," he says, huffing and puffing.

"It was the guy who took us in," Eric confirms. "I couldn't see the other one."

"God, how weird is that," I mutter. "Listen, Devon, we have to get to the old shopping center. How should we go?"

"This way," he says, leading us across the street and down yet another alley. I trip over some car parts and Devon steadies me. "I've got to get to the *Register* to file these with AP," he says as we near the railroad tracks that divide the city.

"You can't take them to the *Register,*" I say between frantic gulps of air. The *New Haven Register* is a rival paper.

"Like there's equipment I can use here!" he says, panting. "So look, go right out of here, and then go left. You'll see an alley that winds around, but it will bring you out farther down on the tracks. You can cross over to the parking lot from there."

"Owe you big time, Dev," I say, pushing off with Eric.

As we spot the alley I hear "There she is!" and think *Oh, God, now what?* But when I look over I see a gleaming pickup and someone frantically waving to get my attention. "Sally, it's us! Sam! And Mom and Dad! I've got your cell phone!"

We jog over to the passenger-side window. Wanda Laurencelle leans forward in the seat to see past her son. "Sally, is that *your* helicopter at the Hub?"

"Yes," I say, trying to get control of my breathing.

There is a brief conference in the front seat and then the passenger door opens and Sam and Wanda slide out. "Come on, get in, Sally," Bob says from behind the wheel. "I'll get you there."

"What about you guys?" I ask Wanda.

"We're cool," Sam assures me, holding a hand out to help me up into the truck.

"Bob, we'll meet you back at the office," Wanda says to her

husband. Eric climbs up, Sam hands his camera up to him and then Wanda shuts the door. "Be careful."

We roar off and Bob explains the only way we can reach the Hub without meeting a police blockade is to go all the way around to the other side of the old shopping center. We go flying down Colony Street, over a bridge spanning the tracks, and then we slow down through a housing development. I take the opportunity to call Will in New York. "Bill Randolph's here with a camera and a truck," I report to Eric when I hang up. "We just have to get your pictures to West End and then Springfield will take over."

"Uh-oh," Bob Laurencelle says as he slows the truck to a stop.

Our helicopter is still there in the parking lot, all right, but so are about three hundred people who have come out of the housing project to stare at it. "We still might make it," I tell Bob, kissing him on the cheek and hastily apologizing for stinking up his beautiful truck. We jump out and hurry into the parking lot through a large tear in the chain-link fence. Eric and I push into the crowd, begging to be excused and allowed through.

"You the star people?" a young man demands of me.

"*Dummkopf!*" says his friend, hitting him on the side of the head with his baseball hat. "That ain't the Life Star."

The Life Star emergency transport is probably the only other helicopter that has ever landed in downtown Castleford.

We break through the circle to find the pilot has done exactly what Eric asked him to do, which was to unfold the portable transmitter tower and set it up on its stand. Eric sets to work, plugging in his camera, and little red lights start twinkling on the delicate ten-foot apparatus as Will verifies over the phone that they're receiving our transmission at West End. There, we're done; Eric and I start breaking down the tower and dish. I can't tell you what a bizarre scene it is here. People of all sizes and shapes and ages and colors fanned out in a circle around us, almost all of them wearing coats and sweaters over nighties and pajamas. It's like an inner-city version of *Close Encounters of the Third Kind*.

"We're good to go!" I tell the pilot, kneeling to close up equipment cases.

"I can't take off unless we get these people back."

"Yeah, okay," I say, frowning. I cock my head, listening. Sirens. Eric has his camera on his shoulder again with the floods on, filming the crowd.

"Everybody has to move back!" I yell at the crowd, waving at them with both arms. "Move back! Move back!"

The crowd surges forward a little, somebody saying he wants to be on TV.

Eric shuts off the camera lights. "Immigration!" he yells, running to the helicopter. A murmur sweeps over the crowd and I see one, two, no, more like ten—no, fifteen people hurrying away. The murmuring continues and then a big group of fifty or so scurry away through the hole in the fence. By the time we're in the helicopter and the blades are starting to turn, the only people even remotely near us are a couple of kids doing wheelies on their bikes, following three old ladies, one of whom is pushing a baby carriage, who are amiably chatting as they pass through the hole in the fence.

I see two police cars, lights flashing, turning into the parking lot. "We've got to move!" I shout to the pilot, and slowly the bird lifts straight up, hovers over the parking lot—the pilot making sure we are well clear of everything—and then we do a kind of sweeping dip to set off that makes me grab the armrest with one hand and Eric's arm with the other.

At the helipad in New York a car is waiting to take us back to West End. When we drag into the newsroom it is a little after five-thirty in the morning and we are pleased to see what the gang was able to make out of Eric's footage and Bill Randolph's reporting. What was so cool was how the camera had picked up far more detail in the blasted newsroom of the *Herald-American* than we could see ourselves at the time through the smoke.

The news editor sniffs the air around me and Eric. "Yech."

"You can't have everything," I say, looking down at my destroyed clothes and shoes.

"Please go away," he tells us. "You did a great job but you really stink, you guys."

I look at Eric wearily. "You were so fantastic I don't know where to begin."

"Shower me with money," he suggests.

"You'll be lucky if that stench comes off in a shower," the editor says.

I take the elevator up to the ground floor of Darenbrook I and hurry outside where dawn is breaking.

Cha-*ching,* cha-*ching.*

"Hiya, handsome," I tell Scotty as I open the pen. Any more dirt at this point cannot possibly matter and so I pat my chest for Scotty to jump up, which he does, gently resting his paws on my shoulders. "I'm sorry I'm so late," I tell him, holding his furry face in my hands. Then I kiss him on the nose and tell him to get down. When he does he starts sniffing my shoes. "I know. They were my favorites," I sigh. Leather Cole Haans, utterly ruined.

I retrieve Scotty's leash, snap it on and lead him out of the run, across the park and into Darenbrook I. (Shhh.) We take the elevator down to the studio level and tiptoe (or as in Scotty's case, clicky-toe) our way through the labyrinth of hallways to reach Alexandra's dressing room. (Mine doesn't go into construction until I move over to *DBS News America This Morning.*) I unlock the door, flip on the light and let Scotty off his leash. It's a fairly small, oblong room, but very comfortable, with well-padded wall-to-wall carpeting. There is an upholstered bench in front of a dressing table and a mirror circled with lights. There's also an easy chair and a daybed with a coverlet thrown over it.

I take off my shoes and thigh-highs, put them in the trash basket and tie the plastic liner into a knot. I strip off my clothes and put them in another plastic trash bag and tie that into a knot. I rinse my hair in the shower and scrub the smell off me. After I towel off I wrap myself in the terry-cloth robe that hangs on the back of the door. I take the cushions and coverlet off the daybed, put them on the dressing table and go to the closet to retrieve a pillow and thermal blanket from the top shelf. I set the alarm on my watch, flick off the lights and cross the room in the dark to lie down on the daybed. I turn on my side, scrunching the pillow up, pull the blanket over my shoulder and let my hand fall over the side of the bed. I feel around until I touch fur.

Scotty is curled up under me, his breath quiet; he is already close to sleep.

Blessed sleep cometh.

The alarm on my watch goes off at noon. I force myself to get up and take a more thorough shower, washing my hair twice. I retrieve some of the clothing I keep in the back of my boss's closet and dress in slacks, a cotton sweater and flats. I sneak Scotty out to the parking lot so he can do his business and then I hide him in the lobby coatroom while I go out to the security hut to bum a cup of coffee. I swing back to pick Scotty up on my way to the newsroom.

"What's new with the Castleford bombing, anyone know?" I call out, crossing the room with Scotty and taking a seat in front of a computer.

"That dog's got big teeth," an assistant producer observes, backing away.

"Nothing," a news writer answers me. "The Springfield crew's still there if anything breaks."

"Why aren't you there?" the assistant producer asks, making a wide arc around us to reach his station. "I thought Castleford was your hometown."

"I was and it is," I answer, logging on, "but I had to come back and sell cereal. Bombings are both unseemly and unladylike."

"Oh," the assistant producer says, still warily eyeing Scotty.

"When do you guys leave for L.A.?" the writer asks.

"Tomorrow night," I answer, swallowing coffee and scanning the news-update screen. (I don't know why, but Security always has the best coffee around here.) I pick up the phone and punch in Devon's cell number in Connecticut. No answer, just his voice mail. "Devon, its Sally," I say. "Please call me and let me know you're okay."

As the writer said, I see the Castleford bombing is on the update screen but with no new information.

At my side Scotty whimpers softly, pressing his nose against my hip. I scoot my chair back so he can crawl under the desk. (He loves caves.) A studio technician cruises by. "Hi, Sally."

"Hi," I say without looking up from the screen. I see the bomb at the *Herald-American* has already dropped to second place on the preliminary run-down sheet for tonight's newscast. Because no one was injured I knew it wouldn't hold the lead. Sad but true.

"Did you really make out with a homeless guy?"

I blink a couple of times. "What?"

"We heard you made out with a homeless guy to get a flashlight."

"That's what you heard from whom?" I ask, turning around in my chair to look at him.

"Can't remember."

"Ms. Harrington?" a young woman's voice says. I swivel the other way. "Mr. Phelps is upstairs in his office and would like to see you when you have a minute."

"Thank you. Tell him I'll be up a in a few minutes."

"Great," she says cheerfully.

"Wait a minute," I say, turning around. "I'm sorry, but who *are* you?"

"Mr. Phelps's new secretary."

"I see. Well, welcome. Tell Mr. Phelps I will be up soon."

"Thank you, Ms. Harrington!" she says, flashing a smile and sailing off.

"Perky little thing, isn't she?" the news writer asks no one in particular.

"Hey, Sal," Will says, striding into the newsroom. "You didn't tell me you made out with a homeless guy."

"How can it be, Will Rafferty," I counter, "that there is a hiring freeze at DBS News and yet Emmett has a new secretary? When, may I remind you, you won't put Margarite on the payroll until June. Margarite—remember her?—she who has been slaving around here for three months for zip?"

"Emmett's overhead is already figured in the morning news budget and you're still on the nightly news budget," Will says.

"So why can't Margarite go on the morning payroll?"

"Because you're still on the nightly payroll, Sally, and she's part of *your* overhead, and you don't have any allocation for a secretary on that budget yet because you are not yet a part of it."

"So little Miss Chicky Poo just waltzes in and gets a paycheck?"

Will gives me a look. "Look, let's get back to the question at hand, Sally. I am willing to break the bank to get you your own flashlight. I don't *want* you to have to make out with homeless guys anymore."

The guys crack up.

"I did *not* make out with a homeless guy," I grumble, swigging the rest of my coffee as if its whiskey and slamming my cup down. "Not unless they have great dental plans and use Listerine breath strips."

"Maybe he was wearing dentures," the news editor suggests, prompting the guys to laugh again.

I don't bother answering this time. It's hopeless. The rumor is no doubt already all over West End.

Will walks over to peer under my desk. "Is that your dog under there?"

I cross my arms over my chest. "He's the only secretary I can afford."

"Come on, Sally, get him out of here."

"Very well," I say, standing and pulling the chair away from the desk. "Come along, Scotty, we've got better things to do, better places to go and better people to see." Scotty rouses himself, bumping his head before coming out. I rub his head and we start across the newsroom.

"I don't know how you did it, Sally," Will calls, "but the charges for the helicopter are coming out of Corporate. Nice going."

"Thanks," I say, having no clue how I achieved this.

I drop Scotty off at doggy day care and continue to Daren-brook III. I stop in at Emmett's office, but he's not there and nei-ther is his secretary, so I walk on to my office at the end of the hall.

"Sally!" Margarite cries, eyes wide in excitement. "That was the coolest! Everybody's stealing our footage from the bombing! I can't believe I missed everything! I wish you had called me! I can't believe we were the only ones to get in the building!"

"Glad you liked it," I tell her, smiling and opening my snail-mail folder.

She drops her voice. "Did you really have to kiss a homeless guy?"

"He stole a kiss, yes," I say, flipping a letter to look at the next one. "But he gave me his flashlight, which is the only way we could have found our way through the building."

"Ick," she says.

I scan a handwritten note from our San Francisco affiliate manager. At least *he's* excited about *DBS News America This Morning.* "The more I think about it, the more convinced I am he wasn't homeless. I think he was wearing Armani aftershave."

"What's that about?" she says. "So who was he? How did he know about the tunnel?"

Good question. "That's what we need to find out. So what else is going on?"

She opens a notebook. "Alexandra wants us to make copies of the pertinent files on Wilson Delafield and send them to Gor-don Strenn."

Gordon Strenn is president of DBS Entertainment. He was also once Alexandra's fiancé. (Oh, it's a long story—if I tried to explain all the love affairs and relatives at Darenbrook Communi-cations I'd be here for years.)

"She's trying to sell the dramatic rights to Mr. Strenn."

"Not a bad idea."

"I'm not sure I understand about the dramatic rights," Mar-garite admits. "How can Alexandra sell the rights to someone else's life?"

"She wants to sell the rights to produce a movie that is based on our information about Delafield. Two books about Delafield have already been signed up by publishing houses and the authors have already contacted me."

"But can't Mr. Delafield's family sue? Doesn't his life story belong to him?"

"He was a publicity hound, Margarite, and you can't deliberately try to be famous and then try to stop people from writing about you once you've become a public figure."

She giggles. "Maybe some day there will be a miniseries about you."

"God forbid," I sigh, wondering nonetheless who would play me. "Anyway, since Delafield's dead anybody can pretty much do whatever they want now."

Margarite frowns.

"I know, it's gross," I tell her, moving past her desk to the filing cabinets set in the wall. "But that's the choice people make when they decide they want to be famous." I slide a file drawer open. "You can download all my computer files on Delafield for Gordon."

"Is there anything confidential?"

"Not that you will be able to find," I answer, thumbing through the files. "My source notes are safely stashed." I pull out a file. "This is something Gordon might like to have. Do we have a box?"

She jumps up. "I think there's one in the supply closet."

A few moments later Margarite returns with a cardboard box and I hand her three bulging files. "Photocopy these first and send him the copies. Make sure the photographs of Delafield are clear. They'll need them for casting." I pull out another thick file and shove the drawer closed. "This should do it," I say, handing it to her. Then I walk back to her desk to get my mail folder, tuck it under my arm, and pick up my copy of the *New York Times*.

"There's fresh coffee," Margarite says. "I just made it."

"Thank you," I say, scanning the headlines on my way into my office. The Middle East. More deaths. Every day more deaths; it's always the Middle East, it seems, which is one of the major reasons DBS News is expanding the newscast from INS to a full hour. The focus of our news-gathering operation has always been on the domestic front; our newscast has the feel of a national local news hour, if you will, and we have always used INS reporters to cover international for us. It was a decision made from the get-go: *DBS News America* is about the news of the day in America. We don't put flak jackets on Alexandra and send her to Iraq to pretend she's an expert on the Middle East; we trust the British news agency to faithfully continue to do what they do best, which is to report international news in a straightforward way almost never seen in the States.

I pour myself a cup of coffee in my office. "Margarite?"

Her face appears around the door.

"How did your test go at school?" I walk over to my desk to sit down.

"Oh. Okay, I guess."

I swallow a little coffee. "Do you want to talk about it?"

She shrugs. "There's nothing to talk about. It was one of those either-you-get-it-or-you-don't tests and I don't think I got it so well. Thanks for asking, though."

"Have a seat for a minute," I suggest. When she takes a chair I lean forward slightly, lowering my voice. "It seems Emmett now has a secretary."

"I know," she says glumly.

"I wanted to explain to you why she is on the payroll already and you aren't. The problem is, I'm still on the nightly news budget and so my office overhead is, too, which would include you. The nightly news budget is frozen, so until I officially move over to the morning news budget, I can't put you on the payroll."

"But you do want to hire me, right?"

She says this in such an earnest way it breaks my heart. "Of course I do! And your title will be assistant."

"Is there really a difference between a secretary and an assistant?"

"'Assistant' means you are apprenticing. Like Benjamin with Alexandra. You guys want to climb the ladder, while a secretary pretty much stays put. Usually because they want a straight nine-to-five job." I sip my coffee. "Did you do as I asked? Did you talk to people in similar jobs at other networks?"

She nods. "Yeah, it's miserable right across the board, just as you said."

"But that's only in the beginning," I tell her. "The industry has to make it tough in the beginning because there are so many people who want to get in and it's a way to screen out everyone but the most able. Unless they happen to be a relative of someone on the board, of course." I open the middle drawer of my desk. "I was going to give this to you tomorrow, since I'm making you come in on a Saturday."

"You never *make* me do anything, Sally. You make me *want* to do things."

I hand her an envelope. "It's just a card saying thanks for all your hard work. And there's something else in there, so don't lose it."

She tentatively takes the envelope from me. "I don't like taking money from you."

"There's no money in there."

She looks puzzled.

I fold my arms on the desk. "I had no money in this world when I started college. I had scholarships and I had student loans, period. I cleared dishes in the cafeteria and I typed like ten million health forms." I pause to smile. "My best friend in college just happened to be a millionaire's daughter, so that helped a lot, believe me, because they only lived a mile from our dorm and we ate there a lot."

She laughs.

"In my first news job, if I hadn't bartended on weekends I wouldn't have made it." I lean forward even more. "Do you have any idea how happy it makes me to now be in a position where I might help out another young woman a little? Since she doesn't have her roommate's millionaire parents to have dinner with on Saturday night?" I nod toward the envelope. "That's a gift certificate for a two-bedroom suite with a kitchen for the week of your graduation so your family will have somewhere comfortable to stay."

Margarite bursts into tears. I pluck some tissues out of the box—guiltily thinking of their urgent purpose yesterday—and walk around the desk to hand them to her. "Publicity got the rooms for me, so if you want to thank anybody you should thank Alec downstairs."

"Sally!" Emmett Phelps says, swinging into my office waving a

DVD. The former USC professor of criminal law is wearing one of his trademark brown tweed jackets, a disheveled white shirt, striped tie and horn-rimmed glasses. "Clem finished the montage—you've got to see it!" He turns to the television in my bookcase.

Margarite wipes her eyes. "I better get the files to the copy center. Oh—and Alexandra wants you to touch base with her."

"Okay."

"Thank you," she says quietly, holding up the envelope. "They'll be so excited, you have no idea."

"You're very welcome." I pick up the telephone and punch in Alexandra's extension. I look over at what Emmett's doing. "Emmett, you have to turn it on first."

"Alexandra Waring's office," Benjamin Kim says.

"Hi. Is she around?"

Benjamin starts humming the theme from *Jaws: dune-dah dune-dah dune-dah dune-dah...* (Benjamin is a little eccentric.) "It's dangerous times in these waters."

Margarite comes back in carrying a large vase of flowers wrapped in cellophane. "These just arrived, Sally."

"Put them on the coffee table. Thank you. Benjamin, what are you talking about?" I say before covering the mouthpiece of the phone. "The button on the right, Emmett. The one that says Power."

"You're about to be called on the carpet by La Presidenta. She was in here screaming at Alexandra."

"Cassy never screams," I tell him.

"Evidently she's learned how."

Uh-oh. "Could you by chance hear what she was screaming about?"

"Nope, sorry."

"Sally?" Margarite says, appearing in the doorway. "Cassy Cochran on two."

I hang up on Benjamin and roll my eyes after I look at Emmett. He's got the DVD carousel spinning around and around. "Hi, Cassy," I say as warmly as possible.

"My office, two minutes." Pause. "If you would be so kind."

"Of course." I guess I shall be that kind.

"You wouldn't happen to know what this is about," I whisper to Cassy's administrative assistant.

She holds both hands to her mouth to whisper back, "No."

"Thanks a lot."

"Sally?" Cassy's voice calls from inside her office.

I take a breath, put a pleasant expression on my face and walk in. (I've already put on earrings and a little makeup and brushed my hair.)

The president of DBS Television is sitting at a small round conference table in the corner of her office. Like Langley Peterson she has a floor-to-ceiling view of the park and the Hudson River. Her reading glasses are sitting on some papers in front of her and she is leaning on the table with one elbow, eyes closed, holding the bridge of her nose with her hand.

More strands of hair are slipping down from the back of her head than usual. This is not good.

"Hi," I say softly, crossing her office. It is lovely in here. It has a gracious French country feel, with light-colored woods, rich burnt oranges, mellow yellows and sky blues—with a dash of papaya-red here and there. Cassy lowers her hand and looks up at me, blinking. "Have a seat."

Also not good. She almost always asks me if I'd like something to drink first. I sit down in the chair across the table from her.

She slips her glasses back on and fusses with the papers in front of her. She finds what she's looking for and glances at me over the top of her glasses before scanning it. "The board of directors has been issued what essentially amounts to a one-hundred-thousand-dollar parking ticket for landing a helicopter in a densely populated urban center."

Oops.

Cassy drops her reading glasses to the table with a clatter. "You told the pilot to land in the middle of a low-income housing project this morning?"

"I told the pilot to land in the parking lot of an abandoned shopping mall that is surrounded by a fence to keep people out." For the moment I'll leave out the part about the gaping hole in the fence. "It *is* in downtown Castleford, but I can prove we took proper precautions in landing and taking off. So we should fight it, particularly since that one-hundred-thousand-dollars figure is coincidentally the exact dollar amount Castleford PD needs to buy new radio equipment."

Cassy's blue eyes are studying me.

"They couldn't figure out where to get the funding," I add, "so ten to one this is now a fund-raising event."

Still, she studies me.

"They're citing the Homeland Security Act, aren't they? Look, Cassy, I *know* Castleford PD. As soon as they got wind it was me for DBS, they thought, 'Wow, Merry Christmas, here's our chance.'"

Frowning, she picks up her glasses and puts them back on to look at the paper again. "They do cite the Homeland Security Act." She looks up. "Your next stop is to Legal, understand?"

"Absolutely," I say. I've spent so much time in Legal lately, Jerry O'Brian, our lead counsel, gets this don't-hit-me look whenever he sees me.

She makes a note. "That was great footage," she remarks without looking up. "I was also struck by the way you handed the story to Bill Randolph and made it appear as though he had gone into the building with Eric instead of you."

"I didn't think a bombing would go over well with cereal sponsors."

Now she looks up. "It was difficult for Alexandra to take you off the Delafield story. I hope you know that."

I shrug, noncommittal.

Cassy takes her glasses off and sits back in her chair as if to assess me all over again. "How are you feeling about the conference?"

"Good," I tell her. "Our presentations are great. The one for the news group is exciting and dashing and in good taste—it has a lot of music, graphics, special effects. Everybody looks great and Alexandra looks like a goddess. I think it's better than anything we've done before. We even worked Kit Whitehawk into it."

"And what about your presentation for *DBS News America This Morning?*"

"It's very, very good," I say, smiling, "even if I do say so myself. Different from the news-group video, but it distinguishes us as the early morning crew. It's lighter—visually, musically—and appealing. Calming, brightly reassuring, I guess you'd call it."

"I'd like to see them today."

"Absolutely. I'll run them up to you right after I leave here."

"You have to go to Legal first," she reminds me.

"Right." I run a hand through my hair. "The only concern I have about the conference at this point is me—physically." I gesture. "I'm a mess. My arms and legs are kind of banged up from this morning."

"Cleo can help." For the first time she smiles. "What about clothes?"

"All set. Wardrobe took me to the showrooms and my dress for the dinner is an absolute killer. Who knows? Maybe somewhere between you and Alexandra and Lydia Southland someone might actually notice me." Lydia Southland is the glamorous star of a new DBS drama.

"My day is long over," she says quietly, moving her papers around again. Suddenly she stands up. "No, sit," she tells me, waving me back down into my chair. She turns to look out over the park, crossing her arms over her chest. She is wearing a pale gray silk suit today; the blazer is left hanging on the back of her chair.

I hope I look this good at *forty*-two. The sheer blouse she is wearing outlines good shoulders and a tapered waist. I wonder if she would look this good if she wasn't married to a billionaire? Probably.

"I wanted to let you know, Sally," she says with her back to me, "that I've shut production down on *The Jessica Wright Show*."

My mouth falls open. I don't know what to say.

Since the substitute host has a three-million-dollar parachute in her contract for such an event I hardly feel sorry for her, but to just pull the plug like this could be a ratings disaster for the nightly news.

"While I don't expect you to fully divert the affiliates' attention away from the fact that our single most successful program has just crashed and burned," she continues evenly, "I am hoping you will give them something to be upbeat about." Pause. "You're going to have to make them love you, Sally. Emmett's important, but not the key. You are."

I blink. "But surely you're going to rerun Jessica's 'best of' shows."

She turns around. "What's the point? It's over."

"But *is* it?" I argue.

"I know what you told Langley—" she begins.

"So *are* we talking to Jessica? Or to Will?"

She looks at me as if I should know better. "It's not that easy, Sally. We have no standing agreement whatsoever with Jessica. She has a four-month-old baby, a husband who insisted she leave here, and, to be honest, I don't want to risk alienating Will over it. He's too important to the news division, particularly now that you're moving over."

This is ridiculous. I know how deeply Cassy sympathized with Jessica's difficulty in carrying a child to full term. I know how Langley and his wife reacted when Jessica miscarried for the second time because they, too, had suffered several miscarriages before conceiving their twins. And I also know how dependent Alexandra has been on Will for fifteen years and that she wouldn't dream of interfering with his personal life.

These people are all too close. There is nothing straightforward about the business relationship between Jessica Wright and

DBS. She started this network with them; she worked side by side with them for a decade; she even married one of them!

"Let me talk to Will," I urge.

"No," Cassy says.

"You can't just pull the plug on the show without asking her!"

"Sally, she *has* been asked," she says, tired.

"And she said no?"

"And she said no," Cassy says, now sounding irritated.

I shift in my seat. "But you didn't talk to Will, did you? I mean, what if he's changed his mind? What if Jessica doesn't even know that he'd be agreeable to her working part-time? What if—"

"Sally!"

"What?" I half yell back.

"Stop it."

"No!" I tell her, standing up. "I'm going to talk to Will because somebody has to find out what's going on with the Raffertys and I'm the only one around here who isn't a member of their extended family. And if you have any faith left at all in Jessica, you'll start rerunning her shows, starting with the very first *Jessica Wright Show* tonight."

Cassy's not quite glaring at me.

"Run them in order," I urge. "That will give you about six years to talk Jessica into coming back. *Anything* is better than just pulling the plug."

I can see she's thinking about it. "We're going to try a sports show in the slot."

"*Sports?*" I practically stamp my foot. "You can't do that to Alexandra!" At this point I'm not sure at all what Cassy is thinking. "Go ahead, fire me," I say, moving to the door, "but I'm talking to Will. There's no way Sports is getting that time slot." I hesitate then, hazarding a look back to see how it's going.

"Well?" Cassy says, walking toward me.

"You mean I can?" I ask, turning around fully.

"I have no knowledge of this," she tells me.

"Of course you don't," I say, getting it.

She follows me out of her office. "Chi Chi, see if you can get Denny Ladler on the phone." (Jessica's long-time Executive Producer.) "And ask Steven from sales to come up as soon as possible."

As I round the corner into the hallway, I hear Cassy call, "Tact, Sally, tact!"

CHAPTER 1

Will Rafferty's eyes are searching mine over the rim of his coffee mug.

I smile slightly. "I didn't mean it as a trick question."

He lowers his coffee mug and his eyes. "Jessica says she's happy."

I wait a few moments. "But you're not absolutely convinced of that."

"I know she's bored." He looks up. "But she's determined to stay with Emily."

"But are *you* determined she stay at home with Emily seven days a week? That's what I want to know."

He scowls at me. "Of course not. Jessica's free to do whatever she wants."

"Then why don't you ask her if she's interested in coming back a couple of days a week? She can bring the baby, the nanny, even the dog. Will, you know they'd build her a house in the middle of the park if that's what she wanted."

He smiles a little, nodding, eyes moving over the scene in the cafeteria.

It is always busy in here. The Darenbrook Café, as they call it, is this huge place with vaulted ceilings and walls that double as exhibition space for employees' artwork and photographs.

Most important, however, is the vast selection of top-quality foods and drinks that are subsidized by the corporation. The café is also in Darenbrook I to take full advantage of the sunlight and view.

"Everybody knows she has no financial need to ever work again," I say.

His head kicks back slightly as his eyes turn to me. "I've done pretty well, too, you know."

"Exactly," I say, delighted he has taken the bait. "So at this point you don't have any financial need to work, either." I pause, trying to maintain an air of innocence. "But your work schedule hasn't changed at all since the baby, Will. Now Jessica's never here—where you are—and she's home all alone with Emily."

"That's not fair, Sally."

"I know it's not fair," I confess. "And that's why I think you should ask your wife if she's interested in coming back a couple of days a week. The question has to come from you, Will, you know that. As long as she thinks you're against it, you know she'll just keep saying no without even thinking about it."

He looks like he's bitten into a lemon. "Why the hell would *I* be against it, Sally? I only wanted Jessica to stay home before because if she lost Emily, like she lost the other pregnancies, I knew she would never forgive herself for not doing absolutely everything she could do to carry the baby to full term." He throws a hand out. "You know, it's not like we were planning to have a carload of kids. We were hoping for two, and pleased if we could just have at least one. And we got the one." He can't help but smile a little. "And what a one she is," he adds softly.

"And of course Jessica wants to be with her as much as possible," I say. "Everybody understands that. The question is, though, is Jessica still the same woman who worked *so* hard for *so* long to make herself a big TV star? Because if she is, then I'm not sure Jessica talking to Gerta—"

"Bertha," he says, correcting me.

"Gerta-Bertha, the nanny," I say with a little laugh, leaning over the table. "That talking to her is going to fully keep Emily's mother happy and fulfilled." I sit back in my chair. "And if Jessica doesn't come back, Will, they're giving her slot to Sports. And you know what that will mean—a huge demographics shift for us as the lead-in."

He flinches.

"Sports!" I cry, hitting the table. "And Jessica's fans will be gone forever, so then if she ever does want to go back on TV, she's going to have to go somewhere else and start all over again, trying to find the right time slot to start building her audience all over again."

Will's pushing the salt shaker around. "Why hasn't anyone said anything to me about this?"

"Because they love you two so much they're terrified of interfering with your family life. Or of seeming to value the fate of their careers over their friendship with you. At least the latter's true with Alexandra, I know that much."

His eyes come up. "So what does that make you?"

"Unfair but desperate." I offer him a sad smile. "And hoping that given your wife's personality, this is actually something that might be a win-win for everyone."

He takes a sip of his coffee and makes a face. "Cold." He puts the mug down. Then he nods once. "Okay."

I freeze. "Okay what?"

"I'll ask her."

I try to stop myself from cheering.

"Well?" he says. "Aren't you going to pressure me to do it within the next five minutes?"

"Well, to be honest," I say, "I was sort of thinking how it might appeal to your wife to ride in and blow the entire network away with happiness just before its darkest moment."

His eyebrows crash together. "The affiliate convention? *This* affiliate convention? Tomorrow. Are you nuts?"

"Just ask her, Will, please. She would love to ride to the rescue, you know she would. That's who she is."

"You are a real piece of work," he tells me, rubbing his eye. He drops his hand, looking across the cafeteria. "Here comes Margarite."

My intern is hurrying through the tables with a worried expression. "The FBI's in your office with a warrant," she says breathlessly when she reaches us.

We scramble to our feet. "They're probably after the Delafield files," Will says.

"May I help you?" I ask from the doorway of my office. "I'm Sally Harrington."

A woman (wearing an armband reading FBI) is holding something behind her back while a man in a navy-blue suit turns around. "Hello, Sally."

"Agent Alfonso," I say, surprised. "I thought your jurisdiction was California."

"It was," he acknowledges, extending a hand.

I shake hands with him. He is a dark-haired, extremely fit man of about forty who tends toward shyness. He once gave me a lift to L.A. from the middle of the desert. I look at the other agent. She brings her hands out from behind her and I recognize the plastic trash bags I put my ruined shoes and clothing in last night. The bags have been untied. (Thank God my office trash was emptied last night or I'd have another plastic bag full of Paul's DNA.)

"You have a warrant for Alexandra Waring's dressing room?" I ask skeptically, eyes on the bags.

"I'm sorry, Sally," Margarite says from the doorway, tears threatening. "They asked me to show them where you had been in the building over the past twelve hours and I took them there."

"For pity's sake," I say to the female agent, "tie those up again, will you? They smell god-awful." I turn to Margarite. "It's fine, don't worry. Really. Go have your dinner now. I'll bring you up to speed later."

Looking dubiously at the agents, Margarite leaves.

Agent Alfonso nods toward the bags. "Giving us those saved us from serving the warrant to search your apartment."

I put my hand on my hip. "It might be helpful if you told me what you're looking for."

"Sally," Will says from behind me, standing with Jerry from Legal.

"Gerald O'Brian, Darenbrook Communications corporate counsel," our chief attorney says, moving in front of me.

As Jerry inspects the warrant my telephone starts ringing. Margarite didn't put the phones on Call Forward so when the second line starts to ring as well, at an alternate interval, it gets pretty noisy. "Is there somewhere we can talk?" Agent Alfonso asks.

"There's a conference room," I offer, looking to Jerry, who hands the warrant back to Agent Alfonso. "It's right across the hall." I lead the way, open the conference room door and flick on the lights.

"We won't require your presence," Agent Alfonso tells Will. He looks to me and I shrug, so he leaves.

I wait for Jerry and the agents to choose seats before I close the door. Agent Alfonso opts for one end of the long table and Jerry takes the other. The female agent moves toward the middle and so I choose a seat across from her.

The door flies open and then Alexandra's standing there. Her eyes go straight to Agent Alfonso. "I remember you."

"And I remember you, Ms. Waring," he says, standing up. "But we don't need you in this meeting."

I take Alexandra outside. "Any Delafield files I should worry about?" she asks me.

"No, everything's clean."

I slip back into the conference room. "Sorry. You now have my full attention, Agent Alfonso," I say, sitting down and folding my hands on the table in front of me.

"I want to talk to you about your visit to Castleford early this morning."

Not Delafield. I clear my throat. "There was absolutely no one in that parking lot when we landed."

Agent Alfonso frowns.

"Let him ask the questions, Sally," Jerry says, which means *Shut up! Don't volunteer anything!*

Agent Alfonso's frown deepens at Jerry. Then he turns his attention back to me. "What prompted you to go to Castleford this morning?"

"One of the *Herald-American* staffers told me their building had been evacuated. For a bomb scare."

"Who was the staffer?"

"Devon Clarke." To the other agent, who is taking notes, "That's Clark with an *e.*"

"Thank you."

I refocus on Agent Alfonso.

"Devon Clarke called you at what time?"

"Around twelve-forty."

"This morning?"

"Yes."

"And where were you?"

"In the newsroom. I was working late."

"Why did he call you?"

I think I'll skip the part about him joking they thought I must have been the one to call in the bomb threat. "He and some other former colleagues were stuck outside. The police wouldn't let them leave—"

"This is before the bomb went off?"

"Yes," I say quickly. "I guess they were bored and they knew there was a good chance I was still here working. So he called."

"And what did he tell you?"

"About being evacuated."

"Anything else?"

I blink. "They had a bottle and someone went to the gas station to get potato chips and dip."

He gives me a dubious look. "What else?"

"The bomb went off."

"While he was on the phone with you?"

"Yes. And then he hung up."

"And what did you do then?"

"I took the corporate helicopter out there to see what had happened."

"Who went with you? In addition to the pilot."

"A cameraman, Eric Patel."

"What was your purpose for going there?"

I shrug. "To scoop other news organizations." He waits. "And to get good pictures."

He looks at his notebook. "You got inside the building? After the police had sealed it?"

"Yes."

"How?"

"There's an old tunnel that runs into the basement of the *Herald-American* from an abandoned building across the street."

"How long have you known about this tunnel?"

"I didn't know about it. Devon found a man who knew about it."

"And who was he?"

"I have no idea."

"And this stranger showed you the way to this tunnel?"

I look at the female agent. "That's where all the gunk got on my clothes and shoes."

"And you were able to get inside the *Herald-American* building?"

I nod. "We came in through a storage room in the basement."

"Without permission?" Agent Alonso asks.

Jerry sends me a warning look. "I was with an employee of the *Herald-American*," I say carefully.

"Did the stranger come with you into the *Herald-American*?"

"No."

"What did you do after you got into the building?"

"We went up the stairs to the newsroom and shot some film."

"What happened then?"

"The police chased us out."

"How did you exit the building?"

"The way we came in."

"Did you see the stranger when you were leaving?"

I hesitate. "The guys said they did, but I didn't see him."

"You seem unsure."

"Two guys tried to grab me as we left the building. But the guys helped me get away. I didn't see who they were."

"So you are saying it could have been the stranger with another man."

"Eric said he thought the other was some kind of cop."

"But you don't know that."

I shake my head. "No."

"So you got away from these two strangers. What did you do then?"

"We made our way back to the helicopter." I'm leaving the Laurencelles out of this. "We evacuated the parking lot, took off and came back to Manhattan."

"And then you returned to the West End Broadcasting Center?"

"Yes."

"And what did you do then?"

"I took a shower and caught a few hours' sleep.

He is quiet for a few moments, looking at his notes. "Did you ever leave the downtown area while you were in Castleford this morning?"

"No."

"You never went to your house?"

I shake my head. "No."

"You didn't go to your mother's house?"

"No."

"At any time were you ever by yourself while you were in Castleford this morning?"

"No. Eric, our cameraman, was with me the entire time."

Agent Alfonso looks down the table at Jerry. "We're going to want to talk to him." He turns a page in his notebook. "Did you see Alfred Royce while you were in Castleford this morning?"

"Yes."

"Where?"

"He was standing near the entrance of the *Herald-American*."

"Did you speak to him?"

"No."

"Why not?"

I shrug. "I had no reason to."

"You didn't want to ask him to get you inside?"

"No."

"Why not? You had one of his photographers with you."

"No. I didn't. Not yet. I found Devon later."

He stares down at his notes for several moments. Finally he looks up at me. "Alfred Royce published an attack on your character recently—is that correct?"

I'm starting to feel a little scared inside and I don't know why. I shrug. "Yes."

"The article upset you, didn't it?"

"It was an editorial."

"But it was an editorial that provoked an unflattering story about you that then appeared in several newspapers, did it not?"

"Yes."

"And the editorial upset your mother, didn't it?"

"My mother has nothing to do with any of this," I tell him icily.

"Oh, but she may."

"Don't you dare use my mother as a way to get to me," I tell him.

"But that's exactly what Alfred Royce did to get back at your mother, didn't he? Humiliate you to get back at her."

I narrow my eyes. "Where are you going with this?"

"Belle Goodwin Harrington," he reads from his notes. "Engaged to Malcolm Cleary, Ph.D., professor of nuclear physics and chemistry, Wesleyan University." He looks up. "Your mother had a falling-out with Alfred Royce a week ago Saturday."

"This is pathetic," I tell him. "I suggest you not waste your time by chasing the good guys."

"Perhaps, Agent Alfonso," Jerry says, finally speaking up, "you should get to the point of your inquiry and tell us how we can help you."

"Help us answer the question," Agent Alfonso says, "who might want to help you in Castleford."

"Help me how?"

"To avenge you and your mother."

"Avenge my mother? What are you talking about?"

"I'm talking about Alfred Royce being beaten and left for dead at your front door in Castleford this morning."

"My doorstep?" I say in disbelief.

"On your front porch in Castleford."

"My God," I murmur. I raise a hand to my face, trying to think.

"In what condition is he now?" Jerry asks.

"He's having a craniotomy as we speak."

"To relieve pressure on the brain," I murmur to Jerry, looking up. "Who found him? I didn't go anywhere near my house and the cottage is in the middle of nowhere." I rent the old caretaker's cottage at what's left of Brackleton Farm, the last large privately owned tract of undeveloped land in Castleford.

Agent Alfonso reads a name from his notes.

"My handyman," I say, understanding at once. "It's recycling day. He must have gone by to see if I had any to put out. The craniotomy—his injuries were to the head?"

"Primarily. It was an angry beating, almost methodical." He pauses. "Probably using a blackjack."

The other agent is writing all this down.

"He was beaten in what might be considered a professional manner."

"A beating by a professional *what?*" I say.

Agent Alfonso cocks his head slightly. "Police, underworld, armed forces, boxer, take your choice."

I think of Paul and find myself shaking my head.

"What is it?" Agent Alfonso lowers his head slightly as if to see me better.

"Nothing."

He meets my eyes. "The beating was so bad they had difficulty determining who he was."

Good God. Under normal circumstances my handyman should have recognized him immediately.

I lower my head, trying to think.

"So it would appear, Sally," he continues, "that someone was very angry with Alfred Royce on your behalf. And they took it on themselves to beat him nearly to death and leave his body in a place they were absolutely sure you would find it."

I close my eyes, starting to feel my head swim. "This is psycho stuff."

"The reason why we are interested in your shoes and clothes is because it appears Alfred Royce was beaten in the same building you used to gain access to the *Herald-American*."

I shake my head slowly. "I swear to God, I have no knowledge of this whatsoever."

It is silent for several moments. I have to close my eyes again; I feel ill.

"Professor Cleary," Agent Alfonso begins.

"Professor Cleary," I say, opening my eyes, "can't put drops in the dog's ear because he's terrified of hurting her."

"He is a nuclear physicist."

"Retired for five years, so what?"

"The bomber went to great pains to make sure no one at the newspaper was hurt by the explosion," he says. "He also knew the explosion would bring Al Royce to the scene." When I don't respond he continues, "Someone got Al Royce to the paper, beat him nearly to death and then transported his body to leave it at your front door."

I look at him incredulously. "And you think someone in my life would do such a thing?"

He looks down at his notes. "Why did you say Devon Clarke called you this morning?"

"Because he wanted to tell me about the bomb scare."

"Why?"

I run a hand through my hair. "Because I was probably the only person he knew who might be still be working."

"How did Devon Clarke know about the underground access to the paper?"

"I don't know," I say honestly. "I've been trying to get him on the phone to ask him that very question. He said the stranger had been looking for me. Asking for me."

"You have a special friend in the police department, I understand."

"I have several."

"That you're dating?" He looks at his notebook. "Paul Fitzwilliam, New Haven PD."

"I strongly doubt a police officer working his way through law school is your man," I say sarcastically.

Suddenly I think about how our family cat used to leave dead mice at our door as a gift. A slight hum starts in my ears and things started turning yellow. Abruptly I push my chair back and drop my head down between my knees. In a moment Jerry and Agent Alfonso are out of their chairs and on either side of me. "I'll get her some water," I hear the other agent say.

"That's it—slow, deep breaths," Agent Alfonso says. I feel his hand on my back.

As the blood rushes into my head I feel better and slowly I sit up, apologizing. The other agent hurries back in to hand me a Dixie cup of water from the cooler. I thank her and take a sip, assuring them I'm okay now.

"I believe Sally has answered all your questions, Agent Alfonso," Jerry says, "and so unless you have something further—"

"No, we've got what we need for the moment," Agent Alfonso says. He smiles at me apologetically, backing away to his chair. "You understand why we have—"

"Of course," I say, waving it off and finishing the water. "I just hope you find who did this as soon as possible." I wish they'd get out of here so I can tell Will and Alexandra about this development—which, I know, will raise the uncomfortable situation of DBS News breaking the story of Al Royce nearly being beaten to death and its direct connection to me. "Thanks again for the water," I say, shaking the agent's hand. She gives me her card, as does Alfonso. When I ask if they know where Al is being treated, they tell me Hartford Hospital.

Jerry opens the conference room door and stands there, waiting for me to leave before they call for Eric. Cassy appears in the doorway, introducing herself and asking if she can assist in any way. Alfonso thanks her but says they have all they need for the moment.

"It is extremely important Sally attends our affiliate convention in California," she tells him. "If we give you our schedule and where to reach her at any time, I trust there won't be a problem."

"When and where is it?" Agent Alfonso asks her.

"We're scheduled to leave tomorrow night," she says. "It's being held at the Manning Convention Resort south of Los Angeles."

"It was renovated last year," Agent Alfonso tells her.

I explain that Agent Alfonso used to work in the Southern California district; that is where I first met him.

"So we're there Saturday, Sunday and Monday," Cassy says, "and then we fly directly to Liverpool, England, for a two-day summit with our international affiliate. You have my assurances, Agent Alfonso, that we will have Sally back in New York by Friday."

"I think this could be worked out," Agent Alfonso agrees. Turning to me, "You must pay a visit to the Castleford Police Department before you leave."

"Of course," I say. "I will go there shortly."

"Castleford?" Cassy says, frowning. She looks to Jerry. "I thought this was about the Delafield murder."

"No."

She turns to me. "Is this about the helicopter?"

I shake my head. "Somebody beat up Al Royce and left him at my front door in Castleford."

Her mouth parts. Then she recovers, telling the feds she will have her assistant make up a schedule and contact numbers for me.

"You're to go right in," Benjamin tells me outside Alexandra's office.

I crouch down to see him at eye level. "I need a favor."

"Am I surprised?" he says tonelessly.

"I need you to track down Bill Randolph from the Springfield affiliate," I tell him while scribbling a note.

"That's the guy covering the Castleford bombing?"

"Right." I keep writing. "Tell him I will be out there as soon as I can, but that he is to follow up on this immediately." I hand him the pad. "Can you read it?"

Scanning it, his eyes widen. "The weirdest stuff happens around you," he remarks, reaching for the telephone.

I point to the phone on the file cabinet. "Can I get an outside line on this?" He nods and I punch in my office code and dial information to get the number for Hartford Hospital. Patient information tells me, yes, Alfred Royce is there, presently in post-op recovery. "General post-op or ICU?" I ask the lady.

"If he was in ICU it would say so."

Thank God for that. "Has he been assigned a room number yet?" A room number will tell me what level of care he requires and what is considered his most serious injury. My guess would be neurology.

"Not yet. But we have a full house today."

"Is ICU full?"

"No." Pause. "If the patient required intensive care I can assure you that is where he would be now."

I thank her, hang up and cross over to knock on the frame of Alexandra's door. She tells me to come and I do, closing the door behind me. Alexandra is watering plants and Will is seated in front of her desk. When he sees me he jumps up. "Did they ask for the Delafield files?"

"No. They wanted to see what I knew about Alfred Royce having his head beaten in and his body left on the doorstep of my cottage in Castleford."

"What?"

Alexandra has abandoned her watering can to return to her desk.

"Benjamin's tracking down Bill Randolph right now to give him the information," I report. "And as soon as I get things squared away here I need to get out there. They'll never let a crew near my house, but I figure they'll have to let me through and then somehow we can get a shot of the crime scene." While I tell Alexandra everything I know, Will gets on the phone with the newsroom to put the studio crew on alert.

When I finish, Alexandra says, "Where's the photographer who got you in last night?"

"Nobody knows."

"Okay," Will says, hanging up the phone, "I'm going downstairs. When you're through here come down." He turns to Alexandra. "You'll get ready?"

She nods, turning to her computer. "I'll write the copy out now with Sally and then we should get her on her way."

Will walks to the door. "Just swing by the newsroom before you go, Sally, all right?"

Alexandra and I write the copy, she sends it into the system and then stretches. "There's no way around it, I guess. We're going to have to say whoever did this left Royce's body for you to find." She looks up. "So much for your privacy."

I stand up. "I need to get going."

"Make sure Bill interviews you on camera," she tells me. "Don't brush your hair and no makeup."

I hesitate.

"What?" she asks, printing out the copy.

"You actually want me to appear in the story?"

"Of course." She reaches for the pages coming out of the printer.

"But with the cereal sponsors—"

"What is the matter with you?" she says, coming around her desk.

"But I thought—"

"There is a huge difference, Sally, between the stories you choose to involve yourself in and the stories that happen to you as a bystander." She flings her door open. "Benjamin, we need a car for Sally yesterday. She's going to Connecticut and the driver must stay with her for as long as she needs him." She turns to me.

"Fine, I just had to get it straight in my mind," I tell her.

"Alexandra Waring's office here," Benjamin is saying into the phone, "we need a car yesterday."

"Oh," Alexandra suddenly says, grabbing my arm and pulling me back toward her office.

"What?"

"Jessica's coming back," she whispers.

If Alexandra thinks throwing my name and face across every media outlet in the country in connection with the brutal beating of Al Royce is a good idea, who am I to argue? Of course this means Al's editorial really will be read in newspapers across the country now (...one can only shudder at what kind of role model the Women's Club would consider unsavory) and so I am not particularly thrilled. Or at least I prefer the propaganda our Publicity department churns out: "Sally Harrington is bright and warmly sunshiny, a combination perfect for delivering the first news of the day."

I sign Scotty out of West End doggy care to ride out to Castleford with me. If, indeed, I really am still going to the affiliate convention and then on to England with the DBS News gang, I would like to leave him with Mother.

It is a very weird feeling I have when I see a police blockade across my driveway. It is also very weird to, after all these years of trying to keep my home private, now be plotting to get it on the national news. As the limo nears my driveway, Scotty barks a couple of times, excited to be home.

A transmitter van from the Springfield affiliate is parked on the other side of the road. Bill Randolph is standing outside of it with a cameraman. Across from them—and behind the heavy wood barrier—is a police car with flashing lights. "Okay, I see them," I tell the newsroom back at West End. Across the street the cameraman snaps to attention, hefting the camera on his shoulder to shoot the arrival of our limousine. I shut off the phone and run a quick hand through my hair. As instructed I haven't brushed it, and I'm not wearing makeup; I'm supposed to look as though I've just rushed out here to see what has happened. Which is true.

"You might be on national TV," I tell Scotty.

"I gotta call my wife," the driver says.

As previously instructed, Bill and the camera remain in position across the street while we pull up to the blockade and I step out of the car. As I pull my identification out of my wallet I can't decide whether it's good or bad that I realize I used to babysit for this police officer. (I suspect people might not call him Greggie anymore.) "Officer," I say seriously, aware of the shotgun microphone being aimed at me from across the road.

"Hi, Sally," he says, stepping forward to give me a kiss hello on the cheek.

So much for rough stuff.

I point across the road. "They're with me. I want to go to my house to get some things."

Officer Doyle squints at Bill. "He's a DBS guy?"

"Yes. From our affiliate in Springfield."

"He's a real pain in the ass," he tells me honestly.

"Sorry."

"It's a crime scene, Sally. They're not going to let you near the front porch."

"That's all right. I'll just go in through the back of the house."

"And you can't take that truck. If they're with you, they need to accompany you in your vehicle."

"Fine." I call over to the boys, "You have to leave the van. Come on!"

The guys scramble for stuff and hurry across the road while the officer talks to someone on his walkie-talkie. Scotty and I have to get in the front seat with the driver to make room for everybody, and Scotty, sitting on me, won't stop barking. (The camera's scaring him.) I open the car door. "Greg?" I say to the officer. "Would you mind taking him for a few minutes?" I get out of the car, holding Scotty's leash out.

"Sure," he says, taking the leash from me. "Come on, girl."

"Boy," I say, wincing. I hand him some Milk-Bones from my blazer pocket.

Scotty lets out a high-pitched whine; he realizes I'm leaving without him. The officer drops down on his haunches to soothe him while I get back in the limo.

"That's a real tough police force you've got," the camera operator observes as we get under way.

I turn around in my seat. "You should have seen him when he carried a two-hundred-pound unconscious woman down a fire escape." A big bump in the road sends the whole back-seat crew bouncing into the ceiling. Even with stabilizers, I doubt we can use much of what the cameraman's getting right now. The old, long, winding, deeply rutted dirt road that serves as my driveway on the Brackleton Farm would be enough to make any viewer carsick.

As we come around the big bend, my little house swings into view, looking sweet as usual. It is a 1920s white bungalow with a lovely front porch, which, at the moment, is somewhat alarmingly swathed in yellow police tape. There is a squad car parked in front of it, with an officer leaning back against the driver's side of the car, arms crossed over his chest, watching our arrival. There is another uniformed officer on the porch and a woman who is dressed in plain clothes.

The Springfield crew piles out of the car first and I take my time, making sure the camera guy is getting the shot.

"This is a crime scene," the officer informs me. I don't know him, which means he must be relatively new. He has his arms crossed over his chest and is still leaning against the car, I realize, because he's nervous. He sees the camera.

"Give us a minute," I say to the cameraman. He backs away, swinging the camera toward the house (zooming in on the porch, no doubt) as I take a step closer to the officer. "I am going to take them into my house through the back, Officer. We'll be ten minutes, tops. Would you like to be interviewed? Be on the national news?"

The color deepens in his cheeks.

"Don't touch that tape!" the officer on the porch barks at Bill Randolph. "Do you hear me, *sir?* Do not touch that tape!"

"Let me know on our way out," I tell my officer, and before he thinks to argue with me, I lead the group around to the back of my house where I unlock the kitchen door. I ask the camera guy not to film the inside, which of course prompts the guys to look around madly as though they might find pornography or something hanging on the walls.

While I call into West End, the cameraman hangs out of my study window to shoot Al Royce's bloodstains on the porch. Bill pops his head out of the living room window and asks the uniformed officer and the woman—who evidently is a forensics person from the state lab—if they would like to speak on camera, to which the officer growls perhaps Bill should just get the hell out of here.

The time is 4:56 and on the phone Will tells me to get Bill into position to do a live feed for the news break at five. I hustle the guys outside and hurry them down the driveway where the camera guy can get Bill with the crime scene behind him as a backdrop. I warn the cops we're going live for the national news.

We wait for the signal from New York and then West End takes Bill live, standing in front of the crime scene where Al Royce's body was found. It is strange to hear myself being talked about in the third person, particularly when I can't hear what it is that Alexandra, who is on the air at West End, is asking him. In two minutes it's over and we walked back to the limo, where I am approached by the first officer who had been leaning on the squad car. "I've been instructed not to talk to you," he tells me.

"You were in the shot, though," I say happily. "So tell everybody you know to watch DBS News tonight at nine. They'll be rerunning it."

We drive out to the road and find that Scotty has somehow wrangled an emergency thermal blanket from his officer to lie down and take a nap on. "He reminds me a little of the academy dogs," he tells me, handing over the leash.

"It's the shepherd in him."

"So listen, Sally, Lieutenant D'Amico expects you to go directly to the police station from here."

"I will," I promise, walking across the road with Scotty to review Bill's instructions for continuing to cover the story for tonight's newscast. I like Bill and have faith in him. He's in his late fifties and has been around a while, and frankly I am relieved to hand this whole mess over to him. "From here on in," I tell the Springfield reporter, "I am officially citizen Sally Harrington and will not influence the coverage of this story."

As I drive downtown in this long black limousine, I wonder if people realize that I'm not just Belle and Dodge Harrington's little girl anymore.

"How is Al?" I ask Buddy D'Amico when he walks into the interview room. The first boy who ever kissed me (behind the coat closet in first grade) has kept me waiting for almost an hour. "All I can find out is he's been moved from post-op into a room, but no one will say where the room is."

"Do you blame them?" he asks without looking at me, dropping a thick manila folder on the table and drawing up a chair to sit. "Whoever attacked him is still out there."

I register this fact to relay to Bill Randolph. "But what is his condition, Buddy?"

He gives me an annoyed look before drawing a large envelope out of the folder. "Lieutenant," he mutters, leaning over to put the folder on the floor. "He's going to be all right."

Thank you, God. I've been saying prayers all day, but worried about their effectiveness since I didn't care very much for Al before now.

"Have you seen your mother yet?"

"I'm going there as soon as I finish here."

"A mob's amassed in her driveway in the last half hour. I have half a mind to bill you for the overtime it's going to take to keep people from trespassing. Thanks for the warning, by the way, that you were breaking the story and bringing the world down on us."

"Thanks for the warning on the one-hundred-thousand-dollar parking ticket," I counter.

"You're welcome," he says succinctly, picking up a pencil and bouncing the point on the table like a small ball. When the point breaks he scowls and I wordlessly dive into my bag for another pencil and give it to him. "Thanks."

"You're welcome." I stay quiet while he sorts through his papers. I'm not sure why we're just sitting around like this. "How is Al's family doing?" I finally ask.

Buddy glances up from his papers. "What family?"

"His wife?"

"A few months back somebody died and left her some money. She left."

"I didn't know," I say softly.

"Kids haven't shown up yet, either."

I rub my forehead. It's sad. And it explains why Al made the big pass at Mother. He *was* taking a last shot at what he thought would be happiness.

Buddy asks if I would like coffee or anything to drink. I tell him I'm fine, that I have a bottle of water right here in my bag. There is a knock at the door and a young policewoman hurries in. Buddy introduces her and she takes a seat in the corner of the room. "Let's get started," he says, picking up my pencil. He looks as tired as I feel. Buddy taps the eraser end of the pencil with his left hand while he turns the tape recorder on with his right. He reads the time and date into the machine, says his name, the officer's name and the name of the person to whom he is speaking, which is me, Sally Harrington.

The interview lasts almost two hours. Buddy first goes over the chain of events leading up to the editorial in last week's *Herald-American:* the award ceremony at the cultural center the week before and Mother's run-in with Al at the country club. We cover the events of the night before and end with the arrival of the FBI this afternoon at DBS.

"Let's go back to when you saw Mr. Royce this morning," Buddy says. "Where was he exactly?"

"Standing outside the entrance," I say. "To the right of the front doors. He was with a state trooper."

"Did you recognize the trooper?"

"No."

"And you say Al didn't see you."

I shake my head. "I didn't want him to."

He thinks a moment. "Okay, so then you circle the building."

"Right."

"And how did you find Devon Clarke?"

"Sam Laurencelle told me he was looking for me."

"Sam? That's Bob and Wanda's son?"

I nod. "Yes."

"How did Sam Laurencelle know where Devon Clarke was?"

"He knew what area he would be in, so we went there and Devon called out to us."

Buddy makes a note. "Have you talked to Devon Clarke since this morning?"

I shake my head. "No. I've left messages, but I haven't heard back from him." I feel a sinking feeling in my stomach. "Have you seen or heard from him, Buddy? Lieutenant D'Amico?"

He doesn't answer right away and nervously I unscrew the top of my bottle of water to take a swig. I would prefer to drink out of a glass, but since there's nothing around to use except a dirty broken foam cup in the wastepaper basket next to me the bottle will have to suffice.

"He's around," Buddy finally says, "but we're still waiting for him to come in."

"He's usually very cooperative."

Buddy starts unfolding an enlarged street map of downtown Castleford. "Devon Clarke called in his resignation to Alfred Royce's mailbox at the paper. Evidently he wished to clarify his status before selling his pictures to the Associate Press."

"You're kidding." I'm sort of surprised at Devon. To cut his long-time employer out like that.

Buddy smooths the map with his hands. There are faint outlines of buildings on the street map. He stands up to come around the table and stand over me as I point out to him the exact route I took early this morning.

"That's the building we went through," I say, "but I don't think this part, that's shown here, still exists. I think it's just a bombed-out space. And the building is not this big. I know it's not. There's a large alley that runs down here where it shows the building extending."

Buddy murmurs agreement, bending to examine the writing

in the key. "Nineteen-seventy-nine," he says in disgust, straightening up.

If things are as bad as this in our police department, that they're using street maps from 1979 that detail buildings that no longer exist, perhaps DBS *should* pay the hundred-thousand-dollar parking ticket.

Buddy walks around to sit on his side of the table again and brings the large envelope back onto the table to extract some five-by-seven photographs. He sifts through, selects one, and spins it around on top of the map to show me. "Is this where you went in?"

"Yes. Devon knocked on one of the boards over the window and the guy opened the door."

"And you didn't recognize the man who let you in?"

I shake my head. "The light was very poor."

He flips back in his own set of notes. "You said he was about five-ten."

"Now that I think about it, there was a small heel on my shoe. You better make it five-eleven."

Both police officers make a note. "What else?"

"He was white. No glasses or anything. At first I thought he was old—I think because of his croaking voice. I also assumed he was homeless because he was dressed for it, you know? He had three or four layers of shirts on."

"Color?"

"The top layer was a jacket, red, with dark running through it. Like a hunter's plaid."

"Good."

"It was scratchy, probably wool." I close my eyes, trying to recall. "The next layer was blue, I think. A sweatshirt, maybe?" I shake my head. "The next layer was dark and had a collar. The T-shirt underneath I remember specifically, because it was pink—shocking pink. You could see the round neckline." I open my eyes. "He also had a dark hat on. I never got a clear look at him, his face, I mean. Any impressions I have come from a microsecond of flashlight here and there. And it wasn't a particularly good flashlight, either."

"Was it a baseball cap he was wearing?"

"No," I say, shaking my head.

"Could he have been wearing a sock hat?"

"How so?"

"You know, like Dopey wears?"

I burst out laughing, I can't help it.

Buddy's laughing, too, which makes it all right for the female officer to laugh, as well. He turns off the recorder for a minute. "We're stuck in a *Snow White* phase at my house right now," he explains. "Over and over, 'Daddy, Daddy, read me *Snow White*. Mommy, Daddy, let's watch *Snow White*.'"

Buddy's wife went to school with us, too. They have a little girl and a fairly new baby boy.

He turns the recorder back on.

"No," I answer Buddy, "he didn't look like Dopey."

His mouth twitches but he quickly sobers. "Stocking cap?"

"You mean like Santa Claus wears?" I ask, laughing again. "Oh, Buddy, I'm sorry," I say, dropping my head to the table.

When we can at last move on, I dismiss a sock hat, tennis hat, visor and decide on a winter cap, "Like the one Johnnie Cochran tried on at the OJ trial."

"Black?"

"Dark, that's the best I can do."

"And it was a white guy."

"White face, narrow jaw. Clean shaven."

"Hair?"

"Couldn't see any. Dark eyebrows, though."

"What about his voice?"

"Raspy, that's the only way I can describe it. Either he's smoked for years or he was disguising it. Probably the latter." I take another sip of water.

"Why do you say disguised?"

I put the bottle down. "At first I assumed he was one of those guys who keep getting into the old factory. But then I noticed he was too steady, too sure of what he was doing, to have been living like that. And the more I think about it, the more sophisticated I think he might have been."

"How so?"

"He was cleanly shaven and he smelled like Listerine breath

strips. The mint kind." I close my eyes. "He also grabbed me so fast and so expertly—" I open my eyes. "He must have had some kind of training. Which would fit in with what Agent Alfonso said, that he thought the assailant was 'a man of combat,' he called it."

"Interesting," Buddy says, making a note.

"Police, military, underworld, boxer, he suggested."

"Could it have been Phillip O'Hearn?" Buddy asks.

You have to understand what a surprising question this is. Phillip O'Hearn is a Castleford construction baron who was once my father's best friend and became my family's bitterest enemy. Now we tolerate each other. O'Hearn even helped my family out not long ago, but even that can never fully heal the wounds he inflicted on us. "Where on earth did you pull that from?"

Buddy sniffs slightly, raising his eyes to look at me, waiting for me to answer the question. "First of all," I say, "O'Hearn must be twenty to twenty-five-years older than this guy was."

"He's sixty-six and in great shape."

"There was no way this guy was sixty-six," I tell Buddy.

"Why do you say that?"

"I don't want to talk about it," I say with a shudder.

"Sally."

Reluctantly I look across the table at Buddy. Al Royce was nearly killed and his body was left on my doorstep. I rub my right temple, willing the nausea to go away. "The guy had an erection. I'd swear he was at least twenty-five years younger."

"Okay," Buddy says quietly, making a note. "But that's important." He looks up. "Did you tell Agent Alfonso this?"

I shake my head.

"Okay," he murmurs, making a note.

"Phillip O'Hearn is at least three inches taller than this guy was," I add. "And I punched him out once—Phil, that is—and there's no way I could deck this guy. His reflexes were that good."

"If you had to guess how old he was?"

I think of Paul at age twenty-five and of my exes in their thirties. "Between thirty and forty. Maybe closer to forty."

"You told Alfonso that when you were leaving the building— the old warehouse—*two* men grabbed at you."

"That's right."

He looks at me. "Was one of them the perp?"

"You mean the guy who let us in?"

He nods.

"The guys say yes, but to me they were just hands out of the dark. Eric said he thought he was some kind of cop, but I didn't hear any sounds a cop's gear usually makes."

"You would know that from Paul, of course," Buddy says to himself.

"But that doesn't make sense to me," I say. "Why would a police officer be with someone pretending to be a homeless guy who led us into the *Herald* in the first place?"

He folds his hands in front of him on the table. "You know just about everybody in Castleford, Sally. Did the perp remind you of anyone?"

"No."

"But he knew who you were," Buddy says, tapping his pencil on the table and looking down at his notes. "I find that interesting." He balloons his cheeks with air and lets it out slowly. "But then, these days, who doesn't know who you are?" He turns to address the officer. "Did you ever hear of Sally Harrington before you came to Castleford?"

She nods. "From the Mafia Boss Murder Trial in Los Angeles. After Nick Arlenetta was killed."

You know, even though many say it was that trial that "made" my career at DBS, I am sick of being identified with it. I am sick of it because I am sick of thinking about what led up to it, the murder Nick Arlenetta got away with of an "inconvenient" girlfriend and an "inconvenient" wife, the murder of his own cousin's wife, the ensuing war between the Arlenetta and Presario families, and then the cold-blooded murder of one of his own brothers.

On top of everything else, there were the years of sexual abuse Nick Arlenetta had inflicted on children and yet the trial was to bring his murderer to justice, as if the murderer had done the world anything other than a service! But no, the trial dragged on, and while I got portrayed as a poster girl for nymphomania, the youngest brother, Michael Arlenetta, was scooping up the reins of power left behind by Nick. I gave the feds testimony that was enough to indict Michael Arlenetta for attempted murder, but he got off, and so the whole experience has left me feeling disillusioned and deeply sad.

But that's how everybody knows me, as the bad witness in the Mafia Boss Murder Trial.

"See?" he says, turning back to me. "Too many murderers around you, Sally. Has DBS provided any security for you? Today?"

"I don't think so."

"Then stay with your mother tonight. It's the least you can do for her with the mob scene you created over there."

I nod. "Okay."

"All right," he says, abruptly turning off the recorder and scooting his chair back to stand up. "Ditch the limo for tonight and I'll take you to your mom's. I'd like to check out the situation for myself." After I've gathered my things and stood up, he says, "I wish you'd keep your mouth shut for a while about this, but I suppose that would be too much to ask."

"Devon, where are you?" I shout into my cell phone after *DBS News America Tonight* is over. I hang up and then decide to call him back and say there's interest in one of his photos for a Pulitzer. That will get his attention. This time, however, I am informed his mailbox is full. Mother, seated across from me in her living room, clicks the TV set off with the remote and scolds, "Sally."

I put my cell phone on the coffee table. "What did I say?"

"Don't make it worse, dear," she advises, closing the curriculum book she's been working on. She looks at her watch and shifts in the wing chair to get a better look at me. "Don't you think it's time you went to bed?"

"What? And miss all the fun?" I say, nodding toward the front of the house. Mother says this is the first time in thirty years the drapes have been drawn over our big front windows.

My father designed and built this house on the last five acres of what had once been the Harrington estate. The house in which my father was born can been seen through a screen of fir trees, an elegant redbrick mansion that today is a convent. My grandfather ran through a staggering amount of money, destroyed the century-old Harrington printing business and then responded to the whole financial crisis by shooting himself in the head. The estate had to be sold.

When Daddy married Mother, her parents gave them the means to build this house as a wedding present. Daddy was killed when I was nine and somehow as a schoolteacher Mother kept body and soul together and hung on to the house. I suppose I should feel the Harrington land carries a kind of curse, then, but I don't. I look at the big stone fireplace in this room and smile when I think of Daddy collecting every single rock for it from this property. He adapted eighteenth-century housing designs to accommodate modern building materials.

Last year I had bound in leather the blueprints and photographs of every building Daddy ever designed. They sit in a place of honor in the built-in bookcases across the room.

It is wonderful to have money to do things like that. Particularly when I still vividly remember the nights when dinner was buttered spaghetti and lettuce with oil and vinegar because there simply was no money in the house for anything else. Those times were usually in winter, when oil bills sabotaged Mother's budget. She was so proud, my mother, and when I think of her skunk brother and the money he drained out of her parents and threw away—it makes me so angry I want to scream.

So sometimes, still, when I look at Mother, my heart breaks a little, remembering how hard she struggled to take care of me and my younger brother, and how hard she tried to hide that struggle from us.

I'm not sure Rob was ever truly aware of our precarious financial condition. He was younger, young enough not to understand until later when things were better. Maybe that's why I will never stop feeling so driven to work and save money and Rob feels okay about dropping out of college and drifting his life away in the mountains of Colorado.

We are like night and day, my brother and I. Of course, he is the male heir (and you know how mothers are about their sons!), so while Mother is my very best friend on the face of this earth, Rob is like the treasured offspring who in olden times would

have been packed off to India or somewhere to pull himself together before returning to public life.

He's good-looking, a fabulous skier and is really rather sweet. The
first and the last attributes have gotten Rob out of fixes for most
of his life, and the second offers him a way to pass the time until
he figures out what on earth he wants to do. There is no sign of
him getting married (a new girl about every fifteen months has been
his MO for the past ten years), and the last time I saw him, this past
winter when I went skiing, I got the decided impression he was
fooling around with somebody's wife. When I asked him about it
he blew up, so I knew I was right, and while I didn't bring it up
again, it did leave a cold spot in my heart. I just don't go for that.

"So tell me again, Mother," I say, scanning the mantelpiece and
bookcases, "why you have five pictures of Rob in here and only
two of me?"

She laughs, slipping her glasses off and letting them drop on
their chain to her chest. "Because he's so much better-looking
than you are," she kids, getting out of her chair. "Darling heart,
you really must go to bed. You're nearly cross-eyed with fatigue."

"I need to find Devon."

"He's probably hiding from the press."

"And how weird is that?" I ask her. "The press hiding from
the press?"

"No weirder than a media star hiding out with her mother
from the media outside," she says. "Listen, little miss, you've got
a very important affiliate convention to attend." She walks over
to pick up the newspapers I made a mess of on the coffee table
and continues to the old seed bin that doubles as a wood box for
us. She raises the lid and tosses them in.

I get up to go over to the front door. I flip the switch that turns
all the lights off in the living room.

"Sally, what are you doing? I can't see where I am going."

"I want to see what's going on out there," I say, peeking outside through the curtains. "I hear the dogs barking."

"You better get them in."

I flick the light back on and open the front door. Bringing
up my thumb and forefinger to my mouth, I make a piercing
whistle.

"Just like your father," Mother muses on her way into the kitchen.

I smile, standing in the doorway. Daddy did teach me how to do that. In a minute I see Scotty and Abigail racing down the driveway toward the house, Abigail pulling ahead. Abigail, a small but superbly sleek golden retriever, is a joy to watch run. Scotty, on the other hand, with his complicated genetics is not fast, nor very graceful. The dogs come bounding into the house and too late Mother calls from the kitchen to bring them in through the back because they're probably muddy.

I chase them into the kitchen with an old towel.

"Did I tell you Paul split more wood?" Mother asks, putting some pots away from the drainage rack.

"He mentioned it," I say, kneeling to start rubbing them down, starting with Scotty. Their feet are damp, but not muddy.

"I think he's darling," Mother says, yawning. It's way past her bedtime. She's up by six every morning. She leans on the counter to watch me. "He loves this house."

"He loves you," I say, moving on to rub Abigail dry. "And why shouldn't he? Without you he'd be skin and bones. He never cooks for himself."

I rise to my feet, looking for somewhere to hang the towel.

"The edge of the chair is fine, dear," Mother says. When I turn back around I find her still leaning on the counter, watching me.

"Why are you looking at me like that?"

"I'm waiting to make sure you go to bed and the counter is holding me up."

I laugh.

"Let's go, pups," Mother says to the dogs, turning on her heel.

"Don't they get cookies?" I ask.

"Cookies," she calls, holding two Milk-Bones over her head. "They get them upstairs."

"You never let *us* eat upstairs," I remind her, following Mother up the stairs.

"The dogs don't talk while they eat—they're never as messy as you were."

I mock a slight shove in her direction.

"I'm sorry you couldn't see Paul while you were out here,"

Mother says a few minutes later, poking her head into my old bedroom. "What are you doing, Sally? Turn out that light. You're exhausted."

"In a minute." I'm thumbing through a history of Castleford the *Herald-American* published a few years ago. I hold up a page for Mother to see. "Do you remember him?"

Mother is in her robe and nightie but still has her glasses around her neck. She puts them on to see. "Al's father? Yes, of course I remember him." She takes the book from me and sits down on the edge of the bed. "Oh, look at this," she murmurs. "When he used to have hair. He certainly didn't have much when I knew him."

I look at her. "You really can't think of anyone who might want to hurt Al?"

"And leave the poor man on your porch? I think not, dear." She turns a page. Then she closes the book. "The police talked to Mack. Did they talk to Paul?"

I prop myself up on one elbow. "Why did you ask that?"

"I'm curious. If Buddy could think Mack of all people could hurt anybody, I should think—I should *hope*—he would also consider someone as young and strong as Paul." She makes a face. "Can you possibly imagine Mack beating up Alfred and leaving him on your porch? With the way his back is? The whole thing is ridiculous." She gives her head a shake.

"But someone did do it," I say gently.

Mother closes her eyes a moment. "I know that." She pulls her glasses off and puts the book on the nightstand. "I think we've had more than enough for one day," she says, turning out the light. "Thank God Alfred is going to be all right." She stands up. "I hope you said a prayer for him."

"All day, Mother, all day."

She leans over to kiss me on the forehead. "Good night, my angel. See you in the morning."

"Do you think we could go to the Bradley Diner for breakfast tomorrow morning?"

"With that crowd outside?"

"I was just thinking we could throw them some business."

She laughs softly. "Well, Mark will love you for it. Good night."

"Good night," I say, turning on my side and adjusting the pillows. "Thanks for letting me stay. And sorry for all the commotion."

"Shocking as it may sound," she says, hand on the doorknob, "I've almost come to expect it. Oh, here's someone we forgot. Scotty, go see your mother."

"Hi, baby," I say to him. I feel the bed rock as Scotty jumps up. He circles around twice on the imaginary grass and lies down at my feet.

"Good night," Mother says, closing the door. A moment later she reopens it, a bar of light falling across the room. "When do you suppose I can answer the phone again?"

"Four days should do it," I say, yawning. "But I still think you should get an unlisted number. I'm going to need one here, anyway."

"Do police officers need unlisted numbers, too?" she asks. "Well, I'll think about it, dear, but it is more expensive."

The door closes firmly this time and I pull the covers over my shoulder. I am so tired I almost feel sick, but my mind is having a hard time shutting down.

I frown. Did Mother ask if Paul would need an unlisted number, too?

I suppose it would be normal to assume that we might one day live together. We have been seeing each other for a while. And Mother really likes him.

I wish I could visualize it, living with Paul. And thinking only about Paul.

But I can't. I keep thinking about somebody else.

"You're to go straight into Alexandra's office," Margarite tells me when I arrive the next morning.

I look at my watch. Eleven. "She's in? On a Saturday?"

"She's in, Will's in and Cassy Cochran's in there, too, with the new sales director," she reports, swiveling her chair in my direction. "The field report from Castleford last night was great. Is Bill Randolph as good as he looked?"

"He's great," I confirm, picking up my copy of the *New York Times* and scanning the front page.

Here it is, front page, on the bottom. Bomb Explodes At Connecticut Newspaper and there is a stunning photograph of the blasted newsroom interior at the *Herald-American*. The photo credit reads: "Devon Clarke for the Associated Press."

I flip the first section of the paper down to look at the Metro section. Ah, here we are; it made the local Manhattan edition but not the tristate editions: Publisher's Body Found At Ex-Employee's Door.

"It's not so bad," Margarite offers, looking over my shoulder.

The paper of record states the facts: a bomb went off at the paper and nobody was hurt (see A-1), but later in the morning the newspaper publisher of that newspaper was found unconscious on Sally Harrington's front porch, suffering from what officials called "A horrible beating to the head." It tells how Al was rushed to the hospital. "According to Lieutenant D'Amico of the Castleford Police, Ms. Harrington, an employee of DBS News in New York, was not at her home in Connecticut when the incident occurred."

"What's his name again?" I ask Margarite, closing the newspaper.

"Whose?"

"The new sales director."

"Ah." She looks around on her desk, spies a piece of paper and draws it nearer. "Steven Kol-sek?"

I lean over to look. "Probably Kol-check. Okay, just let me throw my stuff down." I zip into my office and out again, pen and legal pad in hand. "Anything else important?"

"About a million voice-mail messages, but I think you already got most of them on the way in," she says, handing me her message book. "Nice outfit, by the way. The suit's a nice blue on you."

"Thanks, it's my mother's." I skip how we had to gather the skirt waistband with safety pins in the back so it wouldn't fall down around my ankles. I scan the message book. "Did you get a chance—"

"I got everything from your apartment," she assures me.

"Bless you."

"Your dress for the party tomorrow night arrived and Cleo got your gown back for Monday night's dinner. Everything's packed and in Alexandra's dressing room. They're going to take all your stuff with hers."

"Excellent," I say, suddenly feeling nervous. It's not all that easy to deliberately go from working behind the scenes to being on center stage. It's one thing to trip your way out on a moment's notice, but quite another to rehearse as a star.

I mean, look at me. My hair's a mess, I'm holding together a suit two sizes too big with safety pins and some psycho beat up my former boss on my behalf.

"I guess I better see what my status is in the sales department," I say, handing the message book back and shoving off.

"It should be off the charts after talking Jessica Wright into coming back!"

I retrace my steps back to Margarite. "What makes you think Jessica Wright's coming back?"

"Everybody knows, and everybody knows she's coming back because of you!" She grins. "Everybody's also hoping the hiring freeze will be lifted."

"I never even spoke to Jessica Wright, Margarite."

"Yeah, but you made Will talk to her and Benjamin heard Mrs. Cochran say it's a good thing somebody's not afraid to rattle the family chains around here."

I smile.

When I arrive at Alexandra's office, Benjamin jerks his thumb in the direction of the door in a manner that suggests I best not lollygag.

I take a breath, knock twice and walk in, taking care to close the door behind me.

My future co-anchor, Emmett Phelps, and Alexandra are sitting on either side of Cassy Cochran on the couch. Emmett, as always, is dressed in a tweed jacket, tie and horn-rimmed glasses; Cassy is wearing casual slacks and a sweater; and Alexandra is in blue jeans and a navy top (Saturday clothes). Will, and a man I don't recognize—whom I presume is Steven Kolcek—are sitting in chairs opposite them. Our publicity director, Alec, is pouring coffee at Alexandra's entertaining area in the corner.

"Good morning," I say, trying to mask the nervousness I feel.

Emmett and Will and the new guy immediately stand and there is a chorus of hellos. Alexandra introduces me to Steven and we shake hands. "It is both a pleasure and an honor," he tells me. He's a bit on the short side, but cute. His face appears permanently flushed, though, and I can't decide if he just has that kind of skin or he is a serious party boy. *Director of sales?* Smart money goes on the party boy.

"It's very nice to meet you," I tell him. "And I hope the events of the past couple of days haven't made your job even harder."

Will has dragged another chair over for me to sit in. As I do, Alec comes over to hand me a mug of coffee. "For you, Sally-baby-oh-babe. And ni-i-i-ice suit," he adds theatrically. I thank him and take a sip of coffee, checking out the faces. No one looks upset. To the contrary, they are all looking rather cheery. No doubt because of Jessica. As I reach to put my coffee cup on the table, out of the corner of my eye I catch Steve stealing a head-to-toe look at me. It's not sexual in nature, but professional. I am a mare he is to lead around the ring in the horse-and-pony show.

"How is Al Royce?" Alexandra asks me.

"Better," I say. "He's talking. Now, what he is saying, nobody will tell us yet. *Yet.*" I smile. "We've got our sources working on it."

"And do these sources know you'll be away?"

"They'll contact Bill Randolph directly."

"Good," the anchorwoman says.

"How is your mother?" Cassy asks. "I hear her house got over-run with reporters last night."

"She's fine. But she did make an effort this morning to look especially nice when she left in case they filmed her."

People laugh.

"And how are *you?*" Cassy continues.

"Since I've known Al might come out of this relatively okay, pretty good." My eyes settle on Emmett, whose expression is verging on distraught. "What is it, Emmett?"

"All of it," he blurts. "If this kind of stuff happens to my family, I'm not sure I want to do this."

"But nothing's really happened *to* me," I point out.

"I don't want my kids finding bodies on our porch!"

"We all feel that way, Emmett," Will says. "And we all worry. Because celebrity is a lightning rod for wackos."

"I'll second that," Alexandra says. She turns to Emmett. "We all need to take precautions. But you learn it as you go. It doesn't happen all at once."

"Except to Sally," Cassy says.

"Speaking of Sally," I say, turning to Steve, "have you heard anything from sponsors? I'm almost afraid to ask."

"Why?" Cassy asks. She looks to Alexandra. "Is there something I don't know?"

"She's worried about being connected to this kind of violence."

"Cereal sponsors," I underscore.

"You guys took the Delafield story away from her because of it," Emmett reminds Cassy.

"The only bad publicity is no publicity," Alec says.

"I certainly don't agree with that!" Cassy declares, leaning to look past Alexandra at the publicity director.

"While it's true," Steve the new sales guy says to me, "that early-morning anchors are somewhat more vulnerable to sponsors—which is why you tend to see so many new faces reading the news in the morning—"

Reading the news? I think. *Is that what he thinks we do?*

"Reporting the news," Alexandra corrects him. "Or because we're a broadcast network, not a cable network, it's also correct to say, 'So many new faces broadcasting the news.'"

Steve pauses, a little flustered. Then he nods in Alexandra's direction and turns back to me. "I was telling the group before you came in I've been getting calls today—on a Saturday—from *new* advertisers who are interested in signing up for *DBS News America This Morning.*"

"You're kidding."

He smiles broadly. "I'm not kidding."

"And none of the sponsors who have already signed with us," Will adds, "have complained. Not a single one thus far."

"And it seems you have been offered your first personal-endorsement deal, Sally," Cassy adds, "from a burglar alarm company."

"That's not her first offer," Alexandra says. "During the Mafia Boss Murder Trial we got a call about—" She looks at Will, trying not to laugh. "What was it for?"

"Sexual enhancement through self-hypnosis," he says. "Scientifically proven results!"

Everyone laughs. Unfortunately they are not making this up.

"There was never any question about Sally remaining my co-anchor, was there?" Emmett says nervously.

Emmett and I still don't know each other extremely well, but certainly I know him better than anyone else at DBS. We've slogged through a few battlefields together already. And perhaps most meaningfully, I helped him when he was seemingly struck by amnesia during his debut on network TV. Although Emmett is ten years older, I have developed a kind of motherly attachment to him. I love coaching him because he works so hard at learning the medium and it is gratifying to watch someone as bright as he is become more effective in it. This is a midlife career change for him, and as his confidence continues to grow, I sense that his family life, too, despite their move to New York from California, will be affected in positive ways, as well.

From the network's point of view, the demure former law professor has a TV-Q rating that cannot be ignored. The TV quotient of a person is a measurement of how much people like someone on the small screen. That's right, at face value, for no earthly reason anyone can figure.

That's why the network favors me, too, and why the entertainment division tried to draft me to substitute for Jessica Wright, because I have an inexplicably soaring TV Q that nobody quite understands but which everybody would like to make a dollar on.

No one has been more keenly aware of my viewer appeal than Alexandra and Will. The question in their minds has always been if I had the mental musculature to transform my print journalism skills to TV. There was also a question about whether or not viewers would trust someone who had been as badly portrayed as I had been in The Mafia Boss Murder Trial. Apparently I'm doing just fine and seem to appeal to much of Alexandra's demographics.

I think it's amazing how well Alexandra has done in the ratings after her love affair with the actress Georgiana Hamilton-Ayres became public knowledge. The women were often inadvertently photographed together, but never attending a public function together. Each always has an escort, for Alexandra usually Will or Jackson Darenbrook. Sometimes even Langley. While the tabloids have for years referred to Alexandra and Georgiana as gal pals, when either one is asked if she is gay, they say no and leave it at that. Since Georgiana was once married and Alexandra was twice engaged, and both have a long list of former boyfriends, I suppose literally speaking—or at least semantically—that is true.

At any rate, when Emmett and I were thrown together to do the nightly wrap-up about the trial, it became at once clear something special happened between us on the air. Our personalities, our sensibilities, our areas of knowledge, even our appearances seemed to bring out the best in each other. It was nothing we tried to do; it was something that just happened.

And we really liked each other.

So when Emmett first came to New York to do a story for *DBS News Magazine,* it was me the network asked to coach him through the process. It was a delight. As for Emmett, he believes in me in a way few others do and I feel he is an integral part of my stability on this new journey. (I like the Sally he sees and aspire to be more like her.)

After Emmett asks if there ever was any question of me *not* being his co-anchor, Cassy says "No" at the same time Alexandra says "Yes" and Will says "Sort of," which produces rather an interesting moment.

"I said yes," Alexandra says, "because I knew it might be hard to turn down a million dollars as Jessica's substitute in order to co-anchor the morning news."

Emmett is looking at me. "You must regret it sometimes. A *million* dollars?"

"No, I don't regret it," I say, recrossing my legs. "Speaking of Jessica," I continue, "my assistant tells me everybody knows she is coming back."

Will smiles, shrugging. "The deal was very quickly done."

"Extremely so," Cassy confirms. "Denny will be joining us in L.A. as Jessica's executive producer." I applaud and Alexandra, Will and Emmett briefly join me. "And as of…" She looks at her watch. "Noon—" she lowers her hand "—Jessica Wright is once again part of the DBS family."

We all cheer, Will included. "Man, this really rocks," Steve says to Will. "I arrived thinking, man, get the lifeboats out, and now I'm given a whole fleet of new battleships."

"How many shows is she doing?" I ask.

"Four with a best-of running Friday nights," Cassy says. She adds to Steve, "Which has always been the weak-sister night, anyway."

"She's coming in Monday through Thursday?"

"Tuesday through Thursday," Will says. "She wants to tape two shows on Tuesdays."

"That's a lot."

He smiles. "It's great," he assures me. "She gets two days to prep at home, three days in the studio, and then a proper weekend with her adoring husband."

"I thought there was a baby somewhere," I tease him.

"The baby is always there," he tells me, "seven days a week."

"If you'll excuse us," Cassy says, rising from the couch, "but Steve and I have a meeting to get to." The men hasten to their feet. "And I will see you tonight at Newark. Everybody knows where the Darenbrook plane is?"

There is a general acknowledgment to the affirmative. Steve explains he is flying commercial with some of the reps and will see us tomorrow. He and Cassy leave, and then Alec takes off, leaving the four of us, Alexandra, Will, Emmett and myself.

Alexandra leans on the couch armrest, dropping her chin into her hand. "So what do you think?"

Will sits back into his chair, raising his hands to hold behind his head. "He's either very good or a pathological liar, I haven't decided yet."

"Sally?" Alexandra asks.

"Where did he come from? And why did he leave wherever he was?"

"He's from an ad agency," she answers, getting up and walking over to open the cabinet, which hides a small refrigerator. She names one of the largest ad companies in the country and offers us a Perrier water, which we all decline. "He jumped to this side because he wants to learn about programming."

"Who are we talking about?" Emmett finally asks me.

"The new sales guy, Steve."

"One would hope he jumped to this side because he wants to be a successful sales director," Will says.

Alexandra comes back to us, sipping from her glass. "I think he'll be all right. Cassy knows a lot about him."

"Then for crying out loud, cut him some slack!" Emmett says a little more forcefully than perhaps he meant to. I suspect on some level he identifies with Steve. "Sorry," he mutters, fussing with his tie.

"We're not questioning his abilities, Emmett," Alexandra explains. "We're questioning his commitment to the news division in particular."

"Entertainment will be a breeze for him now that he has Jessica," Will says.

"Oh." Emmett brightens a little. "So did you see our presentation for *News America This Morning?*"

"Yes," Alexandra says, offering Emmett one of her better smiles. "It's terrific, absolutely terrific. You did a great job."

"Thank you," Emmett says.

I avert my eyes; Alexandra and Will know I did ninety-seven percent of the work on it, but it will take a couple of years of experience before Emmett realizes all that went into it.

"It's really good," Will agrees. "Though I noticed you *just—*" he holds up his hand as though he is holding a very little something between his thumb and forefinger "—missed outshining the news division's presentation." He turns to me. "I'm beginning to think you should be a Hollywood film editor, Sally."

"While I think it's wonderful…" Alexandra begins.

"You wonder if we can tinker with the end," I finish for her. I smile. "Benjamin has the most recent version. If you check the end I think you'll find that we've smoothed it out."

There is a knock at the door and Will gets up to open it. There are some whispers and then he says, "She's right here," and backs away for Margarite to enter.

"Sorry to interrupt," she says apologetically, "but Sally, there's a very strange man on the phone who says it's an emergency. He said to tell you it's Pete. And that he has information for you."

"That's Crazy Pete," I say, prompting a groan out of Will. "Forward his call here and ask Benjamin to put it through, please." I stand up.

"Who's Crazy Pete?" Emmett asks.

"Sort of the resident conspiracy theorist of Castleford," I explain.

"Sort of the complete wacko, you mean," Will says.

"Who has a way of finding out things no one else does," I add.

"Ten to one he's got something for us on the bombing or Al Royce."

"Before you are too impressed," Alexandra says to Emmett, "understand this is a man who covers his head with aluminum foil to block alien mind scanners."

The telephone rings and I walk over to Alexandra's desk. I cover my mouth with my index finger and only when they have stopped laughing and are quiet do I pick up. "Sally Harrington."

"It's me," Crazy Pete whispers.

I turn slightly away from the others. "Are you okay?"

"Why, who's after me?" he whispers.

"Nobody. I just meant you sound—well, you sound…" I look over at Alexandra and quickly away again. "You sound tired," I manage to say.

"Who's there?" Crazy Pete demands. "Someone's there!"

"Alexandra Waring is with me," I tell him. "And this is a secure line, don't worry."

Will is practically falling out of his chair.

"It wasn't a local who bombed the paper," Pete whispers.

I grab a pen and paper. "How do you know?"

"The bomb was made from blasting caps used in highway construction." Crazy Pete's father was in construction; he would know. "But the Connecticut highway department doesn't use this kind."

I straighten up. "Do you know who does?"

"Southern Massachusetts, New Jersey, Pennsylvania and Maryland."

I write this down. "And where did you get this? About how the bomb was made?"

"I gotta friend in the state lab." The state crime lab is in Castleford. "And they know there was more than one guy."

"More than one guy?"

"Mr. Royce was with two state troopers before he disappeared. Nobody knows anything about these two troopers, except that they drove away in a black Chevy Tahoe."

I'm writing. "This is excellent, thank you. And nobody knows who they were?"

"They're pretty sure they weren't state troopers."

"How do you know this, Pete?"

"None of the state barracks knows anything about them. It's not much of a description—trooper hats and uniforms."

"Anything else?"

There is a long pause. "I'm supposed to be taking new pills but I'm not sure what's in them. They give me a headache."

I scratch my head, impatient. "Who prescribed them?"

"They're some kind of mind pills."

"Who prescribed them?" I say again.

"He meets me places."

If a doctor is making "house calls" to meet Crazy Pete, it means he's meeting him at midnight somewhere like the third pine tree from the left at the park entrance.

When I get off the phone I tell the others what Pete told me—none of which, as Alexandra points out, we can use until it is substantiated.

I return to my office to call Bill Randolph in Connecticut.

"Is everything okay?" Margarite asks as I breeze by her desk.

"Yes. Can you please track down Bill Randolph and get him on the phone?" I ask over my shoulder.

"Sure thing. Hey, Sally? I left the draft you wanted on your chair. And there's fresh coffee!"

I swerve into my office to pour myself a cup, and when I cross over to my desk I notice the vase of white roses on the coffee table. "Margarite?" I sit down behind my desk and take a sip of coffee. After a moment, Margarite appears in the doorway. "Where did these flowers come from? They can't be the ones from my apartment."

"The ones in your apartment were dead," she says. "I hope you don't mind, but I threw them out so they wouldn't smell."

"Was there a card?"

"It's there on your desk."

I spot the small envelope and pull the card out.

Sorry to miss you again.

I frown. "Is there someone who keeps calling or something, Margarite? It says whoever sent these is sorry to miss me again."

"You don't recognize the handwriting?" she asks, coming closer.

"It's typed." I try to think. "Who would I be missing that knows my home address in New York? Do me a favor and when you get a minute find out from the delivery room where they came from, and then call the florist and ask them who sent them." I glance over to see that Margarite is smiling, eyes twinkling.

"I think it's so cool you have so many admirers you don't even know who's sending you such expensive flowers," she says.

I blink. "I guess." I sit down at my desk, wondering if I think it's cool, too. Or creepy.

III

It is difficult, I find, to fully enjoy flying across the country on a private jet when I keep thinking about someone beating Al Royce "in a professional manner" and leaving him for me to find

The only "professionals" I am friendly with are Paul, Buddy D'Amico and the Presario crime family. I'm actually not supposed to call the Presarios a crime family because the former don, Rocky, is retired and his son has been straight for decades. Still, Rocky, who resides in New Jersey, is the only one I know of who has the staff and resources to carry off something like what happened in Castleford.

But why would he do such a thing? Sure, it's true that because I helped the Presarios protect themselves from Nick Arlenetta they might still feel they owe me something, but surely they would wait for me to ask for help. Not just read the paper one morning and send their guys out to blow up Alfred Royce III's office, beat him up and leave him on my porch. Of course, who knows what a dying don might do.

"Of course they have to consider me," Paul had said cheerfully. "One good mental shove and I could be an avenging psycho on your behalf, fighting injustice and punishing nonbelievers."

"Please, don't even kid about it."

"Sorry. But since it looks like Royce is going to be okay, I gotta say it's hard to believe he didn't have it coming. If not about you and your mom, then about something else."

I just don't understand guys sometimes. How they rationalize someone being physically beaten as a suitable consequence to un-ethical behavior is beyond me.

Occupied as I am with these matters, I nonetheless have enough attention left over to be utterly wowed by the Daren-brook corporate jet, which is a customized Boeing 757. In the front is a smaller cabin with eight comfy armchairs that fold out into makeshift beds. This area is separated from the main cabin by two bathrooms in a divider wall. The main cabin is set up as a large living room and a three-quarter Pullman galley separates it from a café setting where there is a bar, a table for four and two smaller tables for two. The last compartment of the plane, in the tail section, is comprised of a small bedroom and shower.

I am seated on the right side of the living room area, where I have snagged an armchair in front of a plasma screen to watch episodes of NBC's *Starting Over*. It turns out Jessica Wright is hopelessly addicted to the show, too, and until a few minutes ago, when baby Emily started screaming her head off, she had been sitting with me watching it.

Starting Over is a reality show about six women who tempo-rarily live together while they—with the help of myriad psycho-logical, physiological and spiritual teachers—put their lives on a much brighter and happier course. The women have different challenges that are all—or so it seems to me—rooted in the cir-cumstances of their childhoods. (I identify.) When one woman successfully utilizes all the help that is offered to her, she gradu-ates, and another woman arrives with a different set of problems. (I think I'm hoping that watching the life-coach Rhonda will save me from the therapy I've been told most of my life I should be in.)

Jessica and I had a nice chat before she took Emily to the front cabin. She thanked me profusely for talking to Will about her returning to work and said after all the trouble she felt she had caused she didn't even know how to bring up the subject with him. "I was beginning to think Emily and I were going to have to go into the *Starting Over* house in order to talk about it."

"The fact you and Emily are here with Will tonight," I said, "tells everyone everything they need to know."

"Still, I've caused a lot of trouble."

"You've provided the ratings and money from the get-go for DBS to build a network with," I told her.

"That's not true," she said modestly, but the glint in her eye told me the comment pleased her. "This is a gift," she said, rubbing the baby's back. "I felt so homesick for everybody. I felt like my family had been taken away."

No, there's no doubt about it, we are flying to the affiliate convention a very happy group. The return of Jessica Wright to DBS is going to blow the affiliate managers away.

On the other side of the cabin, using the other plasma screen, sits the enemy in the form of Bosco Lawrence, the slick executive producer of DBS Sports. With him is our former news colleague and sports desk anchor. Bosco was the one who engineered the split of Sports from News (taking a third of our operating budget), and while Cassy tells us the split was inevitable, we still view it as treason. The news division bore the financial burden of Sports "trying to find its legs" for years and years, and the second they started making real money they split.

On the same side of the main cabin sits Langley's ancient administrative assistant, Adele. I think she is a little scared of flying. She has a book in her lap but her eyes are shut and she is holding on to her armrests as if she might be concentrating on holding the plane up in the air. I consider going over to talk to her, but I'm not sure Adele entirely approves of me.

Not far from Adele slumps my future co-anchor, Emmett, who is fast asleep. Unlike the rest of us he is not yet accustomed to vampire hours and was asleep before we left Newark.

The plan is to get us to the hotel in L.A. by 1:00 a.m., which is 10:00 p.m. Pacific Time, and get us to bed so our body clocks are relatively well adjusted by tomorrow morning.

The Rafferty's nanny (Gerta-Bertha as I have come to think of her), emerges from the forward cabin to take a seat. She offers me a smile and pulls out a book.

Everybody else—Cassy, Alexandra, Will, our COO Langley Peterson and publicity director, Alec—are in the café. I suppose I should be curious about what they're up to, but I am too caught up with whether or not a housemate is going to get thrown out to get up and find out.

"May I bring you something from the kitchen, Ms. Harrington?" the steward says, appearing in front of me. He is dressed in an impeccable navy-blue suit, and if you look closely at his navy tie, you will see the pattern of white on blue is actually made up of small *D*s. For Darenbrook, of course.

I take off my earphones. "You wouldn't happen to have a chocolate chip cookie, would you?"

"Mr. Darenbrook would fire me if I didn't," he says, grinning. "They're from a bakery in Mr. Darenbrook's hometown."

"Hilleanderville chocolate chip cookies," I say, clicking off the DVD player with the remote, "how can I resist?"

"With or without nuts?"

"Without, please. And a glass of skim milk? I'll be with the others in the back." I put my earphones to the side and stand up, my hands instantly going to my lower back. I pulled something while running around in Castleford and I've got to remember to get a massage at the hotel to work the kinks out.

I walk across the cabin to pull Emmett's blanket back over him, turn off his reading light, slip off his glasses and put them in his jacket pocket. His breathing scarcely alters when I push his seat farther back. I see one lid of Adele's open slightly and then quickly shut again and I feel badly about how white her knuckles are.

As I walk past Bosco I see he's watching clips of the Minnesota Twins from the new reality-based series they're pitching to the affiliates. While he sees baseball on the screen all I see are field cameras lost to the news group. Still, I offer a passing smile.

Langley, Will, Alexandra and Alec are sitting with their heads together over the larger table, where Alec is frantically scribbling notes. Alexandra is the first to see me. "Did you get anything to eat?" This seems to be a cue for everyone around the table to sit back and relax a minute.

"The steward's bringing it to me back here," I tell her.

Alec rises and offers me his seat. "I better get on that release," he says to Alexandra, taking his pad with him.

"Be sure to run it by Cassy," Langley calls to him.

I can see by everyone's expressions that something is up. "Where is Cassy?"

"Trying to get some rest," Langley says.

After a moment, Will gets up. "I better check on Jessica and the baby."

When he leaves, Langley and Alexandra exchange looks and then Langley sits back in his seat and tries to smile. He is not altogether successful. "So let me guess what you ordered, Sally. Fresh fruit and cottage cheese?"

"No," Alexandra disagrees while stretching, "she's tired. So it's got to be grease or sugar." She drops her arms. "Since there's no McDonald's around I vote chocolate."

"Doesn't anyone eat a plain old sandwich anymore?" Langley asks rhetorically. "I don't think I've seen my wife eat a sandwich in five years. You know, with bread."

The steward comes in with a tray. He places a napkin on the table in front of me and then he says, "Your cookie, Ms. Harrington," setting down a plate with—I kid you not—a ten-inch chunky chocolate-chip cookie on it.

"Ha," Alexandra says triumphantly.

The steward sets down the glass of milk and asks if there is anything else any of us want and we say no. Alexandra puts her elbows on the table and holds her face in her hands, eyes on my cookie. "Like all people who can't eat certain things anymore," she says, "I am obsessed with those certain things."

"How am I supposed to eat this in front of you?" I complain. I tip the plate in Langley's direction. "Langley?"

"Please," he says, holding a cocktail napkin forward. I break off a big piece and give it to him. When he takes a bite, I do, too.

"Wait until you close in on forty," Alexandra promises me, sitting back in her chair.

"You could have a little piece if you want," I tell her. I look at Langley. "I have seen her eat, you know, I'm one of the privileged few. Nonfat yogurt, carrots, celery, popcorn, filet mignon, ten million vegetables, all without salt, and maybe a chicken breast. Possibly whole wheat pasta." Chewing, I turn to her. "You once made me bacon and eggs. And you made potatoes. And I saw you eat them."

"Once in a while is okay," she says.

I look at Langley, taking a sip of milk. "The first thing I'm going to do when I'm officially an anchor is tell Alexandra Waring she's too thin."

Alexandra leans forward, suddenly, reaching for my cookie. She breaks a small piece off and puts it in her mouth. Then she reaches for another. Langley and I look at each other. She eats this as well, washes it down with Perrier water, folds her hands on the table and looks at me. "You should know Jackson's not coming to the affiliate convention."

I think I may have dropped my cookie. "Why not?"

Langley seems to have lost interest in his cookie and puts it down.

I look at Alexandra. "But he has to come. It's his gig."

Alexandra glances at Langley and then reaches down to somewhere next to her seat. Her hand comes back up with two pieces of paper taped together. "Next issue of the *Inquiring Eye*," she says.

Learning nothing from her expression, I take the pieced-together fax from her and sit back to look at it in my lap.

It is a page proof. There is a picture of Jackson on a sleek sailboat, looking back over his bare shoulder at the camera. His arm is around what appears to be a naked woman who clearly is not Cassy. To make matters worse, from the angle of the photograph it appears that Jackson is in the throes of receiving, shall we say, oral stimulation from the lady?

Pleasure Boat, the headline reads. And then underneath: "Media billionaire Jackson Darenbrook enjoys himself with an unidentified woman on the Savannah River in Georgia yesterday. Darenbrook's wife, Cassy Cochran, president of DBS, was presumably left ashore to take care of business."

I close my eyes. *No. Not to Cassy.* Slowly I open my eyes. Langley is looking up at the ceiling, upset; Alexandra is now eating Langley's piece of cookie, which I guess says it all. I swallow. "Has she seen it?"

Alexandra nods, slowly chewing.

"Could it be an old photo?" Before the Darenbrooks were married—about eight years ago—Jackson was a notorious play-boy. His first wife had died in a horrible accident and for years after that Jackson bounced from one bimbo to another until he met and fell in love with Cassy, his new employee.

Alexandra shakes her head. "No." She finishes the cookie and swallows more Perrier.

"So he's cheating on her?" I say in disbelief. I've *seen* Cassy and Jackson together in private life and I would swear the love and affection and devotion was real.

"I'm going to check on her," Alexandra says, getting up with-out answering my question.

Langley and I watch Alexandra disappear into the aft cabin. He seems reluctant to meet my eyes. Jackson is not only the CEO of Darenbrook Communications, but he has been Langley's best friend and brother-in-law for more than twenty-five years.

I put the fax on the table and Langley reaches for it, rolls it up and sticks it under the table. The plane takes a little bounce with turbulence.

"Has anyone talked to him?" I dare ask. "To get his side of the story?"

"Cassy spoke to him." He touches at his glasses. "I don't know yet what he said."

"Langley." He looks at me. "Forgive me for speaking out of turn, because I'm sure you guys know best, but I think the Dar-enbrooks should brave it through the conference." He doesn't say anything, one eye twitching. "Having a meeting with the affili-ates without Jackson is like him missing his own birthday party. The whole thing is his show."

"Guys," comes an exaggerated whisper, "there's something I want you to see!" A pair of hands land on my shoulders and a mane of auburn hair appears in the corner of my eye, followed by Jessica Wright's large green eyes—sparkling with delight—peering around at me. "Come on," she urges.

Puzzled, Langley and I get up to follow Jessica through the main cabin to the front of the plane. The talk-show hostess has been working hard with a trainer since Emily's birth, I notice, with the only telltale sign of her new status in the world being an unmanageably large bosom. At the threshold of the forward cabin, where the lights have been turned low, Jessica signals us to follow and holds a finger to her lips. She tiptoes in and we likewise follow.

I almost burst out laughing, but Langley and I both manage to only grin furiously, bringing a hand up to cover our mouths. A blanket is spread out on the floor of the plane and Will is sprawled out on his stomach, facing left, the side of his head resting on his extended right upper arm. His left arm is bent in a circle, inside of which there is a tiny bundle in pink jammies, also lying on her tummy, with her head turned to face her father. What is so darling is that her little right arm is crooked in a circle just like her Daddy's left, and father and daughter are long gone in blissful sleep. They also have the same profile.

Jessica pushes us out again. "I don't want to wake them," she whispers.

"Reminds me of when the twins were little," Langley whispers, giving Jessica's arm a pat before making his way back to the café area.

They are like family; the five key players of the original DBS team are close in ways I will never be. Almost eleven years is a long time, and while their lives have changed mightily, the bond between them—Jackson Darenbrook, Langley Peterson, Cassy Cochran, Alexandra Waring and Jessica Wright—has only deepened. Jessica Wright returning to the air is not simply about economics, you see. To these five it means the immediate family unit is once again complete.

All except Jackson, evidently.

Jessica looks around the cabin. "Where's Alexandra?"

"She's with Cassy."

Her expression has grown thoughtful, green eyes subdued. "Will told me about the picture," she says. "Stupid, stupid, stupid. Are men stupid or what?"

"So you think it's for real?"

She sighs, steadying herself as the plane heaves slightly. "What innocent would put himself in a position like that in the first place? He must have been smashed."

"But do you think…?"

She shrugs. "I don't know. I suppose all the elements were there. He's constantly on the road, she's tied up with us all the time." She notices my expression. "But it might not be as bad as it looks."

"But what do you *think?*" I press, swaying into the wall as the plane bounces.

She leans toward me, holding the wall. "I think I'm very glad I've chosen to stick close to my husband. Day *and* night." The plane gives a small shudder and Bertha, the nanny, approaches us. "I was just going in," Jessica tells her, but as she turns to go into the forward cabin Will appears on the threshold. "You're up," Jessica says.

"I had to strap in the baby," he says, yawning.

"Did you remember her binky?" Jessica asks him, sliding past him into what I have come to think of as Emily's Room, with Bertha behind her.

"I did it right!" he calls after them.

The steward asks us to take a seat and another pocket of turbulence jostles Will into me. "Whoa," he says.

"We must be going over the Rockies."

"Will, come on," Jessica says, reappearing to grab him by the arm. "You're going to get brained and think you're Superman or something."

"You're welcome to join us," Will offers.

"Thanks, but—" There is a sickening drop in our altitude and I hear Adele's gasp all the way across the main cabin. "Later!" I call to Will, and I make my way to the seat next to Adele. "We're going over the Rockies, I bet," I tell her cheerfully. "It will be fine in five minutes or so."

Bosco and the sports anchor, who like the rest of us have flown all over hell and high water, are having a couple of beers and guffawing about something. I look at Adele; she's very frightened. I take her book from her and spread a blanket over her lap, taking care to tuck it in around her legs. "Put your chair back a little and close your eyes," I instruct. She's clutching the arms of the chair so tightly it is difficult to manage, but she seems willing so I push her seat back a little. "Close your eyes," I say, "because I'm going to read to you."

I fasten my seat belt and open the book to where the marker is. I look at the cover. "I love Stella Cameron," I tell Adele, and whether she likes it or not I begin reading, loud enough for her to hear but not loud enough to bother the sports guys.

Adele, of who-knows-how-many years, does close her eyes. A few minutes later, when I begin a new chapter, I hear the click of a seat belt and a moment later Emmett comes groping over to sit in the seat across from Adele. He doesn't even look at me, but yanks his seat belt tight and shuts his eyes as fast as he can.

I continue to read, feeling strangely warm and secure.

It is an absolutely gorgeous Sunday morning in Southern California. It must have rained before we arrived for the skies are free
of the usual pale yellow of car exhaust. The sky is most definitely
blue and the breeze carries the faint scent of the Pacific, which
is less than a half a mile away. We are south of Los Angeles, at the
lush Manning corporate retreat near Mission Gardens.

The hotel proper is five stories of sand-colored stucco, delicate
wrought iron and glazed inlaid tile. The balcony eaves and roof are
made with curved red-clay shingles. I have been given a corner
suite on the fifth floor, which has a full-fledged terrace with amply
cushioned wrought-iron furniture. I look out over the maze of gardens that surround the hotel, in which are strategically shielded
bungalows for guests even more privileged than I, i.e. Alexandra.
There are three swimming pools: one that curves around half of
the hotel (if you like swimming around hotels), one unabashed lap
pool near the health club and a more decorative pool, terraced in
rock, around which are a few lounge chairs and tables for dining.
The complex also boasts twenty-seven holes of golf, six clay tennis courts, an outdoor basketball court and a shuttle to the beach.
There are, too, of course, the palm trees and bountiful citrus trees.

Should anyone ever feel inclined to work here, which I

strongly doubt, there are meeting rooms and office space with every convenience imaginable. All in all, I decide, stretching in my soft hotel terry-cloth robe on my terrace after a sumptuous breakfast, few would guess these grounds were once a dump for the city of Los Angeles. (Like Sutton Place in Manhattan, such things are better left unsaid.)

Donning khaki shorts, a blouse and sneakers, I zip down to the front desk at nine to find out where, exactly, are all the boxes from New York with my name on them. I may start playing the role of celebrity soon, but I am, at the moment, still Alexandra's special projects producer.

A porter leads me to the grand ballroom where I find a crew building staging for tomorrow's big dinner-dance event. I take inventory with two of our guys to make sure all of our equipment has arrived safely and am a little dismayed when I find out we have already lost one gofer. (Last seen last night at Virgin Records on Sunset Boulevard.) I am also more than a little disconcerted when it takes nearly an hour to locate the masters of our presentations.

One of the guys says something about seeing on the news that Jackson's been running around on Cassy, but I dismiss it out of hand, saying the Darenbrooks are targets for whatever the tabloids can cook up.

Unfortunately, if you had seen Cassy after we landed in L.A., as I did, you would be hard-pressed not to believe the story. Her chin was held high, but her eyes were badly rimmed in red, and she and Alexandra quickly jumped into a waiting limo and went ahead to the hotel, which left me and Emmett without a ride. We had to bum a ride with the merry insanity of the Raffertys' "Nursery on Wheels Mobile," as Jessica called it.

Around noon I direct a number of boxes to be taken to another, smaller ballroom where tomorrow's breakfast meeting with the affiliate managers is to be held. The tables are already set for one hundred and eighty and it is a rather splendid show of white linen, silver and crystal water glasses. No place cards yet, though, I notice, and I make a note to come back to double-check my copy of the master chart against the final seating arrangements. (I need to know exactly where a few key station managers are sitting because I have some special stuff for them that was too expensive to produce for the whole group.)

We (which is actually just me) have been busy creating glossy propaganda materials for this convention. Everyone who attends this breakfast will find at their place setting a beautiful four-color razzle-dazzle folder about the news group's programming. Across the front cover a quote from Jackson Darenbrook's speech at the very first affiliate convention, "Build It and They Shall Come." On checking just the top folder, however, I discover the copy center has managed to put the glossy group photo of the DBS News on-air talent (Alexandra, the five "editors" of the nightly news, the correspondents of *DBS News Magazine* and us—Emmett and me) in the folder upside down. Right. Open the folder and see everyone's upside down shoes and legs.

The booklet in the folder on *DBS News America Tonight with Alexandra Waring* looks great. I smile. So does the brochure for *DBS News America This Morning.* And the catalog from *DBS News America Documentaries* looks impressive.

The piece count in the folder is short, though. I check through the folder again. Then I open another folder and look inside that one. Then I open another box and check a folder from there. Nope. The brochure for *DBS News Magazine* is definitely missing.

I have to go through almost all of the boxes before I find the missing insert. I look at my watch. Well, it's now or never. So down I go on the floor to begin the task of turning the glossy photos right side up and inserting the missing piece for *DBS News Magazine* into each folder.

Some guy comes in to mess around with the sound system. "Do you know where José is?" he asks me. When I tell him no he leaves.

I am in a good rhythm and making great progress when a woman's voice exclaims, "Wow, Sally Harrington! You look great!" I nearly jump out of my skin. When I look up from the floor, where I am still on my hands and knees, she adds, "We saw you on TV when you were all beat up at that trial."

"Oh," I say, sitting back on my heels and smiling at a heavy-set woman in a floral print dress and a man behind her who is—if I am perceiving it correctly—cringing.

"We were at the wedding," the woman explains.

"Oh? I didn't know there was a wedding here," I say politely, resuming my collating tasks. I can't stop now, not when there is an end in sight.

"It wasn't here, it was at a church. At least they called it a church, although I never heard such things as were said yesterday in any real church before."

"There was a cross," the man points out.

"A cross doesn't make it a proper church," she insists. "I'm telling you he can't be Christian, that fellow Carl."

I continue with my work and a silence ensues. When I see they seem to be waiting for Sally-Harrington-who-looks-great to say or do something, I ask, "Did they hold the reception here?"

"*Very* fancy-schmancy," she says. "It was Hildy Baily's wedding, my husband's second cousin's daughter. You may have heard of her because she's a singer—although she couldn't have been doing so hot if she was working at Wal-Mart, which is where she was working when she met Carl. He came in to buy a satellite radio. He inherited a bundle from a funny uncle who didn't have any kids but he still likes to save money."

"I see," I say, smiling over my folders. I love America.

Out of the corner of my eye I see the woman is taking several steps closer. "You couldn't sign this for me, could you?" she asks, extending a pen and what turns out to be a hotel luncheon menu.

"I would be delighted," I tell her, leaning back on my heels again to accept the pen and menu.

"I finally have something to show everybody at home," she says. "I wish we had more time to talk."

"We're going to the airport right after we see my cousin," he says.

"Stop," she scolds her husband. "She doesn't care anything about old Sharla."

"Who am I making this out to?"

"Lily and Harold."

I write something nice and hand the menu and pen back to her.

"You're very sweet and you certainly are prettier than when you were all beat up!"

"Thank you."

"We need to go, Lily," Hal says, checking his watch.

"I finally meet someone important and we have to go!" Lily sighs dramatically.

I stand up to shake hands goodbye. Before Lily changes her mind about leaving I drop to the floor again, mumbling about my need to hurry.

Mercifully they do leave and soon I have completed collating all of the folders and have everybody in them right side up. I stand up, wondering just how unsanitary it would be to put the folders on the breakfast tables after working with them on the floor. Well, I decide, it's not as if they have to eat their breakfast *off* the folders. Before anyone comes in, though, I quickly stack them on chairs.

I spot yet one more box behind the serving table that has my name on it. Puzzled, I circle the table to pick it up and balance it on my bent leg to look inside.

These are the postcards that are supposed to be left in the affiliate managers' rooms. I heft the box to get a better grip when I hear from behind me, "You're Sally Harrington, aren't you?"

I turn around, finding a young man of about fourteen standing just a few feet away. "Your timing is perfect," I tell him. "I was looking for a strong young man to take this box to the front desk for me," and playfully I toss him the box. Instead of catching it, however, the kid just stands there, watching it bounce off his stomach like a medicine ball and crash to the floor, exploding postcards all over the carpet.

"Well you *looked* strong," I tell him.

"You can't touch boxes unless you're in the Teamsters union," the kid explains.

"What, are you management or union?" I joke.

He squats down next to the box, but still doesn't touch anything. "I'm Gordon Strenn's son."

Gordon Strenn is president of DBS Entertainment here in Los Angeles.

"Your father didn't explain everything," I tell him, kneeling to begin picking up postcards. "While it's true you can't *transport* boxes in California with any conveyance on wheels, you can *unpack* boxes that don't contain equipment that require a union operator."

"Oh," he says. "Sorry." He starts picking up postcards.

"I shouldn't have thrown it at you." I smile. "I should have at least shaken hands with you first and *then* thrown the box at you."

He laughs, tapping a group of cards into order and placing them in the box. "I remember you from the Mafia Boss Murder Trial. Dad says you have big-time charisma."

"Oh, he did, did he?" I glance over. "I didn't realize any of Gordon's children were quite so grown up," I tell him. He's rather slight, certainly slighter than his father, but has the same curly brown hair. Delicate bones, though.

"My mother was Dad's first wife," he says, walking on his knees to get to the cards.

I didn't know Gordon Strenn was married before. "You have me at an advantage," I tell him. "You already know my name."

"Oh. Sorry. I'm Christopher." He walks back over on his knees to put the last of the postcards in the box.

I can't quite place it, but he has a trace of an accent. "Glad to meet you, Christopher," I say, walking over to him on my knees to shake his hand. "You don't suppose I could talk you into helping me distribute all of those folders over there, could I?"

"Sure," he says.

We get to our feet and I load him up with a stack of folders, showing him how I would like each one set on the table. Then I grab a stack and start on another table.

"I can't thank you enough for your help, Christopher," I say as we race from one table to another. "I'm running behind."

"Everybody's running behind," he tells me. "We're late because Mom made us go to the chapel after church. My half brothers were in a program."

I smile. "I met your stepmother once. I liked her."

"Yeah, she's great." He starts placing folders again. "My mother— you know, my real mother, in Paris—says Mom's like tuna fish."

I turn around. "Sorry?"

"She says my grandmother was like caviar, Mother's like smoked salmon and Mom's like tuna fish, everybody likes her."

Ouch. Mother sounds just a wee bitter.

"Dad almost married Alexandra Waring, did you know that?" he asks me next.

"Yes, I did."

"Did you know Mom used to be Dad's secretary?"

"Yes." It's part of the DBS legend, what happened in that very first year. I scoop up more folders and press on.

"Did you know they fell in love while Dad was engaged to Alexandra?"

I choose not to answer that one. I suspect the situation was far more complicated than Christopher can know.

"It all worked out for the best," he sighs, sounding like a grown-up. "Mother still hates Alexandra's guts, though. Nobody's even allowed to say her name."

I glance over. He's walking over for more folders.

"My mother says Dad married her off the rebound," he says matter-of-factly. "After Alexandra dumped him the first time around. That's why their marriage didn't work."

I have stopped moving. When Christopher looks over I hasten to resume working and try to sound as casual as he does. "I didn't know Alexandra and your father dated before he married your mother. Of course," I add, "I didn't know your father was married before so…" I let my voice trail off. After I move to the next table I notice that Christopher is watching me and I ask him if something's wrong.

"No."

When I finish my table I walk around it to stand closer to Christopher, who has stopped working and is just standing there, looking at me, his face streaked with pink. "What is it, Christopher?"

He glances at the door. "I wondered if I could ask you a question."

I shrug. "Sure."

"How can Alexandra be a lesbian if she had sex with my father for so long?"

He's caught me off guard with this one and I struggle not to appear shocked. "How do you know they even had sex?"

"Mother told me. She said Dad was sexually obsessed with Alexandra."

"Oh, Christopher!" I say, thumping my remaining folders on the table so hard it makes both the silverware and Christopher jump. I put my hands on my hips. "I find it very hard to believe that your mother would ever talk to you about something like that."

After his initial alarm dissipates a little, Christopher hangs his head. "I've heard her talking about it to her friends. She didn't tell me. She always tells her friends Dad and Alexandra's relationship was all sex and Dad was too stupid to notice that Alexandra was never in love with him."

"Christopher, Christopher, Christopher," I murmur, sighing and walking over to him. "Listen, sweetie," I say, placing a hand on his shoulder, "all that you need to know—all that really matters—is that your mother and father loved each other when they had you."

He squints. "How would you know that? You didn't even know my mother existed."

I take him firmly by both shoulders. "Listen to me, Christopher, I'm very old and I know a lot of things. One is that you are one of the luckiest kids on the face of the earth because you not only have a mother and a father who love you, but you have a stepmother and three brothers who love you, too. I know this because all I had was my mother and brother."

"What happened to your dad?"

"He died," I say quietly, lowering my hands. "When I was nine."

"Oh," he says. "I'm sorry."

"Thanks," I say, turning away, wondering how on earth I got myself into this conversation.

"Did Alexandra dump Dad to be with a woman?" he asks me next.

"No."

"But Mother says—"

I whirl around. "Your father and Alexandra called off their engagement because your father knew he wanted to be with your stepmother and Alexandra knew that was the right thing."

"Yeah, but—"

"Christopher, there you are!" a deep voice says.

Oh, great, I groan inwardly, recognizing Gordon Strenn coming into the ballroom. How long has he been at the door and how much has he heard?

"I wondered where you got to," he says, coming over to us.

"I was helping Sally put this stuff out," Christopher says, holding up the folders.

"It *is* you, Sally Harrington," Gordon says, smiling. Gordon is about five-ten, with receding curly brown hair and nice gray eyes. He's wearing a typical Sunday-afternoon-in-L.A. outfit for the well-to-do man: blue jeans, white polo shirt, blue blazer and loafers without socks. He holds out his hand. "Congratulations. Everybody's excited about your newscast."

"Thank you," I say, pushing my hair back off my face before shaking his hand. "I'm very excited, too."

Gordon releases my hand and looks around. "So this is where breakfast is tomorrow?"

"Yes."

"And the cocktails and buffet…?"

"Outdoors tonight, around the pavilion in the garden."

"Sally said you didn't explain everything," Christopher tells his father. "She said I can move boxes in California as long as I don't use a vehicle on wheels and they don't contain anything that has to be run by a union guy."

"Thank you," he says to me, grabbing his son around the head and pulling him playfully to his chest. "He'll be the only kid in Beverly Hills who knows how to lift a finger."

Christopher wrests himself away from his father, laughing, and tells me he's going to finish his folders. We watch him. "He's a great kid," I tell Gordon.

"Thanks. I know. So what is this?" he asks, taking a folder from me and opening it. He pulls out the DBS News booklet and lingers—I could be imagining it, though—over a color close-up of Alexandra. Then he pushes it aside to pull out the other inserts. "This is terrific, Sally," he marvels, feeling the paper. "You guys must be making more money in the news group than I know about."

"My family still has friends in the fine-printing business," I explain. "They produce art books, glossy calendars, that sort of thing. They cut me a big break on it. That's eighty-pound paper, coated two sides."

"I wish I had friends like that," he murmurs appreciatively.

"Maybe not," I tell him. "Since they bought my family's printing equipment for a song after the banks repossessed it way back when."

"Who did the design?"

"We did. Alec—you know, our publicity director—knows a lot of graphic design and he's taught me a lot. And Alexandra knows what she likes and Will knows what we *have* to have in it, so it just worked out. I think our total cost came out to about four bucks a folder."

"No!"

I smile. "Yeah."

"Four bucks," he repeats. "It would be at least twenty-five out here." He closes the folder and holds it up. "May I have this?"

"Sure."

"No wonder Alexandra freaked when she thought she might lose you," he says. "You still know how to do things yourself, an ability we tend to lose very quickly out here."

"Alexandra was going to lose you?" Christopher asks, coming back to us empty-handed.

"We tried to get Sally to take Jessica's place while she was out having Emily."

"Cool," Christopher says. "But now she's back, right?"

"And we're all singing hallelujah," Gordon adds under his breath.

There is movement in the doorway behind the Strenns that catches my eye and I look over. For a moment it feels as though someone has socked me in the stomach. Both Christopher and Gordon turn around to see what I'm looking at. "Uncle David!" Christopher cries, and despite his young-man status he runs over and throws his arms around the man, who in turn picks him up in a bear hug. He sets Christopher back down and the two turn back to look at us.

"So, my man," Gordon says, "you made it after all."

"I made it," he confirms, crossing the room to shake hands with Gordon.

Gordon steps back. "Do you guys know each other? David, this is Sally Harrington."

"Hello, Sally," David Waring says, offering his hand.

My heart is pounding and I still haven't quite caught my breath. I hazard a handshake, trying to recover. "We've met before," I tell Gordon.

"Uncle David was Dad's roommate in prep school," Christopher says. "Back in like 1812 or something," he laughs. "He's my godfather."

Ah. So that's how Alexandra met Gordon Strenn. He was her brother's roommate at Choate.

Ah.

I swallow, trying not to meet David's eyes. It can't be an accident, can it, that the married man I vowed never again to see is here?

"So when did you get in?" Gordon asks David Waring.

"About half an hour ago." His eyes move over to me. "I stopped in to see my sister."

Christopher swipes the folder out of Gordon's hand to show David. "See what Sally made? I helped her set up for the breakfast meeting."

David is attractive in the way all of Congressman Waring's children are. He is forty-five, six foot two, about one-ninety (he is not a rail like Alexandra), dark hair streaked with gray (thinning in the back) and has a milder but nonetheless effective version of his sister's blue-gray eyes. He used to wear glasses but underwent laser surgery. "Look at my little sister," he muses, thumbing through the pictures in the folder. He glances up to flash me a smile. (He has, like Alexandra, fabulous teeth.) "This looks wonderful. She never looked so good."

"Thank you."

"Did you know that Alexandra was a kooky kid?" Christopher asks me.

"Not kooky," Gordon protests. "Just different."

"Definitely spent too much time alone on the farm," David says, and we laugh.

What he says is pretty much right, though. While all the Waring kids made Georgetown their home base with their parents, Alexandra, five years younger than David, stayed on at the Waring Farm in Kansas with her grandparents. She was also the only one who didn't go to private school, but graduated from a suburban Kansas City public high school. She was a three-letter girl (soccer, basketball, tennis), second in her class, student council president and voted most popular. David also told me she was elected homecoming queen, but maneuvered behind the scenes to privately decline the honor before the vote was counted in case she won.

Why she did, no one seems to know. But he did know their mother was very angry with her, which certainly wasn't the last time.

"Why don't you get a bite to eat with us?" Gordon suggests. "We're going to have lunch outside by the pool."

"Thank you, but I've got way too much to do still," I tell him. I try not to look at David again. He is even better-looking than I remember. It seems hard to believe nothing happened between us. Physically, I mean.

"I can stay and help," Christopher offers.

"Oh, no, Christopher, go on and have lunch. I'm sure you men have things to talk about."

"Yeah," Gordon says in a tough-guy voice, jostling his son with his elbow, "we've got *guy* stuff to talk about."

"Yeah, *foot*ball and stuff," David joins in, pretending to flex muscles.

"Oh, no," Christopher says to me, "here we go again with the good old days."

"Yeah," David says. "We can talk about how in the good old days your father dropped that pass in the Lawrenceville game."

"Dropped only because your godfather threw it like a girl," Gordon tells his son.

David falls back a step. "You try throwing a pass with a two-hundred-fifty-pound linebacker on your arm!"

"Can you believe," Gordon says to me, shooting a thumb in David's direction, "that I was roommates with this ambulance chaser? For four long years?"

"The best years of your life!"

"Come on, son," Gordon says, clapping a hand on his son's shoulder, "let's go watch your uncle David eat his words."

"You guys go on," David says, laughing. "I'll be right there. I'd like to speak with Sally for a minute."

Gordon's eyes flick over to me and then back to David. "Yeah, okay. We'll see you out there."

"See you later, Sally," Christopher says.

"Thanks again for your help," I call. We watch until Gordon and Christopher have left the ballroom and the door has closed behind them. I take a breath and look at David.

"I'm sorry to surprise you," he says.

"*Ambush* might be the more appropriate word."

"I've wanted so badly to see you," he says taking a step closer to me. "To talk to you."

I don't say anything, my eyes dropping to the ground.

"My divorce is final."

My eyes fly up. Then I turn away slightly. David's waiting for me to say something, to react, but I can't because I feel frozen. It has taken a lot for me to push David out of my thoughts; the pain was a little less each day after I sent him away. And I tried to put my best foot forward with Paul and not look back. Not allow myself to think about what might have been.

Paul, who was available; Paul, whose baggage was manageable; Paul whom Mother likes so much; Paul, who has only a future to deal with and not much of a past.

David and his wife, Mary Ellen, were Episcopalian and that is how they brought up their son and daughter. Over the years Mary Ellen developed a drinking problem and went in and out of treatment programs, which at least evolved her drinking from a constant problem to a periodic family crisis. About two years ago she started attending a born-again church and has not, to my knowledge, taken a drink since. While David was grateful Mary Ellen was getting help from the church, his gratitude turned to worry and then anger over the increasing influence a certain man in the congregation started to have over her.

First Mary Ellen discouraged David from attending church with her. Then she started spending almost every evening with this man at church meetings and activities. Then Mary Ellen announced she would no longer allow their children to participate in any family event where Alexandra was present because she was in a homosexual relationship. When she forbid their daughter to even contact her godmother in any way, David went ballistic.

Mary Ellen, you have to understand, was once very close to Alexandra, to the point where the anchorwoman flew to California twice to help David and the kids get Mary Ellen into treatment because Alexandra seemed to be the only person Mary Ellen would listen to. But that evidently no longer counted for anything.

This is around the time I met David in New York. He was still trying to talk his wife into third-party spiritually-based but nonreligious counseling (only in California!), but had begun to realize how far gone their marriage could really be. And that Mary Ellen might indeed, after finally putting down the bottle, want to be free of him to start over.

So David Waring was a decent, lonely, married man whose eye faltered and set on me in the same way I might choose a faraway parking spot because I fear there will not be another space for me. So while David may have believed he had found something extraordinary in me, I knew he was looking for something that could make the pain go away.

That was not what I was looking for and that is not what I saw in him. And that is why I had to send him away.

"I'm sorry to show up like this. I set the visit up with Gordon—I mean I wanted to see Christopher while he was here, but I knew you'd be here. I wanted to see you, Sally." I feel his hands on my shoulders. "You're shaking."

"Of course I'm shaking," I say, pulling away. "I'm terrified of anything that feels like it has the ability to kill me."

"Oh, Sally."

"I've had a lot going on, David," I tell him.

"The Alfred Royce thing. It must have been awful."

"Awful for him." I look at him. "You didn't happen to beat his head in, did you?"

He smiles apologetically. "I'm afraid not."

"Oh, David, don't you see?" I say, turning my back to him and bringing a hand to my eyes. "This is classic, what you're doing. Your marriage failed and you're reaching out for someone to get you through the pain."

"Of course it hurts, Sally, but not nearly as much as it did when we were married." Pause. "It was the not knowing that was so awful. Not knowing if she was in love with someone else or did she just hate me, or had we grown too far apart and our kids were right? That we were making their lives miserable, too, with our fighting?"

"But *I'm* seeing someone. *I'm* in a relationship."

Silence. "Paul," he finally says. "Yes, I know about Paul." After a moment. "But you're not living with him or anything, are you?"

I whirl around, making the mistake of looking into those brilliant blue-gray eyes. "And what if I am?"

"Then I'm going to say to you if you want to marry him, you should, but if you don't, you should move out and find the man you do want to marry."

Marry! Where did that come from? I look at my watch. "I have to go." I meet his eyes again. "How long are you here for?"

"As long as you want me here," he says easily.

I shake my head, looking away.

"Sally," he says, reaching for my hand. "Please. Look at me."

Finally I do. I ask, "Do you have any idea how much pressure is on me to do well at this convention?"

"Yes," he says solemnly. "And I'm going to stay out of your way and worship you from afar."

I frown, trying to pull away, but he won't let go of my hand.

"I'm not kidding," he insists, starting to smile. "I'm going to stay out of your way. And if you want to talk, just let me know. Lexy said I could stay with her." Pause. "And she seems to think I should stay. Why do you suppose she thinks that?"

"Because she hates your wife?" I suggest.

"Ex-wife. And no, she doesn't. She thinks I should stay so you get used to the idea of me being available."

My eyes fall briefly to his mouth and then dart away. I find I am no longer trying to get my hand away from him. "I have to do well at this conference, David. Everything is riding on it."

"And you will do very well. Because that's who you are."

I look up at him. "This is so…"

He nods. "I know." His grip tightens.

I want to tell him what a thrill it would be if he stayed, for me to know he was just a phone call away, just a few hundred yards away. I want to tell him about the joy I feel right now, way deep inside, about being able to think about him again, to remember what he is like and how he makes me feel, and how close to him I want to be.

I would like David to see me all dressed up. I would like to look across the room and see him watching me. And I would like to do well in front of him. "I'd like you to stay," I say quietly, still not quite believing this can be real. I raise a hand to briefly touch the side of his face.

"There you are," Will Rafferty says, swooping down beside me on the garden wall where I have been sitting with my eyes closed to the sun. We're near the pavilion where tonight's welcome reception is being held; it is beautifully laid out with white linen, crystal and flowers. A jazz band is setting up nearby and the hotel chef—tall white hat in place—is fussing with the staff over Sterno placement on the buffet tables.

"I am here," I acknowledge, edging over to give him a little more room.

"Thanks." He holds his hand over his eyes to view the pavilion. "So where are we?"

I refrain from crying, "What do you mean *we?* While I've been working all day you've been playing around with the baby in your bungalow. Except, that is, when I saw you carrying a couple of golf clubs in the direction of the driving range!"

Oh, I can't blame Will for wanting to get the last bit of mileage out of me. Alexandra can drive people nuts with her demand for attention to details.

"We're all set," I tell him. I gesture with the clipboard toward the pavilion. "I just have to make sure they set this up right."

"Why are you doing this?"

"I made a deal with the banquet manager." I settle back, crossing my arms comfortably across my chest and closing my eyes again. (I know I'm supposed to avoid the sun like Dracula but I can't help it—it feels so good.) "He said if I signed off for DBS on this setup he would lock down the ballroom for the breakfast meeting." I open my right eye a little. "Which means Sports and Entertainment can't get in there to put anything at the place settings." I close my eye. "Which means only our folders will be waiting there for the affiliate managers tomorrow morning."

"Excellent," he says. "What else?"

"Never satisfied, these guys," I mutter. "Each room has Alexandra's letter of welcome in it, along with two stamped postcards for them to send home, one of the evening news gang and one for *This Morning*." I open my eyes to add, "Emmett and I look positively gorrrrgeous." I smile, closing my eyes again. "The equipment has been checked and rechecked; the presentations are here and cued in the right order—and are now under lock and key. The missing assistant turned up in Pacific Palisades—"

"Pacific Palisades?"

"Don't ask," I advise, opening my eyes again. "And I know you are absolutely dying to know this, Will, but my dresses are pressed and ready to go. The only question that remains is whether or not I can get this body looking like something in an hour."

"You always do."

I smile. "Thank you, boss."

"You're welcome."

"Why didn't you ever tell me Alexandra dumped Gordon Strenn not once but twice?" I ask him. "And that he was David Waring's roommate at Choate?"

He looks at me. "Because you never asked?"

I consider this. "Good answer."

"And where did you find that out? Not from your new best friend the banquet manager."

"Gordon's son, Christopher."

Will yawns, covering his mouth with his hand.

"So?" I say.

He lowers his hand. "So what?"

"So did you know they went out before?"

"I knew they went out in college or something." He yawns again. "It's ancient history." Now he closes his eyes to catch some rays. "It was ancient history even by the time I started working with Alexandra."

A member of the band drops a cymbal and our tranquil sun-bathing is momentarily interrupted. The sun is just right—not too hot—and there is a lovely breeze. I don't know about Will, but I feel as though the chill of the East is being gently lifted from my bones. "So when did you meet Gordon?" I ask him.

"He came around while we were at WWKK in New York. He was married then but he still had it bad for Alexandra, you could tell."

"What happened?"

He shrugs. "Nothing. He disappeared and then when we were in D.C., he just showed up one day divorced and moved in with her."

"Just like that?"

"Just like that." After a moment. "I was surprised."

There's something in his voice that prompts me to look at him more closely. "Did you ever have a crush on her?"

"Everyone had a crush on Alexandra," he says simply. "Everyone," he confirms.

"Did you ever suspect—?"

"No," he says.

"You never—?"

"Never."

"That's interesting."

"No, it was weird," he says, opening his eyes and facing me. His brow furrows slightly. "I never dreamed... It never even crossed my mind."

"How did you find out?"

"She told me." He pauses, thinking. "The day before the first gal-pal story about her and Georgiana appeared in the *Inquiring Eye*."

The drummer of the band clicks his sticks four times, does a furious drumroll and ends the exercise with a light *ting* on a cymbal.

"Were you surprised?"

"Surprise doesn't cover it," he says, eyes on the band members. He glances over at me, smiling. "I know. Jess can't believe I never suspected it, either. I kept telling everyone they were crazy, Alexandra was as gay as I was."

It would seem Jessica has told her husband little of Alexandra's sexual history prior to Georgiana Hamilton-Ayres or Gordon Strenn.

He looks at his watch. "We better start getting ready." He gives me a quick once-over and takes my clipboard away from me. "I mean *you* better start getting ready. Go on. I'll sign off here."

"Make sure they finish the bar," I warn him, getting up. "So is Jackson coming or not?"

"Not." He stands up, looking very official with the clipboard.

"It's going to make people think there's something to the story."

"There probably is," he says, walking away. "Hey! What's with the bar?"

"It's coming," someone says without enthusiasm.

The chef in the tall white hat comes over to Will. "Don't let anyone drink red wine if they're going to eat my chicken."

"I'll see what I can do," Will promises, turning around to widen his eyes at me. He looks at his watch again. "Sally, go! And check on Emmett, will you? He got a suntan sprayed on and I hear he looks orange."

"What does Bill Randolph say about it?" I ask Haydn over the speaker phone as I adjust my towel. I stopped by Emmett's room to stick him in the sun on his balcony, had an emergency manicure, showered and am now sitting at the vanity table in the bedroom of my suite where Cleo is attempting to make me into something glamorous. Since this includes having my hair up in four large rollers, like I'm in some sort of Dippity-do commercial from the sixties, I am a little nervous about how things might come out.

"He said the Presarios once blew up your car in Castleford," Haydn reports.

"Yeah, they did." Cleo is trying to smooth liquid foundation on my neck into the natural tones of my chest and shoulders.

"So he thinks the investigation has gone in that direction. The old don used to be in construction, right? In New Jersey?"

"New Jersey, Pennsylvania and New York. Ow," I tell Cleo, pulling away from her.

"You've got to stay out of the sun!"

"So do whatever you have to do," I whisper to her. "But a little more gently, please."

"What's going on at your end?" Haydn asks.

Cleo leans closer to the speaker phone. "I am trying to make a silk purse out of a sunburned sow's ear."

"Whatever," I tell her. "So he thinks they're looking in the direction of Rocky Presario?"

"Yes."

"Huh. Interesting."

"Who is Michael Arlenetta again?" he asks.

"The youngest brother. He inherited Nick's territory. But he's no fan of mine," I add, "so don't waste your time. It was my testimony that got him indicted."

"Is he in jail?"

"Hell no. He got off, just like his brother used to."

"That's better," Cleo mutters, squinting into the mirror to check her work. Then she pulls my head back and brushes my eyes closed with her fingers so she can work on my eyes.

"Bill's trying to get a copy of the police lab report on the explosives that were used to blow up your car and see if there's any similarity with the bomb at the paper."

"Tell him he might try leaning on Buddy D'Amico for it."

"Quiet for a minute," Cleo says, tilting my head back again.

"One second, Cleo," I tell her. "He should let Buddy know we know a lot more than we're saying right now, and that he would be willing to work some sort of a deal with Buddy."

"Okay."

"You have less than two minutes, missy!" Cleo hisses at me. I close my eyes and lean back so she can start on my blush.

"The Delafield story has stalled out completely," Haydn says, moving on. "Will says to skip Gainesville altogether until it gets moving again. Alexandra concurs."

"Good," I tell him. And then what he says sinks in. "But how could it stall out—"

Cleo curses, taking a step back, threatening to strangle me with her hands.

I hold up a finger to keep her at bay. "How can the story stall out when we know they have a thorough description of the suspect, a complete set of his fingerprints and even samples of his DNA, and the authorities refuse to come forward with any of it? Surely that's news."

"I think there's something cooking down there," Haydn says. "Some sort of a deal."

"Double-check with Will and make sure that's what he wants. And then just skip it, I guess. So what else?" I signal Cleo with my finger that she can come back to work. While Haydn continues to run down everything that's going on in New York, my features begin taking on rather striking proportions.

By the time Cleo moves on to my hair Haydn has hung up to attend to the various emergencies inevitably preceding the nightly newscast. I'm actually starting to relax a bit now, almost even enjoying myself. It's starting to really dawn on me that soon I will be escaping the pressures of being Alexandra's special producer to focus entirely on our work as the morning news team. In the meantime—as I try to objectively assess myself in the mirror—I think few other things could put as much pep in my step tonight as the knowledge that David Waring is here somewhere, and that he is here because he wants to see me.

I hope I get to see him before the end of the night.

20

"The hardest part," I tell Emmett as we cross the center pool area, "is putting one foot in front of the other. And you should be grateful you don't have to do it in spiked heels."

"I noticed those," Emmett says, stopping our progress to look down behind us. I raise my right foot for his inspection like an obedient horse with a blacksmith. "They're pretty." He turns back around, nervously patting my hand resting on his arm. "And you're beautiful, Sally," he assures me.

To be honest, I am feeling rather beautiful. After Cleo "rebuilt" me I wriggled into my hot-pink-and-white shift (terribly sixties, my dear), with my grandmother's pearl necklace and matching pearl earrings (terribly WASPy, my dear), pink spiked heels (terribly sexy, my dear) and matching pink lipstick (back to the sixties we go, my dear), and I feel ready to conquer anything.

Understand I am wearing shocking pink and white by network design. I'm supposed to be the young and trendy, bright and sunshiny one. Also, hot pink was the only color left that looks half decent on me. Alexandra is wearing a dress of blue-gray silk (which knocked both colors out of the running), Jessica Wright is wearing a coral color, Lydia Southland's wearing red, and since

I look anemic in green or yellow and draw the line at purple, here I am in shocking pink and white.

"The orange is gone?" Emmett asks, rubbing his clean-shaven chin with his right hand. His forehead has already broken out in nervous perspiration. Despite the network's plea that Emmett at least forgo his tie for this informal reception, he has stuck to his guns, wearing one of his tweed jackets, tan khakis, dress shirt, tie and high-gloss leather boots (which give him another inch in height). When I explained to him the brass fear some of the affiliate managers might feel a little intimidated by his education as it is, and he would be the only man wearing a tie at this event, his exact words to me were, "Did it ever occur to anyone that I would *like* to intimidate the affiliate managers? That I wish to establish a decorum befitting an officer of the court?"

"The orange is completely gone and you look very handsome, Emmett," I assure him, stopping us for a moment. "Do you have a handkerchief?"

"Yes, of course," he says, reaching for his back pocket but then getting a panicky look on his face as he gropes all of his pockets.

"Hang on." I circle a poolside table to retrieve a clean towel from the stack left for hotel bathers. I come back to Emmett, shaking the towel out and holding it by the corner. "Deep breath, let it out slowly," I tell him. I slip his glasses off and hand them to him, quickly pat the perspiration off his forehead with the corner of the towel, dab under each eye, on his chin, and then toss the towel over the back of a chair. He puts his glasses back on and waits for my call. "Perfect, Mr. Legal Eagle." I take his arm again and we continue on.

"We're due in thirty-one seconds," he says, looking at his watch. We can hear the clinking of glasses, the chatter and laughter, a quiet jazz song being played by the band. He grins at me suddenly. "You're pretty good at this."

"Timing is everything," I say with a wink. Now we can glimpse the party through the garden and my heart has begun to thump. I am far more scared than Emmett knows.

"This is worse than getting married," he says under his breath as we make our entrance from, as we were directed, the walkway to the south.

"Here they are!" we hear Cassy announce.

Most of the talk stops as we near the pavilion. There are at least a hundred or so men and women mingling about. A great deal more men, though. After a moment of hesitation a few people start clapping and then suddenly everyone is scrambling to put their drinks and appetizers down in time to join in. I'm already nodding to station managers I know well and giving a little wave to others.

"Thank you," Emmett says in a deep voice that sounds horribly like Ted Baxter on the *Mary Tyler Moore Show* to me.

I lean into him. "Relax," I whisper through my smile, "normal voice."

"Thank you!" Emmett calls again, sounding better.

Everyone has resumed talking and drinking and eating, but a little crowd of affiliate managers has surged around me, separating me from Emmett. I see that Cassy has stepped up to Emmett's side so I relax.

Jock Hagen comes over to say hello, bringing another tide of affiliate managers with him. Jock was not only one of the best pitchers in the history of the American League, but is one of the most adept on-air announcers around. It was quite a coup for Bosco Lawrence to sign Jock for a sports reality show. Jock's traveling with the Minnesota Twins this season, producing three hours of programming each week depicting the day in the life of a major league baseball team. It's going to be huge.

Like the good ol' boy he is, Jock kisses me warmly hello (though we have never met) and gives me a hug of congratulations. "So is it a publicity stunt or was that body on your doorstep real?" he whispers in my ear.

"It was real," I tell him.

Moments later he is off, dragging his fans with him and moving over to congratulate Emmett, whom he does not, it goes without saying, kiss or hug.

Many at the reception already have a good buzz going; the men and a handful of women are happy to be here, happy to feel appreciated and cared for, and this is a particularly great event for the managers from the smallest stations. Our largest affiliate, WST in New York, employs 283 people, while our smallest affiliate, in South Dakota, employs a total of four.

"So *are* you doing a farm report or not, Sarah?" the Des Moines station manager asks me. I've told him many times that my name given at birth was Sally but I guess he doesn't like it. (I can see the billboard on Highway 80 in Iowa now, *DBS News America This Morning with Sally Harrington and Emmett Phelps.*)

"It's up to you," I tell him. "We'll outline the national weather fronts and then break to local reports. If there is a breaking crop story you know we'll run it as straight news." (Even our New York affiliate will include a fifteen second "farm" report, basically because Alexandra insists on it. Not only is she the daughter of an old Kansas farming family and the owner of a working farm near Far Hills, New Jersey, but she believes that farming is still the symbolic lifeblood of America, second only to clean water.)

"Have you lost weight?" the lady manager from Cleveland asks me.

"No," I tell her.

"You're still not married?" Seattle asks me.

"I'm still not married," I tell him.

"So who was the guy they found at your apartment?" Tulsa asks. "We heard it was your husband. Or ex-husband."

"He was found at my house in Connecticut," I say, correcting him. "And he was once my boss at the local paper out there."

"But wasn't he your ex-husband or something?"

"And your boyfriend beat him up, right?" Lady Cleveland asks me.

"No. We don't know who did it."

"So is *he* married?" Lady Cleveland asks, pointing to Emmett.

"He's very married," I tell her.

"How much ad time do we get in the weather segment?" Des Moines asks me.

"Enough certainly to make some good money," I tell him. "I'll make sure Steve Kolcek talks to you. He's the new sales director we have on board."

"Hi, Sally, how are you?" Ann Arbor asks, pumping my hand enthusiastically but looking at Emmett. "I need to ask the new guy about my divorce."

A drink appears in my hand—Alec gives me a little wave as he moves on through the crowd—and the questions continue and I do my best to charm and entertain while trying to maintain a sense of dignity in my new role as anchorwoman.

Houston, unfortunately, doesn't care about my dignity, he only wishes to openly stare at my breasts. Tucson is embarrassed by this and tells Houston, "Rachel's looking for you."

"Oh, yeah?" Houston asks, looking around. "Which one's Rachel?"

"You know, the hot one from Florida."

"Aaah," Houston says knowingly. "Where is she?"

"Near the bar, I think," Tucson tells him. After Houston leaves, he smiles shyly at me.

I lean forward. "Is there a Rachel-the-hottie?"

He shakes his head. "No." He leans forward. "Is it true his father owns the Houston station?"

"Stepfather," I correct him. We exchange cognizant looks and then talk shop a bit until the noise suddenly lessens and a murmur rolls over the party. Borrowing Tucson's wrist to check the time I figure it must be Alexandra.

The station managers essentially worship Alexandra Waring because until DBS News was launched, their stations, as independents up against the affiliates of the Big Three, had largely been considered a joke in the marketplace. When "The yuppie news at nine" (as a prominent television columnist wrote at the time) started registering significant ratings, our affiliates suddenly became of interest to local advertisers sick of being at the mercy of the Big Three affiliates.

And while it may have been *The Jessica Wright Show* that most consistently delivered strong ratings for the stations, it has been the constant supervision and guidance of the affiliate newsrooms by Alexandra's group that has elevated the stations in the eyes of their communities. DBS News has also given each affiliate a new sense of purpose. Even our tiny South Dakota affiliate offers live coverage of state election returns (something that admittedly had not seemed all that important until the minority leader of the U.S. Senate was turned out of office).

Alexandra looks breathtaking tonight. I keep saying she's too thin, but these guys don't care, they never seem to get past those startling eyes and generous mouth. Throw in all the innuendo about her sex life and their minds positively run amok with possibility. Rarely, however, are crude remarks heard about her. To many at the affiliate level, particularly out West, the Waring family is almost American royalty.

Not long after Alexandra's entrance another wave of excitement washes over the crowd, which this time borders on unruly. Even the band stops playing and everyone starts cheering and yelling and whistling as Jessica Wright comes down the garden walk, sashaying down like the conquering heroine she is, dressed in a brown leather miniskirt and matching cowgirl boots, and a billowing, long-sleeved coral-colored silk blouse. (She couldn't possibly wear one of her former trademark plunging necklines yet; she'd look like a porn star.)

The group verges on happy insanity. If Alexandra Waring gave the affiliates their self-respect, Jessica Wright gave them houses and retirement savings. During the ongoing disaster of her replacement, the managers screamed of pending financial disaster, but now magically here she is, their Jessica, riding to the rescue of the DBS family.

I knew she'd love this role. And she plays it perfectly, making even the most cynical here smile.

By the time Lydia Southland makes her dramatically beautiful Hollywood entrance, I almost think people don't care. Lydia Southland has been a huge TV star for years and is only now coming to DBS (some whisper because she's past her prime), whereas Alexandra's and Jessica's success is of their making. Lydia is just kind of an add-on now. (Mind you, she is one of the most talented and lovely people on the face of the earth, but you know what I mean. She's almost a prop.)

"I had no idea you and David knew each other so well," someone says in my ear. I turn to see Gordon Strenn, freshly showered and shaved, gray eyes looking friendly but amused.

"He helped me sort out my great-uncle's estate," I explain.

"So he said," Gordon confirms, looking around. "He took Christopher to an Angels game tonight. He said if it's not too late he'll give you a call when they get back."

"Oh, that's great," I say, trying to keep my voice light. "Hi," I say, shaking hands with Atlanta, "it's great to see you."

"Congratulations," Atlanta says—meaning it, I hope. "We've got a few headaches to take care of, Sally, but we should be on-board with you."

My smile expands and I cover his hand with both of mine. "Thank you. You know how important Atlanta is to our success."

"Just make us some money," he tells me. "Gordon, how are you? Get outta here, but Lydia Southland looks more beautiful than ever."

"The ratings are going to be more beautiful than anything you've seen before," Gordon promises him. They talk a bit while I say hello to Indianapolis. After a while Atlanta moves on to introduce himself to Lydia Southland and Indianapolis goes with him.

"She still looks fantastic, doesn't she?" Gordon says to me.

I look at him and realize he's not talking about Lydia Southland, but Alexandra.

"Yes, she does. And she's got decades to go with that bone structure."

Alexandra is explaining something to Langley and two affiliate managers, eyes bright with excitement, hands gracefully illustrating her point. Gordon looks at me. "David says you've been a godsend to her."

I look at him. "How so?"

"To start with, you seem to be immune to the Waring spell."

I smile. Little does Gordon know he's just got the wrong Waring. "She's a great boss, a great person. She's been very good to me."

Watching her again, he murmurs, "She usually is."

There is a flicker of something in Gordon's voice I don't think I like. "I should say hi to some more people," I say, moving away. "See you later." A minute later, while I'm talking to Madame Cheyenne, I see that Gordon is sipping on his drink, watching me.

"Do you think you could come to Alaska?" Juno interrupts Madame Cheyenne to ask me.

As the new kids on the block, Emmett and I hang out at the reception long after Jock Hagen, Lydia Southland, Jessica and Alexandra have left. Will stays on as well, playing the man's man with the guy managers and subtly trying to push our newscast as the greatest thing since bottled beer. He also appears to be drinking as heavily as some of the heartier partyers of the station managers, but I know the icy mugs of suds he's chugging down are O'Doole's.

By nine o'clock Emmett and I are allowed to leave and we are sent up to the DBS hospitality suite on the fifth floor of the hotel for debriefing.

I am surprised to find only Langley and ancient Adele (I've got to stop thinking of her like that!) waiting for us. I'm also a little surprised to see that Langley is wearing blue jeans, a polo shirt and Top-Siders. (He looks so white.) Adele is still in her (taffeta?) party dress, taking notes in shorthand.

"Houston's going to be a real problem," I tell Langley, taking a sip of water. I have taken off my shoes and have my legs tucked up under me on the couch. Next to me Emmett has taken off his tie and jacket. He is having his first alcohol of the night, a beer, and keeps examining the autographed picture he got from Lydia Southland. "Their local newscast is so far in the basement it's almost nonexistent, but they say they're not going to carry us."

"They say or he says?" Langley asks, referring to the affiliate manager.

"He says. He says they can wait until we offer them a better cut."

Langley shrugs. "He knows we have to have them."

I nod. "Word has it he's also sleeping with their morning anchor. I believe Will may be able to fill you in more on that."

Langley cinches the side of his mouth. "We have to have Houston," he says again.

"I know. I'm just telling you what he told me. And he thought maybe if I gave him some personal attention this weekend, we might be able to work something out."

Adele's pen stops.

"Is he a problem for you?" Langley asks me seriously.

I shake my head. "He's an alcoholic. That's his real problem. Maybe Jessica could take him to an AA meeting," I suggest sarcastically.

"Alcoholic rapists on Viagra are a whole new problem," Emmett says. "There's case law coming about whether or not there is a difference between a rapist raping a woman and an alcoholic raping a woman during a blackout, a time when otherwise they would be erectly dysfunctional. And can the victim sue the drug company?" Emmett catches Langley's look and stops talking.

Langley briefly touches on the status of each affiliate. At first tally, he tells us, it appears we may get a little less than two-thirds of the affiliates to carry *DBS News America This Morning.* He then assigns us a "hit list" of managers we need to pay special attention to while we're here—Adele hands each of us a list—and explains that my golf foursome in the morning and Emmett's tennis partner have been chosen with care.

"You're joking," I say to Langley after looking at my list. "You've got Houston on here."

"He's in the foursome but he is not your partner," he says. "Look, Sally, if you don't want to do it, I won't make you. But he and Alexandra hate each other's guts, Will slugged him two years ago for something he said about Jessica, and we've got to have Houston, it's as simple as that."

"This is a backhanded compliment if I ever heard one," I say.

"What is?" Emmett asks, looking up from his list.

"Langley doesn't think your legs are good enough to interest the Houston manager."

Emmett looks down at his piece of paper again. "I'm playing with the Milwaukee manager in a round robin?"

"He needs to be your best friend by lunch," I explain.

"His father is a judge in the criminal courts," Langley adds.

"Oh, that's good," Emmett says, sounding relieved. "And they're taking us? Milwaukee?"

"No," Langley says. "They've passed on you."

Emmett looks at me in dismay.

"We've got nothing to lose and everything to gain," I tell him. "And the pressure's on him, not you. *He* has to justify why he doesn't want his station to carry the most distinguished new face in national television news."

Emmett doesn't look convinced.

"Just tell him about yourself," I say, "over the course of the morning. How you were a trial lawyer and how you started teaching and how you came to DBS and then how A&E offered you your own program for a lot more money—"

"That's not true," he says, "the money part."

"How you chose DBS over A&E then, because you knew *DBS News America This Morning* was a winner and didn't want your family to have to wait long to enjoy your success."

"It may not be as hard a sell as it seems, Emmett," Langley adds. "Milwaukee's been yelling for years for a saleable male anchor. And now here you are."

(I feel my feathers ruffling.)

"And by the way," Langley adds, "you can offer your opinion, Emmett, on any current issues, but you are *not,* I repeat, *not* to give advice about anyone's divorce."

Emmett is about to protest, but I nudge him with my foot. "Understood," he says.

"I think Emmett did exceedingly well," I say, hinting to Langley. When our COO fails to take it, I am ticked. "I thought he did a particularly good job of fielding questions regarding Jackson's absence."

Emmett is staring at me. (All he said to people was that they should ask me.)

"And while we're here getting our marching orders," I continue, "perhaps you could tell us what exactly it is you wish for us to say about the absence of our chairman and the picture that is being shown everywhere?"

Adele shifts uneasily in her chair.

Langley coughs a little and looks at Adele. "Did anyone ask you about it?"

She nods. "I'm afraid it's like an elephant in the middle of the room, Mr. Peterson. I think his absence is particularly embarrassing for Mrs. Darenbrook."

Langley looks vaguely stricken by this. He gets up and heads for the bar, where he proceeds to pour himself a Scotch and soda. He takes a big swallow. "There's been a crisis at one of the newspaper printing plants."

"And when they ask which one," I say skeptically, "we are to say the one nearest the Savannah River?"

He looks at me angrily and I hold up my hand. "I'm sorry. That was uncalled-for." I lower my hand. "You don't deserve it."

"I want you to tell people you don't know why Jackson isn't here, but you're sure he'll be here tomorrow night."

"And will he be?"

He walks away from the bar, sipping his drink. "Cassy says he's doing something for tomorrow night's dinner to explain everything."

"Are we sure Cassy wants to hear it in front of the affiliates?" Emmett blurts out.

"I'm sure it will all work out," I say, nudging Emmett again and standing up. "If that's all, Langley—"

He snaps out of wherever his mind is, looking at me as if he only recognizes me this very moment. "Yes, I think so. Adele?"

"I have nothing more, Mr. Peterson."

Langley walks us over to the door. There he turns to Emmett and to shake his hand. "You were terrific tonight, Emmett, and very professional. We're all very proud of you."

Finally! I think, my good spirits renewed.

Emmett looks somewhat startled by this minor onslaught of praise. "Thank you, sir. That's a real compliment coming from you."

"I hope you understand that I've been distracted lately," Langley mumbles, "but that I take a keen interest in your progress. I'm very pleased by what you've already accomplished. I think you were very impressive tonight."

"Thank you, sir," Emmett says again, elated.

"And you," Langley adds, turning to me. Suddenly he bends over to kiss me on the forehead. "Thank you," he says, stepping back. "But stay out of trouble. And get Houston." And then he abruptly turns around, the ice clinking in his glass.

Emmett and I look at each other and scoot.

"My message light is blinking," I say over the bedroom telephone to the front desk, "but there are no messages on my voice mail."

"Ah. Ms. Harrington. That is because you left instructions for us to hold all deliveries until you called for them." Pause. "There were two—no, actually there have been *three* flower deliveries for you this evening."

"You must be joking."

"They're quite beautiful," he assures me. "May I send the porter up with them?"

I kick off my spiked heels and pad over the thick carpeting into the living room of my suite. It's really great. When you walk in, there is a fully stocked bar ahead of you with a big bowl of fruit on it and two barstools. Next to it are sliding glass doors leading out to the terrace. The living room proper rolls to the left with two perpendicular couches and two easy chairs around a massive square ottoman/table thing. It's clearly designed for meetings or interviewers or something, since there is a telephone on the bar, one on the side table between the two couches and another one, a cordless phone, placed between the easy chairs.

The bedroom is simply and beautifully furnished: a king-size sleigh bed, tallboy dresser, vanity table, white duvet and bedding, and floor-to-ceiling silk drapes.

The porter wheels the flowers into the suite on a large brass luggage cart. The first one is a colossal white wicker basket of semitropical flowers. The card reads: "We are so lucky to have you! Love, Jackson."

Jackson? Jackson—our missing CEO, frolicking on a boat near Savannah with some chickeepoo instead of being here with his wife and employees—Darenbrook?

I frown, tossing the card on the bar. "Perhaps you could put those on the terrace," I suggest to the porter. "There's a table near the door that stays in the shade during the day." While the porter acquiesces I move on to a stunning arrangement of English spring garden flowers. I rip off the envelope stapled to the cellophane and take out a card. "Break a leg, kid. Love, Paul."

I grimace. They are very beautiful and must have cost a fortune. "You can put these over there, if you will," I tell the porter, walking over to pick up the mobile phone. While he takes the cellophane off the garden flowers and neatly disposes of it, I reach Paul's answering machine at his apartment. "Oh, Paul," I say quietly, "they are so beautiful, you have no idea. I wish you could see them. I'm also a little put out you spent so much money— I worry now you might not take that one crucial seminar that you'll need as a prosecutor—" I make myself laugh. "There you will be, just about to nail some horrible monster in the courtroom and then you'll freeze. You'll say, 'If I hadn't bought those stupid flowers for Sally in California that year I would have had enough money to take that class that would have told me how to finish this trial.'" I lower my voice. "Things went pretty well tonight and I'll give you a call tomorrow. Thanks again for the flowers. It was very sweet of you."

The porter returns and I get off the phone. "And what about this one?" he asks, gesturing to the much smaller bundle swathed in tissue paper.

"Is there a card?" I ask, walking over. He hands me an envelope, the size of a birthday card. I open it. The card is an ink-and-watercolor sketch of a collie running along the beach at sunset. He sort of looks like my Scotty. I open the card. "I cannot tell you how happy it made me to see you today. D." I swallow and bend to pull the tissue apart. A crystal bowl of water is anchored in a square cardboard carton. Floating in it is a single white orchid.

"Not as big a show as the others," the porter says.

"That's the style of the person who sent it," I say quietly, trying to pick it up. The porter squats quickly to hold the box so I can lift the bowl out. I hold it up to the light.

Lovely.

I place it on the bar and bring out the money I tucked away to tip the porter. After he wheels out his cart and the wrappings from the flowers, I walk back to the bar to look at the orchid. I pour myself a glass of white wine and, standing there behind the bar, lean against it, rest an elbow down on it and consider the gift again from this angle. I don't know how long I've been standing there when the telephone starts ringing. I reach across the bar and pick it up. "Sally Harrington," I say automatically, forgetting I'm not at work. I mean I am at work, but not work-work. You know what I mean.

"Sally, it's David Waring." There is a lot of noise on his end. "I apologize for calling so late but I wanted to explain why I'm not back at the hotel yet."

"You don't have to explain. Unless we made a firm date that I don't remember." Oh, I remember all right. I've been hoping all evening to see him.

"No, no firm date. But I did want to offer you a nightcap and find out how things went." There's some man yelling in the background. He sounds kind of crazy.

"Where are you?"

"In an emergency room in Anaheim. Christopher and I were at the Angels' game and somehow he slipped on the stairs as we were leaving and whacked his forehead."

"Oh, no."

"Oh, yes," he says. "And you know how foreheads bleed. But he's fine." The shouting man's voice seems to be fading away. "He just got a few stitches here, but now Betty Strenn wants him checked out by a plastic surgeon at Cedars-Sinai, so I'm taking him there now. Gordon's going to meet us. I'm talking to Sally

Harrington," I hear him say. "Sally? Hang on, Christopher would like to say hi." The phone changes hands.

"I wish Uncle David would tell everybody I got in a fight," Christopher says. "It sounds a lot better than falling down the stairs."

"How are you feeling?"

"Stupid."

"So you're going to see a plastic surgeon now, I hear."

He lets out almost a giggle. "I think I'll get my eyes done." The phone changes hands again.

"A wise guy," David says. "Any chance we could get together for breakfast or a cup of coffee tomorrow?"

"I have to play golf first thing in the morning."

"Oh, right. I'm supposed to be taking Alexandra and some guys to shoot trap."

"Shoot trap?"

"All I know is my sister says I'm in charge of trap for DBS News tomorrow morning or I lose my room in her bungalow." We both laugh.

"Thank you very much for the beautiful orchid," I tell him. "It's lovely."

"Did they send the white one? I couldn't tell if they were putting me on or not, if they'd really send the one I chose in the shop."

"They sent it," I confirm, looking at the crystal bowl. White. "David?"

"I'll be right there, Christopher," I hear him say. "Yes, Sally?"

"Do you like white flowers?" I ask, thinking of the roses in New York.

"I liked that one. It seemed unusual and beautiful. Just like—" Pause. "No, I'm not going there. Yet."

"You haven't sent me any other flowers recently, have you? In New York?"

"The way you ask that question makes me wish I had. But no, I'm afraid it wasn't me."

I look at Paul's flowers across the room and feel a deep pang of guilt. How can I be so fond of Paul and feel almost dizzy right now from all the sensations I'm experiencing just by talking with

David? And with Paul there was sexual attraction right off, but with David it was something else. Oh, the attraction was there, but there was something even headier at work, just as it is now. A kind of breathless awe.

"I think I have some time tomorrow around one," I tell him.

"Then one o'clock it is. I'll be in the lobby, and if you can't get there, I won't take offense but I will track you down." Silence. "Sally?"

I drain my wineglass and am this close to telling him to come up to my suite no matter what time he gets back.

You're working, I remind myself, putting the glass down. *You sent him away and now you want to see him, just like that?*

Yeah. Just like that.

"Yes?" I finally answer.

"I'll look forward to tomorrow."

"Me, too," I tell him. After I hang up the phone, I continue standing behind the bar a minute longer, watching the orchid. I lean over and gently blow on it, watching the flower drift.

White roses, white orchid.

I meet the *DBS News America This Morning* naysayer managers—
Houston, Denver and Buffalo, markets numbers 4, 19 and 58 of
our 122 affiliates—at the starter's booth at 6:30 a.m. I am dressed
in a blue, yellow and white plaid golf skirt, a blue sleeveless
blouse with a collar and a pair of two-toned golf shoes, all of
which Mother gave me for Christmas.

There are no overtly defined clouds in the sky, but it is already
so humid as to be uncomfortable. I've only played twice since
last summer, but did take some time to drive, chip and putt in
Manhattan at Chelsea Pier before coming out. I'm playing far
better this morning than usual, probably because the golf cob-
webs haven't been fully dusted off yet so my mind is unable to
force my reflexes back into their usual ruts. While Houston—who
looks extremely hungover—and I are playing roughly the same
game, his partner, Buffalo, loses two balls by the fourth hole. My
partner, Denver, who just returned from golf camp in Arizona,
is killing us all, but his play is at least inspiring us to concentrate.

Though Denver is dragging his feet about taking our newscast, I don't think it is a lost cause. He's already got good ratings with a local six-to-seven news hour in Denver, from which,
he keeps reminding me, they keep all ad revenue. I counter that

by citing the new hybrid SUV campaign that has signed with us, a sure sign of the viewer demographics that are expected. So yeah, I tell him, he has to crunch the numbers, but what is better? A few people watching and a lot of Clapper commercials? Or a lot of eighteen- to thirty-four-year-olds and a higher-priced ad from the local mall, car dealerships and computer outlets?

I like him. He's in his late thirties, married with three children and is originally from New York. We have a laugh over how much of Denver is from anywhere *but* Denver.

"Does anybody live where they grew up anymore?" he asks me while we were walking a fairway. Houston and Buffalo fly past us in their cart to look for Buffalo's ball in the high grass. "The kids who grow up in the sticks flock to the city, the city kids head for the suburbs and the suburban kids head for the sticks. Mountain people go to the coast, water people go to the desert, the candlestick-maker's kids go to Wall Street."

On the green of the seventh hole, Buffalo whispers to me there's something about Denver I should know. I say fine and we wait as Houston attempts what's got to be a sixty-yard putt—and sinks it, which prompts the first civil words out of him this morning. On the eighth hole Denver and Houston get great drives; I hit a straight but soft drive and Buffalo whacks his ball out of the t-box into some trees. When I suggest Houston should perhaps play ahead with Denver because he's so good (he beams), I jog over to the trees with Buffalo to hunt for his ball.

"I know all you guys at the network like him," Buffalo says about Denver as we enter the trees. "But you should know he's got a bet going that he can get you in the sack while we're here."

At first I am floored. Then the hot rush of indignation starts to rise, followed by a kind of choking embarrassment, which is replaced, finally, by fury. *I'm bigger than this,* I tell myself. *I'm supposed to take this in stride. I am a target, a goal. This is part of why they pay me, to deal with this crap.*

Buffalo's watching me with a worried expression. "He's an asshole, Sally, he does it every year. This is the first time he's picked one of the network employees, though."

"Did you find your ball?" I ask, trying to keep my voice level but succeeding in making the question sound like a reprimand.

"Screw the ball," Buffalo says, tromping over through the grass to me. "I wouldn't have told you if I knew it would upset you. I just thought you should know what you're dealing with."

I think of Denver's wife and kids I met last year when they came to visit West End. If what Buffalo says is true, the man is not merely a smooth liar but practically a sociopath.

"And I appreciate it," I tell him sincerely. We head back to the fairway to pick up our bags. "So what are the odds?"

He hesitates.

"What are the odds?" I ask him again.

"I think it's up to nine to one."

I glance over at him. "In whose favor?"

"Nine to one he can't."

"Well that's something, I guess."

He drops a ball near mine and plays from there. As we walk up to the green he tries again to make me feel better. "The only reason why anyone would ever bet on him is because the odds are so high."

"Do me a favor," I say, eyes ahead, "and don't tell me who bets on him."

When we finish the hole we find Denver and Houston waiting for us on a shaded bench. Houston has gotten a bottle of beer from somewhere. (It's a little after eight.) We proceed to the eighth hole and I hit what is a rather amazing drive for me. Because the woman's red marker on this particular hole is past a water hazard and is some fifty yards ahead of the men's tee, I land on the green of what is supposed to be a par 4 hole.

"I was wondering," Denver says as we walk the fairway, "if you would mind going over the numbers with me after I meet with Steve. Since you've worked on the production side in New York, I think you could be very helpful in giving me enough ammunition to win over the station owner about carrying your newscast."

I glance over, smiling. "You mean there is a chance for us on your program schedule?"

He offers me a smile that I might have considered an earnest

All-American smile before, but now see only as a signpost to Sleazebag City. "There's always a chance," he says gently. Then he looks ahead. "Some of us have missed our chance. I should at least try to help you get yours."

"Thank you. That's very kind."

"You're great, Sally, really, really great," he says softly.

I see, he's going to play it as the sadly misunderstood unhappily-married man, who is willing to help me so I can soar to great heights while he continues his miserable existence. He will want to see me succeed more than anything. He will take the greatest joy in my success. If only... Sigh. If only what? Oh, Sally, please let me be with you, just one night, so that I may have one wonderful memory before you go on....

I have half a mind to club Denver from behind with my nine iron.

"You shot a forty?" Jessica Wright asks, swinging baby Emily from one hip to the other while she looks up at the scoreboard posted by the pool.

Denver shot a thirty-five, which has put us in first place. The guys have gone to shower and change; they have to attend the noon luncheon with our sales, finance and production people. As a producer I would normally attend this meeting with Will, but this is one of the big changes in my duties: I'm supposed to be a special attraction here, not everyday Sally, the producer that's been yelling at their newsroom staffs.

"Yes I did," I declare, thumping my glass of Gatorade down on the table. "And everything I know I learned from this outfit my mother gave me for Christmas."

"The same principle as a clean car driving better?" Alexandra says from across the table, where she has just finished a strawberry-and-banana smoothie. Unlike bedraggled me (who hasn't even brushed her hair since leaving the golf course), Alexandra looks like a cool, sleek cover model from *Town & Country*—you know, the special "Shooting Trap in Southern California" issue? Her outfit sort of looks like a beige linen pantsuit, though it can't be since there does not appear to be a single wrinkle in it. It is a softly folding material that looks like linen but falls like silk.

Jessica whirls around, her tropical wraparound skirt ballooning colorfully around her, and flip-flops her way in our direction. She is wearing a one-piece blue bathing suit and Ray-Bans, and her auburn hair is being held up on the back of her head with two hotel pencils. The baby is in a little green bathing suit and matching hat and her skin is slathered white with sunscreen. "Who gave you permission to be better than I am?" Jessica asks, stopping next to the table.

"Trust me, it was a fluke," I tell her, running my hands through my hair. They both look so nice and I feel so ratty.

"I've got to get this little one inside," Jessica announces. Alexandra scoots her chair back and stands up to say something to the baby and kiss the top of her head. (She is Emily's godmother.) Jessica looks over to me. "Rehearsal is when?"

"Three."

After Jessica and Emily take off for the Raffertys' bungalow, Alexandra and I are the sole people left in the pool area.

"I heard from Kit yesterday," she tells me.

I finish swallowing some Gatorade. "About?"

"He heard Bill Randolph was sitting in as anchor last night."

I slowly lower my glass. "You're not going to tell me he wants to know why *he* isn't sitting in for you."

She smiles slightly.

"No," I say, appalled.

"He couched it well. He said since the Delafield story's on hold and the Castleford bombing still has legs he thought maybe Bill might prefer to stay in the field."

I shake my head. It doesn't take long for an ego to develop on TV.

"He also says he's getting an agent," she continues. "A big one in New York."

I can't take it anymore. "He thinks just being part Native American is all it takes? That no experience is necessary?"

"Who said his being part Native American has anything to do with it?"

"Hello? It's me, Sally? Who knows you've wanted a Native American on the air forever?"

"And that's why," Alexandra says, toying with the straw in her empty glass, "I'm making Willa Trueblood a regular contributor to the magazine show." She is clearly delighted by the surprise on my face.

"So how do you think Bill did?"

She tosses the straw on the table and sits back in her chair. "Great. I'm anxious to see how well he does tonight."

"You know he was an anchor years ago, in Little Rock, I think."

"So I hear. How old is he?"

"Fifty-eight. And he was a stringer in the Gulf War for CNN."

"What is he doing in Springfield?"

"He moved there for family reasons. I don't think he ever said what it was, but he was grateful to get the job."

"Do me a favor and find out what his family status is. And see if he would be willing to relocate. Or at least travel during the week?"

"Sure."

"No, never mind, Sally, I'll get Will to do it. This isn't your problem anymore."

The comment makes me feel a little lonely. As ridiculous as it sounds, I'm already starting to miss Alexandra. It's going to be very strange not working so closely with her day after day.

"I got flowers from Jackson last night," I tell her. "A huge basket of them."

"He knows what a big convention this is for you." Alexandra's eyes are their usual stormy Atlantic color, but seem softer somehow.

"I would have preferred his presence over flowers."

"Don't be so hard on him," she tells me. "And let's see what he's got planned for tonight."

"You mean he's coming?"

"He'll be appearing. How and from where I'm not sure."

I am puzzled by Alexandra's forgiving attitude. She must be fairly certain he is not totally in the wrong.

"So what's the story with them? Cassy and Jackson? Are they still going to be together?"

She holds my eyes for a moment. "I don't know why not."

"Because maybe he's having an affair?" I suggest.

She checks her watch, backs her chair away from the table and gets up. "I've got to get moving. I'll see you at three?"

"Yes," I say, pushing my chair back and getting up, too. "But wait—you never told me how you did this morning. I don't know how you score trap, but how did you do?"

"David won by one," she says, walking backward down the path.

"Who came in second, as if I don't know."

"There is no such thing as second," Alexandra tells me, turning around. "Either you win or you don't." She offers me a wave over the back of her head and disappears into the gardens. A few moments later I hear her call, "There is, however, such a thing as a second chance, Sally."

I spend almost an hour in the shade of the pool gazebo on the phone talking to the newsroom staff back at West End. I also have a quick chat with Bill Randolph.

"Did you see the newscast?" he asks me.

"I watched a replay before I went to sleep," I tell him. "And I have to tell you…" Over the terrace wall of the smaller ball-room on this side of the garden, I can only see the reflective glass and none of what is transpiring inside. I wonder how our DBS News folders went over.

"Come on, Sally, what?" Bill says.

"You were terrific. And Alexandra wasn't surprised and is feel-ing very good about what she saw. She's anxious to see how you do tonight."

After a moment. "Yeah?"

"Yeah. Have you heard from Will?"

"Not directly, except to say I am to sit in again tonight." We talk a bit about logistics, about the status of the Castleford story, about what my opinion is about the likelihood of the Presarios having carried out the beating of Al Royce.

"I can't even imagine it," I tell him.

"Rocky Presario's got very bad emphysema," he says.

"I know."

"A lot of people say he's not really with it anymore. Dementia from oxygen deprivation."

I try to see where he's going with this. "So you think he's nuts?"

"It's a possibility, Sally. It's getting harder and harder to pretend this wasn't planned by professionals."

"But I don't get it," I tell him, shaking my head. I look back up at the ballroom where the managers are meeting and wonder if anyone is watching me. Or placing bets on me. Or against me.

"Here's the sixty-four-thousand-dollar question," I tell Bill. "How did you end up in Springfield? I hate to be a nosey parker but there's a reason why I'm asking. A reason you might like."

"I knew my mom had about a year left," he tells me. "I was globe-trotting and I'm an only son and she was all by herself and, well, my wife actually suggested it. She was very close to my mother. And she thought it would be good for the kids and that it would make Mom really happy if she saw us living in the old family manse."

"So your wife took care of her?"

"Mom had her care already set up. She and my dad had planned very well. She had 24/7 care for the last six months." Pause. "She passed almost two years ago."

"So you guys are still in the house?"

"My wife and kids are wild about living there." Pause. "Oh, no, you're not going to ask me to move to another affiliate, are you, Sally?"

"Alexandra wanted me to find out if there were any options."

Reluctantly, "I think not. At least not until my kids are out of high school. One's a freshman and one's a junior."

I make a note, *three and a half years.*

"She's not thinking about another affiliate," I tell him.

The silence is so long this time I wonder if he's still there.

"Really?" he says softly.

"Really," I say, grinning.

"To be honest, I thought at this point I was too old for you guys."

"To be honest with you, Bill, I think it's an outrage we didn't know how very, very good you are."

"How could you have known when my own station hated to use me? *They* think I'm too old."

"Good, then let's screw them," I suggest cheerfully.

It is twenty after twelve when I decide I better get upstairs to pull myself together before meeting David. To be truthful, I've kind of been sitting out here because I was hoping he might pass by. I was willing to look like a mess in exchange for appearing happily surprised at running into him.

(What is the matter with me?)

Before going up I stop by the front desk to check for messages. The nice lady clerk disappears into the back and reemerges with a large manila envelope. "You received all of your flower deliveries last night, Ms. Harrington?"

"Yes, thank you," I say, accepting the bulky envelope. Curious as to what this unwieldy thing could be, I rip it open and pull out a walkie-talkie. It has a red blinking light flashing on it. I check to see if there's anything else in the envelope, but no, there's no note, nothing, there is just the walkie-talkie.

"You push that when you want to talk," David Waring says quietly by my right ear. "We used to use them skiing with the kids."

Startled, I turn, my face inches from his. His eyes are happy and it is nice to see him. "Yes," I say, staying as close as we are, "but to talk to whom?"

"There's only one way to find out." He places his hand over mine and makes my index finger press down on a button. "Okay," he prompts, guiding it up to my mouth.

I smile, ducking my head a little. "Calling all cars, calling all cars," I say, laughing.

"Thank God, is that you, Sally?" Emmett's voice comes blaring out a moment later, making us jerk the walkie-talkie away from us.

David is still holding my hand and I realize the desk clerk is watching us with interest.

"Where have you been?" the walkie-talkie squawks again.

"Emmett?" I ask, gracefully pulling my hand away from David's.

"You were supposed to take the walkie-talkie this morning so I could talk to you!" scolds the walkie-talkie.

I push the button. "On the golf course?"

"How else was I supposed to reach you?"

I look into David's eyes. "He's not a golfer."

"So I gather."

"Are we having a rehearsal?" the walkie-talkie says, demanding my attention again.

I push the button. "Yes. Three o'clock. Now, Emmett, listen, I'm leaving this hideous thing for you at the desk. Goodbye." I hold it out to David. "How do I shut it off?"

"Like this."

"Excellent," I say, turning to the front desk and sliding the walkie-talkie over to the clerk. "For Emmett Phelps, please." I turn around again, looking at my watch. "I was just going upstairs to clean up before meeting you."

"You look wonderful," he says. In his navy polo shirt, gray Dockers and laced leather sporting boots, he does, too.

"I hear you won this morning," I say, waving at Bertha-Gerta, who is crossing the lobby. She waves back. She must have finished the Stella Cameron novel because now she's carrying a Heather Graham.

"The only real competition was my sister," he says, shrugging, "and all I've ever had to do is say something awful to her and she misses."

"David!"

"She needs to strengthen her mettle," he protests.

"That is the last thing your sister needs," I say, shaking my head at him. "So how's Christopher?"

"He's fine. He's home with Betty today."

"I hear we won last night," I add.

"No," he tells me, "we lost."

I take a step back, making a face. "You're an *Angels* fan?"

He takes a step back, imitating me. "You're a *Yankees* fan?"

"Of course I am," I declare.

"You're from Connecticut, you should at least be a Red Sox fan!"

"Red Sox fan?" I cry indignantly. "What, are you on drugs?"

We're doing the classic Yankee versus Anyone face-off, which is making me feel inanely happy for some reason.

The desk clerk, I see, is still watching us.

"All right, I will temporarily forgive you," he says. "At least long enough to have a bite to eat."

"Well, maybe," I say, with mock reluctance.

"I was going to suggest we eat by the pool. It was pretty good yesterday."

"If you don't mind, it's just that I've been out there all morning and I kept feeling like the managers were watching me from the ballroom. I could use a little time offstage, if that's all right. The hospitality suite's open on the fifth floor. It's got sandwiches and salads and things."

"Sounds fine to me."

As we cross the lobby to the elevators, a porter inadvertently veers in front of us with his heavily laden baggage cart. David lightly places his hand on the small of my back to steer me out of the way. Our eyes lock for a moment and it is crushing inside, the surge of feeling that comes over me. I think he must have felt something, too, because we scarcely speak on the way up to the fifth floor, as if what we just felt should be denied. Suddenly it feels as though we are right back to that last moment we said goodbye in New York.

In the upstairs hallway I have recovered enough to explain how everyone's in meetings or resting before we have our rehearsal and how we should have the place to ourselves. I am wrong, of course. As I go sailing through the door Cassy's and Langley's startled faces fly up from the table they have been huddled over. "I'm so sorry," I say, stopping in my tracks. "I thought you guys would be in a finance meeting."

"We're *in* a finance meeting." Langley nearly scowls, looking down at his papers to finish jotting something down.

"David?" Cassy says, taking off her reading glasses and leaning around to see behind me. "I heard you were here."

"Cassy." David warmly acknowledges her, crossing the room.

"You look wonderful," Cassy tells him, standing to exchange a kiss. She takes hold of his hand. "Have you met Langley Peterson?"

"Many times," Langley says, prompted to stand up now, too,

but seemingly more agreeable to our interruption. "Good to see you again, David," he says, shaking hands.

"And good to see you."

While they make polite conversation about the trap shoot this morning, I take a tray and start compiling a selection of food for lunch: a cottage cheese and fresh fruit plate, oriental chicken salad, a ham-and-cheese sandwich, cheese Danish, banana, an apple and some cheese, an Atkins protein bar, a glass of milk and a thermos of coffee. Since I like everything on the tray, whatever we don't eat I will save in my refrigerator for later. I grab some silverware and napkins and just as I am picking the tray up, I feel a hand on my arm.

"We're not going to be long," Cassy tells me in a low voice. "We needed to run some numbers away from the group. We've got so many deals going on *America This Morning* we needed to double-check the overall numbers to make sure it can work."

I must look worried or something because she quickly adds, "It's all doable, Sally. We just need an accurate accounting to know exactly where all these deals land us."

"The Denver manager's taking bets he can get me in the sack," I hear myself say. "He's already hinted he needs private time with me to make his decision about the newscast."

"The Denver station is going up for sale," Cassy says, "so it doesn't matter what he thinks."

I look at her. "Does he know that? That the station's going up for sale?"

"Does it matter?" She smiles sympathetically. I envy the precise beauty of her features. (She's definitely had her eyes done, I decide.)

If, indeed, it turns out that Jackson is cheating on our fair president, ten to one it is a straightforward sex thing. It's hard to imagine Cassy being asked to do certain sexual acts—she's just too, too, you know, refined. Classy. Ladylike. And my guess would be Jackson has taken what he might consider his baser desires elsewhere. Heaven knows he was into some wild stuff until he married her.

I hope he hasn't done it. I want so much to believe in a good marriage. And if Cassy Cochran can't have one, I don't know who can. A more kind, gentle, smart, funny, beautiful woman doesn't exist—except for my mother, of course.

"No, I suppose it doesn't matter," I say in regard to the Denver affiliate, picking up the tray. "At least the odds are nine to one against him."

"Be polite, Sally, that's all I ask of you. And remember, it goes with the territory, this won't be an isolated incident. You're a big target now."

"Gee, thanks, boss lady," I tell her, shoving off. "Come on, David, we're going to my terrace."

"We'll see you at three for the rehearsal?" Langley says.

"See you at three," I promise, turning as David opens the door for me.

"And Sally?" Langley calls.

I turn around. "Yes?"

Langley smiles. "You should know Houston signed on for *News America This Morning.*"

"Houston?" I say, thunderstruck. "How did that happen?"

"We're not sure," Cassy admits, sitting down next to Langley. "But I got the station owner on the phone—"

"His Texas stepdaddy," I clarify to David.

"And his Texas stepdaddy has confirmed it," she finishes. "He came into breakfast and went right over to Will to tell him." Langley says something to her I can't hear, and she leans closer to tell him something. Then she looks at me, smiling again and waving us off. "Go have your lunch. And enjoy yourself. You've done brilliantly this morning."

"I only wish I know what I did," I murmur to David, walking out. There is definitely pep in my step now. Houston out of the blue. David has taken the tray from me to carry and at my door I use my key card to pass over the electric-eye lock. I go inside and hold the door open for David.

"Wow, what a view."

I lead him across the living room and open the sliding glass doors to the terrace. (I see David looking at his white orchid on the bar as he passes by.) We walk onto the terrace and I direct him to set the tray down on the wrought-iron coffee table. I urge him to sit and help himself to whatever he wants. I tell him that

I like everything on the tray, and go back inside to retrieve a couple of glasses from the bar, an icy bottle of Saratoga sparkling water from the refrigerator and two coffee mugs. When I return I see he's gone for the cottage cheese and fresh fruit plate. I take the plate of oriental chicken salad inside to put it in the refrigerator. On this trip I notice that my message light is blinking. "Please start eating!" I call to David. "I need to check my messages."

"Sally, hi, it's Buddy." Buddy D'Amico from Castleford PD. "I wanted to let you know that Al Royce is being released from the hospital sometime this week, maybe Thursday. So it looks like he's going to be okay." Pause. "I thought you would want to know. I already called your mom to let her know. Um, what else? You may also be interested to know I stepped in to keep Crazy Pete out of jail. It seems he's been skulking around the state lab and I know better than to ask who it is he's skulking around for. So you better tell Pete to stop anything and everything connected to this case or he's going into the slammer. And this time it would be state prison and there will be very little I can do for him." And there the message ends. I make a note to leave a message for Crazy Pete.

Next message. "It's me again," Buddy says. "Um, so you don't worry, I got a hold of Peter Sabatino and he swears he won't do anything else for you. I've talked to that Randolph guy. And look, Sally, it was a bombing so it's a federal investigation. I can't give you any information I don't have myself. Anyway, have a good trip and I'm keeping an eye on your mom."

The time stamp says the calls were two hours apart.

I walk out to the terrace, sit down and pour us both a glass of sparkling water. Then I start in on the ham sandwich—first cutting the crust off and then slicing the halves into quarters, not because I'm picky but because it is a few less calories this way—and I tell David the good news about Alfred Royce.

My telephone starts ringing. I put my sandwich down, excuse myself and go in to take it, wiping my mouth with my napkin on the way. "Hello?"

"Hi, babe, it's me," Paul says. "I'm really glad you liked the flowers."

"I loved them, thank you," I say, turning away from the terrace. I debate whether or not I should close the sliding doors but decide it will only serve to make things more awkward. "Where are you? It sounds like a party."

"I'm at the train station. We had a call here and now we're taking a break and I took the chance you might be there. So how is it going?"

"Pretty well, actually. Tonight's the big night."

"Hang on a minute," Paul says as a voice over a loud speaker booms in the background. When it stops he says, "Sally? I'm sorry, but I've got to go. Promise me you'll call, no matter what time it is, to tell me how it all goes tonight."

"I promise," I tell him. And then he is gone. I walk back out to the terrace. "Sorry about that," I say, settling down again at my place. David is more than halfway through his salad.

After a while, he puts his fork down to use his napkin and drink some sparkling water. "I saw the picture of Jackson and that woman this morning on the news. It certainly doesn't look very good, does it?"

"Langley says he's still coming tonight, or is appearing via some other way. Video-conferencing maybe. And Cassy looked pretty good, didn't she?"

"I thought so."

"Certainly she looks a lot better today, so there must be hope on the horizon." I finish eating another sandwich quarter. It is made with brie and is very good. "Alexandra seems to be trying to just ignore the whole thing."

"She's very upset," he tells me. He takes another sip of water, watching me over the top of the glass. He lowers the glass, swallowing. "Of course she could be upset about other things."

I look at him. "Like what?"

He puts his glass down. "Something's going on with her and Georgiana."

"I know."

"They're not going through with the baby thing."

"Oh," I say, reaching for my water. "Well, maybe it's for the best."

"There's something else I'd like you to know."

"And what is that?" I say carefully, knowing I couldn't swallow anything right now if my life depended on it.

"Lexy gave me a copy of the confirmation that my—you know, donation—was destroyed."

My eyebrows rise slightly. "I see." David had been the sperm donor for Georgiana to conceive. Before I knew him well, I thought it was great.

"I don't know if they decided it was just a bad idea, or if there's real trouble."

"And of course your sister's not saying, which is your sister all over."

He smiles slightly. "Yeah." He looks down at our dishes. "I was disappointed. For her, I mean. I've got my kids—regardless if they're talking to me or not, I've got them. Lexy has a lot to offer a child."

"It's so hard, though, David." His eyes come up to me. "Just take Georgiana—forget the gay stuff—and look at how hard it is for a working movie star to stay married. They're gone so much and for so long, and unless your spouse can come with you, which Alexandra can't, that means six weeks here, eight weeks there, shuttling back and forth to L.A., and a partner who has little or no flexibility in her schedule."

"I guess," he says, sitting back against the couch. "But they really care about each other. It was a good match."

"And it may not be over." I point to his plate. "Come on, buck up and finish your fruit." Am I relieved David won't have any more children around? By another woman, frankly yes.

He sits forward and picks up his fork, pushing the food around a little. "So how was your golf outing?"

"Oh, fun and god-awful at the same time."

He swallows some cottage cheese. "That's the game."

I have finished another sandwich quarter. I think I'm in love with this sandwich. "Do you play? Of course you play," I answer myself. "Warings play every sport known to man."

He laughs. "I actually love golf."

"Of course you do. You're an attorney."

"No," he protests, "I'm a pretty good golfer, that's why I like it. Though I must admit," he adds, reaching for the cheese Danish, "taking clients out is a great way to get outside and call it work."

I smile. "You *are* a lawyer."

When I lower my eyes, reaching for another piece of sandwich, he says, "How is Paul?"

"He's very good," I tell him. "He just got promoted. To detective."

"That's impressive. And he's going to law school?"

"Yes. And he seems to like it, although he's feeling a little…" I think about how best to phrase it.

"Dumb?" David offers with a knowing smile. "The whole first year of law school is designed to make you feel like a hopeless idiot so that you'll forget whatever you think you know and just memorize everything they want you to know, and memorize it in the exact context they want you to understand it."

I'm thinking how one of my exes, Doug Wrentham, an assistant D.A., used to say the same thing. "And how is Mary Ellen?" I say to him in turn.

"Depressingly thrilled we're divorced." He puts the rest of the Danish down and wipes his hands on his napkin.

"That must be difficult," I say diplomatically.

"No," he says, reaching for the coffee thermos. "Would you like some?"

"I'm fine, thanks."

"No, it's not difficult," he says, pouring coffee for himself, "because I don't feel like the pathetic spouse anymore, trying to stagger on." He puts the thermos down, probably harder than he meant to. He picks up the mug and takes a sip of black coffee. "Mary Ellen doesn't get it, though. Her new messiah will never marry her because then the alimony would stop and he doesn't seem inclined to hold a proper job. It's going to be interesting to see how they resolve sinning. Of course I'm not convinced he likes women much, anyway," he says, putting his mug down and sitting back. "But that's not my problem, is it?"

"No."

"I just don't understand how she could want a man like that," he says.

Somebody's got to say it and it might as well be me. "Maybe

Mary Ellen doesn't really want him, David. Maybe she's using him as an excuse."

His expression makes me hurt inside.

"She just might not want to be married anymore. She might feel it's all she can do to learn how to take care of herself, that she's just not up to the task of being a wife. And staying sober. That it's too much."

He studies me a moment. "But look at Jessica."

"Jessica's been sober for ten years and is still very much into AA," I say. "It sounds like Mary Ellen's trying to use her church the same way, but it doesn't necessarily work that well. Not everybody was driven there by alcoholism. They had different problems."

He's frowning. "But, Sally, this guy went right to her from the beginning."

"And who, in Mary Ellen's mind, could be safer? You said he probably doesn't even like women sexually. He doesn't have a career that demands her to be a hostess." He winces slightly. "He has no children to take care of and neither does she, which leaves them free to focus on the church—which makes them both feel good. At least a lot better than when they first came in."

"You make this all sound so logical," he says, rubbing his jaw.

"Only because it has nothing to do with me. I'm just an outsider looking in."

"I think what makes me angriest," he finally says, "is how pressured Mary Ellen and I were to get married to begin with. If I had been just a few years older I would have seen her drinking problem even then. But everybody drinks too much at twenty-three—because at twenty-three you can get away with it. But then when everybody started cutting back, I look back and realize Mary Ellen was just getting warmed up. By the time I could really accept what had happened—what a huge problem her drinking had become—we had two kids and fourteen years of marriage and families where divorce was unheard of. And what are you supposed to do, Sally?" he says, suddenly getting up to pace the terrace.

"What are you supposed to do if your wife's an alcoholic and refuses to get help? I'll tell you what you do—you take the car keys away so she won't kill the kids and then you start taking money away, but then her parents send her money and there we are again, with her on a bender, the kids freaking out and me not knowing what to do short of hiring a full-time cop to watch her, which is basically what I did. Somebody had to look after the kids until they were old enough to go away."

He squares off at the end of the terrace and comes back this way. "They told me to leave her, so I did. Took the kids. Less than twelve hours later there we are at the hospital, wondering if Mary Ellen's going to make it or not because she swallowed everything in the medicine cabinet. So they tell me to do an intervention and we do that. And Alexandra, of all people, convinces her to go into rehab. We go into therapy as a family and everything's great, only the kids walk in one day while I'm tearing the house apart because I found Mary Ellen not only drinking, but screwing the bathroom-tile guy."

He stops, turning to the terrace wall and leaning on it, clasping his hands together and taking a breath. "I'm not proud of my part over the years. It wasn't just Mary Ellen. There was something wrong with me, too. I should have acted years before I did." He lowers his head and lets it hang there. "The worst of it is, Sally," he says quietly, "my kids think Mary Ellen drank because she couldn't stand to be married to me." He raises his head, looking out over the garden. "And there's got to be something to that. Because she's certainly not drinking now." Pause. "As they so often throw in my face."

I pour myself a cup of coffee and stir some milk and a little sugar into it. I put the spoon down and pick up the mug to take a sip. Swallowing, I say carefully, "From what I understand, when one parent is an alcoholic and the other one isn't, the children take their rage out on the parent they perceive as the strong one, the one who can take it and won't collapse on them—even if they're enraged with the alcoholic."

He lifts his head, turns around, walks over to the settee and throws himself down. He looks at me sheepishly. "Gee, I'm not carrying any anger and resentment, am I?"

"I'm not sure how you could feel otherwise," I say, putting my coffee down.

He rubs his face and drops his hands, sighing. "At least it's over."

"David," I say gently, standing up. I walk around the table and sit on the edge of the chair nearest the settee and take his hand. "It's not over. It's not going to be over for a long time."

He lowers his head.

"You need to heal," I continue quietly. "Your children need to heal. And it's a terrible burden to bear, having your children think bad things about you. But you know that eventually it will all come out, that eventually they'll have a much better understanding of what really happened." He looks up at me. "You can't ever give up on trying to help your children to understand. It would be a kind of death for you if you did."

He lowers his head again in such sadness. I slide my arm around his shoulders and slowly rub his back.

He has traces of dandruff on his shoulders and I find it endearing. Mr. Perfect is vulnerable and perhaps that is why I've always cared for him. Like all the Warings he appears at first blush to be invincible—fiercely bright, healthy, athletic, strong. Very strong. And good-looking. But he is gentle-hearted and loyal and that can bring down any man down in this world. And that is what makes him such a wonderful man in my eyes. He doesn't run. He tries. No matter what.

Maybe I shouldn't run anymore. Maybe I need to try. No matter what.

"Your friend Paul is young enough to be my son," David says with his head still bowed.

I laugh. "And this signifies what?"

He raises his head to look at me. The beautiful eyes are sad, but a trace of sparkle is still in there. "It signifies that at forty-five I should be a lot more together than I am."

Now I throw my head back and really laugh. When I finish, I say, gesturing to myself, "And here, ladies and gentlemen, is the amazing Sally Harrington. Now, if the first twenty-two rows of people could please move back to make room for her baggage!"

David smiles for real now, eyes locked on mine. A breeze is playing with his hair. "You know, don't you, how I feel about you?"

I look down. Classic, isn't it? A man heartbroken by divorce seeking a way out of the pain.

"Sally?" He takes both of my hands to hold between his own. "I don't expect you to believe that I am a man who knows his own heart."

Tentatively I bring up my eyes.

"I can't let you go." He smiles, but his eyes are not smiling.

A pigeon flutters down to sit on the railing, startling us both. "Poor guy's probably hungry," I say getting up. "If the hotel management sees me do this they'll probably shoot me." I pick up my bread crusts and walk to the other end of the terrace to fling them over the wall. The pigeon nearly flies into me in his haste and swoops down into the garden after them. As I watch, three, no four, five—eight!—pigeons descend on the scraps.

"Here," David says, coming up behind me. He has torn up his Danish into small pieces.

"Okay, guys, dessert!" I call, throwing the food. "Oh, I can't watch them," I say, turning around, "or I'll be out here all day trying to make sure everyone gets the same number of pieces."

"I'm surprised the hotel hasn't done something to keep them away," he says, looking down at them.

"We have fake owls on top of West End." I walk back to the table, pile our plates on the tray and carry it inside to put on top of the bar. David comes in and slides the screen door closed.

"Look at this hair!" I say, frowning at myself in the mirror over the bar. "And I suppose it might have been nice if I had at least washed the dirt off my face."

"I guess I better let you get ready for your rehearsal," he says, looking at his watch. "You've got a big night ahead of you."

"Yes, I do," I say, crossing my arms over my chest. I realize I am holding myself, as if trying to protect myself.

He takes a step closer to me. "Sally."

I wait, but he doesn't say anything else. Just stands there in front of me, looking down into my eyes. "What's wrong?" I ask him.

"I'm in love with you," he says.

I study his eyes intently, which seem almost fearful. My heart is pounding and I know what he would like me to say, but this is exactly what I have warned myself against.

"I love you, too," I hear myself say, and in the next moment I am in his arms.

I have little memory of the rehearsal except that I was late.

It's difficult to describe what I was feeling in David's arms, except to say something seemed to break inside of me and then that something wholly gave way when I realized he was hanging on to me even tighter than I was to him.

After that I felt as though I was standing next to myself, watching the proceedings of the outside world with dull interest. I had better things to think about.

I am in love with David Waring.

I don't remember the rehearsal as very long, but afterward, on the terrace where a dance band was setting up, the next thing I knew Cassy and Langley were standing in front of me in all their evening finery, asking me if I was all right. I looked at my watch and now am hightailing it for my suite.

It is twenty-five to five when I blow into my suite and find Cleo there fuming. She orders me into the shower and tells me she's going to work on Jock Hagen at the other end of the floor because unlike *some* people who keep everybody *waiting,* he is *ready.* (She's not really all that mad, I know, only very nervous. She's got a lot of ponies to trot out with great hair and make-up tonight, and neither the humidity outside nor the icy-dry air conditioner inside is helping her cause.)

When Cleo returns I have nothing on but a towel and moisturizer. Looking in the mirror, I find it is difficult to believe I can be downstairs in twenty-six minutes. Cleo starts putting goop in my hair and blow drying it, yelling the latest convention gossip over the noise: one of the sales guys fell in the carp pond (no carp were killed); Langley's good glasses are MIA so he can't really see anything; and one of the affiliate managers made a pass at a fourteen-year-old girl who turned out to be the daughter of actress Lydia Southland.

"Who did?" I say, scandalized, looking at her in the mirror.

"That beefy guy from Texas—the one who keeps staring at everyone's boobs."

"Oh, no," I murmur, frowning. "Houston. And we just signed his station to carry us."

"You may need a little Wite-Out on that contract," Cleo says, "since Langley had him thrown off the hotel grounds."

My jaw drops. "You're kidding."

"Close your eyes," she instructs, dabbing foundation on my face. "Long gone, history, *hasta la vista,* baby. Lydia's husband's flying down from Toronto to be with the daughter tonight. Calm her down, I guess. But she still wants to see her mother at the dinner. Apparently this new series is a bigger deal for Lydia than people think."

"What do you mean?"

"She's calling it her swan song. She's want to be number one just one more time."

"Before what?"

"I don't know," she says, shrugging.

"So have you seen any sign of Jackson?"

"Mr. Hot Pants?" she growls, throwing the sponge down and fussing over her tray of makeup. "He's teleconferencing in from New York." She grabs a soft brush and starts on my blush. "Dumb cluck. Running around with floozies again, just like the old days. What a nightmare this Viagra crap is."

"He might be innocent, you know."

"Yeah, and I saw a pig fly the other day," she acknowledges, dropping the brush and picking up eye shadow. "Close," she directs. "So guess who's been asking about you."

"I almost afraid to ask."

"Jock Hagen. He thinks you should be part of the sports team." While she trades one color blush for another, I open one eye to see if she's serious. It seems that she is. "Close," she tells me. "He says you have the right look. He says your dad was a big deal at Yale—is that true?"

"I think Mr. Hagen is accustomed to being revered," I say, "and has caught on that the news division is at war with Sports. I think he's more interested in making friends with me than drafting me."

"I wouldn't be so sure about that," she says. She puts the eye shadow away and reaches for eyeliner. "And you know what? Close."

"What?"

She pauses while getting her hand positioned. "I think I am making you very beautiful, Sally Harrington, and I think you will be very pleased."

They have lined us up, if you can believe, in a darkened room on the far side of the grand ballroom, which is also the kitchen relay station from which dinner is to be served to two hundred people. Lydia Southland and Gordon Strenn are at the head of the line; Jock, our sports anchor and Bosco are next; me and Emmett; Alexandra and Will; and, finally, Jessica Wright and her executive producer, Denny Ladler. The men are all wearing white dinner jackets and black ties, we ladies as a group are aglitter in long gowns. We made quite a hit when we were led through the staff corridors to get here, a glamour parade on high.

We are a rather amazing-looking bunch, I have to say, which is a good thing since we're in television.

Cassy and Langley are up at the podium on the dais staging in the front of the ballroom and are explaining how many kazillions of dollars the affiliates are going to make on DBS programming. (Two hundred people clap and whistle.) "We are also," Cassy says, "substantially increasing the participation of our affiliates in the charitable events of their communities."

Four or five polite people clap.

"That went over like a lead balloon," Jock observes, peering through the crack in the doors.

"It's catching on something," Will complains to Alexandra, jerking his right arm up and nearly hitting her.

"Easy," the anchorwoman says, holding a protective hand over her glistening black hair.

"He always does this," Jessica sighs, walking behind her husband and plunging her hands into his jacket pockets. "It won't catch, dearest darling, if you take out the cell phone, take out the pager, take out your index cards and take out your pen," she says, pulling all of this stuff out and handing it to Alexandra. She tugs on the bottom of his jacket and smooths the pockets. "Or at least balance it out."

"The screen is coming down," Jock says from the crack in the doors. I move around Bosco to see. A large movie screen is descending from the ballroom ceiling behind the dais and everyone is applauding.

"Who needs me?" Cleo whispers, arriving with her toolbox.

"Me, please," Lydia Southland says, raising her hand. "Something's in my eye."

"And Cleo," Alexandra whispers, moving toward her, "can you see that this stuff is given back to Will after we are seated on the dais?"

"Sure."

"It's Jackson Darenbrook," Jock announces.

Several of us move closer to the head of the line to see; Gordon opens one of the doors a few inches, pleading with us to be quiet.

There's Jackson up on the big screen. He is sitting in an easy chair that is normally used on *The Jessica Wright Show,* which tells me this must be coming from Studio B at West End. Of course it is. Studio A will be a madhouse with the newscast going on the air in less than an hour with a substitute anchor. "Hey, there, guys," Jackson says in his unmistakable drawl. Jackson's fifty-six, and his short hair is almost entirely gray, but his cornflower-blue eyes—his best feature—are alive with obvious good humor. His face is tanned and weathered and he, too, is also wearing a white dinner jacket and black tie.

"So y'all think I've been playing around, do ya?" He laughs. "Although we know the press never lies—" There is laughter. "I may have to take exception." He raises a blowup of the photograph that appeared in the *Inquiring Eye* and it looks worse than ever, with Jackson's face frozen in discovery and the head of the woman in his lap. "I had to spend a lot of money tracking that photographer down, but I did, and I would like to show y'all something."

A wave of murmurs breaks out when Jackson holds up a bigger blowup, from which you can see the first was cropped. The boom of a sail is lying across Jackson's leg and two men and the woman are evidently trying to lift it off him.

The camera pulls back and there is an audible gasp as we see that one leg of Jackson's black dress pants has been cut off to accommodate a cast up to midthigh.

"The real picture will be running in tomorrow's papers with a complete retraction and apology," he says. "It seems the *Inquiring Eye* is quite shocked and appalled that anyone would dare sell them a misleading photo." He bursts out laughing and so does everyone else in the ballroom.

"So listen, guys, I wish I were out there in sunny California with you and my beautiful wife, but it's going to be a day or two before I can get around. So I just wanted to tell you the bang-up job I think you're doin' and how excited I am about what's being done at DBS. May you all work hard and well and retire wealthy and healthy." Flash of the Darenbrook smile. "Have fun." And the screen goes black. There is huge applause.

"So he's not a scumbag," Cleo says aloud, fussing with the makeup over Lydia's right eye.

Outside there is a booming soundtrack and I look out to see that the entire screen over the dais is filled with what looks like a full-fledged major motion picture. This is the promo for DBS Entertainment in Los Angeles, a dazzling introduction to their programming, and the introduction to their new drama, *Nationale,* starring Lydia Southland. (Think Xena meets Interpol.)

Alexandra, Will and I keep looking at one another because we know Gordon must have spent ten times what we did and we're wondering where he got the money. An hour of Entertainment's programming normally runs between two and four million in overhead, whereas an hour in the news division is usually under five hundred thousand. In the short run we make far more money for DBS than they do, but in the long term, with syndication and overseas sales giving their productions a long shelf life, they ultimately win out, but not by what I would consider an impressive amount. When you consider Alexandra's hours and the fact she is paid a little more than two and a half million a year (her counterparts at the big three make between nine and thirteen) and that Lydia Southland will make eighteen million for thirty weeks of work, one should hope there would be a lot more profit margin on that kind of investment.

It's like comparing apples with oranges, I know, but I am annoyed with this lavish Hollywood production. Oh, ours will stand up next to it, because we *are* the news group, and our presentation should look and sound like the news group. (I think it's all the oohs and aahs I'm hearing out there that's getting to me.)

Cleo does a last-minute touch-up on Lydia's long, honey-colored hair, making it perfect. The actress is in a stunning black dress with silvery spangles and a neckline plunging almost to her waist.

Alexandra and I certainly are the tamest of the women: Alexandra is wearing a navy-blue sequined gown (which makes her look like one tall, sleek glass of water), diamond earrings and a diamond necklace. I am wearing a shimmering gray silk dress I never would have tried on had it not been for Cleo. (She says Carole Lombard once wore a similar gown to the Academy Awards, but since I'm not really sure who Carole Lombard was, I didn't say anything.) Jessica, dear Jessica, our network heroine riding to the rescue, is wearing a sparkling and spangling red (I mean *red*) gown that one suspects might be sewn on her, it fits so tightly, and her ample bosom has been stuffed down into it in an effort to make it somewhat in the same proportion as the rest of her.

Lydia does this kind of gig blindfolded and doesn't display the slightest sign of nervousness. Why should she? She's gorgeous and has a proven track record. She's a big star and actually a pretty good actress.

Gordon Strenn, on the other hand, whom one would presume has done stuff like this for years, seems extraordinarily nervous. He keeps clearing his throat and touching at his bow tie. I see Alexandra is also watching him; she whispers something to Will, who moves over to say something to Gordon that makes him laugh.

"Who is Carole Lombard?" I whisper, moving closer to Alexandra.

The luminous eyes blaze a moment. "Only the funniest and most beautiful comic actress that ever graced the face of the earth."

I smile. "Oh."

"Why?"

"Cleo says I remind her of her."

"She died in a plane crash," Alexandra says.

"Great."

"But she was married to Clark Gable."

I remember Carole Lombard now. One of my mother's favorite movies in the whole wide world—one of the few she's actually kept a VHS copy of—is *Our Man Godfrey.* I think Carole Lombard played the spoiled daughter who falls in love with the butler.

The movie has ended and on stage Cassy is saying, "Ladies and gentlemen, it is my great honor and pleasure to introduce to you the star of *Nationale,* Lydia Southland, and the president of our entertainment division, Gordon Strenn." The musical soundtrack of the new series is played over hidden speakers around the room and a spotlight appears on our doors as two attendants open them. Lydia and Gordon begin their walk across the ballroom. The group is suitably awed by Lydia as she makes her way to the stage, and they are all standing as they applaud. Gordon holds Lydia's hand as she steps up on the stage, and then you see what makes Lydia Southland such a star when she makes a deep and graceful curtsey to her audience. They go nuts and she merely smiles and waves at them.

It takes a while for the group to quiet down and when they

do, Lydia steps up to the podium. "Have you ever met someone for the first time and feel as though you've always known them? Now, I'm not going to go 'Shirley' on you—" everyone laughs, the reference being to Shirley MacLaine and her belief in reincarnation "—but I've been in this business for a while and I have never had as good a feeling as I do about working with you at DBS." They stop her with more applause. "There is an air of genuine excitement at this network," she adds, "that is the envy of the industry. DBS is small and creative and, let's be blunt about it, you guys know how to make money." More applause and now whistles. "I am deeply honored to meet you all and I thank you for so graciously welcoming me into the extended family that is DBS. Thank you."

Well, that puts everybody back on their feet applauding and cheering. Lydia exchanges kisses with Langley and Cassy and, on Gordon's arm, she takes her place for dinner at the dais.

When everyone settles down, Langley starts talking about the success of the Sports division and the lights are turned down low for their presentation. It's a marvelous cut-and-paste job highlighting the division's highest-rated events, which then flows into Jock Hagen and his on-the-road with the Minnesota Twins reality show. It's simple and great and when it's over, our sports anchor, Jock and Bosco jog out of our little room, the theme music going and the spotlight playing over them as they start clowning around on their way up to the podium. Our sports anchor holds his arms up like the signal for a touchdown, Jock sweeps his hands across like a ref signaling the runner is safe, and Bosco champions his hands over his head like a prize fighter. The affiliate managers have started cheering, D-B-S! DBS! like a stadium cheer.

While Jock addresses the affiliate managers, I discreetly coach Emmett to take a deep breath, and then Cleo touches up my lipstick. "You know everybody out there," I murmur to Emmett, pulling him close, my heart about to pound out of my chest. "This is the fun part, when they get to see the presentation you worked so hard on."

He smiles, swallows and fiddles with his bow tie. I reach for that hand, give it a squeeze and bring it down to his side. "You're perfect," I tell him, clearing my throat and facing forward.

Sports has cleared the podium and the lights dim in the grand ballroom and our presentation starts to roll. The DBS News theme music (modified to be identified with our newscast) brings a smile to my face as it booms from the speakers and the screen goes from black to an explosion of light that diffuses to reveal me and Emmett on our new set. Then a montage of clips run, reminding everyone of the wild coverage of the Mafia Boss Murder Trial; there are snippets of Emmett and me from our daily posttrial program, the best part of which cut back and forth between Emmett in the studio and me running outside with a cameraman to cover the arrest of Michael Arlenetta, the mobster who was to come in for an interview. Then it shows the bags and bags of mail and overloaded e-mail boxes sent to the network about us; there are shots of Emmett on the air as "Crime and Punishment" editor in New York; of me working in the newsroom and studio—writing, editing, orchestrating people—and reporting for the magazine show. The effect, if I may say so, is electric, and by the time we reach the end of it—when the type announcing *DBS News America This Morning* explodes across the screen—even I feel like watching us.

"And we are thrilled," Cassy is saying, "ladies and gentlemen, to introduce to you the co-anchors of *DBS News America This Morning,* Sally Harrington and Emmett Phelps."

I have to strong-arm Emmett to step into the spotlight on time and—ow—now I can't see beyond ten feet of red paisley carpeting in front of us. As we have been taught, we are smiling broadly in all directions as we walk in the direction of the stage. I can't really hear the music anymore; I've kind of lost a sense of where we are, it's all so overwhelming, kind of like tides of sensation and attention washing over us. It takes a few seconds before I realize we are being loudly cheered, and then I see David suddenly, in a black tuxedo, beaming, standing and applauding as if he's begging for an encore and suddenly I feel so beautiful and so happy I can scarcely contain it. Fleetingly I lock eyes with him before moving on. It takes us fifteen seconds to reach the stage but it feels much longer.

Emmett is now the stable one, pressing a hand over mine on his arm to calm me as we ascend the stairs. I think my spine is quaking. Cassy kisses me on the cheek and Langley surprises me by giving me a hug and then Emmett and I hold hands at the podium looking over the audience, which is quickly settling back into their seats.

When it is quiet, I say into the microphone, "Hello and welcome to *DBS News America This Morning*. I'm Sally Harrington—"

"And I'm Emmett Phelps," he finishes with a flourish.

They love it and most of the audience applauds. Thanks to Cleo we've never looked so good and our presentation seems to have hit them just right. They can really see the newscast now; they can visualize us on the television sets of their communities.

We hemmed and hawed about what to say and finally decided the best thing to do is what Emmett now does, which is to step forward and say, "Thank you very much. We will do our very best for you."

And so we're done and are moving along to sit at our places as Langley steps up to the podium. "I scarcely know how to introduce this next presentation," he says. "I can tell you, however, that my career is divided into two parts, B-A-W and A-A-W... Before Alexandra Waring and—" That is as far as he gets before everyone jumps up to cheer. And well they should. Alexandra's name is synonymous with the five thousand hours of news coverage that has elevated the importance and respectability of everybody in here.

As we knew it would, the sound of a piercing emergency siren pushes people back down in their chairs with their hands over the their ears. But when the alarm is dropped a few amps and they see our (sometimes kooky) meteorologist strapped to a Florida flagpole during a hurricane, they begin laughing. He is shouting his report over the roar of the wind, and then the montage gives over to nine successive clips of DBS News reporters covering breaking stories around the country. Then we zoom into the newsroom at West End, the crews hustling in the studio, techs running through Engineering and the satellite room, the production staff in the control room and in editing booths, and then we're back out in the field with correspondents and field trucks. Suddenly there is silence as we cut to the park at West

End. A little bird sings and then we fly off with it into a whirlwind of documentary series titles, *DBS News America Goes to World War I, World War II, Korea, Vietnam,* the *Gulf War, Iraq.* We see classrooms of children watching DBS News video disks, quality cable shows crediting DBS News for our footage, and then we see thousands of people in Times Square looking up at Alexandra broadcasting the news on our huge electronic billboard. We roll into *DBS News Magazine* and snippets of our best stories of the year and then glimpse what is to come with our partnership with INS in England. Then nine little screens appear along the edge of the main frame, inside of which are various shots of DBS News in action, and in the center flashes a list of the awards the news division has won in the past year, including three Emmys and a Peabody. These all fade to blue and then we zoom out to see Alexandra and Will under the hot studio lights of the set, correcting copy. They look up and smile and that shot freezes. Then the presentation ends, the spotlight comes on and Langley says, "Ladies and gentlemen, I give you the managing editor and executive producer of DBS News, Alexandra Waring and Will Rafferty!" and the floor starts to vibrate under the ensuing roar.

Alexandra and Will are just smiling and waving, gliding across the room like Cinderella and her prince, the theme music of DBS News playing almost unheard. They climb the stairs onto the stage and there is another wave of enthusiasm and the affiliate managers break into the chant, "Al-ex-an-dra! Al-ex-an-dra! Al-ex-an-dra!"

Finally the group settles down. "Good evening," Alexandra says in that famous voice, "I'm Alexandra Waring and clearly this is what's happening in America tonight."

They go nuts again and we're all back on our feet—"Al-ex-an-dra! Al-ex-an-dra!"—laughing and clapping. It really is wonderful.

"On behalf—" she tries to begin. People eventually quiet down and take their seats. "On behalf of every member of the DBS News team, which now numbers more than three hundred affiliated professionals across the country—" More applause, this time for the managers' own people at their stations. "I offer our

heartfelt thanks and grateful appreciation for your ongoing support of the basic premise of DBS News—that the United States
of America is the single most influential nation in the world and
it is our job to keep an eye on it!" Applause and whistles. "Will?"
she says, turning to him.

He leans over to the microphone. "You guys are great." There
is a little more applause as they walk over to the table but it is
nothing like before. I think the group must be getting hungry.

Cassy steps up to the podium. She raises a hand and then drops
it, looking as though she was going to say something but changed
her mind. Quiet has fallen across the grand ballroom. "Where do
I begin?" Silence. "There was no presentation prepared for this
part of our program because until seventy-two hours ago not only
did we not know we would *have* this part of the program, but we
were heartbroken because, after ten years, *The Jessica Wright Show*
was going off the air. Permanently." There is a lot of murmuring in the audience. "But who needs a glossy presentation? If
there was ever any doubt what Jessica Wright means to this network—"

That's as far she gets before everyone is on their feet, roaring
approval and a moment later the chant has broken out—*Jess-i-
ca! Jess-i-ca! Jess-i-ca!*—only this time the affiliate managers are also
pounding their tables and the noise is unbelievable. The spotlight goes on but only Denny is there because Jessica is already
running through the tables hugging everybody. When the spotlight finally catches up with her it is just in time to see her trip
and nearly fall, turning the chanting into a frightened
"ooooooh," but which gives way to more wild cheering as the
manager from Buffalo not only catches Jessica, but sweeps her
up in his arms and carries her up on the stage like a newlywed.
After being gently set down, Jessica kisses Buffalo on the cheek
and then the spangling vision in red is squired to the podium by
Denny, her dress sparkling madly under the lights.

She takes hold of the microphone and leans into it. "She's
baaaack," she says, and the crowd erupts all over again. And she
just grins and grins, absorbing the attention, eyes starting to glis-
ten with tears. I turn to look at Will and his eyes are full, too, as
are Alexandra's. "Hello, hello!" she says, trying to bring order to

the room. "Okay, guys, now listen to me, you have to promise to be quiet and not to make noise. Okay? Do you promise?"

Puzzled, the group promises.

Jessica presses her finger against her lips and the lights dim. "I want to show something to you," she whispers into the microphone. An image appears on the screen and when the audience recognizes they are looking at a sleeping baby the whole room melts.

"That's our daughter, Emily," she whispers into the microphone. She points to Will. "And that's her daddy." A few people start to applaud, but Jessica shushes them again and steps back from the podium to look up at Emily once more before signaling that is enough. The lights come back up. "So that is my immediate family," she tells the audience. Then she turns to gesture to Cassy and Langley and Alexandra, "And they are my extended family." She smiles, looking out over the room. "And so are you. You know I could never have left you for good."

The room explodes and Jessica leans a bit on Denny, openly crying. It's been a while since she's had this kind of attention.

Dinner can't help but be anticlimactic, but the food is excellent and the spirits high and most of the managers seem to be interpreting Langley's invitation to relax and enjoy themselves as an invitation to get drunk. An army of waiters and waitresses attend to us with great attention and I eat too much. When it is time for coffee and dessert we step down from the dais to mix with the managers and I make a beeline for David. "Do your stuff," he urges in my ear, "but I will be claiming the first dance."

Delighted, I move about the ballroom and practically talk with everybody, I think, over the next hour. I am on cloud nine, no doubt about it. Life is good.

At nine the band on the terrace strikes up and several people go outside to dance. One couple is Jessica and Will. Another is me and David.

"They absolutely love you," he tells me, holding me close in a fox-trot.

I smile, thinking who cares, all I want is for you to love me.

He looks into my eyes and pulls me closer; I rest the side of

my face against his shoulder. When I open my eyes a few moments later, I catch Cassy and Langley, dancing next to us, staring at me. I close my eyes.

When the number ends, David steps back slightly and smiles
down at me. Neither of us is ready to let go. "This is the deal
I'm willing to make," he murmurs. "Fast dances with anybody
and all slow dances with me."

I smile, feeling blissfully happy. "I'll fax you a deal memo."

"Sally?" It's Emmett, and he is not terribly steady on his feet.
"Am I allowed to ask you to dance or can I only dance with managers?" Around us everyone has started jumping around to that
perennial wedding reception favorite, "Taking Care of Business."

"I don't think one dance can hurt," I call over the music. An
affiliate manager cuts in about halfway through, but Emmett's got
the hang of the event now. He circles out to scoop up one of the
female managers and bring her out on the floor. We change partners again for the next fast song, then again for yet another one,
and I begin to worry about perspiration.

I've danced with five different guys by the time another slow
song is played, but the minute the beat slows, David appears.
"May I have this dance?" he asks, bowing magnificently. I laugh
and move into his arms as if we've been doing this for years. We
fit together well.

"Happy?" he asks, holding me close.

"Extremely."

"I think my sister would like it if I stopped dancing with you,"
he says. "She's looking daggers at me from across the terrace."
He laughs and so do I.

"What time is it?"

He looks at his watch without disrupting our step. It feels better, though, when his hand returns to my back. "Ten twenty-three."

"I get off at eleven, mister," I tell him. "Think you might buy
a girl a cup of coffee?"

"I can think of nothing nicer," he says quietly, dancing. He
holds me so close I imagine I feel his heartbeat.

I use the last half hour well, making a point of connecting with
the only three managers I have managed to miss thus far. I have

no idea where Emmett is and Alexandra doesn't know, either. While Will checks the men's room I scout the dance floor and Alexandra scans the ballroom. "If you're looking for Emmett," David whispers, appearing at my side, "look down there."

I look over the balustrade into the garden. Sure enough, there's Emmett, sitting among the plants next to the path.

"He's outside," I report to Will and Alexandra. "And if you have no objection, David and I are going to get him safely back into his room."

"Jessica said he drank a lot of wine," Will says.

"He was nervous," I say.

"Ah, loyalty," Alexandra says. "Go on. You were absolutely the best tonight, Sally. It's going to work, I know that now." She looks past me to David. "Big brother, do me a favor and don't let Emmett throw up in public, okay?"

I feel a little twinge, thinking how much practice David must have from his ex-wife.

I try to make it look as though I'm just going to the ladies' room instead of altogether leaving the party. I don't wish to be stopped. I want—I need to talk to David. There is so much to be discussed about where we go from here and I don't have a whole lot of time.

"Hey, Sally," Denver says, sliding between me and Alexandra, "you promised me a dance."

"She'll be right back," Will lies.

"She can't disappoint her golf partner, can she?" he asks Alexandra. "We won." He moves closer, sliding an arm around my shoulders. "We're a great team." He turns to whisper in my ear. "Vertically." He holds my eyes as he backs off, and then looks meaningfully down at my mouth.

"She'll be right back," Will says again, pulling me away by the arm. "Go," he says to David, "get her out of here and make sure she triple-locks her door."

"I take it that was the nine-to-one-odds guy," David says as we walk out of the ballroom.

I look at him, horrified.

"You should hear the things they've done to Alexandra. One year someone hired a call girl to come on to her."

"Somehow that doesn't make me feel better," I say, accepting his arm. We hurry outside to the garden path and wind our way over to underneath the balustrade. It smells wonderful out here and the low lights are lovely. "Emmett?" I whisper, glancing nervously above at the dancers.

"I think he's there," David says, stepping off the path and holding back some plants. "Emmett?"

"Did you find him?"

"He's asleep," comes the answer from behind some bushes. "Emmett, come on, get up, fella, we need to get you to your room."

"You're Alexandra's brother," I hear Emmett say.

"Yes, that's right. Come on, I'll help you. That's it. Okay, let's move along here."

"I'm really tired," Emmett complains.

"You can sleep in your room," David says. A few moments later, Emmett comes crashing out of the foliage and trips over the walk.

"Hi, Emmett," I say, grabbing him.

He stares at me a moment and then closes one eye. "Hi, Sally," he finally says.

"We're going this way, Emmett." I look back over my shoulder to David. "Could you get his other side?"

"Sure."

"I can walk," Emmett says irritably, shaking us off.

"Fine," I say, gesturing, "you lead the way. To the left, Emmett—toward the lobby."

Emmett obediently scuffles along in the direction of the lobby. There is a dreadful green stain on the shoulder of his dinner jacket I doubt will every come out. He stops and turns around, squinting at David. "You're Alexandra's brother," he says again. He looks at me and turns around again, muttering that we're going to the lobby.

"That goes to Alexandra's bungalow," David says, pointing to an offshoot to our path.

As Emmett wrestles with his bow tie in front of us, David takes my hand. The music has faded in the distance. Emmett finally gets his tie off and stuffs it into his pocket. He's looking a little steadier now. He keeps walking, muttering about hating carp because they're bottom feeders, and David pulls me off the path to kiss me. I am amazed at how familiar it feels. Perhaps I've seen it so much in my mind that I somehow have come to know it.

I've never been with a man this tall and it's strange to feel slight. So feminine.

"I have been in love with you since the day we drove out to Connecticut," he whispers, hugging me.

"It was at the rest stop," I whisper back. "When you thought I didn't feel well."

He brings his head back to look at me in the dim light. "How did you know?"

"I didn't. Until now." I reach up to kiss him and effortlessly we unfold into each other. I've never felt anything like this before.

"Sally?" Emmett yells.

"Uh-oh, duty calls," I murmur, brushing my hair back and smoothing my dress with my free hand. "Coming, Emmett." I let go of David's hand and hurry toward the hotel. Emmett is standing at the lobby door. He is holding it open by slumping back against it.

"I lost you," he complains.

"Let's get our keys, Emmett," I tell him, pulling him inside. We cross the marble floor and I shiver—it's freezing in here—and negotiate the turn with him into the front desk area.

"Hello, beautiful lady," says a voice. I turn around. It's Paul. Paul Fitzwilliam. He smiles, holding his arms out to me. "Surprise."

I walk over to Paul, smiling uncertainly, and he gives me a big hug, lifting me off the floor. "I wanted to see you before you left for England," he murmurs into my neck. He puts me back down on the ground and holds my face in his hands. "Look at you. The most beautiful woman in the world." He kisses me once and releases me. "How did it go?"

"Great," I say vaguely.

"Emmett, how are you?" Paul asks my co-anchor, moving to shake hands. Paul is wearing the Ralph Lauren blue jeans I gave him, a red-and-white pinstripe shirt (I also think I gave him), a blue blazer and sneakers.

"Sally thinks I'm drunk," Emmett tells him. "She's making me go to my room."

"I'm sorry," Paul says quickly, spinning around, "is it not over? I was waiting until I knew for sure everything was over."

Where is David? He was right behind me and now I don't see him.

"Sally?"

"No, I'm through for the day," I say. And then I give my head a little shake. "Paul, what are you doing here?"

When I first met Paul, here in Los Angeles, he was darkly

tanned and his hair streaked almost blond by the sun. One winter in the East has darkened his hair to brown and his complexion is decidedly pale. He looks so terribly young.

"I had a couple of days coming and an unused ticket and so I thought I'd catch you before you left and then go surfing with Jack." He has his arm around my waist.

"I'm still sort of working," I whisper, and Paul nods once, letting his arm slip away.

"So you're Alexandra's big brother," a booming voice says near the front desk. "Geez, you look like her." We all turn to look. It is the Ann Arbor affiliate accosting David. "I hear you're an attorney."

Emmett whispers, "Watch. He's going to ask him about his divorce."

"Can I ask you a question?" Ann Arbor says. "See, I'm going through a divorce…"

I could be imagining it, but I sense Paul's body stiffening beside me. "Isn't that David Waring?"

"Yeah," Emmett says. "And I still don't know why he got to come and my wife couldn't."

"Because his sister's the boss," I tell him.

"He lives out here, doesn't he?" Paul says, giving David a wave. "Hi, how are you?"

"Up north somewhere," I say.

"Good, thanks," David says, walking over with Ann Arbor following behind him. "It's Paul, isn't it?"

"Paul Fitzwilliam." They shake hands.

I feel like the lowest form of life. "I need to get my key," I say, walking over to the desk.

"So do I," David says. "Emmett, did you get yours?"

"No."

"I'll get it," I volunteer. I ask the clerk for the keys and when David stands next to me, I say, without looking at him, "I'm sorry, I had no idea he was coming."

"It's all right."

"It's not all right," I say, feeling my throat tighten.

"Ms. Harrington," the clerk says, handing me the key cards, "there was another flower delivery for you this evening. Would you like me to send it up?"

"Sure, whenever," I tell him. "But have the porter leave them outside the door."

"Very good."

"Key to bungalow 3, please," David says. As soon as the clerk steps away, he says, "Don't worry about me."

"I'm worried about me," I say. "Everything has changed. Everything." As I turn around I glimpse the misery on his face. We've officially been in love with each other for about nine hours and we're already miserable. "Here you go, Emmett," I say, holding out his key as I walk back. "It will be much more comfortable than sleeping in the garden."

"He says you were the hit of the convention," Paul says, smiling.

"Hardly. Where are your bags?"

"At Jack's. I didn't know how kosher it would be for me to show up here."

A group of affiliate managers comes stumbling in through the door from the pool. "Hey, Sally, I want my dance!" Denver declares.

I suppose I could use this intrusion as an excuse to send Paul away, but that would only be postponing the inevitable. I need to say something; I *have* to say something to Paul before another day passes. And I should do it now, while he's here on his own home turf, visiting his best friend.

"I'll meet you in the bar a little later," I tell Denver.

"Good night, everybody," David says, giving a wave and disappearing outside.

"So do you guys want to have a drink?" Emmett asks us on the way to the elevator. Whatever he sees in Paul's face has him backpedaling immediately. "Oh. Well, I'll ride up with you guys. Sally and I are on the same floor."

On the fifth floor we say good-night to Emmett as he heads in a different direction. Paul takes my hand, swinging our arms as we walk. "Wait until you see this suite. It's unreal," I say, opening the door.

"This dress is unreal," he murmurs, sliding his hands around my waist and kicking the door closed behind him. I stand there, unsure of what to do.

"I need to get out of these shoes," I finally say, hobbling to the bar. I hold on to it while I take off my sandals.

"Are those my flowers?" he says, pointing to them across the room.

"Aren't they beautiful?"

He takes off his blazer and opens the closet door to hang it up. "So what is David Waring doing here?"

"Would you like a beer?" I ask as I walk barefoot around the bar.

"Sure."

"They've got Amstel Light or Heineken," I say, opening the refrigerator.

"Heineken's great."

I pop the cap off with an opener and pour the beer into a glass. Paul slides up to sit on a stool. "Best-looking bartender I ever saw."

"I did used to bartend, you know."

"I know," he says, accepting the glass. "Thanks." He waits until I have poured myself a glass of white wine and then raises his glass. "To your good health and happiness and brilliant career."

"To your good health and happiness and brilliant career," I say back. We clink glasses and drink.

"Boy, that's tastes good," he says, lowering the glass. "So why did you say he was here?"

I almost say "who?" but that's going overboard. "To see Alexandra, I think. He's staying with her. They haven't seen each other in a while."

"He's married, right?"

"Mmm," I say noncommittally, sipping my wine.

He nods thoughtfully and takes another swig of beer.

"Oh," I say, remembering, "that photo of Jackson and that woman on the boat turned out to be bogus. In the real picture there are two guys with the woman trying to lift rigging off his broken leg. They're rerunning the picture and a retraction and an apology tomorrow."

"I'm glad for Cassy," he says. "So who's that from?" he asks, nodding at the orchid.

My mind seems to be frozen.

"Who is it from?" he asks again.

"I got all these flowers at once," I say. "This one, yours, a basket outside—" I stop when I realize he has picked up David's card.

"Looks like Scotty," he says about the outside of it. He opens it. "'I cannot tell you how happy it made me to see you today—D.'"

"Denny Ladler," I say. "It was his first day back."

He puts the card down. He picks up his beer glass and looks at it in his hand. He takes a sip and puts it down, looking at me. "I can't get married until I'm financially stable. I know you make eight times the money I do, Sally, but it wouldn't be right unless I could at least afford to feed us both."

If he is trying to take my breath away he has succeeded. I think Paul just asked me to marry him. "I'm a lot older than you are," I say quietly, seemingly stuck in this spot behind the bar. "We're at two different places in our lives." I pick up my wineglass and move around the bar and Paul slowly turns on the barstool to watch me as I sit down in one of the easy chairs, drawing my legs up into the chair with me.

"It's normal to be scared," he says. He is resting one foot on the rung of the barstool and his legs are splayed so as to offer me a view of what is transpiring in his pants. I think I know what Paul is thinking about; he's thinking about us doing it against the terrace wall while the other hotel guests come and go below.

I feel absolutely nothing.

Had David not been here I know I would have been thrilled to see Paul on this, my victory night, and I would have loved to have used up the last of the adrenaline from today by making love in every nook and cranny of this suite. I wouldn't have gone for the terrace wall, though, not with the DBS crowd around. On the settee on the terrace, though, surely.

But I don't feel anything now. I don't feel as though I even really recognize Paul at the moment as someone I know very well.

"He came here to see you."

I am startled to attention. "I'm sorry, what?"

"David Waring came here to see you," he says, sliding off the barstool and walking to stand in front of me. "He was after you before, too, I remember. But I figured since he was married you wouldn't be interested."

He turns around and makes his way back around the bar. "And to my way of thinking, Sally, I don't think you're indifferent to him." He bends down and comes up with a bottle. I hear the clink of glass. I'm looking down at the carpet, wondering what I should do, what I should say, but I am at a loss.

"Son of a bitch," Paul says, coming back around to fall in the chair across from me. He is holding what appears to be a glass of Scotch. "I should have known why you didn't ask me to come out." He takes a gulp.

"It never occurred to me you could get the time off," I tell him honestly.

He takes another gulp. "You knew he'd be here, didn't you?"

"Absolutely not."

He takes a sudden breath, turning his head to look back at the orchid. "I can't take you lying to me, Sally."

"Paul, I haven't done anything."

"Clearly you *have,* Sally," he snaps, turning back around to look at me.

"Paul, listen to me," I plead, but when he turns to glare at me I have trouble continuing. *But you must.* "You know how deeply I care about you. But you also know how the difference in our ages has always troubled me."

"But *why?*" he says. "I will be successful, it won't be long—"

"Paul, you're very successful now!" I am very near tears. "That's not it, Paul. You know it's not. It's about our lives going in two separate directions. We barely see each other as it is."

"I can practice in New York."

"Right. The closer to New York the happier you'll be? Are you trying to tell me you're going to undergo a personality transplant? You can't even hack being in New Haven, Paul. You hate the city, you want to live in the country—"

"Castleford's fine," he says.

"But it's not fine for me."

"David Waring lives out here—what are you going to do with him?"

"This is not about David Waring," I say stubbornly. "It is about me being self-centered, about me wanting to have you in my life because I do love you as a friend, and as a lover. But I know, I've always known, Paul, it couldn't work in the long run."

"He's waiting for you to call him, isn't he? As soon as you get rid of me?" He hunches forward, holding the glass in both hands. "Are you that scared of commitment? The second a relationship might count for something other than a decent lay and you can't handle it? So now you're moving on to a married man? So you don't *ever* have to commit?"

I only, I fear, look at him blankly.

"I can't believe I moved to Connecticut," he mutters, vaulting to his feet and spilling Scotch in the process. "What was I thinking?" He's standing at the sliding glass doors now, looking out. "You're not that good in bed. I've had a lot better."

I suppose I deserve this.

He sighs, shaking his head and looking down at the floor. "Goddamn it, Sally. You're just going to throw it all away?" He turns around. "You're just going to throw *me* away?"

My telephone starts ringing.

"That's probably him right now," he says angrily, taking another hit of his Scotch.

I shake my head. "It's not like that, Paul."

"Oh, you mean it's *Denny* calling?" He snatches the phone and I am truly scared. "Hello?" Pause. His eyes dart around the room. "Yeah, she's here, Emmett, hang on." He thrusts the phone at me and walks away.

"Hello?" I say softly.

"Robby Palermo's been murdered," Emmett says breathlessly.

I squint, trying to think.

"Remember at the trial? He was one of the guys linked to Michael Arlenetta when they firebombed the house?"

"He was never arrested," I say, grabbing the pencil on the side table. I jot down the date and time and make notes in shorthand. "Palermo, you said?"

"Yeah. And he's dead for sure. They found his body in San Diego without a head. Will says they think it was blown off."

I frown. "Blown off with what?"

"I don't know, but Will's meeting me downstairs in five minutes to take me to the Burbank studio. He wants me to break the story."

"You break the story? Why you? The guy nearly killed me—*I* should break the story."

"That's why I'm calling you," he says. "I think I might have had too much to drink."

"What about Alexandra?"

"All I know is I have to meet Will in four minutes now. I'll meet you in the lobby," and he hangs up the phone.

"I'm sorry, but I have to go to the studio in Burbank," I tell Paul, hurrying into the bedroom. "A guy from the Mafia Boss Murder Trial was just found with his head blown off in San Diego." I peel off my dress and yank the closet open, reaching for the blouse and clean blue suit I always travel with in case of things just like this. No panty hose; no time. I grab the phone and punch in a number. "Thank heavens you're there, Cleo, we're leaving for the studio and we need you. That's okay, no straight lines are necessary, just brush my hair out. I'll be waiting for you in the lobby." I hang up and hastily put on a pair of blue pumps.

"I'm sorry," I say again, zipping into the living room to unplug my laptop. "This is one of the guys who almost killed me." I slip the laptop into its bag and hurry to sort the electrical cord and put that in, too. "You can stay here if you like."

"No thank you," he says in a voice so angry it stops me. He strides over to the closet, flings the door open and yanks his blazer out of it. "I want you out of my life once and for all," he declares. He opens the door to the hallway, bends down and comes back in carrying a large vase of flowers in his right hand. "You've got more fucking flowers from Denny!" he cries, hurling them at the mirror behind the bar. The mirror explodes into a million pieces, making me duck and cover my head.

When it is over, I lower my hands and straighten up, a shard of glass falling from my hair.

Paul slams the door so hard it flies back open and crashes against the wall. A minute later a man is peering in at me from the hallway. "House detective, Ms. Harrington, are you all right?"

"Yes," I say dully, nudging broken glass with my shoe. "I'll pay for the damage, of course, but if you could ask someone to clean this up while I'm gone I would appreciate it."

"What was it he threw?" the man asks, stepping in to look around.

"A vase of flowers. Into the mirror over there."

He gingerly makes his way through the glass to take a look. "These roses?" he asks, holding up a single white rose.

"I guess so. I didn't see what kind they were. Oh, no," I say, putting my computer bag down and walking toward the bar. "There's water all over these—" I bend over to pick up the five DBS News folders off the carpet I was saving for England and look for something to dry them off with. I hurry into the bathroom to wipe them off with a towel.

Build It and They Shall Come, it says on the front cover. *Be Sally and have trouble,* it should say, I think, carefully drying each one.

And then I stop. *Build it and they shall come.* A slight hum begins in my ears and I feel a horrendous sinking feeling in my stomach. *Looking forward to seeing you again. Sorry to miss you.*

"Ms. Harrington?" the detective says in the doorway. "Are you all right?"

"Was there a card?"

"I'm sorry—"

"Was there a card with those flowers?" I ask, hurrying past him. I hunt around, glass crunching under one of my bare feet. But I see it, the small envelope, and pick it up.

See you tonight!

"Careful, you've cut yourself," the detective says.

"I need my date book," I tell him, feeling dazed. I stagger across the living room to the desk and flip my date book open, rifling through the pages.

"Your foot's bleeding," he says, coming over.

"Give me a minute," I plead, trying to think. I turn another page of the calendar. *Two weeks ago. Then last week.* I flip forward a couple of pages. *Was it Tuesday or Wednesday?*

"Oh, my God," I say, covering my mouth and sinking into the desk chair.

I get it now. I think I get what is going on.

A mere hour passes from the time I call Agent Alfonso in New York and the arrival of Special Federal Prosecutor Sky Preston at my hotel suite. He is accompanied by FBI Agent Sasha Punjab. Sky used to operate out of the D.C. area, specializing in racketeering and money laundering, and his career path and mine crossed several times over the course of my involvement in the war between the Presarios—the family that had gone straight—and their cousins, the murderous Arlenettas.

"We moved out here last month," Sky tells me as we settle in the living room. The night maid came in to at least vacuum the glass off the furniture, and the house detective brought me a first-aid kit to bandage my foot. The hotel offered to move me, but I don't want to do anything until I get this sorted.

"Prosecutor Preston is now a director of the organized-crime unit for the western United States," Agent Punjab explains, eyes on the shattered remains of the mirror over the bar.

"The real reason why we moved here," Sky says, "is so my wife's aging lab can go swimming every day. She's got hip issues." Sky's wife is a former Wall Street whiz kid who does casework for the feds in the area of international money laundering. He turns to Agent Punjab. "Sally's a dog person."

He's making an effort to calm me down, I realize.

"Ashley, right?" I say. "Black Lab with a dash of Chow?"

He looks at me incredulously. "You've never even seen her."

"You told me enough to make her memorable." I manage to smile slightly. "Purple tongue, hip dysplasia, great ball catcher."

"For a person who used to have such problems with her memory…" He looks around. "So what happened here?"

"It's unrelated," I tell him.

"Hotel security said it was a domestic dispute."

"Then why are you asking me?" I say, feeling close to tears.

"Because there's obviously been an act of violence—"

"Do you want to know why I called Alfonso or not?" I nearly yell.

He holds out a cautioning hand. "All right, all right." He senses now how careful he needs to be with me, how far out on the edge I am.

Agent Punjab has taken out a small notebook and pen.

"Why isn't anyone here from DBS security, Sally?" Sky asks gently.

"Because I haven't told anybody else. I just called Agent Alfonso."

"And we're very glad you did." He bites his lower lip. "Do you want to start at the beginning?"

"I'm not sure I even know when the beginning was," I say, getting up to retrieve my calendar from the desk. I think I'm in some kind of shock. "I had a brandy," I hear myself say, "but it seems to have had little effect." I return to my chair, draw my legs up under me and open the calendar on the chair arm. I reach to the side table to take a swig from the large bottle of club soda I have there. (Paul broke all the glasses. I suppose I could get one from the bathroom, but it seems too far.)

"I think someone from DBS should be here, Sally," Sky says quietly, watching me. "But not someone from the news division." He means Alexandra. He wants to avoid having to make a deal to keep his investigation off the air until he is ready. In this instance he knows that I must agree with him, otherwise I would have called Alexandra before I called Agent Alfonso.

"Is Cassy Cochran here?"

I nod.

He stands up. "I'm going to ask her to come here, all right?"

"All right."

"Why don't you take a quick look around," he suggests to Agent Punjab, picking up the phone at the bar. With his left hand he picks up a piece of glass and holds it up to the light. "Cassy Cochran's room, please." He turns to me. "How did you hear about Robby Palermo?"

"Will Rafferty called my co-anchor, Emmett Phelps. They're at the station now. Emmett's breaking the story on the air and then completing a full story for the morning. You know, that ties Palermo to the Mafia Boss Murder Trial."

"Nice timing for him," Sky observes. "It's how people remember Emmett Phelps, covering that trial. It's Sky Preston, Cassy," he says, turning away slightly. "I apologize for waking you—oh, good." He takes a breath. "I'm here at the hotel and we've got a situation unfolding around Sally Harrington and I think she should have somebody with her. We both think you're the person because no one, Sally included, would like this information to get out yet. Okay, good. Thanks. Five thirty-two." He hangs up the phone. "She's coming right up. Sally—"

I look over.

"Which flowers were the ones you told Agent Alfonso came tonight?"

"The white roses," I say dully. "I picked them up with the ice tongs and put them in a plastic bag. They're over there in the corner."

"I see."

"I also put whatever glass and paper and stuff there was in the trash can under the bar. The only other thing in the trash can was bottle cap, so it should be all right."

I hear the snap of Agent Punjab putting on latex gloves and she confers with Sky. I can't hear what they're saying and I'm not sure I want to.

"Who threw the flowers, Sally?"

I look at him.

"He destroyed evidence," he adds.

"He didn't know it was evidence." I take another swig of

soda, but this time keep the bottle with me in the chair to hold on to.

"The hotel detective says a man stormed out of here and out of the hotel." Pause. "I can read a description of him if you would like."

"For Pete's sake, he's a cop," I sigh.

"This isn't the cop from the trial, is it?"

"It is," I tell him angrily. "And he has nothing to do with this. Nothing."

"And almost every time in the past you have told me something was unrelated to the matter at hand, Sally, it's turned out to have a direct bearing."

"Not this time."

"I need his name, Sally."

"Paul Fitzwilliam. Detective. New Haven Police Department. In Connecticut."

Sky comes back to sit down across from me. He's carrying the little notebook Agent Punjab had been using. "I thought he was an L.A. cop," he says to me.

"He was. West Hollywood. And then he came East. He's going to law school, a four-year program."

He scribbles and looks up. "Was he staying with you?"

"No. He was out here on his own. He's staying with a friend." I look in the address-book part in my calendar and give him Jack's address and phone number.

"Did he throw the vase at you, Sally?"

I meet his eyes. "No. I would never have such a person anywhere near me."

He continues to hold my eyes.

"What?" I snap irritably.

"Can you also give me his Connecticut address and number?"

I sigh, shaking my head, but do as I am asked.

There is a knock at the door and I let Sky answer it. A moment later Cassy is rushing to my side, asking if I'm all right. I assure her that I am, not to worry. Sky tells her to have a seat.

Sky sits down across from me again while Agent Punjab is still doing something with the evidence.

"Tell me about the connection you made tonight with the flowers."

"As I told you, Emmett called to tell me about Robby Palermo." I look at Cassy, who nods and says she knows about it. "I remembered him, of course, because we always thought he was one of the principals in the attempt to kill actress Lilliana Martin, the granddaughter of Rocky Presario. But, as you know, he was never arrested."

"Right," he confirms.

"When Emmett said Palermo had his head blown off, something clicked. That he was involved in the rocket attack and now *his* head was blown off. And then the flowers came—" I look at Cassy. "Paul found them outside the door when he was leaving and he got mad and threw them." I clear my throat, looking back to Sky. "When I saw what the flowers were, white roses—the first time I got a dozen white roses was the day Wilson Delafield was murdered."

He confirms the date with me. "And where did you receive those flowers?"

"At the apartment I sublet on One Hundredth Street. Which was strange because so few people have that address." I take a swig from the club soda bottle. A tiny shudder runs through me.

Cassy gets up and disappears into the bedroom.

"Did you ever think that Paul Fitzwilliam may have sent them?"

"Briefly. But he knows I like colorful bouquets. He sent me that one." I point across the room as Cassy emerges with a hotel robe.

"Put this around your shoulders," she says, helping me do just that. I must be in shock because I'm freezing.

"And the flowers outside on the terrace?" Agent Punjab asks.

"Those are from Jackson Darenbrook. Our CEO. They were congratulatory." I glance at Cassy, who smiles slightly, sitting near me again. Only now do I realize she is wearing khakis, a blue fleece top and clogs, and her hair is hastily clipped into a ponytail. She hurried.

"There also appears to have been orchids here," Agent Punjab says.

"Just one. It was swimming in water."

"And who was that from?" Sky asks.

I hesitate just a fraction of a second. "David Waring, one of Alexandra's brothers. It was also congratulatory."

Sky picks something up in my voice. "You have a friendship with David Waring?" he asks, looking up.

I nod.

"He's here in the hotel," Cassy offers. "He's staying with Alexandra in bungalow 3."

Sky turns back to me. "Does he have anything to do with why Paul Fitzwilliam hurled the vase of roses across the room?"

"Come on, Sky," I plead.

"It's important, Sally. You have to give us all the pieces to the puzzle. Otherwise we can't help you."

"It's not me I'm worried about you helping," I tell him, taking another slug of water. "I'm worried about everybody I hate. Because something might happen to them."

"When was the next delivery of white roses?"

"The day the *Herald-American* was bombed and Alfred Royce was beaten up. The card said, 'Sorry to miss you again.'"

"And those flowers are where?"

"In my office at West End. Or I may have told my assistant to take them home since I was going to be away. You can check with her." I give him Margarite's number.

"So you believe the white roses are connected to these events," Sky says a while later. "Delafield's murder, the bombing and beating of Royce, and now the murder of Robby Palermo."

"Wouldn't you?"

Sky bites his lower lip. "Can you clarify that?"

"Everyone in America knew I had a problem with Wilson Delafield when I did that story for the magazine show. I hated the guy for what he did to those animals and it showed. He burned his horses to death and then shortly after my story ran *he's* burned to death, but before that I get white roses at home saying, 'Looking forward to seeing you again.' Al's hatchet job on me went out over a national wire service and a day later his office is blown up. I go out there and then come back to New York and Al Royce gets his head beaten in, his body left on my doorstep and I get more white roses, saying 'Sorry to miss you again.' Now I come out here and get flowers that say, 'See you tonight!' and tonight Palermo is found dead with his head blown off. The same Palermo who nearly took my head off with a rocket, who the whole world knows the feds—*you*, Sky—failed to get an indictment against."

"It could be coincidence," Sky says, scribbling. "Some fan sending you flowers every few days, wanting to show you he knows where you are."

"And that's supposed to make me feel better?" I ask, pulling the robe tighter around me. I look down. I've been cradling the club soda bottle so long the front of my blouse is wet from condensation. I can't seem to let go of it, though.

"You also realize those messages would fit the timing for Paul Fitzwilliam," Sky adds.

"Just give that up, will you?"

He looks over at Cassy. "Or even David Waring."

"Damn it, Sky, listen to me! This is not an amateur."

"I wouldn't consider a police officer an amateur. He could have had help."

"Cassy, talk to him!"

There is a knock at the door and Agent Punjab answers it. Some guy comes in wearing a blue windbreaker. They talk in whispers at the bar for a while and then he leaves with the plastic bags of flowers and glass and stuff.

We slog on for another hour, going over and over the same things. Two more law enforcement people have joined us, but I didn't catch their names. I'm not sure how much longer I'm going to be able to hold up. At least Sky's interest has moved on from Paul and David.

"How do you spell that?" one of the recent arrivals, an older man, asks me.

"*D*—apostrophe—capital *A-m-i-c-o*. He's a lieutenant in the Castlefield Police Department."

"I will call D'Amico first thing," he promises Sky. Then he looks at me again, scratching the back of his neck. "And they have no suspects in the bombing?"

"I don't know."

He looks at Sky. "It sounds like the Presarios, doesn't it? Delafield had a connection to the Gambinos, so there could have been something there. The bomb and the beating definitely sound like a favor to Sally. And Palermo tried to murder Rocky's granddaughter in that rocket attack."

"Rocky's very sick," I tell him. "They say he's dying. He's got very bad lung disease and is bedridden, on oxygen, the whole nine yards."

"Then let's look at the Presario grandkids. We know they're not above a little murder when it comes to relatives, don't we?"

That's, of course, what the Mafia Boss Murder Trial had been about. Which Presario had murdered their cousin Nick Arlenetta in cold blood. But then, Nick had murdered their mother when they were kids.

"What about Phillip O'Hearn?" Sky asks me. "I heard he ran interference for you with the mob in upstate New York."

I am startled. "How do you know about that?"

"What interests me is why Phillip O'Hearn did that for you." Cassy is looking back and forth between us, confused. Sky continues, "You were convinced he was involved in your father's death, Sally."

"But—" Cassy begins.

"Why would O'Hearn run interference for you, Sally?"

I hesitate. "Because he offered to."

"But *why,* Sally? The Phillip O'Hearn I know would have preferred to see you dead."

"What are you talking about?" Cassy asks me. "When did Phillip O'Hearn—"

"You trusted Phillip O'Hearn but you didn't trust her?" Sky says, gesturing to Cassy.

"It wasn't appropriate for me to talk to you about it," I tell her. "And it's still not, Sky. My family was put at risk, Sky. I'm not going there."

"Are they at risk because of Phillip O'Hearn?"

"No! He's the one who helped me."

"But *why* did he want to help you?"

"Because he was trying to make amends." Silence. "He found out some things he never knew. And he honest to God is decimated now by what he did to my father. And my family."

Sky exchanges looks with the older guy. "O'Hearn's got the means to do it."

"Phillip O'Hearn is not killing people on my behalf," I say, losing my temper. "But because of the DBS story that ran—implicating him in the death of my father—I will tell you what I'm scared of. I'm scared that this friggin' psycho's going to try to kill Phillip O'Hearn because he'll think he's doing me a favor. Almost no one knows what my relationship is with O'Hearn now. The world still thinks I hate him."

"Who does know of your relationship?" he asks quietly.

"My great-uncle Percy. And David Waring. Why?"

"No one's tried to hurt Phillip O'Hearn that we know of," he says.

"Stop it, Sky," I say, covering my face. "If you're implying that O'Hearn is alive and well because David knows I don't hate him anymore and thus hasn't tried to kill him…" I drop my hands. "My eighty-five-year-old uncle Percy's a better bet."

"I don't think David could possibly have anything to do with this," Cassy says.

"I have to have a break," I say, putting the club soda bottle down and stiffly trying to get up. I've been in that chair so long I can scarcely stand upright. "I'll be right back." I walk into the bedroom and throw off the robe. I grab some blue jeans, a long-sleeved polo shirt, a golf sweater and some underwear and take them into the bathroom. When I see myself in the mirror I am almost scared. I look like a tormented creature I do not know.

I use the john, strip, wash the worst of my makeup off, brush my hair and change. I also put on socks and sneakers before returning to the living room "I have come to a decision," I announce as I retake my seat. "I'm going to formally request that you, the federal authorities, take steps to protect the well-being of all my enemies."

"Are you going to give us a list?" the older guy asks.

"Yep. Starting with Phillip O'Hearn. You've got to warn him. Crazy Mr. Murder's on the loose."

"Who else?" Sky asks.

"The guy you *did* indict but failed to convict," I tell him, "Michael Arlenetta. The whole country knows he was *there* with Palermo at the rocket attack—and everybody knows he got off and he's taken over his brother's rackets. He's practically a movie star in New Jersey at this point so I would think he's probably a likely target."

"Why should you care what's happened to him?" the older guys says.

"He was going to give me an exclusive interview when Sky had him arrested. I still don't know why he wanted to do it." I look at Cassy. "I'd still like to interview him, now more than ever. But they're going to have to keep him alive if I'm ever going to have the chance."

"Verity Rhodes," Cassy says, naming the publisher of *Expectations* magazine.

"Right," Sky says, making a note, "she's no fan of yours. And you were named in her divorce, weren't you?"

"She didn't name me, Corbett Shroeder did, the creep. I had absolutely nothing to do with any of it."

"Except her present husband was your boyfriend—"

"Just write Corbett Shroeder down, Sky."

He does but then looks up quickly. "What about that intern at DBS you had a problem with? Do you think he would be capable of these murders?"

"What intern?" Cassy says.

"This could be a progression from what he did at West End."

"*Who* did *what* at West End?" Cassy demands.

I shake my head at Sky. "No. He's in Australia now. And he got treatment. He's fine."

"I'm going to check on his whereabouts," Sky says, making a note.

"Damn it, Sally, " Cassy says, "who are we talking about?"

Sky and I look at each other. We made a deal on this a long time ago. The kid was mentally ill. "Sally's right," he finally says, looking down at his pad. "It's not worth discussing."

"Who else do you hate?" the older agent doggedly continues.

"Um," I say, rubbing my eyes, trying to think. "Frank Sabatino. But he's in Europe somewhere."

"I have a file on him," Sky says. He catches my look. "The

case is still open, Sally. There's no statute of limitations on murder."

"Who else?" the older guy asks. "Think hard."

But I can't think of anyone else. And neither can Cassy nor Sky. That's pretty much it: Phillip O'Hearn, Michael Arlenetta, Verity Rhodes, Corbett Shroeder and Frank Sabatino. Five enemies. Is that a good or bad number? I wonder.

Cassy announces it is now a quarter to four in the morning. "And Sally is scheduled to fly to England today," she tells Sky. "And we need her there if it's possible."

"Where are you going?"

"Liverpool. She'll be back in New York by Friday."

"You don't have to worry about anything happening to *me,*" I tell him, "I just keep getting flowers."

"Sometimes thrown at you," Sky adds. "Sasha?" he calls over his shoulder.

Agent Punjab appears in the doorway from the terrace, where she has been making phone calls. "Yes, sir?"

"Is your passport up to date?"

"Yes, sir."

"I want you to go home and pack a bag for three days. You're accompanying Sally Harrington to England and then to New York."

Against her darker skin, Agent Punjab's smile is very white. "I suppose I will have to suffer the hardship, sir," she says.

"Good idea," Cassy says to Sky. "The Darenbrook plane is going over so she can ride along at no additional expense to you."

"That would be great," Sky acknowledges.

Cassy turns to me. "You've got to get some rest."

I yawn in agreement, stretching. I feel much better having them worry about the well-being of my enemies.

After twenty minutes more of instructions and telephone numbers and beeper numbers and being introduced to the man who will be standing guard outside my suite, mercifully everyone is leaving. I walk them to the door and tell Sky I feel relieved that things are in his hands.

"Excuse me, sir, but where are you going?" we hear the guard say in the hall.

"I'm waiting to see Sally Harrington." I recognize David's voice. "When she is free."

"It's all right," I say, stepping out into the hallway.

Poor David has to approach the door with all these serious-looking feds staring at him. He's still in his tuxedo pants and shirt, but with no cummerbund and his sleeves are rolled up over his forearms. He nods to Cassy and guesses that Sky is in charge and extends a hand to him. "David Waring, a friend of Sally's."

"Schyler Preston, federal prosecutor."

"We've worked with Sky and his associates on some stories in the past," I explain, taking David's hand.

"I heard about Robby Palermo," he says, tightening his hold on my hand. "Is that what this is about?"

I look at Cassy. And remember our agreement. Not a word to anyone for now.

I turn to address the feds. "If there isn't anything else…"

They take the hint and file out, Sky and Cassy leaving last. "You're sure you'll be all right?" Cassy asks. She's looking every bit of her fifty-two years this morning. Her eyes move to David. "Will you see that she gets some rest?"

He nods. "Yes."

I thank them all again and almost shove them out the door, closing and locking it behind them. Then I turn around and collapse against it.

"Do you want to talk about it?" David asks, coming toward me and offering his hand.

"Absolutely not," I answer, taking his hand and letting him pull me into his arms.

I remember this same feeling from a long, long time ago. Was it tonight?

"What in Sam Hill are you doing in here?"

My eyes flutter open. Next to me David jerks upright into a sitting position. "I'm not sleeping anymore, that's for sure," he grumbles.

I roll over and smile at him and then prop myself up on one elbow to look at his sister, who is standing at the foot of my bed. With the exception of our shoes, David and I are still fully dressed, just as we were when we basically passed out this morning.

"And may I ask what are *you* doing here?" I say. "And how you got in?"

"I'm trying to find out what is going on around here," Alexandra says, plunking a hand on her hip. "The FBI's been here, your suite's been trashed, I heard Paul was here but now you're in bed with my brother. Cassy's not talking and you let Emmett go to the studio last night smashed."

"Would you like some breakfast?" David asks me, rolling off the bed.

"Water, blueberries, yogurt, granola and coffee with milk, please." My eyes move back to Alexandra, who has dropped down to sit on the edge of the bed in resignation.

"What happened? Cassy's not talking."

"She can't," I say, covering a yawn. I look at the clock. Eight-thirty, no wonder I feel horrible. I notice Alexandra is glowering at me. *"Yet,"* I tell her. "Of course, we will have the inside track on whatever it is when it's ready to be news. Sky's word is good, you know that."

"Sky Preston was here? Oh, no, you're not back in with the mob again, Sally, are you? This Robby Palermo murder—"

"No, no," I say, waving her off. "Don't worry."

"Who smashed up your living room?" she asks next.

"Paul Fitzwilliam," David says, hanging up from room service and walking to the bathroom. He closes the door carefully behind him. In a moment Alexandra and I pretend we don't hear him whizzing.

"Paul was here?"

I nod. "He wanted to surprise me."

The toilet flushes and we hear the water running in the sink. I don't know how they can call this a luxury hotel if you can hear all this.

"So he knows about David," she surmises. "You guys were pretty chummy last night. It's the talk of the neighborhood. Denver lost his money, by the way. He had to shell out more than four hundred dollars."

Now I hear David gargling. "Paul thought some flowers were from David and so he chucked them at the mirror."

"Ah," she says, nodding. The bathroom door opens. "But that hardly warrants a visit from Sky Preston in the wee hours of the morning."

"If a guy who almost killed Sally is found murdered while Sally's in town," David says, sitting on the edge of the bed, "that could warrant a visit, don't you think?"

I look at him longingly, remembering how safe and warm and happy I felt earlier.

That's all we did. Hold each other.

And it was enough.

"How do you know?" his sister asks.

"I don't," he says, shrugging, "I'm guessing."

She refocuses on me and I can almost hear the cogs and wheels of her brain at work. "Did you hear from Palermo while we've been here?"

"No, it was nothing like that, I swear. Otherwise they wouldn't let me go to England with you. And they are letting me go, by the way."

"Well, that's good." Then she smiles a little, looking at David with obvious fondness. "And what are you doing in Sally's bedroom, brother dear?"

"Telling her I'm in love with her," he says simply.

Alexandra blinks, kicking her head back a little. Then she looks at me.

"And I told him I was in love with him, too," I tell her.

"I see," she says, mulling this information over. Alexandra sets those large eyes on me again and it feels like she is trying to peer inside me. "You trust me enough to tell me that you're in love with my brother, but you don't trust either one of us enough to say why Sky was here. Am I getting this right?"

"She always was a rotten kid," David tells me.

"Look," I begin, "it cannot get out. I made an agreement."

Her face lights up immediately, sensing that I'm already starting to cave.

"It's possible the Delafield murder, the Royce beating and Palermo's murder may have been committed by the same person or persons. On my behalf."

Alexandra's mouth parts slightly.

"This isn't good news, Sally," David says.

"Not for any enemies of mine, it's not. The feds are running down a list of people to warn in case this proves to be true."

"We figured the Royce beating was done for you," Alexandra says, amazed, "but Delafield's murder?"

"It doesn't make sense to me, either," I tell her. "But now Sky and the FBI are on it and I have to say I am relieved."

"Did they come to you?" she asks.

I shake my head. "I called Alfonso last night in New York and Sky showed up here."

"And you called him because…?"

"Things fell into place for me."

"They were here until four this morning," David says.

Her eyebrows shoot up. "*You* were here?"

"I came after they left," he explains. He smiles at me and I feel that funny feeling again, a mixture of thrill and fear and longing. "And we fell asleep."

Alexandra swings her head back to me. "And why was Cassy here?"

"You're just not going to give up on this, are you?" I ask her. "How's it going to look when Cassy wouldn't tell you anything and now you'll see her and you'll know everything?"

"She won't know I know," she says, standing up. Only now do I notice that she is wearing tennis whites. "But I know now why she's not going to England and she's sending Jackson instead with his broken leg."

"Why?"

"She's going back to New York to get the background on this story ready so we can roll with it later at a moment's notice."

"No."

"I know so," she says with conviction. "She's going back to New York to put the story together for us. She gave Sky her word and so she'll do it herself."

"She used to be in news, didn't she?" David says.

"For years," Alexandra confirms. "And so," she says, plunking her hands on her hips, making the hem of her tennis skirt sway slightly, "if she's worrying about it then I don't really have to, do I?"

"I'm not," I say, shrugging.

"You think it's safe for you to travel?"

"Sure. But an FBI agent's coming with us to England, anyway."

"Great!" she says, clapping her hands. "That means I am free to worry about other things. Okay," she says, pivoting around, "you guys can go back to being in love." A moment later we hear the sound of the front door closing.

"How did she get in here?" David asks, crawling across the bed.

"She's scary that way," I tell him, fluffing up the pillows. We shift around until I am comfortably ensconced in his arms.

Someone starts knocking at the living room door.

"Room service," we say simultaneously.

IV

CHAPTER
28

My mother always said when I found the right person I would know it. She also said if it was meant to be, then in time things would simply fall into place.

She said there would be no tricking or trapping, no pretending or fabricating, and I would have no real control over the process except in regard to my own behavior. (This is Mother's euphemism for sex.)

She said there would be no great obsession, but certainly plenty of wonderful daydreams. She said there would not be any crazy behavior. (This is Mother's euphemism for wild sex.)

She said an all-encompassing love would present itself and I would recognize it at once because it felt right.

No guilt. No sin. Just right.

And when I found it, she told me, I should expect to spend the rest of my life staying aware of all the small and big things I could do to nurture that love. Because, she said, the passion would be the first thing to go—and yet it would be an ongoing gift, reawakened in different ways over the course of our lives—and it would be the underlying friendship of love that would keep us going.

Mother said all of this to me this morning when I called her.

I have not undergone a conversion in the past thirty-six hours, exactly, but I can tell you I suddenly resent almost every sexual minute of my life to date as much as I resent almost every sexual minute of David's. We have been intimate with others; it's not that I'm jealous, I just hate it. I hate the idea I have missed any time and any specialness with him.

Strange, isn't it? That after all this time I have found someone whose every nuance I adore, whose mind, heart, touch and body I crave, and yet the last thing I want to do right now is to have sex with him? Oh, yes, I'd love to. But I can't. This is too important. Too big.

We need time.

David drives me separately to the Darenbrook jet at John Wayne Airport this afternoon, and what is so remarkable is my feeling of contented calm. We hold hands and keep looking at each other, feeling a bit stunned about it all, I think, arriving apart on Saturday and leaving on Tuesday as a couple. He says something about a sublet in Manhattan and a part-time paralegal to keep up with his California practice.

I feel no surprise when he says this. Nothing amazes me anymore. I merely smile, watching his profile as he negotiates traffic. "We can't do this long distance," he says, glancing over at me. "We need to be near each other, really get to know each other."

"I agree," I say, but I almost laugh out loud because I am suppressing the urge to tell David he is not as unlike his sister as he might like to think and that I have a pretty good idea of what he *really* might be like in his worst moments already. I suppress it for all of about twenty seconds before telling him that very thing.

No tricking, no trapping.

He roars. And then he grins, shaking his head, eyes on the road ahead of us. "That's not very masculine, is it? To remind people of your little sister?"

And so this is how we leave things at the airport, that in a few weeks I can expect him to be living at least three weeks of the month in New York. When I ask him how he can be so certain about that, he confesses he looked into the possibilities shortly after we first met. "But you were right," he says, touching the side of my face with a gentle hand. "I needed to follow things

all the way through with Mary Ellen. And now I know. For sure."
He smiles. "And I love you, Sally Harrington." And then he kisses
me in such a romantic manner as to prompt a little girl in the
terminal to pipe up, "Is he her prince, Mommy?"

"Definitely," I tell the little girl. And then reluctantly I let go
of David to show the security guards my DBS News pass and
paperwork. I look back and he smiles and waves. *I love you,* I
mouth to him.

"Hey, Sally, glad you could make it," Will says to me in the
main cabin. Langley is in the corner quietly dictating to Adele.
On this leg of the journey we're minus Cassy, Jessica, Emily,
Bertha-Gerta, Dash, Bosco and Alec, giving us all the space in
the world. "Your secret agent's in the back having tea."

"Oh," I say, bringing a hand up to my mouth, "I forgot about
her."

"Fortunately she didn't forget about you," Langley calls without looking at me.

"Cassy brought her," Will explains.

"I thought Cassy was going back to New York."

"She is." He checks his watch. "And she better get going
soon. She's flying American with Jess and the baby and Ger—
*Ber*tha." He hits the side of his head with the heel of his hand.
"Now you've got me doing it. Jess said I called her Gertha last
night after the party."

I laugh and the steward comes in to ask me if he can get me
anything. I ask for water, stow my laptop and carry-on in a cabinet and walk back to the café area.

"Ah, there she is," Cassy says, pushing off the wall where she's
been leaning. She must have been entertaining Agent Punjab,
who is enjoying a cup of tea and a sandwich at one of the tables
for two. "I've given Alexandra a sleeping pill," she says in a low
voice, walking over to me, "because if she doesn't get some sleep
soon she's going to get sick. She's been up almost two nights
straight and I still practically had to tie her down in the cabin."

"You're allowed to get some sleep, too, you know," I tell her.
"I wanted to thank you again for staying with me this morning.
I don't know what I would have done without you."

"You just take care of yourself, and keep an eye on Emmett—"

"Where is he?" I say, looking around.

"Asleep in the forward cabin."

"He did well," I say. "I saw his report."

"No, it wasn't bad," she agrees. "It was being slightly drunk the night before on the air that's a problem. Well, progress not perfection. He should sleep all the way through and he needs it. You will check on Alexandra, won't you?"

"Sure."

She points a finger at me. "And mind, you let Sasha do her job."

"I will."

"Excuse me, Mrs. Darenbrook," the attendant interrupts, "but the tower has given the captain permission to taxi to the runway."

"Yes, certainly," she says, looking at her watch. "I need to catch my flight, too." She rests a hand on my arm. "Do your best with INS, Sally, that's all I ask. Watch how Alexandra deals with the issue of you two anchoring the half hour instead of her. And keep an eye on Emmett. He should be fine, but he still needs to work on a stronger air of confidence."

"I'll work on it with him," I promise.

"Jackson will be there to meet you when you arrive. He and Langley know them all very well, so feel free to go to them for pointers. Particularly Jackson. If you need me—day or night— you know how to reach me." She starts moving away, but turns around again to point to the rear of the plane. "And please get on her about sleeping. She's running on empty."

"Got it," I assure her.

I sit down with Agent Punjab and fasten my seat belt. I apologize for forgetting about her and she says, along the same lines as Langley did, "As long as I don't forget about you, Sally, things will be fine."

The hatch is closed and a short time later we are pushing back from the gate.

Agent Punjab is willing to talk a little about herself. (I am to call her Sasha.) Her father was from New Delhi and her mother is a first-generation Pakistani-American. She was brought up in

Brooklyn and freaked her family out by demanding to play sports at a public school. So long as she wore traditional dress and observed customs on family holidays, they got over their horror when Sasha was offered athletic scholarships to college in two different sports. She went to Penn and played Division I soccer and got an Ivy League education. From there she went into the CIA where she trained in an antiterrorist unit, but when her photograph was later circulated over the Internet by Jihad, she was moved over to the FBI.

"Aren't you nervous about going overseas?" I ask her.

She smiles and I wonder how white her teeth really are. She has pretty liquid brown eyes, very dark and sleek black hair that is pulled back. She is wearing a tan skirt and blazer and brown shoes with a small heel. She's not heavy, but she is not slight, either. I can easily imagine her disguised in feminine robes, on the prowl in a Middle Eastern marketplace, but I can also imagine her picking someone up and throwing them across the room.

"I'm not afraid," she says easily. "When it's my time to go, then it will be my time to go. I was moved to domestic duty because it doesn't look good when one of our American operatives gets killed."

"You're a far better woman than I," I tell her.

There has not been much headway on the Palermo murder evidently, or if there has been Sasha's not saying.

"Do you know if anyone has been warning those people on my list?" I ask, almost having to shout to be heard over the roar of our liftoff.

She nods. "They've all been contacted."

"That's good."

She leans forward, holding a hand up to her ear.

"I said 'That's good.'"

She nods. "You shouldn't worry."

I offer a quick smile. "I'm not."

Not anymore.

When we land at Manchester Airport we are whisked through Customs and find two limousines waiting for us outside Terminal 2. Alexandra, Will, Langley and Adele get into the first one and Emmett and I climb into the second one with Sasha. It is almost midnight over here and we can't see anything of the countryside, which, the driver tells us, is not as big a crime as we might think since we are driving through the birthplace of Industrial England—which then became the birthplace of the collapse of Industrial England. Only in recent years, he explains, has the area started to come back in earnest.

I explain that I'm from a similar city in America called Castleford and our discussion gets thoroughly confusing until Sasha whispers she thinks he's talking about Castleford, Chesire and Wallingford, England, and I'm talking about Castleford, Chesire and Wallingford, Connecticut. She's right. He is and I was.

As we near Liverpool we get off the M6 and take about five million turns on what pass for direct routes in Lancashire and then suddenly, right across the street from a housing development, there are the magnificent Victorian gates marking the entrance to Hollistan House. An attendant has hurried out of the small brownstone gatehouse and approaches Alexandra's limo in front of us. Then he dashes back into the house and the iron gates start to open. We drive along a wooded drive, past what I think are fields, and then turn up a gravel drive to view the house in all its nighttime glory.

There are towers, turrets and pillars, windows, a balustrade and a dual set of stairs leading up to the great front doors. "Wow," Emmett says. "Who owns this place?"

"Unfortunately the Hollistan family is no longer here," the driver tells us. "They lost the estate to death duties when the last marquis died. The Bennington Corporation bought it. It's one of the nicest private luxury hotels in Europe."

The Bennington Corporation, I know, is also owned by the outfit that bought International News Service two years ago, the network we're visiting.

"Almost all the great Lancashire families are gone now," the driver says.

"What about Croxteth?" Emmett asks. "I keep seeing signs for it."

"It's in the hands of the Trust, sir. One of the older houses to be sure, but the family has nie been here for fifty years or more."

"I know I've read about an old family estate around here

somewhere," I say, ducking to better see the gargoyles on the house. "It's not open to the public or anything, though."

He follows the first limo around the circular drive, glancing at me in the rearview mirror. "You must mean the Derbys, miss. The Nineteenth Earl and The Countess are still in residence at Knowsley Hall. They've done a magnificent job of restoring the place—the wife got to visit there with her history club." He eases the car to a stop. "Twenty-five hundred acres, all enclosed, and parts of the hall are more than six hundred years old."

"That's okay," Emmett says, opening his door, "I'm okay with this house."

As badly as I feel for the Hollistan family to lose their ancestral home, I too am thrilled to be staying here. We climb out of the car and are greeted by the head butler, William. The limousines speed off to the servants' entrance where our baggage will be unloaded.

"Langley says they keep a stable," Alexandra whispers as we go in. "If you want we can probably take a ride tomorrow."

"I'm there," I assure her, looking around in amazement. The entrance hall mimics the outside with twin staircases curling up to the second landing. A huge crystal chandelier hangs over us, and although I can see the old master paintings are copies (they must be; who in their right mind would let people near them if they were real?), they are large and beautiful and the whole place has cast a hush over us.

"Oh, Mr. Peterson," Adele finally says, "thank you so much for including me."

"And me," I add.

"And me," Emmett says.

"Well, hey, guys," a friendly southern drawl calls from somewhere on the second floor. Jackson Darenbrook then appears at the railing, pulling himself along on crutches. "Have a good flight?"

A chorus of yeses ensue.

"Ya'll are going to be shown to your rooms. Don't bother changing, just wash your hands and go to the Walnut Room for a nightcap with the INS fellas. They've been waitin' up to make sure you got here okay, what with Sally's psycho fan base and all."

I roll my eyes.

"Sally's brought the FBI with her," Langley calls to his brother-in-law. "Jackson? Where are you going?"

"Gotta take the elevator," comes the answer from the shadows. "Already fell down the damn stairs once today."

"Did he really?" Alexandra asks the butler.

"Yes, Miss Waring, I must reluctantly confirm that he did." The butler turns away to call, "Dennis." Moments later a fresh-faced young man, dressed smartly in dark slacks, a white shirt and dark tie appears. "You may show Mr. Peterson, Mr. Rafferty and Mr. Phelps to their rooms, Dennis, and I shall show the ladies to theirs. Madam," he says, bending slightly to offer an arm to Adele.

She accepts the assistance and they lead the way over the rich red carpeting on the right-hand staircase. The steps are shallow and wide, perhaps one stair for every one and a half we have in the United States.

"You've got to take a picture of me for the kids," Emmett tells me from the other staircase across the entrance hall.

The hallway leading to our rooms is extremely narrow but has a high ceiling with occasional small domes of opaque glass. William explains the width as an attempt to discourage drafts in the days before central heating and he adds the skylights were a means of utilizing natural illumination during the day.

Adele is dropped off first, to a door on the left, where, William explains, her bags will arrive shortly. Sasha is then shown to a door on the right side of the hall. "As requested, Mrs. Punjab, there is a door adjoining Miss Harrington's dressing room."

"There go my private parties," I joke.

My quarters are unreal. To start with, the bedroom is huge and looks out over the front of the house. There is a lovely beige-and-mahogany canopy bed and a gas fire burning in the fireplace. The desk and chairs are at least a hundred years old, the windows at least ten feet high and the heavy velvet drapes at least eleven feet long. Then there is the bathroom of white tile and brass fixtures, and in the very center is the biggest old-fashioned claw-foot tub I've ever seen. Suspended from the ceiling is a circular shower curtain. Hot water pipes run through the towel racks and there is a separate closet for the actual pull-chain toilet. The far side of the bathroom opens onto a dressing room, which contains a large vanity table, two walnut wardrobes and three standing mirrors.

I cross the dressing room to turn the key in the door there and knock. After several moments I hear Sasha say to come in. I open the door and immediately feel sort of bad because I think my dressing room is bigger than her whole bedroom and bath put together. There is only one window in here, too, but I realize this is still a very special accommodation, smaller but in some ways, more charming than mine. The full-size bed is piled high with comfy quilts and pillows, the single armchair is upholstered in a soft chintz, the wallpaper is stunning, and there is a gas fire going in the little marble fireplace that makes it warm and inviting. Sasha, it appears, is utterly delighted.

"I'm afraid to show you my room," I tell her.

"I already know all about it," she assures me, waving a folder at me. "I have the floor plans."

"Oh. So do you want me to keep this door unlocked?"

"Whatever makes you most comfortable."

"I'll leave it unlocked," I tell her. "The dressing room's here, then the bath—" I wave her off. "But you just told me you know all that."

"Excuse me, Miss Harrington," a voice says from behind me. I turn around. It is a young woman dressed in a uniform. "Do you require some assistance with unpacking, miss?"

At first I tell her no, but end up sending her racing out with a crumpled skirt from one of my suitcases.

I take care in washing up, brushing my hair and applying a little makeup, and by the time I emerge from the bathroom the girl is knocking on my door to deliver the skirt, freshly pressed and still warm from an iron.

A person could get used to this.

Alexandra stops by to pick me up (nodding in approval at my skirt) and we stop by Sasha's room. We skip Adele's because Langley told her to go straight to bed. A houseboy backs himself against the wall as we pass; he is holding a small silver tray holding a mug of cocoa and a single rose in a vase, which I assume is being taken to Langley's administrative assistant.

"This must be costing a fortune," I murmur to Alexandra.

"Synergy, they say," she whispers.

"Why can't our synergy include a hotel like this?" I whisper back.

We descend the main staircase and find our way to the Walnut Room. Alexandra and I tentatively smile at each other as we go in and Sasha stays outside. Langley, Will and Emmett are already there and have drinks in their hands. Two gentlemen turn around as we enter.

"You shouldn't have waited up for us," Alexandra says, crossing the room with an extended hand and one of her better smiles. "But I'm so glad you did. It is wonderful to see you again."

Jackson is throwing a log on the fire in the massive stone fireplace. He straightens up, holding an iron poker, and gives me a little wave. If I am not mistaken, he may be half in the bag.

I am introduced to the financial director of INS, a rather stiff fellow named Manifred Slatts, and am slightly dismayed when it becomes clear that I am expected to call him Manifred. Not Manny, not Fred or Freddie, but Manifred, as if I'm speaking to a seventeenth-century soothsayer. The man is shy, awkward and uncomfortable. "A great pleasure, Manifred," I tell him, shaking his hand.

He mumbles something I can't understand and I am introduced to the president of INS, a finely chiseled and vaguely swaggering man called Reggie Hume. "Hume, like the philosopher," he says, "my grandfather eight times removed."

I look over to see how Alexandra reacts to this announcement but find that everybody is rushing over to Jackson because his sock, on the foot of his broken leg, appears to be on fire. I don't think anyone's particularly worried about Jackson; I think it's the prospect of somehow damaging this elegant room that has everybody panicked. But Jackson has it all under control, simply bending over to yank off the offending sock and throwing it into the fire.

"I *am* sorry, Manifred," Jackson says, sounding suspiciously close to sarcasm. "First I nearly break my neck on your staircase and now I'm going up in flames. I'm your worst liability nightmare."

People laugh politely but because Manifred doesn't react at all, it turns into an awkward moment. The financial director looks upset and Jackson looks ill-tempered. Alexandra and Will have pulled Reggie aside to talk about a documentary they wish INS to be involved in, Emmett wanders off to look at a painting and Jackson and Manifred seem glumly stuck with each other.

Whatever happened here earlier couldn't have been particularly good.

"Manifred," I say, stepping forward, "are *you* related to any philosopher?"

He bows his head slightly. "No."

"Good, then we have a lot in common," I tell him. "I'm not, either."

Manifred's eyes dart over to meet mine. His brow furrows slightly, unsure. But then there is a hint of a smile and he says, "May I offer you something to drink, Sally?"

"Half a glass of white wine would be lovely, thank you, but let me walk over there with you." I glance back over my shoulder to look at our CEO. He offers a wink to me in gratitude, but it is without the jovial spirits that have always been his trademark. If I am not mistaken, he's even scowling at Alexandra.

"He's very angry," Alexandra later confirms while she's changing for bed in the bathroom.

If I thought I was the honored guest, you should see Alexandra's rooms. She has a corner bedroom with four windows, two overlooking the park in back of the house and two facing east over an elaborate garden. There is also a single French door leading out to a small cement balcony. Her fire is real; chunks of wood blazing cozily in an iron grate.

The bathroom door swings fully open and Alexandra comes out in a fluffy Hollistan House robe, tying the belt securely around her narrow waist. "He's on painkillers and his tibia's smashed and INS started backpedaling on aspects of our deal today."

"I thought it was a done deal." I'm sitting by the fire, drinking water from a glass.

"Nothing is a done deal in life," she says absently, looking through her briefcase. Her cell phone starts to ring. "Now what?"

she sighs, walking to her night table. She flips the phone open, looks at the screen, says, "What do you suppose area code question mark, question mark, question mark is?" and clicks it on. "Hello?" She immediately smiles. "Not yet. Sally and I were just rehashing the bizarre welcoming festivities, which included your husband looking as though he wanted to go fisticuffs with Manifred Slatts. Oh, and he caught on fire." She looks at me. "No, Jackson did. His sock. He was throwing a log on the fire and suddenly there was smoke coming from his foot." She smiles, a little sadly, I think.

"She did great. She charmed Manifred, if you can believe." She glances over at me. "I don't know, I'll have to ask her." She yawns, walking into the bathroom. She signals for me to wait and closes the door. "I hope so," I hear her say, but then I hear another door closing and I don't know where she's gone, but I can't hear her anymore. She must be in her dressing room; I can't believe she'd talk to anyone while she was in the john.

I walk over to the bookcase to see what she has in here. I pull out what looks to be a very old slip-cased volume, *Proper Codes and Conduct for the Young Gentleman,* and sit down by the fire to look at it.

"Me, too," I hear Alexandra say. The bathroom door opens and Alexandra emerges, holding the phone out to me. "She'd like to speak to you."

I take the phone. "Hi, Cassy."

"Can this be true?" Cassy says. "*Manifred* smiled at you? Manifred Slatts hasn't smiled at anybody or anything in the ten years I've known him."

"Was that a smile?" I ask Alexandra. "I didn't realize."

"Sally, was Jackson as bad as Alexandra says?"

"He wasn't bad," I say. "He just wasn't himself."

Pause. "He's got a lot on his plate," she says quietly.

"Alexandra slept on the flight," I report, watching the anchorwoman frown at me, "and now it appears she's going to bed."

"Great," Alexandra mutters, "the sleep police."

"See that she does, Sally, thank you. And thank you for being you. Alexandra says this is the kind of situation where you shine and she's right. You have no idea how much easier it is for every-body to have you there."

I'm not sure I've ever received such generous praise from Cassy.

After hanging up with Cassy, I agree that if Alexandra can swing some horses from the stable tomorrow, I will go riding with her during our late afternoon recess. We say good-night and, feeling exhausted suddenly, I return to my room. I find that my bed has been turned down and a small box of chocolate truffles has been left on my pillow.

I smile.

I change into my nightie and prepare for bed. Then I wrap myself in a robe, turn out the lights and sit in one of the win-dow seats, looking out at the night. The windows are tall and the panes large. The drive is lined in small lights; the flags are flap-ping wildly in the wind.

A wave of sadness comes over me. Paul. I've done my best not to think about him, about how awful the scene in Los Angeles was. I called him and left a lengthy message, but he has not called back. I doubt that he will.

I started to cry while leaving the message because I am upset with how it all came about. The idea that Paul had so happily planned his surprise visit only to arrive and think I was cheat-ing on him just kills me. I told him again in my message that I had not been sexually involved with David Waring or anyone else since the day we met, but yes, it was true, I do have feelings for David. And only just now had I learned he was divorced. I swore to Paul again I never cheated on him, told him I would always care about him and that almost any woman had more to offer him than I did.

I dreaded telling Mother what happened, but I needed to talk to someone. When David's name came up, she said a soft, "Oh." She knew there had been something between us before and she seemed not in the least surprised when I told her I was in love with him.

"The worst thing is," I told her, "no matter what I tell Paul, he will always think I chose David because he is more successful."

"How could anyone at his age be considered more successful than Paul?"

"Mother, he just doesn't get it. He thinks it's about money and prestige. I don't know why, but he's just so focused on that."

She was silent for a while and then said, "I won't call him, Sally, but he might call me."

Poor Mother. Paul wouldn't be the first.

"There are some things I can say that maybe he can hear coming from me. Just make sure you do talk to him, Sally, or maybe write to him, and give him some kind of closure."

I rub my face. Love can be so horrible and so wonderful at the same time. I sigh, dropping my hands in my lap. Of course, I bared my soul to Mother about everything except the fact that some psycho is running around killing people for me.

But they'll find the guy, I know they will. They always do.

I close the velvet drapes and feel my way across the room and climb into bed. The sheets are fine and the bed very comfortable.

I say my prayers, spending a lot of time on the long list of thank-yous and please-watch-overs.

A knock on my door in the morning is followed by the appearance of the same sweet maid as the night before, only this time she is carrying an impressive tray of breakfast silver. She sets it down on the ottoman in front of the easy chair by the window and begins lifting silver covers to show me the various foods being kept warm beneath. Two poached eggs. Potatoes. Fruit salad. Bacon. Kidneys. (These are an accident and she takes them away.) Toast. I tell her I've never seen such a lovely breakfast, particularly the bacon.

"The American predilection for what we call fatty bacon does leave us a bit puzzled," she admits, pouring me a cup of coffee.

"We don't choose it," I explain, "we're force-fed it. So do you work here full-time?"

"Only when they have guests in the house, miss, and my schedule permits." She pronounces this *shedule*. "I'm at university in Manchester."

"Oh, that's wonderful." So is the coffee. "What are you studying?"

"Art history, miss."

"Ah." I take another sip of coffee. I thought English coffee was supposed to be terrible. "And what paintings would you suggest I look at in the house?"

She hesitates, coloring slightly.

"They're all copies, eh?"

"Many are rather good, miss," she hastens to say. "I wouldn't want to suggest you could not enjoy them."

I smile. "You'll do well," I tell her. "Do you happen to know if Alexandra Waring is up yet?"

"Oh, yes, she went out early this morning, for a run, I believe."

After Miss University has departed, as I have now come to think of her, I return my attention to my laptop as I start eating my breakfast. I downloaded last night's newscast from West End and have been watching it.

It was Bill Randolph's third night sitting in as anchor and I have to say I am a bit in awe. He is one of those people whose appearance alters for the better with the distortion of the camera lens. The studio setting seems to do something for him as well: he has an all-encompassing sense of knowingness about him; he is not vain, not posturing. He's just got *it,* whatever that quality is that makes you trust someone on TV.

Of course experience never hurts and Bill has a lot of it.

There is a knock on my door and I take a last bite of eggs before getting up to answer it. "Hi," Will and Alexandra say, waltzing in past me.

"You *are* watching it," Will says, walking over to my breakfast tray. "I saw in the log you downloaded it."

"So what do you think?" Alexandra asks, plunking down on my bed. She is still in her jogging clothes and sneakers and frankly looks wonderful. The color is high in her cheeks, her eyes are wide and rested, and her hair looks amazingly nice simply slung back in a ponytail.

"You can have the potatoes," I tell Will, "but if you touch the bacon you're history." I hand him a salad fork and the silver serving dish they're in. He drops down in the chair opposite me and happily digs in.

"I have to say," I begin, looking over at Alexandra, "Bill is the first substitute anchor I've seen who can hold his own in your absence. And I'm stunned. I had no idea. He doesn't have all of this—" I gesture to my laptop. "Whatever it is he seems to have in the studio, when he's out in the field. But he's good in the field. But different."

Alexandra is nodding. "I agree."

"He anchored years ago—maybe twenty?—in St. Louis," Will says.

"He's officially my number-one substitute anchor now," Alexandra says.

I blink several times, a little surprised.

Will swallows some potatoes. "She's trying to get over her unhealthy reliance on you, Sally. She's been making decisions all by herself all morning."

"I had a dream last night," I tell them as I cut my bacon with a knife and fork, "that Jackson sold me to INS and I was Manifred's girlfriend."

"It's funny you should say that," Will says, "because that is exactly what's happened. You've been sold and Manny's asking for you."

I throw my napkin at him. "So what is going on, anyway? Is the deal on or off?"

Alexandra shrugs. "We're supposed to go into town as planned and tour the studio. They had scheduled a photo shoot and as far as I know that's still on. Oh, Sally, Cleo says for you to wear the pale gray suit and I am to wear the blue."

"You always get to wear the blue," I say.

"And I think the dinner must be still on," Will says. "Dennis took my white dinner jacket this morning to get it cleaned and pressed."

"Our dresses are downstairs somewhere," Alexandra says. "They're ready to go. We're bringing back some hair-and-makeup person with us from Liverpool."

"Where's the secret agent?" Will asks me.

"She's around," I assure him. "I think something might be happening back in the States because she's been on the phone for most of the morning." I look at Alexandra. "What exactly is wrong with the INS deal, do you know?"

"Well," she sighs, getting up to help herself to a bottle of water, "they do business differently from the way the past owners did. And I think Jackson resents how they bought INS in the first place, in a hostile takeover, and Lord Hargrave, whom we were all great friends with, died shortly after that. Jackson thinks it was the stress of the takeover that did it."

Lord Hargrave's title was given to him for revolutionizing English television with the first satellite-distribution system. As I understand it, it was he who first interested Jackson in a satellite for the Darenbrook newspapers, which, in turn, gave birth to DBS.

"So we're just supposed to pretend there is a deal in place?"

"For the moment," she says. She takes the cap off the water and drinks from the bottle. Then she pushes back her sleeve to look at her watch. "We better get ready, guys."

When I am dressed and ready and emerge from my rooms I find Sasha in the hallway waiting for me. She could be taken for one of our producers the way she is dressed and I ask her if she would like to pretend to be one. "That won't be necessary," she tells me.

We descend the front stairs and walk outside where three limos are waiting. The first is a Rolls, the second a Jag and the third a Bentley, all of them glistening under the bright spring Lancashire sun. Alexandra looks like a million bucks and is standing with Emmett, the latter of whom looks not only totally at home here in his tweed jacket and brown dress slacks, but appears to be almost dashing. He's bucking up. Will is talking on his cell phone, pacing in the driveway. In the distance there are sheep grazing in the fields and I can hear the bleating of lambs. The only unharmonious aspect of the scene is Jackson, who twenty yards away is gesturing wildly with his crutch at Langley. Langley just keeps talking and shaking his head, refusing to back off, regardless of how close Jackson yells in his face.

"It doesn't seem to be going very well," Alexandra says to me, noticing my arrival.

"You look great, Sally," Emmett says.

"But you look the best," I tell Emmett, slinging my arm through his.

"I feel great," he announces. Then his face darkens little. "But Alexandra says it may not happen, the deal with INS."

"I'm sure something will be worked out," she says. "And I think your half hour will do just fine."

"Oh, I hope so," Emmett says. "I've got cousins in Birmingham who want to see it."

When Emmett starts making small talk with Sasha Punjab—he's fascinated with a bombing case she once worked on—Alexandra edges nearer. "The overhead they want to charge us is outrageous. They've put London labor costs in for a Liverpool production. It's ridiculous."

"But why would they do this? At this late date?"

She lifts her eyebrows. "They must have another suitor."

"I wish Cassy was here," I say.

"No, you don't."

I look at her. "Why?"

Alexandra walks toward Will, pretending she did not hear me.

We leave Hollistan House without our CEO. After Jackson savagely bangs and crashes his way on his crutches into the house without speaking to us, Langley asks that Alexandra and Will ride with him in the Rolls and that Emmett, Sasha and I take the Jaguar.

Our ride into Liverpool is short and pleasant. We come into the city on a route showing several grand eighteenth-century buildings that have been restored. I am surprised by the light and air of the city because I had always heard it was, well, a dump.

It's not. To the contrary, there seems to be an extraordinary amount of building under way and on a scale I haven't seen since Dublin was flooded with money from the European Union.

"Liverpool is a UNESCO World Heritage site," Emmett says. "United Nations Educational, Scientific and Cultural Organization."

"A world heritage site built on the blood of the slave trade," Sasha says.

"It was the port of everything for everybody all over the world," Emmett protests.

"I thought it was the home of the Beatles," I say, trying to lighten the mood.

If our executives are having problems with one another it is not evident in the warm reception we receive at the INS studios. The co-anchors of the half hour of international news we

already import from INS, Leona Thistle and Ronald Law, give
us a tour of the facility, where employees are touchingly kind in
their praise.

TV "newsreaders," as they call anchors over here, are not stars
like they can be in the U.S. They are allowed to have imperfect
smiles, normal faces and are even allowed to age. Those who do
happen to be very good-looking usually get their teeth bonded,
their hair bleached and take the first plane to America. "It's
frankly a relief, Sally," Leona confides to me. "I look at you and
Alexandra and thank *God* I'm in Blighty because in America I
would be out of work."

"But you are popular in the States," I tell her.

"I've seen our ratings, Sally," she says, "and besides you and
my son at Harvard University I'm not sure many people are
watching."

"The demographics, though, Leona, surely you've seen those."

She meets my eye almost shyly. "A highly educated lot, it
would seem."

"I'll say. Who's ever heard of the Ford Foundation advertising
on a commercial newscast?"

At noon we are taken into a surprisingly large conference
room off the INS newsroom. They have placed the anchors at a
long table in front, where we share a couple of standing micro-
phones, and the employees sit in rows as an audience. Box lunches
are handed out to all and a refreshment stand along the side of
the room has tea and coffee and soft drinks.

I like this. Make it casual and on the traditional employee lunch
hour so anybody from the company can come.

I have no idea where Langley has disappeared to.

We begin by Ronald Law briefly outlining what is proposed
as a partnership between our news groups: that DBS will increase
its international news coverage from a half hour to one full hour
nightly; and for the first time DBS News will provide a live half
hour newscast for INS, which will focus on news out of
Washington, D.C., Wall Street and Hollywood.

"Not to detract from Sally and Emmett, Alexandra," a woman
asks, "but why aren't you doing the newscast for us?"

"Because I'm exhausted," the anchorwoman says, making

them laugh. "Seriously, that is a real factor. The idea is to maintain a certain level of excellence and even I'm not getting any younger."

"You're a hell of a lot younger than I am!" Ronald says, making everyone laugh again.

"There was also a request that the half hour be live," Alexandra continues, "and it works out much better with Sally and Emmett doing it. On their early morning newscast for us in America, Sally and Emmett will be largely drawing on the stories not only from my newscast the night before, but from your morning news over here."

"So are you doing international news at all during your newscast?" a man asks Alexandra.

"We do a headline service on breaking international news and then refer them to your newscast for in-depth coverage."

"How are we supposed to keep a straight face when you keep pretending the American president has a brain in his head?" a snide young woman asks, which, sadly, prompts some laughter.

"Not only should you keep a straight face," Emmett says in his teacher voice, "but you would do well to offer the respect that is due the most powerful man on earth."

An uncomfortable silence ensues, so I lean forward into the microphone. "Emmett happens to be running for president," I deadpan.

"Alexandra, you said something before about the caliber of writing being so important," a woman says.

"Yes," Alexandra says, nodding.

"So if writing is the key to a good newscast, then why are all of you so good-looking?" A little laughter.

I lean forward. "Because our ancestors left England?" I suggest.

There is laughter mixed in with a few good-natured boos. As I assure them they are indeed members of the finest-looking lifeforms in the universe, I see Manifred Slatts slipping into the back of the room. Still no sign of Langley.

Emmett is asked about how well is he acquainted with English law, and when he explains how he switched classrooms for two years with a dean of law at Cambridge they seem pleased.

There is some discussion about the ability of normal working people in England to identify with us and I talk a bit about my upbringing in Castleford, a background, I explain, which I think is helpful.

"Where I grew up in New England is not terribly unlike the Liverpool-to-Manchester area," I explain. "The young people, if they have stayed—and most don't—don't do what our parents did for a living, often because the way they made their living doesn't even exist anymore."

There are murmurs of recognition in the group. Birmingham, Manchester, Liverpool, they identify.

"But this has nothing to do with how I present the news," I tell them. "It merely offers a comfortable avenue for me to participate in community events in this particular area of the country, and I think Emmett would be great in London, Oxford, Cambridge. Do invite us over for a charity fund-raiser or two each year." I gesture to Emmett. "We both do it at home and we'd love to help here if we can."

"What about big Hollywood stars?" someone calls. "We want that on your newscast."

"And you will certainly get them," Alexandra says. She explains what they have heard is true, that Jessica Wright is returning to DBS, and that DBS News—and therefore INS—will have first excerpts from her celebrity interviews.

The discussion turns to the difference between what INS is airing in America and what DBS will be airing in England. "The idea is to expand each other's viewership," Emmett says.

"And we're offering your viewers a window on what makes America tick," I add.

"And what does make America tick?" Manifred Slatts asks from the back of the room. His employees appear somewhat astounded he has spoken.

I glance at Emmett and then Alexandra; they defer to me. "What makes America tick," I say, "is the use and abuse of our Constitution, the power and pitfalls of money, and a need to escape the harsh realities of the use and abuse of our Constitution and the power and pitfalls of money!" There is scattered applause and Emmett and Alexandra nod in approval.

Alexandra goes on to talk about some of the *DBS News Magazine* stories we will be offering to INS and then we wrap up, the hour being over, and promise a fun visual presentation tonight at the Hollistan House dinner. Leona asks the group for one last question.

A man stands up. "Should we be scared of getting beaten up if we say anything bad about you, Sally?"

The group breaks into whispers, seemingly scandalized by the reference to Al Royce. I'm surprised they even know about it. When they are quiet I smile at the man who asked the question and say, simply, "Yes." The room breaks into applause.

They like me. It feels great.

I wish David were here to see it.

"No, they're okay," I say, flexing my feet in the stirrups, "it just feels strange to be wearing someone else's boots."

"It's not as if anyone still wears them," Alexandra says, breaking into a posting trot.

"Oh, great, whoever these belong to is dead?" I ask, commencing a trot on my mare, a chestnut named Sybil. (Let us hope she is not the multifaceted American kind.)

"He said they were left in the stables years ago!" she calls back.

We drove back from INS in as good spirits as one could be, given the fact our chief operating officer, Langley Peterson, did not return with us to Hollistan House and our chief executive officer, Jackson Darenbrook, had evidently commandeered our plane and left the country.

When Alexandra swung into my room to tell me we could get a couple of horses from the stable, I jumped at the chance. To ride across a Victorian estate like this is a dream. I was outfitted at the stable with ankle-high laced riding boots, but Alexandra stuck with her running shoes since, at this point in her riding life, she scarcely needs a saddle. Donning velvet-covered riding hats (read pretty helmets), we were off.

The sky is blue with fleecy white clouds, the wind is blowing and the fields are rippling in new green. We pass though a field of daffodils and look back to see an amazing view of Hollistan House. There are birds out here who sound like nothing I've ever heard before ("Partridges and grouse, possibly," Alexandra says). As we ride past pastures we hear the bleats of the newborn lambs learning to walk on their own and see calves lounging clumsily around their mothers.

We find the nicely tended trail the groom told us about and Alexandra coaxes her dapple gray, Windemere, into an easy cantor, and Sybil just seems content to simply do whatever Windemere does. As the trail narrows around the lake, we slow to a walk and Alexandra starts pointing out plants and bushes and trees, telling me what can grow at home in the northeast and what can't. We see a crane standing on a half-submerged log; ducks are swimming in the shallows; the breezes send ripples across the lake and shimmer the reflection of trees and blue sky.

As we emerge from the woods around the lake, the trail widens again and Alexandra falls back to ride next to me. "I hope you're pleased with yourself," she says, "because I am very, very proud of you."

"I thought Emmett was wonderful."

"The proper response to a compliment," Alexandra says, leaning my way to catch my eye, "is to hear it, let it register and then say thank you."

"Thank you," I say, meaning it.

"You had thirty people in that room who are going to scream if the deal isn't done. Once they get over the we're-good-looking-because-our-ancestors-left-England remark, that is."

I laugh. "I meant it as a compliment."

"I don't think it was taken as one."

"They certainly don't seem like a very happy lot at INS, do they?"

"They've been through a lot. A hostile takeover is rough."

"Speaking of turmoil, what is with Jackson? He was a nutcase this morning."

We ride along.

"Alexandra?"

"I don't know what to tell you," she says, watching a bird flying overhead.

"Because you don't know what to say or because you don't know what's wrong with Jackson?"

She stands up in her stirrups, flexing her back. "A little of both."

I prod Sybil. She's taking a very unproductive interest in the new spring shoots, trying to sneak little munches in here and there. "So you do know what's going on?"

Alexandra and Windemere break into a cantor.

"Come *on,* Sybil," I urge her, pulling her head away from a sapling and giving her a little kick. Alexandra is way the heck down the trail and turning onto a smooth dirt lane. When I finally catch up with her Alexandra's not even on Windermere anymore, but has dismounted to open the gate to a field. We walk through and then she follows, pulling Windemere through, and reaches over to lock the gate. She leads Windemere around, steps up on the first white rail of the fence and swings herself up in the saddle in a way I couldn't do in a million years.

"I don't want to scare the lambs," I say, pointing across the field.

"We're just going over there," she answers, pointing down along the fence. "The groom said there was another good trail on that side."

The lambs are darling, fuzzy little animals. "What will happen to them?" I ask. "Never mind, don't tell me, I don't want to know," I add quickly, vowing never to eat lamb again. I can't think about the calves, either. Veal.

"Let's hope they're being raised for wool," Alexandra says, taking care to steer Windemere around some rocks and pits. "And the calves will replenish a dairy herd."

"I don't see a great future for boy calves, then."

"Boy calves," Alexandra repeats, laughing. She looks at me and not for the first time do I realize how at home she is out here. This is a woman who belongs outside. It shows in the sparkle of her eyes and the glow of her smile. "I thought you grew up on a farm."

"*Next* to a farm," I correct her.

"Well, it's a good thing because I'm not sure the world is ready for boy calves." She's still laughing to herself; I can see her shoulders still shaking in front me.

"I'll get this one," I offer as we approach the gate. I slide off Sybil and reach through the fence to pull up the latch, then walk it back. Sybil chomps down on a tree branch and seems determined to rip the tree out of the ground by the roots to take it with us.

Alexandra and Windemere walk on to the promised trail and take off. Muttering under my breath, I have to get the branch out of Sybil's mouth, walk her through the gate, lock it, and then find a tree stump to get back on her. By now Alexandra could be home in New Jersey. Still, once I am back on Sybil and cantering along at a comfortable lope, I wonder if riding ever gets better than this.

About a quarter mile down I come upon Alexandra and Windemere waiting for us. I am reluctant to break our pace, but slow Sybil down to a walk.

"Don't look now," Alexandra says quietly, as we draw near, "but to your right, behind the stone wall, there's somebody there."

"Probably one of the estate workers," I say, resisting the urge to look.

"If it is, he's a creepy one, because he's been skulking around following us on a bike since we left the lake."

I frown. "Why didn't you say anything?"

"I wanted to make sure," she says. "I think he might be a photographer."

"Finally, a photographer when we aren't doing anything to be embarrassed about!" I say to the sky.

"Come on," she says, reining Windemere around in a tight circle, "let's find out who he is."

"Why? Who cares? Let's just get out of here."

But Alexandra prompts Windemere into a cantor and heads for the stone wall, and sure enough, I can see somebody scrambling behind a big oak. Alexandra and Windemere sail over the wall with room to spare and on that side she circles around and I urge Sybil forward to see better. There is a gunshot and I see Windemere rear in terror. Alexandra stays on him, but then there is another shot and Windemere skids madly to the side before rearing up again, and this time Alexandra is thrown. In a second I am off Sybil and climbing over the stone wall while a guy in a brown jacket and brown pants pedals furiously down the lane on a tan mountain bike. Windemere has galloped out of sight.

I can see immediately by the way she is lying that Alexandra's broken her arm. Thank God she had on a riding hat. She is looking up at the sky, seemingly stunned or in shock. I yank off my hat and pull off my sweater. I lay it over her chest and take the moment to move her arm into a natural position. She does not seem to feel it.

That's not good.

"Let's just wait a minute before you try to move," I tell her. I am terrified she's broken her back. She's blinking, at least, which is a good sign. Then tears start to pool in her eyes. She's scared, too.

"Okay now," I say quietly, pulling a strand of her hair from her mouth, "can you move your feet at all?"

Merciful God, thank you, I think as she moves her feet.

"Excellent," I murmur. "Your right arm? Do you know which one is your right arm?"

She moves her right arm.

"You've broken your left arm just below the elbow," I tell her. I look around. Sybil is merrily grazing at the side of the wall. I shouldn't leave Alexandra. But how am I going to get her out of here? "We need to borrow Sybil's saddle blanket," I tell her, hurrying back over the wall. I take Sybil's reins in hand and, much to her joy, draw up a stirrup, unbuckle the saddle and drop it on the ground. I take the damp gray saddle blanket from her back and leave Sybil to do as she may.

The sun is starting to go down and I need to keep Alexandra warm. I cover her with the damp blanket, saying, "We need something for a splint." I hope I sound confident. "I think one of those branches might work." The dead branches turn out to be too crooked to be useful but I find a huge hunk of tree bark that seems promising.

"Are we making a canoe?" she asks, eyeing it upon my return to her side.

Thank God she's with it again. "If I use two pieces of this, one on top of the other, we can keep your arm straight in the smooth part."

"And when I start screaming," she begins, grimacing.

We both hear the rev of an engine and moments later a green Land Rover comes bouncing up the lane on the other side of the wall. It stops near Sybil and the groom and another man jump out. "She's broken her arm," I call to them. "We need a blanket and a first-aid kit if you've got it."

The men briefly confer and then the groom hurries over the wall while the other man runs back to the truck. "I knew something was wrong when Windemere came back to the stable," the groom says, squatting down on the other side of Alexandra. "I thought I heard shots."

"There's a guy running around with a gun," I tell him. "He's on a mountain bike and he fired twice to deliberately scare Windemere."

"Was he out here to shoot?"

"I never heard of anyone shooting game with a handgun," I tell him.

The other man arrives with a large towel and a first-aid kit. "An ambulance is coming," he tells us.

"I don't need an ambulance," Alexandra says, still lying there on the ground with her helmet on. "Help me sit up."

We look at each other, fearing that moving her might do something awful.

"You start and we'll help," I say. If she can't get far then we'll know how badly damaged she is.

Alexandra moves her head around a little and slides one foot back, bending her knee. When she tries to push herself up with her good arm she pales and falters. Then she faints dead away.

"Quick," I tell the groom, "those scissors, please. We need to see what's going on under here." I start at the end of her sleeve and make progress cutting my way up. I tell the man to call the police, about the guy on the bike deliberately scaring the horse.

"That's a nasty one," the groom says on an intake of breath.

The jagged edge of Alexandra's broken bone had punctured her skin, but now that the arm is aligned it's at least not bleeding too badly, but bad enough that we need to bind the wound.

The groom takes over from me, dressing the wound with hands that have helped to heal heaven only knows how many horses over the years.

Something called an "ambulette" arrives at the same Sasha and Langley are driven up in an estate pickup truck. As the emergency workers tend to Alexandra—handing me, in succession, the horse blanket, my sweater and then Alexandra's riding helmet—they fire questions at her. What is her name? Does she know what day it is? Where she is? Is she pregnant? What allergies does she have? They give her a shot of morphine, and when that kicks in, they put a splint on her arm and lift her onto a stretcher.

"They got him," Sasha says to me as we watch the doors of the ambulette close.

I turn around to look at her. "The guy with the gun?"

She nods. "And I want you to come with me now to see if you recognize him."

I don't suppose it is appropriate to call a police station adorable, but when it is housed in a such a charmingly maintained Victorian cottage it's difficult to call it anything else. We have arrived just behind the Lancashire police. When we walk inside the perp is still in the reception area, his arms handcuffed behind him, and when he sees me his eyes widen slightly. So he knows who I am, I surmise.

"You don't have to go any closer," Sasha says, touching my arm.

The man is about five-nine, stocky, square actually, with dark tightly curled hair and blue eyes. He's in his late twenties, maybe early thirties, and looks as though his nose has been broken once or twice.

"I have no idea who he is," I tell Sasha, turning around and walking out of the station. I wait for her outside and become preoccupied, watching villagers who are driving by take a particular interest in me. I finally look down and realize my blouse has blood on it. Sasha comes out with a young bobby. "This officer will take you back to the house, Sally, and I will be along soon."

"I hope you find out who he is," I tell her.

"I intend to."

"And I hope you find out he has nothing to do with me."

She meets my eyes. "We already know he has something to do with you, Sally. He was carrying a picture of you."

I look down at the ground. "Do you think he was going to hurt me?"

"If he wanted to, he could easily have shot one or both of you," she says.

I bring a hand up to cover my face. "I just don't get it."

"I want you to go back to the house and get some rest," Sasha says.

I turn to the bobby. "I want to see how my friend is."

"She is a fair piece away, Miss Harrington," he says politely. "They've taken her into Liverpool."

When I am driven back to Hollistan House I am more than astonished to find the tent on the near side of Hollistan House bustling with activity as if nothing has happened. Barrels of ice are being hand-trucked across the lawn; kerosene space heaters are being set up; a stream of workers, in smart black skirts or pants and white shirts, are streaming from the house into the tent and back again. When I step out of the police car I smell the most delicious aromas.

The fact that one of the guests of honor has been terribly hurt is evidently not to be viewed as a damper on corporate festivities. William, the head butler, attends to me at once when I come in the front door and I beg to simply be allowed to go to my room. In the hallway upstairs, with the bobby behind him, I hear Langley call to me. He is buttoning the sleeves of a clean white shirt "The deal is on, the dinner is on," he says. "Do you think you can do it?"

Every bone in my body is screaming, *What, are you nuts?* "I suppose it depends on whether Alexandra is dead or not," I say sarcastically.

"Alexandra is fine," he tells me, finishing his second cuff. "Bad break, very painful, but otherwise she's going to be fine. They're bringing her back tonight." He looks at his watch and then at me, biting his lower lip. "It's okay if you can't do this, but I've got to prepare Emmett if you're not up to it."

"Of course I'll do it," I tell him. Behind Langley I can see the Lancashire police officer looking sympathetically at me. It helps that someone seems to get it.

"Everyone has been told Alexandra had a fall and broke her arm," he tells me, starting to back down the hall. "Will is going to bring you the talking points of her speech."

"That won't be necessary," I tell him wearily, "because I wrote them."

A hot bath and the INS hair-and-makeup lady help restore me to the living. Actually, looking at myself in the three mirrors of my dressing room, I find it hard to believe I am the same person who came back from the police station. To cover my new scratches and bruises the makeup artist produces a flimsy white wrap. We try it over my shoulders and it looks okay.

My hands are a mess. She does her best with a quick manicure and some foundation to lessen the appearance of the cuts.

I have not seen Sasha Punjab at all.

While I am waiting for Will and Emmett to pick me up, I check my cell phone for messages. The most recent one is from Alexandra. She sounds groggy and tired, but herself. "The good news is," she says, "I've got a cast and enough painkillers to fly to the moon and back, but the bad news is, I tore ligaments in my elbow, which means surgery down the road." Pause. "I heard they caught the guy, which is great. I'm close to talking someone into giving me a lift back there. Will says you're pinch-hitting for me and I don't have to tell you how relieved I am that you feel up to it."

Will delivers me and Emmett to the banquet manager, who walks us through the torches to the central entrance of the tent. We are to stand with Leona Thistle and Ronald Law so people have a chance to meet us. (He cannot imagine how loath I am to do this, how jumpy I feel.) After relating the approved version of Alexandra's injury, I listen with envy as Leona bemoans how dull their lives at INS are, and that the only broken bone sustained by either anchor was when Ronald broke his little toe running from the bath to answer the telephone.

The INS employees and major area sponsors are arriving in vans from Liverpool, which must have given them each a license to drink because they certainly start putting it away the second they arrive. All and all they are a nice group of people, although

I am beginning to be able to tell the long-time employees from the ones hired under the new owners. Is it too transparent to say the long-time ones seem to have more consequential things to say?

There is one moment where I feel as though I am watching myself from the other side of the tent. And in this moment I think of my father, and I think of how proud of me he would be to see me like this. He would love the idea I am all dressed up (Daddy was one of those fathers who loved to see his daughter in a frilly little dress and his son in a smart little suit and tie when we went to church), and he would be pleased at how I am conducting myself.

For, despite all the insanity of this trip, I am very excited about this deal with INS, and am perhaps even more excited by being seen over British television because I never dreamed I would ever be. ("Wouldn't it be marvelous if we knew The Queen watched you?" Mother said.)

As I am chatting with an older gentleman in charge of studio props at INS (and see in his eyes the delight of receiving the attentions of a pretty young woman), I think of David and wish he could be here. And then I wonder about thinking of my father and then David, and then think, *Oh, no, don't tell me this is a father thing,* but in the next moment I know it most certainly is not since Daddy was the dreamer and the maverick of the family and David is much more like Mother, a stable, quieting force of the universe.

I will call him as soon as I know for sure Alexandra is safe and sound. In fact, I might make the call to him with Alexandra.

The people keep coming. Yes, Alexandra will be just fine and is returning to Hollistan House tonight. No, not for the party, unfortunately, but I am sure she will be back over soon. Yes, she is extraordinary. No, I believe she has always been registered as an independent. Yes, I suppose it is an unconventional lifestyle for a news anchor. No, I wasn't aware Georgiana Hamilton-Ayres attended the opening of Scottish Parliament with her father. And so on it goes.

Emmett is doing beautifully, having gained more confidence by the minute on this trip. He is a little pink in the cheeks from the attentions of so many women (and one young man) and is playing the role of a gallant.

When we are finally led to the head table I am a little perturbed to find that I am seated next to Manifred Slatts. He's just weird, there's no other way to describe him. Since there are only two women at the table, I have the INS president (heaven forbid we forget, the philosopher eight times removed) Reggie Hume on the other side of me. Next to Reggie is Emmett, then Ronald, and then Leona, with Langley at the end of the table.

The dinner is very good, with an army of waiters and waitresses filing in and out of the tent with almost military precision. Then Reggie philosophizes for a while at the microphone over dessert and then Langley tries his best to fill in for Jackson (the jokes don't go over so well with his style of delivery). I am pleased when the group seems delighted it is my turn to speak and I do my best to express the happiness we are feeling at DBS News to be working with them. I make Emmett and Leona and Ronald get up to at least say hello, and then we all sit down again as our specially prepared presentation is screened on the side of the white tent. It is a remix of our promos for DBS News, *DBS News America This Morning,* and the film INS created for its own affiliate convention the week before.

It's rather good. And it's kind of cool how we keep switching back and forth from American to English accents. Somehow it works and, as I am seen saying at its conclusion, "It makes me wonder a little about the need for the American Revolution."

The dinner has gone amazingly well and I feel surprisingly energized and happy, until, that is, I am walked up to the house and find Sasha lingering inside the front door and I wonder why she's here. I go upstairs and wait for her.

"Everyone says you were wonderful," she first tells me thoughtfully as we walk to my room.

Inside my room I ask her about the guy with the gun.

"He says he's a freelance photographer."

"And he was going to take our picture with a gun?"

"It had blanks in it."

I blink. "Blanks?"

"And he did have a camera on him, a digital. But he hadn't taken any pictures."

I try to think this through.

"Sky wants us to return to the States first thing in the morning. I agree with him. Whatever the story is on this guy we both would prefer you be at home while we find out."

I walk over to the windows to pull the velvet drapes closed. "So it really is about me, not Alexandra." I turn around. "Please tell me straight out what you think, Sasha."

"We're considering the possibility of a kidnapping attempt."

"Kidnap me," I say, pulling the silk wrap off my shoulders and laying it across the back of a chair. "In England."

"A van was found in a cattle barn that no one seems to know anything about. The things found in the van seem to support that theory. There's also evidence there may have been an accomplice."

I move on to close the drapes over the second window. "And the guy was carrying a photo of me, you said."

"Yes."

I turn around. "Sasha, I would be delighted to go home with you tomorrow."

I find there are now two uniformed bobbies stationed in the hall as I cross barefoot over the lush carpeting to knock on Alexandra's door. I knock softly, in case she is asleep, but she calls for me to come in. At least I think she does—the doors are so thick in this place I can't be sure.

By the single lamp illuminated next to her bed Alexandra looks terribly pale. But she is clean and sitting up, lounging under the bedcovers in white silk pajamas. The left sleeve of her pajamas has been removed and her arm, in a cast, is resting on a pillow beside her. She's on painkillers—you can always tell by looking at a person's pupils—and she offers me a woozy smile. "You did beautifully, I heard."

"But everybody missed you," I say quietly, pulling a chair over to sit next to the bed. There is a little fire going and it is cheery in here. It certainly beats a hospital room, although looking closely at Alexandra I am not convinced she shouldn't be in one. While I tell her about the dinner I refill her water glass and throw more chunks of wood into the fire grate. She asks a few questions but listens to my answers with her eyes closed.

Sitting again and watching her in this vulnerable state, I see how much like her brother she is. That same underlying Waring steel is there in the chin and the nose.

"Langley got through it okay," I tell her. "But the INS old-timers were all asking about Jackson."

"What did you say?"

"A problem at one of the printing plants. I'm afraid this myth-ical problem has begun to take on somewhat catastrophic pro-portions."

She smiles, eyes still closed.

"That Manifred creep said Jackson picked a fight with them, that there wasn't anything on the table yesterday that couldn't have been worked out if Jackson had calmed down." I look at the fire. "And I think it's very nice he wasn't getting a blow job in that picture and everything, but people wonder why Cassy isn't here."

Her eyes open.

"I said she was working on something in New York in our absence, that we had to make a choice." I look at the molding along the ceiling. It looks like carved plaster. "The timing had everyone wondering, though. You know the picture, Jackson banging around in that cast, Cassy not here."

There is a nice crackle to the fire.

It is several moments before I realize Alexandra is crying. I have no idea what to do. Alexandra never cries, but she certainly is now, albeit silently, her head bowed into her good arm.

I move to the side of the bed and touch her shoulder and am surprised when she sits up to cry on my shoulder for real. I tell her it's all right and lightly rub her back, a million possibilities running through my head. When her bout seems to have sub-sided a bit, I lean forward to get a tissue from the nightstand and press it into her hand. She clutches it a moment and then sniffs, backing away from me to wipe her eyes. "I'm sorry." I hand her some more tissues and she blows her nose and tightens her fist around the tissues, shielding her eyes from me.

"Medication can do this to you," I say softly. "You know that."

"Oh, Sally," she sighs, still shielding her eyes.

"Is it something in particular or is it just everything?" I say quietly, gently pulling her hand away from her face.

She takes a breath and then looks at me. "Jackson found out about us."

"About who?"

"Me and Cassy."

"But that was like twelve years ago," I say, surprised. "Surely he can't—" Something in her eyes makes me stop speaking.

"No, Sally," she says, dropping her head, "it is now. And has been for years."

V

I certainly have been given a lot to think about during the flight home.

Few times in my life have I ever been as shocked as I was last night. "Wow," I think I said to Alexandra, and then I remember looking down at my hands in my lap.

I didn't know what to say. I have been privy to almost every area of Alexandra's life but clearly there's a big part I missed. Right under my nose. What I always understood was that during the collapse of her first marriage twelve years ago, Cassy had a relatively brief love affair with Alexandra and then had sent her on her way because, well, Cassy wasn't gay. And they've been great friends ever since. Alexandra was with Georgiana Hamilton-Ayres and the Darenbrooks were married and in love with each other.

Where the hell have I been?

The implications of their deceit is staggering.

"Before you think badly of Cassy," Alexandra said, "after around the third year of their marriage, she knew Jackson—" She took a breath. "Was stepping out. No love affairs or anything— just sex, evidently."

Hmm. As I suspected.

"She came to me a while later." Alexandra wasn't crying anymore but, on the contrary, seemed on the verge of smiling. "And then things happened and then we said we couldn't do it anymore. And then she came back again." She looked at me. "It's been like that ever since. Until recently."

I nodded, having a lot of questions but scared to ask even one, she seemed so fragile.

"Jackson knew Cassy once had an affair with a woman. She told Jackson about it before they were married, but she never told him it was me." She started picking at the bedcovers with her right hand. "When she caught on to what Jackson was doing on the road, he said that he loved her and wanted to be married to her and share their family life, but that he needed something more to make it work. It wasn't about love, it was about sex." She raised her eyebrows. "So as long as he was discreet about it, careful about it, Cassy turned her head the other way."

"She should have left him then and there," I said, looking at a knot in the headboard behind Alexandra.

Her eyes come back to me, glassy from the drugs. "Why? To do what? Break up her family a second time?"

My God, I remember thinking, *Cassy's a grandmother. Alexandra's having an affair with someone's grandmother?* "But don't you want to be with her?" I finally asked.

"No," Alexandra said simply, wiping her nose again with the tissues, "because she couldn't take the fallout. And I don't want her to leave DBS, and I don't want to leave DBS News."

"But Alexandra…" I began.

She looked at me with an almost hopeful expression.

"Can you really live like this?"

"I can't go on living like this with Georgiana," she said, eyes starting to fill. "She knows. Not who it is, but she knows there's someone. And it makes me feel sick that she might be willing to put up with it."

I don't know if you have ever held someone up as a role model, a person or persons against whom all others seem to inadequately measure. When it turns out that your idol, or idols, as it is in this case for me, are capable of living such a lie as this, it makes you feel betrayed. It's not a pleasant feeling, not with people you've come to love.

Good God, I'm the one who's always aspired to have a marriage like the Darenbrooks!

So I am not particularly good company on the flight home. Emmett and I sit together in the last row of first class and he just keeps talking, ecstatic about how our trip went, and after a while I pretend to sleep so I can have time to think. Sasha is sitting behind us in the first row of tourist, on the aisle.

We land at JFK, and when we reach passport entry we groan— at least two other flights have arrived ahead of us and the line goes on forever. Sasha speaks to an official, shows him her credentials and we are sent ahead of the line. We collect our luggage at the baggage carousel and it requires two carts to move it all. Emmett and Sasha each push a cart while I call West End to say we're in. I also see I have a text message waiting:

AM HERE IN NYC I LOVE YOU D

"Good news?" Emmett asks, noting the change in my expression.

"Excellent news," I tell him, putting my phone away.

Sasha and I breeze through Customs, but Emmett is stopped and asked to open his bags. We're asked to please move along and I call to Emmett we'll be waiting for him outside. When we emerge from Customs we find a large crowd of people crushing around the exit, obviously waiting for other passengers arriving on overseas flights. Several drivers are waving signs at us, but it is a while before we find one holding HARRINGTON. He takes the baggage cart from Sasha and says this way to the car, but I explain we still have one more passenger we need to wait for who has been detained in Customs. After five minutes of standing around, the driver starts getting antsy, saying something about the limo getting towed.

"Maybe we could ask somebody, Sasha? What's holding up Emmett?" I feel like I'm about to drop in my tracks. Sasha and I dutifully take on the crowd in the direction of the hall where we have just come through and I hear the driver say in my ear, "If you value the life of Belle Harrington, your mother, then you will come with me now. Quickly."

I whirl around to look at his hard expression and numbly allow him to lead me away by the arm. I look back but can't see Sasha in the crowd. Outside at the passenger pickup area a black car with darkened windows pulls up to us and the driver opens the back door for me. I know if I get in, all is over, but what am I to do? It's my mother.

I climb into the back seat, the door is closed behind me, and I look at myself in the reflection of the mirrored partition between me and the drivers. We are heading in the direction of Atlantic City.

I am standing in what I think is a beach bungalow. There is a raised stone fireplace to the left of me and a leather couch flanked by end tables, lamps and two matching chairs to the right. There is also a large coffee table with a few recent magazines spread in an array: Time, Vanity Fair, The New Yorker, Barron's. There is a wood floor and in this part, the living room area, there is an oval braided rug. There is a kitchen area behind the couch, set off by countertops, and to the right there is a dining area with sliding glass doors leading out to what appears to be a deck. With the exception of the couch and matching chairs, the furniture is all faux Stickley. There are two thick round candles on the table, never used.

I don't see a phone. Or a TV. There are handsome bookcases with nothing in them.

Everything appears to be new. The bungalow itself isn't, but the furnishings are.

Behind me is the door I came in, which I find, not surprisingly, to be locked. I walk through the only other door in the place, which leads into a small bedroom, lit by a single brass lamp over a queen-size bed. Again, faux Stickley. Opposite the bed are sliding glass doors onto the deck. I walk over and find I cannot budge the doors, and then see the contraption near the ground on the outside that has jammed them shut. I figure the drivers are probably outside, watching me, and draw the drapes closed over the doors.

I go over to use the bathroom. Judging from the pink tile in here I think the bungalow was probably built in the fifties. There is a pile of thick white towels on the edge of the tub and an unopened bar of Camay soap. In the medicine cabinet, which is new and isn't fitted into the wall properly, I find two unopened toothbrushes, toothpaste, Oil of Olay body lotion, a bar of Secret and a box of tampons. I close the door and wash out the plastic pink cup on the sink and drink a glass of water.

The water's hard, really hard. It tastes awful, but I make myself drink two more glasses because I know I am dehydrated.

In the bedroom I pull back the levered panels that serve as a closet door. Empty.

I walk over to the single chest of drawers and pull one open. Empty. And obviously new.

I head back into the central room, to the kitchen, and look around there. The refrigerator is on, but nothing is in it. It also appears to be new. I open the freezer, which is empty. The combination stove and oven is not new, but is as clean as a whistle.

There are some pots and pans in the cabinets that look as though no one has ever used them. There are a few cooking utensils in a drawer, a couple of kitchen towels and a gleaming set of stainless-steel cutlery. Blocking the view from the window, I wrap a dishcloth around the knives and take them with me. There are exactly four dinner plates, four bowls, four bread plates and four cups and saucers. There are four light green glass tumblers. There is an unopened pack of fancy paper dinner napkins.

For spices there is an unopened pack of disposable salt and pepper shakers.

I walk over to the sliding glass doors by the dining table and am not surprised to find they are jammed shut, as well. Next to the door is a switch that turns on an outside light. There is an impressively large weathered-gray deck out there with stairs leading down to what I think might be sand dunes. I keep that light on so I can see if anyone comes from that direction.

I walk over to the window on the side wall and find that hardware has been soldered into a metal lump.

Great. A firetrap with no means of exit. There are two tiny skylights over the kitchen and dining area, but there's no way I could fit through them.

Son of a bitch.

I put down my knives, pick up one of the dining chairs and swing it like a Louisville slugger into the sliding glass doors. It bounces back with such violence it kicks backward out of my hands over the dining room table. I march into the kitchen and rumble through the lower cabinets until I decide on the heavy frying pan, bring that with me and then slam it as hard as I can against the window. That goes flying out of my hand, too, stinging my hand with vibration. I pick up my dishcloth and make a tour again of the little house, secreting one knife under the couch cushion, one under the chair cushion, one under the mattress in the bedroom and one in the tank of the toilet.

I return to the living room, my eyes on that window again. The only way I can get past that shatterproof glass would be to knock the entire window frame out. My eyes travel to the fireplace in hope of a log I can use as a battering ram, but the fireplace is empty, not even a grate.

There's nothing I can do but wait. Almost four hours have passed since they snatched me from the airport.

And who is they?

I hear and feel a slight rumble in the floor and a minute later there are the telltale sounds of baseboard radiators heating up. Must be the furnace. Under the house? Is there a basement? I get up and jump up once, feeling the floor shake when I come down. Yep, there's a basement. There must be an outside entrance to it since there's no door to it inside that I can find. I go back into the bedroom and open the closet doors again, checking the ceiling for maybe an attic crawl space.

No.

I pull up the rug in the bedroom. Nothing in the floor.

I go into the bathroom and drink some more water. About all I can do now, I decide, is pray. I mean, who else can help me? And so I go back into the bedroom and get down on my knees

next to the bed to pray. I have a lot to say. That if it is my time
I won't be too disappointed because so much of what I've always hoped for in my life has happened. That it wouldn't be as
though I died without ever knowing what it feels like to fall in
love, and to feel loved. I've realized my potential at work. And
for the first time in my life I have no debts and some savings,
and I have a will, which Mother has a copy of, and a term life
insurance policy of $500,000, so Mother will be able to take early
retirement with Mack and sail around the world or do whatever
she would like to do.

It is only now, when I think of Mother and how she will feel
if I die before her, that I start to cry. First Daddy and then it
would be me.

My head jerks up at a sound. Sniffing and wiping my eyes, I
stand up and walk to the living room threshold. The door I came
in is being unlocked. I hear men's voices and then it opens. A
man comes in, who, with his back to me, slips off a gray trench
coat and tosses it over the back of the chair. He's not a tall man,
not fat, not thin, but seems vaguely familiar. The back of his head
shows black hair carefully combed over a bald spot. He shrugs
his shoulders to shift his jacket, smooths his tie and at last turns
around.

"Ah, Sally, there you are." He smiles and takes a step toward
me.

It is Michael Arlenetta, mob heir to his slain older brother, Nick.
He was the second name on my list of people I asked Sky to warn.

"You certainly are a very difficult woman to get the attention
of," he tells me.

I hold on to the door frame of the bedroom for support.
"What do you mean?"

He shrugs a little, choosing his words with care. "One would
think you would have had the courtesy to cover Wilson Delafield's death. Considering it was your story that got him murdered in the first place."

"How do you know my story got him murdered?"

He smiles and walks over to the couch and bends to pat the
seat. "Why don't you sit? You must be tired. I know I am." He
yawns slightly, moving toward the easy chair. "Jet lag."

I don't want to sit, but I'm feeling a little light-headed. I try to gather whatever dignity I have left and walk over. I sit down, lean back against the cushions, cross my legs in the direction opposite Arlenetta, and take one of the throw pillows into my lap to hold while calculating how long it would take me to grab the knife and lunge for the chair.

He looks me over blatantly, from head to toe. "How do you feel?"

"Upset. Your driver said my mother would be hurt if I didn't come with him."

"I know. I'm sorry. But they were getting desperate." He looks at me sincerely. "I wouldn't hurt your mother."

"Who was getting desperate?" I ask him.

"You didn't come to Gainesville. You took off from Castleford. You didn't even bother going to the station in Burbank to report Robby Palermo's terrible misfortune." He licks his lips and smiles. "Remember when you were supposed to interview me? In Burbank? And you had me arrested instead?"

"I didn't do that. I wanted to interview you," I tell him honestly. "What I could never figure out was why you wanted me to."

"Because I wanted you," he says simply.

I will not let him stare me down. And I try to remember the man who had almost seemed vulnerable years ago, when Alexandra and I ambushed him with TV cameras. Michael Arlenetta had been an illegal weapons dealer, among other things. Just a small branch in New Jersey and Pennsylvania of his brother Nick's empire. He had been a young and respected businessman in Fort Lee, New Jersey, with a wife and children, who gave a tremendous amount of money to charitable causes.

Surely this can't be the same man, not this strange creature with glittering eyes.

"Then you went traipsing off to England with an FBI agent, but you even bolted from there, not even waiting to find out who was tracking you."

I try not to look afraid. "I presume you were nearby."

"I was waiting to see you, yes." He looks down and brushes imaginary lint off his pants.

I catch my breath. "It was you at the *Herald-American* that night. You're the one who took us through the tunnel."

He smiles. "Maybe, maybe not."

"And you killed Wilson Delafield."

"I haven't killed anyone." He drums his hands on the arms of the chair and narrows his eyes. "You really don't know what Delafield was planning. Which means the feds probably don't yet, either. Interesting. And not very impressive, I'm afraid."

"Don't know what?"

"That Delafield was looking for someone to kill you."

I blink. "I don't believe it."

"You should, because I know the guy he was trying to hire to do it." He pauses. "He wanted your throat cut, Sally."

Could this be possible?

It's possible.

Arlenetta is biting his thumbnail, eyes still on me. Abruptly he stops biting his nail and lowers his hand. "But I wasn't going to let him do that. Because we never got together, did we?" He smiles. "You might call this my parting shot to America." His eyes travel down to my breasts.

"You're leaving?"

"I wanted to spend some time with you first."

I feel a chill. "Okay," I say, trying to brave it out. "How are you?"

He throws his head back to laugh. I finger the handle of the knife. He's just too far away. "You certainly are something," he says. "Both of my brothers had a thing for you. First Cliff—"

"Whom you killed," I interject.

"I did not," he says firmly. "But since he betrayed everyone in the family, I should have."

"Nick killed him?"

"Not personally."

"Excuse me if I don't seem impressed," I tell him.

His eyes take their time traveling down my body. "But I am impressed, very impressed."

I try to swallow.

His eyes come back up. "So this is the drill, Sally. You and I are going to spend some time here together. Then I will go my way, and you will be free to go yours."

This would be too much to hope for.

"I'm afraid I had very little notice of your arrival," he continues, uncrossing his legs, "so we haven't shopped for you and I need a little something done in the bedroom before we can be alone." He splays his legs and I can't help but glance down. "I'm having a hard time waiting, as you can see."

I look away.

He gets up out of his chair and comes over toward me. I clench the knife under the pillow. "Look what you do to me." Suddenly he grabs the pillow out of my lap and clenches my wrist, turning it until I cry out and drop the stainless steel knife. "What are you going to do, butter bread with that?" he mutters. He grabs a handful of my hair and forces me to look at his groin.

"I don't want you to kill me," I tell him honestly.

"Then let's enjoy ourselves." He reaches down for my hand and presses it against his erection. "I'm a lot bigger than the cop—the Arlenetta boys are kind of famous for it." He forces my hand to start rubbing him. "He does fuck you pretty good, I have to admit," he says, his voice growing weaker. He pulls his hand away to undo his belt, unzip his pants and expose himself. "Come on," he says, holding himself in one hand and pulling my head toward him with the other.

"Not like this," I plead, turning away.

He yanks me by the hair. "Come on."

I close my eyes. "I can't like this. I'm gross, I'm dirty, I need a bath. If you make me do it like this it will ruin everything. I'll feel dirty and ashamed." He lets go of my head and I look up at him. "I swear to God if you let me take a bath—just give me an hour to pull myself together and I promise you…" I force myself to smile. "You know what I'm like, Michael."

He pulls me to my feet to roughly kiss me. He tastes like mint Listerine breath strips. Yes. It was Michael Arlenetta at the bombing. He starts pulling up my skirt. "Please. My bath."

He steps back slightly to study my eyes. "You're scared."

I nod.

One side of his mouth hitches. His eyes still on me, he zips himself up and buckles his belt. "You like Chardonnay, right?"

I nod.

He looks at his watch and back to me. "Take your bath, but be presentable because I have to have a guy do something in the bedroom for us."

My rapist wants me to look decent in front of another man. "Okay," I murmur, edging away.

"You got any more knives?" he asks me.

I nod. Then I move around the room to retrieve the other three and hand them to him. He laughs a little, shaking his head. "It's all right, keep them," he says, pushing them back into my hands, "I don't feel like eating soup tonight." He turns to pick up his coat and slip it on. "You've got about an hour, Sally," he tells me in a voice that almost sounds respectful.

"And you're bringing food?" I ask. "Because if you are, I'll set the table."

He turns around, adjusting his coat, smiling. He's a happy camper now. "That would be nice."

"Open up!" he suddenly yells, pounding the door. A moment later the door opens.

I go into the bedroom. I stand inside the door, listening to the living room door being locked.

Oh, what's the use? I think, hearing a car start up. *The guy's got people working for him all over the place, I'm never going to get out of here.*

But what can I do? I wonder, going into the kitchen. I glance over at the glass doors and wonder if the guys who brought me here are out there watching the house. I look at the candles and wonder if there's anything to light them with. The burner on the stove, maybe. I turn to look.

A gas stove.

I look up at the ceiling. Eight feet high. Two closed skylights. I look across the room at the fireplace. I wonder if there's a damper. I walk over to look and, yes, there is one, and it's closed.

Excellent.

I hurry back into the kitchen and pull out the utensils and open the package of napkins to set the table. I set two places, side by side. I come back to the stove with the candles and for the benefit of anyone watching, set them on the counter. I twist a paper napkin into a taper and then turn on a burner of the stove.

Taking the taper, I bring it over to light the candles, but after doing so the napkin really catches fire and I fling it toward the sink, but it lands—as I intend—on the stove top instead. I turn on the water, grab the sprayer and pretend to put out the napkin, but in reality am flooding the stove top and burners with water.

As I pretend to clean up the ashes, I shield the stove with my body and turn on another burner. There is the hiss of gas, but the burner won't ignite. The pilot light is out.

Good.

I turn on the burners and the oven, nearly reeling back from the gas smell, and carry the candles to set on the dining table. I bring over two glasses to the table. The sickly odor is almost unbearable now. Then I stand by the sliding glass doors and turn off both the outside light and the overhead dining room light, leaving the candlelight scene looking romantic.

I go to the bedroom and close the door behind me. I make sure the bedroom drapes are tightly drawn and then hurry into the bathroom to start running warm bath water. I race back to grab the four pillows from the bed and bring them into the bathroom. I align two pillows in the tub and make sure they're wet. Then I run back to tear the comforter, blanket and top sheet from the bed and bring them inside the bathroom, too, and center them in the tub. I go back out to the bedroom door and open it just a crack—yes, it reeks of gas out there—and close it again. Then I walk back to the bathroom, lock the door (as if that is going to do anything to keep anyone out) and climb into the tub, pulling the two other pillows and wet blankets over me. When the tub starts to run over I sit up to shut the water off and then lay back down, carefully arranging the wet blankets and pillows around me.

And then I wait.

And wait.

The gas must have mushroomed across the ceiling by now and the layer of gas should be dropping. But if Arlenetta returns before the gas level has reached the candles…

At least I tried, I think, starting to shiver under the wet blankets.

And then the living room blows up.

I grope the bathroom wall and tile falls off in my hands. I step out of the tub and water is pumping over my feet. I feel my way to the door, which is still standing and still locked. It feels a little warm. I wade back to feel for one of the wet blankets and drape it over my shoulders and make my way back to the door. I squat down and open it. The smoke is bad; smoke alarms are screaming; there are small burning embers everywhere, but there is fire light coming in surges from the living room. I cut my foot on the remains of the bathroom door and push on, the smoke making me cough. I drop to my hands and knees and try to see, crawling in the direction of the living room. I burn my hands and try to stand up, shielding myself with the blanket.

I don't know if I'm going to make it.

I have to drop down again and keep going though the smoke and debris into what was the living room. I keep going until I find the far wall and see that smoke is being sucked away and realize that where there had once been a window is now only a huge hole. I shrug off the blanket and try to climb out; I catch my knee on a piece of something, making me cry out because it has torn my skin, and then when I try to find something to hold on to there is nothing and I fall ass over teakettle out of the house. Half of me lands on high grass and sand, the other half, my bottom half, hits a cement walk.

I see headlights behind the house and hear men yelling and I start crawling through the cool sand and grass. It feels good and I just keep crawling, my ears ringing, my eyes burning, and I keep coughing and coughing. I push myself up a dune and then tumble down the other side; then I just let myself lie there on my back, trying to stop coughing, trying to clear my eyes to see.

With a shift in wind I feel the heat from the house and the uncertain light is filled with floating ash. Some guy is yelling. The burning wood sounds like a tinderbox. I start crawling again, now toward the sound of the ocean. I look back.

The house is engulfed in flames, spewing sparks and red embers high in the night sky. I duck when I see headlights again, but it doesn't matter because now they are speeding away.

I stand up and run toward the ocean, falling a couple of times but finally making it to the icy water. I don't care. I just drop down in the salty wash. I've got so many small wounds, everything aches and stings. I hear a muffled explosion from the direction of the house and wonder what happened. The flames have diminished on one side, on the side of the living room, but now the bedroom is going up.

A silhouette appears on the back deck, weaving wildly and then falling flat. I stagger to my feet and take a few steps toward the house and hear the faint sound of sirens. I also hear someone screaming. A man. The man in back of the house.

The sirens, someone must be coming. I find myself slogging back up the beach toward the fire. A large man is heading down the deck stairs to the beach. He is screaming, clutching his head, writhing to the left and to the right. It's not Arlenetta.

"Come on!" I shout, pulling his arm. The man grabs on to my hand so hard he pulls me down. "Can you stand?" I shout. He doesn't answer but manages to sit up, coughing horribly, and that is when I see the black area where his eyes and nose should be. I put his arm over my shoulders and we stagger to our feet. The guy is huge and I think we're going to go down headlong. I shift him a bit, shouting, "You've got to walk!" and in a crippled maneuver we start to move and I don't even know what

I'm yelling at him but I know I'm yelling, urging him forward. The mainframe and roof of the house go down and fiery ash is everywhere as we lurch and stumble toward the water.

The big man is screaming again, saying I don't know what, but I keep pulling at him. The sand is suddenly hard under our feet and then it is cold and wet and I tell him we must go in, he must dunk his head, the water will help him, and then a wave hits us and I lose him when I am thrown down. Coughing water I scramble up and see him crawling toward the beach. Another wave rolls over us and I am thrown down again. This time I manage to get up to the backwash and see that he has crawled up to make it, too, and we both collapse there, the tide washing over our legs.

The man starts gagging and I try to pull him up to sit and tell him help is here, someone's here, and I see searchlights playing over the area and I hear things I can't identify. I can't identify the sound of anything except the crash of the waves, and I bring my hand up to my mouth to make the piercing whistle my father taught me how to do, but my hand is messed up and I can't make my fingers go the right away. "Help is here!" I cry at the giant. He reaches toward me and I think he wants to get up but he shoves my arms aside and grabs me by the throat with one hand, his thumb pressing down. I couldn't protest if I wanted to because I am gasping for air, frantically clawing at his hand with both of mine, thinking, no, God, not after all this, no, and then suddenly his grip slackens and I fall backward into the sand. Now I'm the one who's sobbing, curling up in a tight little ball to protect myself, waiting for another attack.

A hand is gently shaking my shoulder. "Ma'am, it's all right," someone is saying. "It's all right. We're here to help you."

I can't let go of my legs, I just can't. And finally, gently, my hands are pried loose and now two voices are telling me that everything is going to be all right.

VI

CHAPTER
35

"Where does she keep picking it up?" I hear Alexandra asking her tenant farmer.

"The east pasture, where the goats got in and tore up the grass. The clay's come up to the surface." He is holding one of Astra's front hooves on his knee, gently picking inside the white mare's shoe with a tool while Alexandra brushes her. Astra is Latin for star, as in *Ad Astra Per Aspera,* To the Stars Through Difficulties, the motto of the anchorwoman's native state of Kansas. Alexandra's wearing blue-jeans jodhpurs, boots and a sweater, and her cast is slung tightly against her chest. She has been with her horses for the better part of the day. As her houseguest I am not complaining. I feel like I've done nothing but sleep, eat and watch old movies since I got here to the farm.

I feel a lot better than I did. It has been nine days since my rescue from the beach house and four days since I was released from Lenox Hill Hospital in Manhattan. DBS found a terrific plastic surgeon who also performs surgery on the hand, for I was and still am in need of both.

I won't be winning many beauty pageants for a while.

Mother and Mack came to New York immediately and Alexandra very nicely put them up in her apartment for a few days.

Then the question was where should I go after the hospital, and while I assumed I would just go home to Castleford I was relieved when Alexandra suggested I come out to the farm where, as Sky Preston and Agent Alfonso echoed, I knew I was safe.

David wouldn't leave my side at Lenox Hill until I begged him to go, pleading that I wanted to be miserable on my own without having to worry about him. I know I hurt his feelings, but I was still beyond caring about such things then, looking in a hand-held mirror over and over again, wondering if my eyebrows would ever grow back and if the doctor was really sure all these cuts and burns on my face wouldn't scar. And then there is the matter of how much of my hair was scorched and how much of my scalp will be permanently damaged.

If I didn't think I was vain before, I confess to it now, because I am heartbroken about the way I look. And angry, so angry at this point I wonder how I might ultimately choose to express it. And the likelihood of me actually doing it.

My arms are covered with burns and cuts. I broke bones in the palm of my right hand and splinters of glass had to be taken out of both. Somewhat amazingly, the thing I worried most about at first, the torn bottoms of my feet, were both easiest to treat and first to pass worry of the doctors. After a few days of bed rest I could walk fairly well and since then have scarcely thought again of soldiers at Valley Forge.

The feds have stayed in touch. Two days ago Agent Alfonso came to tell me the blinded giant Arlenetta abandoned in the fire finally rolled. The feds now have a name for the guy who set the bomb at the *Herald-American* (now they only have to find him) and they obtained an arrest warrant for Arlenetta because, the giant man swears, he watched Arlenetta beat Alfred Royce's head in with a piece of heavy plastic piping and then instructed him to dump the bloody body at my house. Information from the giant also led the authorities to a secluded one-bedroom house in central Florida where I was to have been taken after the Delafield murder. The house had steel grids soldered over the windows and was outfitted with sliding bolts on the outside.

The giant apparently knows little about who actually murdered Delafield, virtually nothing about Robby Palermo's murder in San Diego and absolutely nothing about what happened in England except that Arlenetta had come to the beach house straight from Newark Airport after flying home from England.

All of these points are rather moot, though. Arlenetta knew the feds were within months of busting him for selling arms in the Middle East and had planned his exit from America with the ease that comes of money, boredom and no conscience. He's gone. Somewhere. Maybe they'll find him, maybe they won't. I suppose if I ever feel better I'll have the energy to worry.

"Ah, there you are," Alexandra says, smiling at me as I stand in the doorway of the tack room.

Her tenant farmer looks over. "How are you feeling today, Ms. Harrington?"

"Much better, thank you. And please call me Sally. Ms. Harrington was the good-looking one."

"Your color's coming back," Alexandra says. Astra nuzzles her shoulder. "No, she doesn't have carrots for you," she tells the horse.

"Frank Presario called," I tell her, carefully crossing my arms so as to not knock any bandages askew. "He said his father wants to see me."

"Forget it," Alexandra says, resuming her vigorous brushing. Little white hairs are floating in the air around her.

"They think Rocky only has a couple weeks left," I continue. "Lilliana also asked me if I would go. Frank is on the West Coast and she's shooting outside Prague and they can't get here for a couple of days and they're scared it will be too late. It's the last thing their father has asked of them."

"Forget it," Alexandra says, walking around to do Astra's other side.

"A car is coming to pick me up," I tell her. "Agent Punjab is coming with me. You remember Jocko? Who works for Rocky?"

Alexandra doesn't answer.

"He's picking us up."

"I have half a mind to throw you out," she finally says.

"I think it's important I go. At the very least to say goodbye, if he's dying."

"Take David with you, then," she says. "If you're well enough to see Rocky then you're well enough to see my poor brother who's been climbing the walls."

"But the car's coming now and David's in New York," I say.

"He's at the bed-and-breakfast a half mile down the road," she says. "The number's on the refrigerator." She tosses the brush into a bucket and walks around to examine Astra's gums.

The same black limousine with dark windows I remember from the Presario mansion pulls around the circle in front of Alexandra's house and I invite Jocko in to wait until David gets here. He confirms how ill Rocky is and says he's glad I'm coming, it will make his boss happy. In a few minutes David arrives, a bit breathlessly, pulling a blue blazer over jeans and a pinstriped shirt. When he sees that it is me opening the front door his face lights up and he says I look so much better its unbelievable.

I almost believe him until I pass the front hall mirror.

Agent Punjab sits in the front with Jocko and David and I sit in the back. We've been talking every day, at least twice a day, so neither of us has any news. He makes no move to touch me since he knows by earlier experience there aren't many places on me that aren't painful.

The brick-and-white-wrought-iron fortress belonging to Rocky Presario is flooded with light. Jocko takes us up to the front door and jumps out to open the door for me. Without knocking or ringing the bell, he shows us through the front doors and gestures to the doorway on the far side of the spacious rotunda. It is, if I recall correctly, the door to the living room. I tell Sasha she better wait out here and I make sure Jocko closes the double doors behind us.

The room is much as I remember. I first came here to produce Alexandra's interview with Rocky for the magazine show. Seems like a million years ago.

Seems like a million years ago the sins of the fathers Joe Arlenetta and Rocky Presario came crashing down onto the next generation, inadvertently dragging me into it in the process.

The old man is lying in a hospital bed near a picture window. He has an oxygen line in his nose and appears to be sleeping.

His face is bloated and his color is bad. A woman I presume is a nurse stands up when we come in and gently touches Rocky's shoulder. "Someone is here to see you."

His eyes open slightly and I recognize the signs of morphine. It really is near the end, then; Frank and Lilliana had been telling the truth. Of course had I not believed them I wouldn't be here.

"Hi, Mr. Presario," I murmur, touching his hand with my left one. Instinctively he takes hold of it and I try not to flinch. "It's Sally Harrington."

His eyes widen a little and then recede and the nurse repeats my name to him. "Get me—" he starts, raising his other hand and then dropping it. Then his eyes come back to me and I know he can't remember what he was going to say. The nurse knows what he wants, though, because she takes a legal-size envelope from the table and holds it in front of him. He seems to recognize it. He lifts and drops his arm. "Give it to her," he rasps.

I swear to God I will never smoke a cigarette.

"Read," he urges.

I open the envelope and pull out a three-page document that looks like a will. My eyes move to David and I gesture that I wish he would look at it with me.

It is a codicil to Rocky's will, dated three days ago. By David's expression I think he is thinking what I am, that there's no way in the world this would stand up in court with the shape Rocky's in. Nevertheless I skim the document and I think my eyes are growing larger and larger. In essence the codicil says two million dollars is to be set aside from Rocky's estate to pay for my protection until such a time Michael Arlenetta is either dead or imprisoned.

"Yes, she's reading it," the nurse is saying to him.

Rocky is nodding, his eyes closed. "Another," he slowly rasps, "pervert nephew." His eyes open and he looks at me.

I smile and nod. "Yes, another pervert nephew. But it's not your fault, Mr. Presario. There is no reason for you to do this."

He closes his eyes, frowning. I look across the bed to the nurse. "He has been very determined about this," she says, placing a hand on his shoulder. At her touch Rocky instinctively looks up at her. "His son and granddaughter are also determined to see that his wishes are carried out. You've done so much for them in the past."

It is getting dark outside and I see the ghastly reflection in the picture window that is me. I look down at the dying man. "Who told you about your nephew, Mr. Presario? It's not the kind of bedside story I would like to hear." Again Rocky looks up at the nurse.

"His grandson came here to tell him."

"Taylor Presario?" I ask, using the name of the boy before he went into the witness protection program with his father so many years ago.

She nods.

Great. The grandson who may or may not have killed Nick Arlenetta ran to Gramps on his deathbed to tell him what happened with Cousin Michael.

The nurse clears her throat, nodding to Rocky. "Yes, I will," she says, raising her eyes. "He would like me to tell you the situation is going to be taken care of." She pauses, her eyes taking on a somewhat steely look. "The codicil is in case it takes longer than he foresees."

I look down at Rocky, who is smiling, closing his eyes. He makes a sound of agreement.

My eyes come back up. "You must be a very trusted nurse," I tell her.

Her mouth expands in what I guess could be considered a smile. "Poppy's my grandfather," she says, "which means I've got another pervert cousin to deal with, too."

At Alexandra's house I show Sasha and the anchorwoman the codicil. When I fail to mention the last part of my interview at Rocky's, about certain matters being taken care of, David doesn't say anything, either.

"The original clash between the Arlenettas and the Presarios was about union turf in Atlantic City?" Sasha asks me.

I shake my head. "It was about Rocky's son, Frank Presario, who was trying to extricate the family from illegal activity. When Frank stopped playing ball with the Arlenettas, Nick put a bomb in his car—which killed Frank's wife."

"And then Frank took his kids into the witness protection program—"

"And put Nick's father, Joe, in prison," Alexandra finishes, "where he died. Nick—" She shrugs. "Well, you know what he did."

"What is Michael Arlenetta's problem with you?" David asks me.

"I don't want to talk about it," I say, getting up and going into the kitchen. He doesn't know the details of Arlenetta's obsession with me. To hell with the medications; I flip the cap off an Amstel Light and plunk myself down at the kitchen table to drink it out of the bottle. In a little while Alexandra comes in. I hear the refrigerator door open and close, the telltale click of a bottle cap, and then she sits down across the table from me, carefully placing her cast on it, and drinks from a bottle of Amstel, too.

I'm not sure I've ever seen her drink.

"After I was shot in Washington," she says, "I had to make a decision about what I was going to do." She takes another sip and puts the bottle down. "I knew I couldn't go back to covering the Hill. I knew I couldn't go back out as a reporter, period. I was too scared."

I meet her eyes and see the earnestness in them.

"When Jackson offered me the chance of launching DBS News, I jumped at it, not because I really wanted to be an anchor again—I had tremendous doubts about DBS ever getting off the ground—but because it gave me an excuse to come in from the field."

"But you went out on the DBS News America tour when the network was launched," I point out.

"And nearly got shot again," she reminds me. She takes a swig. "Now you know why I was so against your touring idea last year." She sniffs slightly. "I was scared. I won't do it." She shrugs, peeling at the label. "It's a sick world, Sally. For every thousand wonderful people, there's one sicko out there dreaming and scheming how to get to us." She swallows, raising her eyes. "And some of them have money. Like Arlenetta."

"He was going to kill me in the end," I say. "I knew that. He said he wouldn't if I cooperated, but I knew he would."

She doesn't say anything for a while. I push my beer away, losing the taste for it. I'm just so scared of everything.

"You don't have to come back if you don't want," she says. "And we'll honor the contract. Heck," she shrugs again, picking up the bottle, "you can sue us for a billion dollars for letting it happen to you and you'll probably win."

"I'm not the suing type."

"Who knows, if you're married to a lawyer?" she says.

I can't seem to look up from the table.

"Look at me, Alexandra. Who could want this?"

"I do," David's voice says from the doorway, "more than anything else on the face of the earth."

I look down.

"I think she's feeling broadsided," Alexandra tells him.

"No, it's not that." I look up. "Why don't you get a beer and join us?"

"I don't need a beer," David says, coming over to sit on the bench next to his sister. "And I don't want to bug you, Sally, and I don't know if my being here is bugging you or—"

"Oh for Pete's sake!" I thump my elbow on the table and cover my eyes. There is no sound from the other side of the table. I finally bring my hand down, tears streaming over my wounded face. "I'm in love with you, David. I'm just scared you won't be able to deal with this life of mine." I look into his eyes. "I'm so screwed up," I wail, and then I start sobbing for real, covering my face again.

"If you're screwed up then I'm screwed up, too," he says quietly from beside me, touching my back. "Hopefully we're screwed up in the same way—or at least in a way that works."

I choke a little, laughing, and accept his handkerchief. I raise my head, wiping my eyes. Alexandra appears to have left. "You're not screwed up," I tell him. "You're wonderful. You're the most wonderful man I've ever met."

"I'm boring, Sally." He takes the handkerchief from me and dabs lightly here and there. "I am a creature of habit and a devotee to the fixed and the finite." He ventures to lightly kiss my lips, the first kiss I have been able to accept. "I'm scared you'll get bored with me when you realize there isn't much more to me than what you see."

I cluck my tongue in annoyance. "Don't be stupid."

"I know my limitations. I can offer you stability and love and fidelity, but that may not be enough."

I swipe his handkerchief and blow my nose, flinching because it hurts. "You're unbelievable," I tell him, throwing his handkerchief down on the table.

"I'm forty-five and boring as hell and you've got it all, Sally Harrington—brains, beauty, talent, a brilliant future and *youth*. And while I don't know why you'd want to share your future with me, I'm hoping that you will."

I squint at him. "David, look at me. Where are we going to go? A rest home?"

He takes my hand gently. "I don't care where we go, Sally," he says, "I only care that we go together. And be together."

I am amazed at how easy this feels, how right it sits inside. "I don't care, either," I tell him. "As long as I'm with you."

36

It was almost six weeks before I returned to work and I am somewhat ashamed to say that I continued to stay at Alexandra's farm because I felt safest there. I let Emmett interview me once on camera while I was at the farm, but I didn't watch any of the coverage. Until three days ago I was still only reading newspapers and magazines, things I could absorb at my own pace.

David stayed on at the farm with me and spent most of his days working in Alexandra's study. The phone and fax machine started ringing about ten o'clock and usually didn't stop until around eight-thirty or nine. We went on walks together every day, morning and night and held hands most of the time. He slept in another bedroom, and as I came to feel better and stronger I came to sometimes wish our sleeping arrangements were different, but DBS kept sending out this shrink for me to talk to who kept telling me to take my time.

We talked a lot, David and I, and the weeks were a slightly magical time for us. Because we *had* time; for once neither one of us had to leave, nor did either one of us want to. We rode into town a couple of times to see my surgeon, but other than that, stayed on the farm and simply got used to each other.

I talked to Paul Fitzwilliam twice, too, and even offered to go to Connecticut to see him, to talk about what had happened between us, but he said he didn't want to see me. He just wanted to know if I was all right. I assured him I was, and that I was in good hands. The last time we talked he asked me if David was here with me and I told him yes.

Mother and Mack came to visit and brought Scotty. Mother and David went off together horseback riding in the afternoon and when they came back Mother had a smile so happy I could only wonder at what they had talked about. "About his children and his former wife," she told me later. "He told me everything, including what parts of his marriage went wrong and which parts he thought were his fault." Then she looked puzzled. "It sounds odd, dear, but in some ways David reminds me of myself—in the same way you remind me of your father."

No higher praise could be given.

Until I get my living arrangements settled DBS has requested I stay in a hotel near West End. Last night, my first night at the hotel, I couldn't sleep and I wondered at my growing anxiety. Was I so used to David being with me that I was scared to be without him? Or was I just scared being in this strange place? Or was I just scared, period? Scared of going back to work, scared of the cuts I felt sure would never heal and the hair that would never grow back?

Cleo said I could wear a wig if need be.

A wig. In my early thirties.

At my request there was no rousing welcome waiting for me Friday morning, my first trial day back at West End. Alexandra and Will were waiting in the lobby and walked me up to my office. Margarite couldn't help but throw her arms around me and Benjamin came over to flash me a peace sign and say he was really glad I was back. As I started through my mail (which wasn't so bad since I had started having it sent to me once I decided I would go back to work), one by one people came up from the newsroom to say hi. Margarite must have told them not to touch me because no one tried to.

One e-mail memo, blind-carboned to me, I found rather interesting:

TO: Steve Kolcek, Director of Sales & Advertising
FROM: Cassy Cochran
CC: Jackson Darenbrook, Alec Lertzman, Langley Peterson,
Will Rafferty, Alexandra Waring
This is to confirm that every DBS affiliate will be carrying *DBS
News America This Morning* from its new launch date of
June 1.

Nice to know all this time and trouble didn't go to waste.

I pick up the telephone and dial David's cell phone. He picks
up immediately. It sounds as though he is in a car. "How's it
going?" he asks me.

"I feel so strange."

"You're bound to, Sally. You've been through a lot."

"No, I meant about you not being with me last night. I hated
it. I couldn't sleep."

He pauses. "I couldn't, either."

I smile, turning my chair to look outside. It really is spring now.
Maybe summer will get here after all.

"I don't suppose I could talk you into driving back out to Alexandra's tonight for the weekend, could I?" he asks.

"If it means you'll be there, yes, you can easily talk me into
it."

"Then I will pick you up. How about three?"

"How about eleven, when I normally get off?"

"Sally, no one expects you to stay that late."

"I do."

"Great, let's fight about it, then," he jokes. "All right, darling,
I will pick you up at eleven o'clock."

"Don't pick me up. Just come over and we'll ride out with Alexandra. If she'll have us—have you asked her if she wants us back
out there? We've only been living there for fifty-eight days, exactly fifty-four more than any self-respecting guest should stay."

"She's the one who suggested it."

"Ah."

"And if you do decide to go, she will send a car to pick up
Scotty from your mother's. She got the okay from the hotel for
him to stay there with you, but you and the dog walker have to
use the service elevator."

I laugh, delighted.

"As a matter of fact," he adds, "the car she is sending out to pick him up is the one I'm driving at this very moment. I'm about five minutes from your mom's house."

My spirits are soaring now and I feel energized. And I almost don't care about how I look. Almost.

After I make my reentry into the newsroom, the afternoon and evening fly by. Although my duties have now officially been re-assigned to the development of *DBS News America This Morning,* I can't help but offer a helping hand tonight on the nightly news. Things don't seem to have transitioned very well in my absence. ("It's been the Chekov school of production," Clem whispers to me, "all these giant cockroaches crashing into one another.")

I swing into things, enjoying myself, actually, running the er-rands and doing the grunt work of the assistant producers. I am quite happy to let everyone else have the nervous breakdowns.

"Your script," I say, handing it to Alexandra with a great flour-ish while Cleo is doing her hair.

"It's late," the anchorwoman says.

"You're welcome," I tell her.

She looks up. "What are you holding behind your back?"

"Well, that's the script that I got, but this one's the one—" I hold out a second sheaf of paper "—I rewrote."

"Bless you," she mutters, tossing the first onto the floor and taking the second and opening it immediately. Reading, she holds up a hand. "Pen?"

I hand her a pen. "So you have two new people starting on Monday, I hear."

"Yes," Alexandra says absently, flipping a page.

Cleo rolls her eyes.

"Okay, I'll see you later," I say, edging to the door.

"Oh, *man!*" Jessica Wright yells, clomping into the room in purple cowgirl boots, purple suede miniskirt, flowing white blouse and rhinestone-and-purple dangling earrings. "Our show was an absolute killer!" She does a little dance, kind of a cross between a jig and a rumba, singing to herself.

I am laughing, but Alexandra pays no notice as she continues

to flip pages and make notations. She is used to Jessica's ongoing monologues.

"Thank you, Lord, for not letting Sally sub for me!" Jessica
cries to the heavens next. "Man, is it great to be back." She comes
over and gives me a big kiss on the cheek. "You look fab."

"Yeah, right," I tell her.

"Well at least you won't scare the baby like before."

"Thank you," I tell her.

There is a chuckle from Cleo's chair. I look over. "You do look
good, Sally," Alexandra says.

Frowning, I turn around to examine myself in the mirror. I
look horrible. "Thanks."

The newscast goes fairly well and at ten forty-five Alexandra
and I go out to the driveway where we find David and Scotty
waiting for us by Alexandra's limo. When Scotty sees me on the
other side of the glass doors, where I am signing out, he purses
his mouth in a perfect O and starts to howl.

"Look at how gentle he is," Alexandra marvels, watching
Scotty's and my reunion.

"He knows I'm not quite up to scratch, don't you, boy?" I say,
squatting to endure a few licks on my face.

"He's been as good as gold," David says.

"Hi," I say to him, standing up to kiss him briefly.

"Argh, first the dog and then me?" he laughs. He holds the
door open; Scotty and I climb in, followed by Alexandra. Then
he crawls in to sit on a jump seat across from me.

"I don't know, Davy," Alexandra says once we're on our way,
zipping up the West Side Highway toward the George Washington Bridge. "The dog gets to sit on the seat and you have to sit
over there."

"I'm not worried," he says, smiling at me.

Something's up with David, I can tell. It's not that he's never
an overtly happy man, it's more that he is reserved when other
people are around. And tonight he is overtly happy, just smiling
and smiling, and I know something is up. "Why are you smiling
so much?" I finally ask him.

"Because I'm happy," he says. "I was miserable last night without you."

I glance over at Alexandra. I am surprised he says this in front of her.

"So he kept me up and made me miserable, too," she adds.

Brother and sister exchange looks.

"What's going on?" I ask them. "I know something's going on."

David hesitates a moment and then says, "Lexy and I had a long talk last night about everything."

I look at Alexandra. *"Everything,"* she accentuates.

I look back at David, who has turned around to make sure the partition is closed. "As much as I would love to monopolize your time this weekend," he says to me, "I think maybe it would be good if the four of us got together at some point."

"How would you feel if Cassy came out tomorrow?" Alexandra says.

Weird, is what I want to say. While I've talked to Cassy a couple of times over the telephone and she sent flowers and books and things to me at the farm during my recovery, I haven't laid eyes on her since the affiliate convention in California. I didn't see her around West End today, either, and, I must admit, it has crossed my mind perhaps she is avoiding me.

"I would feel fine," I say, trying to make my voice light. "I'd love to see her."

Brother and sister exchange looks again. "Great," David says.

"We can have dinner or something," Alexandra says softly, looking out the window.

At the top of the stairs in Alexandra's farmhouse (*farmhouse* is a loose term; it's more like a mansion with a farmhouse facade, remodeled to hide its size) there is Alexandra's suite of rooms to the left and a long hallway to the right. There are two bedrooms off the hall and at the end there is a door leading into a guest suite, which consists of a bedroom, living room and bath. This is where I had been living for the past three months and where most of my stuff, at least my informal stuff, is still and so I feel right at home taking a hot bath before bed.

As usual, David knocks on my door to say good-night and, as usual, I am in my nightie and terry-cloth robe, reading in bed.

What is not usual is having Scotty boy asleep on a beach towel on the top of the bed next to me. I smile as David comes in, putting my book down in my lap, once again wondering at the happiness that seems to spilling from him. "You've had a long day," he says quietly, sitting on the edge of the bed and taking my hand.

He is wearing blue jeans and a pale blue denim shirt I love, because they make his eyes bluer than blue, and for him the outfit is extremely informal and for some reason that makes me feel closer to him.

"Thank you for everything you did today," I tell him. "I'm worried you never get any work done anymore because you're always doing something for me."

He raises my hand to kiss. "Do not worry about anything."

"But I do." We look into each other's eyes for a long moment. "How did I ever send you away?" I ask him.

"Because you had principles," he says, turning my hand over to kiss the palm. He looks at me again. "And because you knew if what I felt was real, that I would be back."

My stomach turns over a little. Sometimes he says things like this and I feel like I'm falling off a tall building or something.

It is different when I sit up to kiss him this time. I have lost all thought of anything but him in this moment, and how I feel about him. I don't care about anything but being with David and making absolutely sure he knows it.

CHAPTER 37

The sheets feel wonderful against my skin, so smooth and warm. I take a deep breath and roll over, pulling a pillow with me to shield the light from my eyes, and my eyes fly open then when I feel a faint burning. My chest, my neck, my cheeks and between my legs. I jerk up into a sitting position, running a hand through my hair, looking around. No Scotty. No David, either. I look at the clock. Eleven forty-five. I fall back against the pillows and look up at the ceiling. Then I close my eyes. Thank you, God. Thank you so much.

I take a breath and slide out of bed, naked, and hunt around for my robe. No such luck. I go into the bathroom and close the door, use the john and then slip into a hot shower. If I had any difficulty remembering what we did last night, what we did for most of last night, the hot water is acutely reminding me of where most of the action took place.

I laugh out loud, letting the water run over my head.

When I come back out to the bedroom with one towel around my hair and one around my body, it is to find David reading the paper in the corner chair with Scotty lying at his feet. He puts the paper down and stands up as I come in. I just stand there a moment, looking at him, smiling.

"I brought you some breakfast," he says. "It's in the sitting room. But the coffee's right here," he adds, reaching for the mug he left on the nightstand.

He's nervous and I can't tell you how deeply moved I am by it. I walk over, make him put the mug down and pull him around to face me. "Good morning," I murmur, sliding my hands up around his neck to kiss him. After, I let my head rest against his chest as he closes his arms around me.

"Where do I begin?" he whispers, gently pulling the towel off to kiss the top of my head. He tosses it on the bed and holds me again. "I've never been so happy in all my life."

"I haven't, either," I say softly, listening to his heart quicken.

We kiss and we are quickly lost in each other, and I am excited all over again by how much he wants me. After such a long night it is amazing, really, how urgent our need is again. Undressing David is the most wonderful and incredible thing, and as I feel him moving against me, on top of me, I feel helpless, totally helpless against withholding anything from him. And so when David shudders, crushing me in his arms, I don't worry that I haven't climaxed, because it doesn't matter anymore, because for once that is not what I am after. For I am after everything now. Absolutely everything. And I know I will shudder with him many, many times, and twice was more than enough last night, and this morning all that matters is that all of it is real and really happened.

"Do you want me to—"

"Shhh," I tell him, pulling his head back down next to mine.

"But aren't I crush—"

"Shhh," I tell him again. He is not deadweight. He is heaven. Though in a minute or two breathing might become more difficult if he falls asleep, which, I suspect, he is about to.

But he surprises me, pulling away, laughing to himself. "I can't believe the dog doesn't say anything."

I turn my head to look at Scotty. He has taken refuge under the TV table in the corner, politely waiting until someone tells him it's safe to come out.

I watch David as he walks to the bathroom. I've never been with anyone his age. He must have been amazing when he was younger because he still is. I think I wish I could get the first twenty years back for him and fourteen back for me so we could have that time together.

But I was pretty much crazy until now, I decide, so I wouldn't have known what to do with David before, anyway.

When he emerges from the bathroom he has a towel around his waist and has brought a warm washcloth over to me. "Thanks," I murmur, wiping my face and hands, and putting it on the night table. I reach for the coffee mug.

"Are you sure you don't want me to—" he begins.

"Trust me," I tell him, "I would tell you."

"That's cold," he says, and before I can protest, he has taken the mug out of my hands to take into the sitting room. When he comes back David hands me a different mug, which is not hot, but a lot warmer, and walks across the bedroom to find his pants.

"Don't you dare put those on," I tell him between sips. "At least not quite yet."

He glances over, drops his pants over the chair and comes back to sit on the edge of the bed. "Here, this is for you." He is holding out a small square box.

I seem to be frozen.

He takes my mug away and holds the little box closer. "Open it, Sally, please, I've been dying to give it to you." I look into his eyes. "Please," he says again, and then he hovers over me while I take the box and open it.

Inside is the most gorgeous ring I've ever seen. There is a sapphire, sparkling blue, with a glittering diamond on either side of it.

I look up in shock. I am speechless.

"This is from your grandmother Goodwin's engagement ring," he says, pointing to the sapphire. "This diamond is from the engagement ring your father gave to your mother and this diamond is from me—I had it cut to match the other one exactly. It's a platinum setting so you shouldn't have to worry about the stones ever falling out." He laughs nervously. "What do you think? Is it okay? Do you like it? Your mother thought you would."

I start to cry.

"Oh, please, Sally, don't cry," he pleads. "But can you try it on?"

I try it on.

David laughs. He's like a little kid. "So you do like it?"

"I love it," I say, tears falling over my cheeks as I look at my hand. Yes, it was made for me. I look up at him and he lurches toward the bathroom to grab some Kleenex for me. "Please, don't cry," he says, coming back to the bed to wipe my eyes, "you're not supposed to cry."

"I can't help it," I say, sniffing and taking the Kleenex from him.

"Sally, will you marry me?"

I look up at him, feeling as though the wind has been knocked out of me.

"Please?" he says.

"Yes, of course I will," I tell him.

It is a spectacular day, I decide as I put Scotty on his leash and head toward the barn. It's warm and there are so many birds in the trees there is practically a racket.

The barn door is open and I tentatively take Scotty in there, unsure how he will react. Astra is in her stall, but the big male chestnut is gone and I figure Alexandra must be riding. Scotty starts to whimper a little as we approach Astra, but I keep telling him it's okay. (He probably thinks Astra is the biggest dog in the whole wide world.) I gently bring him along with me to the stall door and pet him while petting Astra, too, but it's a no-go, I can tell, Scotty's too freaked out by her size and is beginning to tremble, so we go outside to the corral. Sometimes there are goats in here but not today. I let Scotty off his leash in the corral, put my mug on the post and then climb up to sit on the top rail to drink it.

A gorgeous day.

I smile into my cup, sneaking another peek at the ring on my hand. *I get him and this, too?*

Mother was in on this. I'll have to call her. And I suppose I should call Rob, my brother, and tell him.

I hear a horse neigh behind me and I turn around, expecting

to see Alexandra riding bareback on the chestnut, which I do, but hardly expecting to see Cassy sitting behind with her arms around Alexandra's waist. As they walk toward me, I see Alexandra say something to Cassy and bring a hand down to keep Cassy's hands exactly the way they were. "Hi," she says.

Scotty starts barking his head off, which gives me a chance to regroup. It is very strange, to say the least, to see our network president like this. I put Scotty on his leash, tell him for the last time to stop barking (he does) and loop the leash over the gatepost. Still sitting high on the chestnut, Alexandra has her good arm around Cassy, helping her to slide down off the horse. "Ow," Cassy says, trying to stand upright. She is elegantly attired in well-fitting jodhpurs, a fisherman's sweater and gold earrings. And her hair is, of course, falling out of the clip on the back of her head as usual.

"Where are your riding helmets?" I scold.

"Where are my leg muscles?" Cassy groans, rubbing her thighs. But then she straightens up and smiles, her color high. "You look wonderful, Sally. Alexandra said you were mending well, but I'm still relieved to see it for myself."

"Thank you." In this light, the sunshine, Cassy's looking her age, but there's no doubt about it, she's still a beauty. She may talk a tough game on occasion, but is hopelessly gentle-natured. "And you look beautiful as always."

She smiles, a little embarrassed. "Thank you." She comes closer to peer at my temple. "Let me see what they did."

"It's a graft," I explain, holding my head for her inspection. "And then they put in a few implants."

"That's amazing," she murmurs. "You'd never know."

"Oh, I'll know," I assure her, touching my scalp self-consciously.

Alexandra has slid down off the horse, heavily favoring her right arm. "You didn't happen to see the farm truck at the house, did you?" she asks, tying the reins to the fence.

"No."

"Then I'll have to rub you down, boy," she says, patting the horse.

"So, Sally," Cassy says in a voice that sounds oddly formal.

"Cass," Alexandra says. Cassy looks at her. "We have all day. Maybe we should just hang out a while?"

Cassy holds her look for a long moment. "No, I want to get this over with," she finally says, turning to me. "So, Sally—now you know. About us."

I smile. I've been thinking about what to say. "I'm tremendously relieved." Cassy looks openly surprised. "Because I've always thought Alexandra was still in love with you."

She blinks a few times. "I see," she says softly, turning to look at Alexandra, who is examining the chestnut's left front leg. She turns back to me. "Alexandra wanted to tell you. But I asked her not to. It seemed like too much of a burden to place on you at an all-too-important time in your career. I didn't want you to get caught up in—" she gestures "—a complicated situation."

"It's only complicated if we make it complicated," Alexandra says, coming over to stand next to Cassy and take her hand.

It is a very natural gesture. And as odd as it may sound, they seem right together, relaxed. Happy. The vibe is definitely warm and low-key, and there is a sense of quiet foreverness between them.

"I'm embarrassed, Sally," Cassy explains, "because when we first met, when you returned my journal to me that had been stolen, I know what you read and I let you go on thinking that what that poor neurotic woman wrote so many years ago was the truth."

Alexandra squints at her. "What did you write?" She looks at me. "What did she write?"

"Why she thought it best to send you away," I explain.

"You probably know more than I do then," she says, looking at Cassy. "She burned it."

"Good riddance," Cassy says, a slight furrow appearing in her brow. "I was in therapy for years before I could even figure out what I felt."

Alexandra puts a reassuring arm around Cassy's shoulders. "People your age, Sally, just don't carry the same baggage."

"People your age," Cassy repeats, kicking her head in Alexandra's direction, "listen to her. She's so much older than you are, Sally. Why all of those years—"

"Darling, please shut up," Alexandra says. I am amazed at how natural it seems for them to be together.

Cassy turns to me. "I wanted to apologize to you, Sally."

"We both want to apologize," Alexandra says, pulling Cassy more tightly to her side. "And I hope you understand why we've been doing what we've been doing."

"And make sure to explain it to me if you do," Cassy adds with a smile.

"Thank you," I say. They both look at me. "Really, thank you. I feel honored. I've always looked up to you, to both of you—"

"I know," Cassy says, "and I don't want to make a skeptic of you about marriage—"

"I didn't fall off the Castleford turnip truck yesterday," I tell her. "And who am I to judge?"

"I think when the CEO throws crutches on the front lawn of Hollistan House you might possibly be entitled," Alexandra says.

Cassy closes her eyes, shaking her head. When she reopens them, she says, "Jack was in love with Alexandra once, you know."

"He was not," the anchorwoman protests. "He only thought he was," Alexandra adds, walking over to untie the reins.

"When we started the network," Cassy continues, "Jackson's first goal was to break up her engagement."

"She's making this up," Alexandra says, leading the chestnut over.

"That's how I got to know Jackson," Cassy continues, "while I was trying to stop him from blasting poor Gordon into oblivion."

"You never told me this," I say to Alexandra.

"To the barn, ladies, to the barn," Alexandra says.

I retrieve Scotty and fall in step with Cassy behind Alexandra and the chestnut. "It seems a shame to keep him on the leash," Cassy says.

"I'm afraid he'll bolt for the wide-open spaces."

"There's a chain-link fence all the way around the farm," Alexandra says.

True. I look down at Scotty, who is looking up at me with hopeful eyes. Please? "Okay, boy," I tell him. I unhook his leash. He just stands there. "Go on, boy."

"Maybe he needs you to throw him a stick or something," Cassy suggests.

The horse snorts and Scotty dodges away as if he's been zapped by lightning. "It's okay, boy," I tell him, and he cocks his head at me for a moment, sort of smiles, and then—poof—he is gone, bounding away to the woods. "I'll never get him to come in," I say, watching his fluffy tail disappear into the bushes. "Which is not a bad thing," I decide. "Not when I make him follow so many rules most of the time."

Cassy catches my drift and smiles.

"Does he have tick stuff on?" Alexandra asks as we continue on our way.

"Yes." After a few paces I look over at Cassy. "I hope you're staying over tonight."

"I was planning to."

"Good, because I will be cooking."

"You are?" Alexandra asks, turning around.

"It's sort of a special occasion." I stop walking and hold out my left hand. Both women stop dead in the their tracks. "I don't believe it," Alexandra says, dropping the reins and coming over to grab my hand for a better look. "He was talking about it—"

"Absolutely beautiful," Cassy murmurs.

"Oh, my God," Alexandra says all of a sudden, "Sally Harrington's going to be my sister-in-law." She shakes her head, laughing, and gives me a hug. "I'm thrilled, absolutely thrilled."

"And not in the least surprised," Cassy adds. "Alexandra's been trying to engineer this for I don't know how long. Congratulations," she says, giving me a hug, "it's wonderful, wonderful news."

"Thank you," I say. I've been smiling so hard my jaw is beginning to ache. As we continue to the barn, I explain the significance of each stone. And then I look up. David is coming down the path to greet us.

And I wonder, in this moment, how it was I ever wanted to live without him.

Acknowledgments

Sometimes real life actually happens to novelists but I am fortunate to have so many dear people around me to weather them with. My sister, Susan Ault, is my hero(ine), period. I am also blessed by my brother, Bob Ault. I am so very grateful to Peter Authier for all of his strength, wisdom and dedication. My love and thanks also go to Lindsey Ault-Authier, Jocelyn Ault, Taylor Ault, Victoria Ault, Ryann Robinson-Halloran, Justin Robinson-Howie, Ruthanne Robinson and my sister Frances Van Wormer.

My unflagging gratitude to Vilma Nunez, who was so good to both of our parents, and to the grand ladies of Marjorie's infamous bridge group—Susan Varney, Ann Marshman, Hope Koback and Evy Lawrence—for all of the joy and laughter. Speaking of which, I'd like to thank Molly and Ed Savard for their friendship and the Friday night dinner gang at the Friends of the Library Bookstore: Bea O'Brien, Frank Ridley, Kerry and Marilyn McEntee, Sharon Carabetta-Jodon and Lynn and Ron Hastings. Thank you, Nancy Bradstreet, for being so smart about things and Marlene Galligan, thank you for your inspriation.

A special thank-you goes to Tom Barton of Web Solutions for traveling through electronic oblivion to find and rescue

Mr. Murder and to Kelley Moore and Lisa Golebiewski for championing my work.

Loretta Barrett, thank you for being such a godsend in my life. Thanks also to Nick Mullendore and Gabriel Davis for their hard work. To the wonderful Dianne Moggy and the gang at MIRA, your support in every way has been incredible and I thank you with all my heart.

Finally, it all comes down to you, Chris. It all works because of you.

About the Author

Laura Van Wormer was raised in Darien, Connecticut, and graduated from the Newhouse School of Communications at Syracuse University. She began her publishing career as secretary to the editor in chief of Doubleday and worked her way up to become an editor before leaving to pursue her own writing. To support herself while writing her first novel, Laura wrote books for the creators and producers of the television programs *Dynasty,* *Dallas* and *Knots Landing.*

Her first novel was RIVERSIDE DRIVE and she has been a full-time novelist ever since. Laura divides her time between Meriden, Connecticut, Manhattan and Shelburne, Nova Scotia.

She cordially invites you to visit at LauraVanWormer.com.